THIEVES' WORLD™

is a unique experience: an outlaw world of the imagination, where mayhem and skulduggery rule and magic is still potent; brought to life by today's top fantasy writers, who are free to use one another's characters (but not to kill them off . . . or at least not too freely!).

The idea for Thieves' World and the colorful city called Sanctuary™ came to Robert Lynn Asprin in 1978. After many twists and turns (documented in the volumes), the idea took off—and took on its own reality, as the best fantasy worlds have a way of doing. The result is one of F&SF's most unique success stories: a bestseller from the beginning, a series that is a challenge to writers, a delight to readers, and a favorite of fans.

Don't miss these other exciting tales of Sanctuary: the meanest, seediest, most dangerous town in all the worlds of fantasy. . . .

THIEVES' WORLD
(Stories by Asprin, Abbey, Anderson, Bradley, Brunner, DeWees, Haldeman, and Offutt)

TALES FROM THE VULGAR UNICORN
(Stories by Asprin, Abbey, Drake, Farmer, Morris, Offutt, and van Vogt)

SHADOWS OF SANCTUARY
(Stories by Asprin, Abbey, Cherryh, McIntyre, Morris, Offutt, and Paxson)

STORM SEASON
(Stories by Asprin, Abbey, Cherryh, Morris, Offutt, and Paxson)

THE FACE OF CHAOS
(Stories by Asprin, Abbey, Cherryh, Drake, Morris, and Paxson)

WINGS OF OMEN
(Stories by Asprin, Abbey, Bailey, Cherryh, Duane, Morris and Morris, Offutt, and Paxson)

THE DEAD OF WINTER
(Stories by Asprin, Abbey, Bailey, Cherryh, Duane, Morris, Offutt, and Paxson)

SOUL OF THE CITY
(Stories by Abbey, Cherryh, and Morris)

BLOOD TIES
(Stories by Asprin, Abbey, Bailey, Cherryh, Duane, Morris and Morris, Offutt and Offutt, and Paxson)

AFTERMATH
(Stories by Abbey, Brunner, Drake, Morris, Offutt, and Perry)

UNEASY ALLIANCES
(Stories by Asprin, Cherryh, DeCles, Morris, Williams, Bailey, and Paxson)

STEALERS' SKY

Edited by
ROBERT LYNN ASPRIN & LYNN ABBEY

ACE BOOKS, NEW YORK

This book is an Ace
original edition.

STEALERS' SKY

An Ace Book/published by arrangement with
the editors

PRINTING HISTORY
Ace edition/December 1989

ISBN: 0-441-80612-0

PRINTED IN THE UNITED STATES OF AMERICA

10   9   8   7   6   5   4   3   2   1

CONTENTS

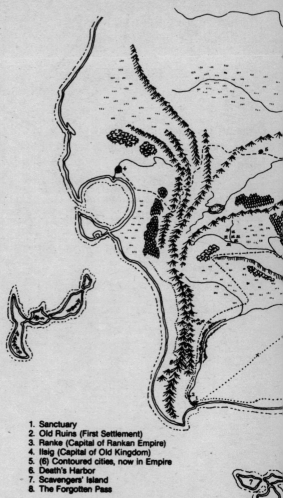

1. Sanctuary
2. Old Ruins (First Settlement)
3. Ranke (Capital of Rankan Empire)
4. Ilsig (Capital of Old Kingdom)
5. (6) Contoured cities, now in Empire
6. Death's Harbor
7. Scavengers' Island
8. The Forgotten Pass

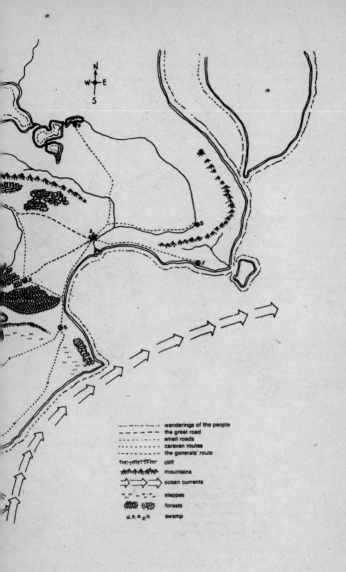

wanderings of the people
the great road
small roads
caravan routes
the generals' route
cliff
mountains
ocean currents
steppes
forests
swamp

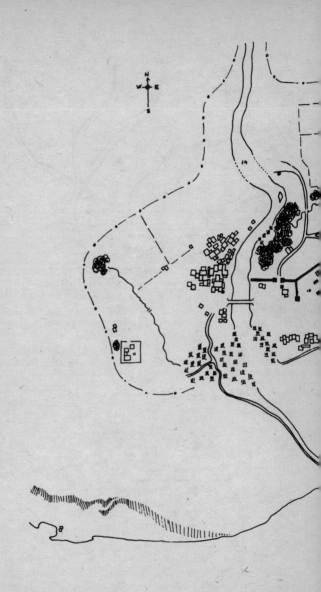

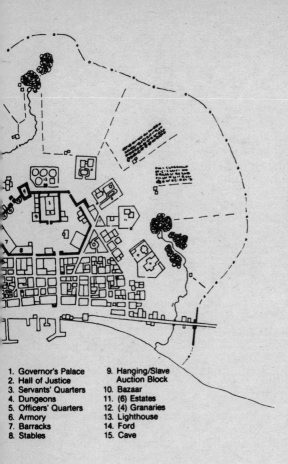

1. Governor's Palace
2. Hall of Justice
3. Servants' Quarters
4. Dungeons
5. Officers' Quarters
6. Armory
7. Barracks
8. Stables

9. Hanging/Slave
   Auction Block
10. Bazaar
11. (6) Estates
12. (4) Granaries
13. Lighthouse
14. Ford
15. Cave

⊢──── ~1 mile ────⟶

STEALERS' SKY

Dramatis Personae

The Townspeople

ABOHORR—*One-thumbed proprietor of the Vulgar Unicorn, now owned by Strick.*
   SILKY—*A barmaid at the Vulgar Unicorn.*

AHDIOVIZUN; AHDIOMER VIZ; AHDIO—*Proprietor of Sly's Place, a legendary dive within the Maze.*
   THRODE—*An employee at Sly's Place.*
   CLEYA; JODEERA—*The woman Ahdio loves, and who works for him at Sly's Place. Since she is far too beautiful to travel safely through the Maze, Ahdio has arranged for her to be protected by a disguise of ugliness.*
   OULEH—*A doubly endowed denizen of Sly's Place.*

AMOLI—*Madam of the Lily Garden brothel, a place of ill repute and endless possibilities.*

CHOLLANDAR; CHOLLY—*A master of glues and rendering.*

FELTHERYN THE THESPIAN—*Actor, director, and producer of Feltheryn's Players, a small theatrical company which has found a better audience in Sanctuary than in the capital city.*
   GLISSELRAND—*His wife and partner in all things.*
   LEMPCHIN—*The youngest member of their acting company.*
   SNEGELRINGE—*The romantic actor of the company.*
   ROUNSNOUF—*The company comedian.*

HAKIEM—*Storyteller and confidant extraordinaire.*

HANSE; SHADOWSPAWN—*Native thief of Sanctuary, with often surprising friends and connections. He has recently returned from a lengthy stay in the north.*

JUBAL—*Prematurely aged former gladiator. Once he openly ran Sanctuary's most visible criminal organization, the Hawkmasks; now he works behind the scenes.*
  SALIMAN—*His aide and only friend.*

LALO THE LIMNER—*A native Sanctuary artist whose paintings are more than they seem.*
GILLA—*His indomitable wife.*
    VANDA—*their eldest daughter, employed as a companion to Lady Kurrekai at the palace.*
    WEDEMIR—*Their eldest son, a member of Walegrin's guard, in love with Vanda's friend, Rhian.*
    LATILLA—*Their younger daughter, just on the edge of puberty.*
    ALFI—*Their son, a lively nine-year-old.*

MORIA—*Once one of Jubal's Hawkmasks, then a servant of Ischade. She was physically transformed into a Rankan noblewoman before the magic died, and the transformation endures. She is in hiding with Stilcho.*

MYRTIS—*Madam of the Aphrodisia House.*

STILCHO—*Once one of Ischade's resurrected minions. He was "cured" of death when magic was purged from Sanctuary.*

ZIP—*Bitter, young terrorist. Leader of the Popular Front for the Liberation of Sanctuary (PFLS). Now he and his remaining fighters have been designated as officials responsible for peace in the city.*

The S'danzo

ILLYRA—*Half-blood S'danzo seeress with True Sight. Wounded by PFLS in the False Plague Riots.*
  DUBRO—*Bazaar blacksmith and husband to Illyra.*
    TREVYA—*A crippled foundling presented to Illyra by Walegrin.*

MOONFLOWER—*Seeress of considerable talent and greater bulk mistakenly slain by Beysib bodyguards.*
  MIGNUREAL; MIGNUE—*Her daughter, who loved Hanse and went north with him, but now dwells alone in Firaqa.*
  JILEEL—*Another, younger daughter.*
  TERETAFF—*Moonflower's husband.*

THE TERMAGANT—*Oldest of the S'danzo women practicing her craft in Sanctuary.*

The Magicians

ILSIGI MAGES:

MARKMOR—*A powerful, ambitious, youthful wizard.*

MARYPE—*His arrogant, yet blundering, apprentice.*

RANKAN HAZARDS DWELLING AT THE MAGEGUILD:

RANDAL; WITCHY-EARS—*The only mage ever admitted into the Sacred Band of Stepsons or trusted by them. Now a teacher at the Mageguild.*

DARIOS—*An apprentice accidentally imprisoned in the Mageguild during the False Plague Riots. He was freed by Lalo, from whom he is now learning a different sort of magic. Before his imprisonment he was Rhian's fiancé.*

THOSE WHO ADHERE TO NO HIERARCHY OR DISCIPLINE BUT THEIR OWN:

ISCHADE—*Necromancer and thief. Her curse is passed to her lovers, who die from it. Since the diminution of magic in Sanctuary, she has been in isolation at her house on the White Foal River.*

STRICK; TORAZELAN STRICK TIFIRQUA—*White Mage who has made Sanctuary his home. He will help anyone who comes to him, but there is always a Price, sometimes trivial and sometimes not, for his aid.*

AVENESTRA; AVNEH—*Strick's increasingly obese assistant.*

Visitors in Sanctuary

THE SHEPHERD—*A figure of considerable mystery. By his panoply he might be an Ilsigi warrior—but all such men have been dead for years.*

The Rankans living in Sanctuary

CHENAYA; DAUGHTER OF THE SUN—*A beautiful and powerful young woman, the prince's cousin, who is fated never to lose a fight. In her arrogance and innocence she made more enemies in Sanctuary than even fate could handle and has left town until her reputation repairs itself.*

DAYRNE—*Her companion and trainer.*

LEYN, OUIJEN, DISMAS, AND GESTUS—*Her friends and gladiators at her father's school.*

DAPHNE—*Rankan noblewoman and first wife of Prince Kadakithis. Ostensibly sent to safety before the arrival of the Beysib, she was actually kidnapped and sold into slavery on Scavenger's Island, where Chenaya rescued her. She is now divorced from her husband.*

PRINCE KADAKITHIS—*Charismatic but somewhat naive half-brother of the assassinated Emperor, Abakithis.*

LOWAN VIGELES—*Half-brother of Molin Torchholder, father of Chenaya. A wealthy aristocrat self-exiled to Sanctuary and hoping to return to the Rankan capital in triumph someday. He operates a gladiator school at his Land's End estate and has built a small, temporary arena there.*

MOLIN TORCHHOLDER; TORCH—*Archpriest of Sanctuary's war-god (whichever deity that is at the moment). Architect for the rebuilt walls of Sanctuary. Supreme bureaucratic adminstrator of the city.*

    ROSANDA—*His wife, from whom he has been estranged for several years. She lives with Vigeles at the Land's End estate.*

RASHAN; THE EYE OF SAVANKALA—*Priest and Judge of Savankala. Highest ranking Rankan in Sanctuary prior to the arrival of the prince; now allied with Chenaya's disaffected Rankans at Land's End.*

RHIAN—*A young woman who has taken service with Lady Kurrekai.*

STEPSONS; SACRED BANDERS—*Members of a mercenary unit loyal to Tempus. Their years in Sanctuary were among the worst in their history. Many of them have already left town.*

    CRITIAS; CRIT—*Tempus left him in charge of peacekeeping in Sanctuary when everyone else left. Also the partner of Straton, though that pairing has been in disarray for some time now.*

    STRATON; STRAT; ACE—*Partner of Critias. Injured by the PFLS at the start of the False Plague Riots. He has been Ischade's lover and, though her curse has not killed him, most of his former associates count him among Sanctuary's damned.*

WALEGRIN—*Rankan army officer assigned to the Sanctuary garrison where his father was slain by the S'danzo many years before. He is now one of three officers responsible for the peace in Sanctuary. He is also Illyra's half-brother.*

The Beysib

SHUPANSEA; SHU-SEA—*Head of the Beysib exiles in Sanctuary; mortal avatar of the Beysib mother goddess. Lover of Prince Kadakithis, whom she wishes to marry.*

KURREKAI—*The Beysa's motherly cousin.*

INTRODUCTION

Robert Lynn Asprin

Zalbar bristled and glared angrily as a passerby jostled his back, nearly dumping his lunch off his lap and over the edge of the wharf where he sat. The Hell-Hound's annoyance went unnoticed, however; the pedestrian continued on his way without a backward glance, picking his way through the crowds. Letting his tight-lipped frown soften into a twisted grimace, Zalbar shook his head with an inward sigh.

He'd have to find another place to eat his lunch in the future if he wanted any peace and quiet during his midday break. It used to be that the wharves were nearly deserted during the day between the time that the fishermen went out with the morning tide and the afternoon when they returned. Now there were trade ships arriving from the Beysib Empire loaded with goods, merchandise as often as not hawked directly from the boats, and the bargain hunters they drew were no different from the noisy, haggling crowds in the Bazaar proper.

Normally, Zalbar avoided tracking, much less participating in, the politics that seemed to thrive in Sanctuary like slime in a stagnant pond, preferring instead the narrow view of a career soldier. By that view, he simply followed his orders without concerning himself with the motivations or machinations of those who issued them. Lately, though, there seemed to be things afoot which affected him directly to a point

1

where he could not purge them from his mind, or avoid speculating on their cause and effect.

One such thing was the town's growing prosperity. Apparently the Beysibs-in-exile who had taken up residence in Sanctuary were approaching some kind of peace or understanding with the powers-that-were in their old homeland. In any case, trade was beginning to develop with Sanctuary as the main port. That, coupled with the new construction (which required constant appraising and reappraising of one's habitual routes through town), was bringing money and jobs into Sanctuary at levels unheard-of when Zalbar first arrived here escorting Prince Kadakithis. Of course, prices on everything from food to women were going through the roof, at a rate that was rapidly outstripping his meager soldier's pay.

Even more noteworthy, however, was what was going on with the Rankan Empire itself, the authority to which the Hell-Hound was ultimately accountable for his actions.

Zalbar had been assigned to Kadakithis, and since that time had received his orders from the local power structure. The chain of command in Sanctuary had become incredibly convoluted over the years, though, with some units answerable only to faceless players in the capital itself, bypassing the prince's authority, and it had all but collapsed completely when Theron murdered his way to the Empire's throne. Now the Empire was in trouble to a degree that it was impossible to ignore, even for those such as Zalbar who would prefer to leave politics to others.

The Hell-Hound shook his head again, remembering with no small measure of disbelief the last briefing he had attended.

The big news of the briefing was that Theron was recalling the Rankan 3rd Commando and the remaining elements of the Stepsons back to the capital ''for reassignment to assist in suppressing the civil disorder within the Empire.'' Even more surprising to Zalbar was the discussion which followed the announcement.

Rather than working out the details of how to effectively police the city in the face of this sudden loss of manpower, the meeting degenerated into an argument as to whether or not the units in question would comply with the Emperor's orders! Even now, there was little sign of them even going through the motions of preparing to leave.

To a career soldier like Zalbar, this was unthinkable . . . and a far more chilling commentary on the Emperor's fading power than any idle street or barracks gossip. Once this door was open in his mind, countless little observations and oddities flooded through, turning his thoughts and speculations onto paths normally shunned.

He knew it had been some time since a tribute caravan had been sent from Sanctuary to the capital, as there had been no call for guards for such an expedition. Originally he had shrugged this off, thinking that perhaps the Empire had authorized that the extra tax monies be spent on the new construction in town. Now he wondered if the prince had simply decided to withhold the monies. If Ranke was unable to even collect taxes . . .

This had come to a head when someone in the barracks had speculated that the units being recalled were actually going to return as a tax-collecting force. This was, of course, pooh-poohed by the other soldiers. If that was to be the new assignment, then why not give them their instructions while they were still here rather than having them travel all the way to the capital?

No, every indication was that the Empire itself was in dire straits, and in its desperation was turning its back on Sanctuary . . . cutting it adrift while it tried to muster its strength and forces elsewhere. With the exception of a few isolated households who were conspicuously noisy in their loyalty and preference to all things Rankan, the Empire's influence was all but gone from Sanctuary . . . and the recall of the troops was simply a final, confirming gesture.

It was with no small surprise that Zalbar realized that he no longer thought of the prince . . . or himself . . . as being Rankan. They had been absorbed into the permanent structure of this strangely addicting town. Sanctuary was their home now, and as much a part of them as they were a part of it. Ranke was just a name, at best annoying when it couldn't be ignored . . . and it was getting easier to ignore it.

Realizing he was dawdling with his thoughts rather than eating or returning to duty, Zalbar rose and threw the uneaten

portion of his lunch into the water. The scraps rippled the
steel-grey water which reflected the blanket of clouds above.

Peace and prosperity had come to Sanctuary, the Hell-
Hound thought, but it was like the indeterminate cloud cover
which hung over the city. Would the sun burn through and
bathe the town with warmth and light, or would the clouds
thicken and darken into a storm?

A soldier could only watch and wait . . . and adapt.

NIGHT WORK

Andrew Offutt

> Hanse believes in very little and perhaps nothing. Therefore he's always ready for anything, particularly the unexpected. It's a trait that has served him well. Because he has to be a pragmatist, Shadowspawn is a pragmatist.—Strick
> Wisdom is the ability to believe only what you have to.—the Eye

Shadowspawn ranged through Sanctuary like a hungry tiger on the prowl.

His real name was Hanse and Hanse was mad. Better put, he was angry, but he was mad, too, in a manner of speaking: mad with anger. Shadowspawn was hardly the first or the last person to be driven into a sort of madness by anger. He had done heroic deeds: he had broken into the manse of that sorcerer and stolen the earring that saved Nadeesh's life and enabled Strick to buy the Vulgar Unicorn from the old physician. And then by all gods, by the will of Injustice Himself—that evil gnomish dwarf who was left hand of ever-fickle Lady Chance—the heroic Hanse had been hit by a stagger spell, punched by three big toughs, drugged, bound, gagged, and popped into a big cloth bag. He had been hauled down to the dock, hauled onto a ship, and dumped into its hold. Destination: slavery, in the Bandaran Isles.

Yet that did not happen. The next time Shadowspawn

emerged from the shadowless sack and saw light he was in
the murky keep of that most sinister of men, Jubal. Jubal had
bought him. True, after some smirking and sneering and
taunting Jubal had freed him, but not as an act of decency or
in exchange for the pitiful price the crime lord had paid. Oh,
no. He had named a ridiculous sum, close to sixteen *pounds*
of gold, and Hanse's only choice had been to agree. A
ridiculous, monumental sum—five hundred pieces of gold!
Ridiculous!

Ole Jubal, Hanse thought, *must have been thinking with his
nose, not his brain. And he wants to take over peacekeeping
in Sanctuary. Right. And put me in charge of guarding all the
jewelers and shops.*

At least Hanse knew now that one of his kidnappers had
been Tarkle, whose main occupation was being a bully. And
Hanse was just as sure that Tarkle with his brain borrowed
from a minnow hadn't acted solely on his own. No, the mage
Marype with his pretty silver tresses must have thought up the
vengeful plan for the *disposal* of Hanse/Shadowspawn, a plan
that truly did involve a fate worse than death and so was truly
wicked, and clever. Marype probably paid Tarkle, too.

Hanse knew four more things, all Musts. He would find
Tarkle. He would find Marype. He would have his vengeance. And somehow, somehow he would pay Jubal his
damned ridiculous price.

Of course I'm worth it, but that's beside the point.

Shadowspawn ranged through Sanctuary like a hungry tiger
on the prowl. And he could not find Tarkle.

Strick gazed across his blue-draped desk at the young
woman there. From beneath a great mass of fiery hair that
dribbled straggly red bangs over her brows and even eyes like
an unkempt hedge, she stared anxiously back.

"I have interesting news for you," he told his visitor,
whose name was Taya and whose scarlet mop of hair was a
disguise, "from the prince-governor. He is without malice
toward you. A small house and a guarantee of funds await
you. They are sufficient to set you up in some business
venture. You could also use it to leave Sanctuary, if you
wish. This is genuine and only truth, Taya. As to my chang-

ing your appearance—yes, that is possible, but such a thing is
not a matter of a few minutes and the Price may not please
you. Meanwhile, you are best advised to go into hiding for a
week or so. It is hardly what you're used to, but I'd recommend a room upstairs over the Vulgar Unicorn.''

Her eyes had widened when he began, returned to something approaching normal as she took in his words, and now
flared wide again. She flounced narrow and shapely shoulders. ''That . . . *place*?!''

The very big man spread his hands in a ''why not?''
gesture and his eyebrows said the same—he who looked like
a swordslinger, a wealthy wizard's bodyguard, perhaps, and
who was instead a wealthy wizard who was at the same time
friend to prince and thief, Rankan noble and Ilsigi banker,
carpenter and smith, whore and orange-pedlar.

He said, ''Who's going to think of looking for you there?''

She swallowed, stared at the close-fitting blue coif or hood
without which no one had seen this man; she visibly considered, and at last nodded. ''B-but I wouldn't dare even set foot
in that—that . . .''

''Careful, Taya,'' the spellmaster told her. ''I own the
place.'' He mirrored her nod. ''The person waiting to see me
right now will make the perfect guide, Taya. He will do it for
me.''

Two people sat in Strick's waiting area below. One, muffled in her costly shawl, was a mildly attractive noblewoman
with a ghastly hairy wart erupting from her nose. Yes, Strick
could and would deal with that, and be well paid for making
her presentable again. The other, from whom she kept herself
well clear, was an oldster with a voice out of a gravel pit. It
was he that Strick's young assistant, Avenestra, beckoned to
rise and follow, and he did, banging his staff as he walked.
He was surprised to find someone else in Strick's office, and
peered closely at her. Unusually keen of eye—especially at
night—he recognized the softly weeping girl there with the
white mage. She, meanwhile, glanced up at him and shrank
at sight of wrinkled brown hands emerging from an old
tan-once-brown robe with its hood all crumpled on his back
and around his shoulders. His face was darkly shadowed by a
funny feathered hat from some far place, doubtless to hide

features ravaged by time and disease and even worse—if anything could be worse than time and disease to a very attractive young woman who had been concubine to the prince-governor from Imperial Ranke. Once-Imperial Ranke.

"Skarth," Strick said, "this is someone who needs to vanish in the Maze for a while."

The big hat nodded and its big bright yellow feather waggled tiredly. "She also resembles someone I once was so rude as to bind and gag in a certain bed in a certain large building!"

Taya gasped and looked at him sharply. He had entered with a limp, bearing a staff or cane in one of those dark, aged hands. Now she also saw an overdone black mustache, floppy as the feather and big and droopy as Strick's oversized blond mustache.

"Taya is in disguise. Taya, this man is in disguise. Please, just wait outside for a moment, will you? I need to impress on him the importance of his job in escorting you."

"Uh—oh, oh, all right," Taya said, who was accustomed to being asked to leave someone's presence and wait somewhere or other while more important things happened than a prince's mere bedwarmer, and hardly accustomed to thinking much for herself.

She rose, bulky and silly in yards and yards of S'danzo garb that hardly went with the lavishly proportioned red wig. The white mage's pneumatically overweight young assistant/receptionist/fetch-and-carrier smiled at her and showed her along the corridor past that burly man who looked like a swordslinger, a wealthy mage's bodyguard, and was. Like the beyond-plump Avenestra, he wore garments of the color that had already come to be known as Strick blue.

"What'm I supposed to do with that?" the one called Skarth was meanwhile asking Strick. He gestured after Taya. Abruptly losing his limp, he paced with uncommon grace to lean on the back of the chair she had just vacated.

Across his blue-draped desk, the man all in blue told him.

"Uh." A withered old brown hand gestured. "No problem with that. Iffen any of these young jaybirds try to cock their combs at that fair young lass I'll whock 'em with my stick, I will!"

Strick winced. "Next time you consider a disguise that

elaborate you might try to gain a lesson or a little advice from Feltheryn.''

"Wh—oh, that actor? Not a bad idea, though. What did you find out about Tarkle?''

Strick sighed and looked morose. "Nothing, yet.''

In an astonishingly young and vibrant voice for such an oldster, the man called Skarth said succinctly, "Shit.''

"Wait.'' With a smallish smile twitching at his mouth, Strick dropped a small brown and yellow tiger-eye into the brown old hand.

"Glass,'' Skarth said in instant appraisal, and Strick laughed.

"True. But it's also today's message token. Hand it to Abohorr and ask him what you want to know. By tonight either he or Ahdio will know where Tarkle stays.''

On the way out of Strick's, Skarth offered the ridiculously disguised girl his hand. She shrank away. She hustled along beside him, while he walked bent, rolling along like a sailor, clonking the hard-packed earth of the streets and "streets'' with his staff.

She had one sentence of him as they made their way through a nice calm windless Sanctuary; Taya asked how it was that he was obviously of considerable age and yet his mustache was so black.

"Dye,'' Skarth said, from the throat. "The only way a S'danzo could have red hair.''

Taya clamped her soft and sensuous lips and wasted no more words on so surly an escort.

When at last they entered the area called the Maze with its noise of yapping dogs and bustling, jostling people amid the odors of cooking and sweat and the ordure of yapping dogs, Taya shrank, bundling into herself and her acres of clothing. Someone jostled her hard and she sought Skarth's hand. He jerked it away.

"Clay might come off,'' he muttered in manner snarly, and led her on, on to that tavern with the laughably obscene sign featuring an impossible animal performing an impossible act upon itself.

Marype, apprentice to the master mage Markmor until the latter's timely demise, stood gazing down at the smallish pile

of white ash in the bottom of a bowl of pure silver. The face
of Marype was serene, brows up and eyes large and contem-
plative.

"You had a short and decent life but not too much fun of
late, hmm, Marype?" he murmured. "Once I was out of the
way you took over this fine palatial home of that slimy
krrf-dealer trapped forever in un-life . . . tricked that doltish
slut Amoli into helping you without knowing your master
plan . . . only to lose that old leech's earring to that most
uncommon of common thieves! Next you showed my training
well: actually succeeded in bringing me back to come up with
an ingenious vengeance on that thief . . . and yet got us both
defeated by a gluemaker with a belly the size of the barrel of
beer he must store in it. Demeaned and shamed me in the
process . . . *and* forced me to yield up my secret name to the
gluemaker *and* those other two. In the event you wondered
why, *why* as you felt your self leaving you, Marype; why,
why I would take your body and leave you in mine and make
sure that this time it is dead without possibility of return . . .
well, that was it. To be demeaned and shamed by those three,
to know they were laughing at us. Are laughing at us. That,
darling apprentice, *that* I could not and cannot bear."

Looking down at what had been Marype and Markmor, the
Marype who was not Marype heaved a mighty sigh. And still
he stared down at the ash that had been both he and his
apprentice. Nearby a happy little rodent in a golden cage
glanced up from its dinner, worked its mouth and whiskers
rapidly, and went back to dining.

"Your first plan was good, boy. The Empire of Ranke has
failed and is dying. The battle of those two power-seeking
females nearly destroyed this town, and Kadakithis the *Rankan*
was lax and late—is late—in coping. Simple matter to spread
poison words and poison thought about him. Simple matter to
see his outré wife dead and bring about his complete fall; to
take full control of this town! Firaqa is well governed, ruled
by wizards . . . why not Sanctuary by a wizard!"

The face of Marype, a not unhandsome one, smiled. He
glanced over at the cage of pure gold on another of this large
chamber's three worktables. Within was a happy vole—a
darkish gray mouse but for its short tail—happily dining on

choice foods. In that rodent of necessity reposed the soul of the mage Markmor, else he could not have assumed the body of his apprentice. Markmor was long dead, resurrected by Marype only to run afoul of the gluemaker Chollander. Now Marype was dead; now the essential intelligence of Markmor resided in this body. That created anomaly, for a body could not house two souls—and yet without the soul of Marype this one would be impossible to maintain. Markmor had no desire to have the well-made, youthful body he now occupied rot into putrescence about him.

The brain of Markmor guided the body of his apprentice and son of his former chief rival, years agone. Within the body necessarily remained the soul of Marype, and so—the vole. It was a happy vole, mindless, well taken care of, and well guarded in this spell-warded chamber.

"Shadowspawn, that street slime Hanse, is disposed of," Markmor said, pacing over to a mirror to look into the face of Marype and watch its mouth move. "A city cannot be taken without money, and plenty is coming in, thanks to your plan." He smiled, watching Marype smile at him.

Long ago Markmor had learned to make gold. Good gold; real gold. He was not sure that any other sorcerer had ever succeeded. Yet if he simply *created* the gold necessary to bring about his ends in Sanctuary, he would need more and more and ever more, for he would have destroyed its precarious economy. No, money must not merely be created but be generated; earned, brought into Sanctuary, to aid the economy rather than harm it. That had been Marype's ingenious plan, for while he had been a stupid boy he had not been ignorant or without cleverness.

The same as Shadowspawn, the master mage thought. And so the rising number of persons missing from Sanctuary. They were not missing. They were merely relocated in the Isles of Bandara, to the considerable profit of Markmor of Sanctuary.

Markmor of Sanctuary strode to the door, slim and young and leggy in black tights and boots under a belted tunic the color of old gold. "Tarkle!"

The hulking fellow appeared, a man beyond homely but looking respectful—ugly both inside and out, Markmor knew,

with hair a brown tangle like an overgrown bramble patch fit
only to hide a fearful rabbit. But then Markmor also knew
without caring that his own new beauty was external only.

Respectful too were Tarkle's manner, and tone, and choice
of response: "Sir?"

"You and your associates will do tonight's work in Downwind, Tarkle."

"Downwind."

"We leave the Maze alone for a while—and who misses
anyone in Downwind? After—"

"Nobody."

"That, damn it, was a rhetorical question. Be quiet and
listen. After tonight's work in Downwind, return here. But
tomorrow it is time you got out of that dingy hole you live in.
You will go there and decide what you have that you consider
of value, and fetch it here."

"Here?"

Markmor fought his exasperation with this semi-intelligent
semihuman. "Yes, here. The room done in greens is yours."

Tarkle's eyes showed joy. "Yes, sir! Oh, I do thank you,
sir!"

"I want you close by me, Tarkle."

Immediately Tarkle moved a pace closer.

Markmor took a pace backward and lifted a staying hand.
"I don't mean now, you . . ." He broke off and sighed. "Be
prepared for a new appearance."

Tarkle looked around as if expecting a new appearance.

The wizard ignored that and wished he knew how to make
brains. Or to transfer one from, say, a cat to a human, for
instance, thus increasing Tarkle's intelligence severalfold.

"Be prepared for a new appearance," Markmor said in
Marype's voice from Marype's mouth while he twitched a
lock of Marype's long silver-blond hair. "I am tired of all
this hair. Today I cut it off and color it, and I don't want you
taking me for someone else when you see me tomorrow!"

Tarkle smiled and nodded. "No chance, sir!"

He saw Marype nod, and wave a hand, and a happier
Tarkle louted out.

Markmor secured the door and returned to gaze into the
mirror. "That big beast is useful, but his mother must lament

the fact that she never had any children. Shadowspawn is disposed of," he repeated in a low, controlled voice Marype had seldom used, "and three more must go. Three who know my secret name. The white wizard they call hero of the people . . . that mail-shirted pretender at Sly's Place, and the gluemaker." Markmor chuckled and again the plump vole looked up. "Best he go into his own kettle. What a lot of glue he will provide for the good citizens of *my* city!"

Skarth showed the Vulgar Unicorn's new man the glass tiger-eye. Shmurt dragged his gaze off Taya, said "What d'you need?" and reached for it.

Skarth snatched it back. "Can't. I have to show it to Abohorr tonight, to get a message."

"Irregular," Shmurt said. He had been caretaker of an apartment building now mostly rubble, then unemployed, then construction laborer. Only recently had the Vulg's new owner installed him as day man.

"Strick said to tell ye a word," Skarth told him, and dropped his voice so that Shmurt leaned forward across the bar. "Boodoovagoolarunda," Skarth whispered.

Shmurt smiled and shook his head. "Don't know where he gits them words! What d'you need?"

Skarth told him.

"*She* wants to stay *here*?"

"Right."

"You sure?"

"Shmurt . . ."

Shmurt nodded hurriedly, raising both hands in a fending gesture, and soon they had Taya installed, happily or un-, in one of the rooms upstairs over the tavern.

"Classiest roomer *this* place ever had," Shmurt said as he and Skarth came back down. "Don't believe I know you. Live close by?"

"Name's Skarth. You've seen me often enough. I live over on Red Court. Sure ye don't know me?"

"Can't say that I do, Skarth. Sorry'f I should."

Skarth chuckled and ordered a small pail of beer. While Shmurt saw to that, the old man glanced in surprise at an unlikely pairing in a dim back corner of the main room of the

already dim dive. There where eyes less keen might have
missed them sat Furtwan Coinpinch, changer and sometimes
pusher, and Menostric called the Misadept, the cheapest mage
in town. Well, the least expensive, anyhow.

"Watch those two, Shmurt," Skarth said, his staff banging
the floor as he headed for the door. "They could steal your
eyeballs and ye'd not notice till ye tried looking for 'em!"

The two men in back looked up. "Who in the fart was
that?" Furtwan demanded.

"Skarth," Shmurt called. "Don't you know ole Skarth?"

Then he returned his gaze to the empty doorway, trying to
fathom who in the fart Skarth was and why he seemed almost
familiar.

Ole Skarth was making his way up the street and into the
market area, his staff bang-banging rather than tap-tapping.
So many people thronged here that it felt a lot warmer.
Business was brisk these days, what with all the employment
available to anyone who could dig, cut stone, lift stone, carry
stone, mix or carry or spread mortar, or swing a hammer or
pick or sledgehammer. He saw Hummy and her daughter
buying meat, real meat, and he was glad; that meant Hummy's
husband had gotten on with the many others working in
construction: the rebuilding of a better, handsomer, safer, and
prettier Sanctuary, according to the official documents tacked
up here and there for everyone to read or pretend to read,
after nature and two viciously maniacal women and some
dyspeptic gods and those outlanders of Tempus's and what
some referred to as Nature had done their best to make this
old city only a rubble-strewn memory. There was Lambkin
buying food for her brothers and father, too, which meant that
the latter was no longer taking odd jobs but "workin' regular" in the current popular phrasing, at some aspect of
construction.

Skarth bang-banged his way among them and the noise of
their comments and dickering, trying to remember to stay
bowed and to lurch, when a voice sliced right through all the
others:

"Hanse!"

Skarth didn't think fast enough, and did the worst thing
possible: he froze and started to turn. He arrested the move-

ment, but knew it was too late. The point was, the voice was an impossibility: Mignureal's. After so many years of noticing each other more than somewhat and then living together up in Firaqa, he and she had agreed to irreconcilable differences. Besides, she had good work and was happy. She remained in Firaqa. Even though this and that had happened along the way so that he had hardly come directly back down to Sanctuary, he knew perfectly well that Mignue could not be in Sanctuary.

The voice sounded like hers just the same, and startled him enough so that he responded and gave himself away. Now he stayed bent while he turned the rest of the way around. He saw her, and sighed. Yes, she sounded like Mignureal all right; and with reason. He was gazing at her younger sister, Jileel, the one who used to peep at him around her mother's voluminous skirts and who now was nearly five feet tall and looked at him steady on from large eyes made even larger and lovelier by kohl, and who appeared to have bought two good melons and stuffed them down her blouse.

His roving gaze showed him that no one seemed to be paying attention, and he lifted a finger to his lips. At the same time he shook his head slightly and moved toward her.

"Shh, I'm supposed to be disguised. How'd you know?"

"Oh, I'd always recognize *you*, Hanse," she told him almost breathlessly, as if he were unmistakably and indisputably just the best-looking thing in the hemisphere. He stood beside her now, head bent so that the big feathered hat from Firaqa shaded the movement of his lips.

"Why are you disguised, Hanse?"

"Stop saying that." He glanced around. "I'm Skarth, girl, Skarth. Some people bagged me and sold me to slavers. I should be 'way out at sea right now, in the scummy hold of a scummy ship. They don't know I got away. I don't want them to know until I'm ready. Right now I'm trying to find out where the main one lives."

"Oh. Oh, Han—Skarth, how awful!" Her hand rushed to her heart in a girlish way and when it banged her chest he'd have sworn it bounced. "You were al-almost, you were almo—oh, oh!"

He rolled his eyes for no one's benefit but his own and

nodded. "Right. It hurt, and cost me a lot of time and trouble. Worse, I owe a certain grasping snake a fat favor *and* a lot of gold."

"Gold!"

Again Hanse rolled his eyes. He had to get away from here, from her. "You know what they call me?"

She nodded with some pride and an after-all-I'm-not-just-a-child attitude. "Of course. Shad—"

He interrupted quickly. "Right. Well, watch that shadow right over there and you'll know why."

She turned her head and partly her body to look in the direction he indicated, and Hanse took a sideward step and a backward one, grunted when he backed into someone's fat bottom, turned, and hurried down a narrow street. More walking and a few turns brought him to Red Court, where he did indeed live, in a decent second-floor room equipped with a huge old wagon wheel of solid wood. By the time he had opened the door he had straightened up and stepped into the room with his normal gait, a smooth gliding pace that jarred no part of his body.

An emphatically red cat of improbable size greeted him with an emphatic and distinctly accusatory noise. Somehow the animal's eyes looked accusing, too. Then its nose twitched a few times and its entire demeanor changed to one of loving cajolery while its emerald gaze fixed in a stare on the small pail its man carried. It banged its sinuous body constantly against its human's legs while Hanse moved to the little kitchen area and poured beer into an orange bowl that was larger than anyone would expect to be a cat's.

"Sorry I had to leave you so long, Notable," he was saying, "but Skarth can't be seen with that big red monster too many people already know is Shadowspawn's shadow. Here you—dammit, Notable, ease up, you'll spill the beer and me too!"

He had to hold the bowl up while he squatted to restrain the cat long enough to get the bowlful of beer on the floor with the other hand. That operation was no simple one; Notable was large, heavy, and squirming like a barrel of worms. Released, he attacked the beer like an army of thirsty horses finding an oasis after days on the desert.

Hanse, called Shadowspawn and more recently Skarth, stepped back and away, paused to set his sense of direction, and thrust his left hand up his right sleeve. That hand whipped up and back just past his ear as he spun. The arm snapped forward and a long flat piece of steel appeared with a *thunk* in the wagon wheel set up against the far wall. Getting the thing up here had not been easy, but it was perfect, a solid wheel of wood joined by wooden pegs, not nails. He had removed the iron rim. Now the wheel showed numerous holes and gouges, the marks of throwing practice with hiltless, guardless knives and stars. The hub was particularly chewed up, while the wall above and around the target was unmarked.

"Damn. I was so concerned with getting beer for you and trying to be a limpy old man I forgot to buy anything to eat. Anything here or have you eaten it all? A couple of big rats haven't come in and emptied the larder, have they?"

Notable glanced up from his bowl, whiskers dripping, and gave Hanse a cold stare.

All in blue as ever, Strick sat alone. Before him on his blue-draped desk rested a small box and, on a scrap of parchment, several strands of human hair. Hair and casket had come to him from the hands of Shadowspawn, who had them from the privy chambers of Marype the mage. The hair was the puzzler; to a man of Strick's talents its aura was distinctly that of Markmor, and yet it was not brown or gray, but silver-blond. Both Avenestra and his own examinations assured him that these hairs had not been dyed. The hair was Marype's. The . . . *owner* seemed to be Markmor.

"Impossible," the spellmaster muttered. "I saw him that night with Marype in Ahdio's back room. He was alive, talking, snarling at his apprentice and even told us all three his secret name—a valuable gift, if he'd been alive. But both of us sensed that he was not, not really. Marype had given him temporary life. Yet this is not dead hair. That is, it didn't come from a corpse; a revenant. It's Marype's. *And* Markmor's . . ."

From pale blue eyes he regarded the wall opposite without seeing it. His fingers moved over the strands they held, moved and moved while he contemplated. Since his arrival in

Sanctuary he had made it his business to learn and learn, about the city and its denizens both present and past. Markmor had preceded him, and been one of the most powerful and dangerous wizards in this sad city just before the arrival of the Rankan governor. Markmor had been beyond competent, and everything Strick had learned indicated that his apprentice had not come close to learning all the master knew, or approaching his talents.

Strick's big orange-yellow mustache writhed as his lips began to move. Almost inaudible words emerged. It was a practice that aided thinking, of gathering facts and matching them, piecing them together into hypotheses and conclusions. Or maybe it was just a habit.

"For some reason Marype brought Markmor back. I know that; Ahdio and Cholly and I saw them both together, and Marype wasn't pulling strings. What does this tell me? That they are one?"

He shook his head. "No."

He stared longer at nothing, and abruptly those almost watery-pale eyes blinked and came alive. "Unless Markmor has taken the body of his aide! Oh, what a monster that would be; another Corstic to waste a young man's youth! But worse— not to destroy his body but to seize it, to use it . . . By the Flame Itself, this is a very, very bad man and this poor staggering town cannot afford another such!"

After a time he heaved a sigh from the barrel chest any fighting man would have been happy to gain. Now Strick of Firaqa was torn. His burden, the Price he had paid for his powers, was twofold. One part of that Price was forever hidden beneath the flapped skullcap he wore, always. The second part was that Strick cared, cared, because he must. He had to. He must help people, not harm them. That meant he wove the spells that people called white magic, and that only.

"But . . . isn't harming Marype/Markmor helping people? Does it serve good to—try to; maybe with Ahdio's help—to try to send an anti-sorcerous spell on Marype/Markmor?"

In blue skullcap and tunic over blue tights as ever, Torazelan Strick ti Firqua sat alone, and fought himself.

*   *   *

"That you in there, Hanse?"

"Thanks for keeping your voice down, Abohorr. You know—you must have less belly than any bartender in this town or any other!"

"I'm startin' to put it on again," the man behind the Vulgar Unicorn's bar told him. "This work is all standin', but hardly the work carpenterin' is. I'm a lot happier, too. You? Is that a disguise?"

Abohorr couldn't see the roll of dark, dark eyes within the deep shadow of the large hat. "Must be. Here." A wrinkly brown hand stretched out to leave an imitation gemstone in Abohorr's thumbless one.

He squinted at it. "Some of your skin seems t'be flakin' off, uh, Skarth."

"Damned clay! Strick asked you to find out where somebody lives. That says he wants you to tell me."

Abohorr nodded, but didn't look happy. "I understand. But I haven't found out. That fellow hasn't been in and my casual tries to find out anything about him got me nothin'. I'm sorry, Hanse."

"Damn. Not as sorry as I am." He glanced around and paused to watch the girlish woman moving among the tables delivering cups and bowls and collecting coins. "Silky looks good. Odd; she's wearing more'n I ever saw on her! She working out all right, Ab?"

"She's all right. Most customers leave her pretty much alone. Ah, she don't mind a pat on the butt now and agin, but she does hate t'be pinched. Broke a good jar over Harmy's head a few nights ago when he pinched 'er. Drenched 'im with beer and stretched him right out on the floor, she did! So she made an announcement—sure can be loud when she's of a mind to!—an' I did, and the boss sent over that sign."

Abohorr jerked his head at the wall behind him. Hanse looked, and sighed.

> PINCHING HURTS. PINCH AND
> YOU'LL GET HURT WORSE.
> GUARANTEED.
>   —The Management

"Ab."

"Hmm?"

"What's it say?"

Abohorr reared his elbows up off the counter and turned to gaze at the sign. "Pinchin' hurts," he enunciated slowly. "Pinch and you get hurt worser. Somethin'—I guess that word is 'signed'—the Management." He turned back to Hanse, who had made a chuckly sound. "That's Strick. An' me, I guess. I got to ask him . . . do I call myself manager?"

The large hat with the large droopy feather wagged. "Better ask him. Seen Gralis, Ab?"

"You ain't heard? He tried to mug the wrong man. Him and several others—but I hear Gralis swears he was by hisself. Anyhow he got his collarbone broke."

"Damn. I wanted to ask him to help me with something." Hanse thumped the bar with a wrinkly brown hand. "Got to go, Abohorr. Thanks. Pinch Silky for me."

Abohorr stared down at a flake of brown wrinkle on his counter, then lifted his eyes to watch Skarth depart, banging that staff on the floor all the way to the door. With a wag of his head the new One-Thumb picked up his bar cloth to wipe away evidence of Skarth's apparent leprosy.

The two youths accosted the old crip just as he was about to emerge from an alley onto the Serpentine. Teeth flashed as they grinned at the silly oldster who had to lean on a staff but still walked with a rolling limp.

"Nice hat you got there, citizen!"

"I'll have that feather, paw-paw. You don' need it."

"This here hat is all I got in the world that I love," an old voice quavered from under the outsize headgear, "an' it ain't for sale. You two nice boys just git along now."

They laughed. "Who said anythin' about buyin'," the leftward one said, moving in.

"Got a shock for you, citizen," the other said, with a chuckle that more resembled a giggle. "We ain't nice boys." He was moving in.

"Well, y'oughtta be! Look atche—Synab's boy Hakky an' you're Saz's little brother Ahaz, ain'tche?"

The youths paused to exchange a glance. "He knows us!" Ahaz whispered, high-voiced.

"Shu'up," Hakky told him. "So we have to leave some work for Cholly the gluemaker, then."

Each took a deep breath, fixed his gaze on the crippled man under the big hat, and again started toward him. Hakky's knife was in his hand.

Their quarry underwent a miraculous cure, but rather than straighten up he remained stooped. Neither accoster recognized it as a combative crouch until he shoved his staff between Hakky's legs and jerked it up hard, and even while Hakky was sucking in an audible, high-voiced gasp of pain, the quarry danced back and gave Ahaz such a crack in the side of his shin that the youth squealed and went down. After bouncing off the alley's right wall.

When they got their groaning selves together after a minute or so, their intended prey had vanished, seemingly into the shadows.

"Damned old faker!" Ahaz whimpered. "What a mean trick! And us just boys, too!"

That was when Hakky kicked him in his other leg.

And cried out at the pain his violent movement sent sizzling into his bruised and swelling genitals.

A few minutes later the damned old faker used his staff to poke aside several of the thirty-one dangling strands of Syrese rope hanging before the entry to that low dive called Sly's Place. He step-clonked in, glanced around at a fine big crowd of drinkers and babblers, and step-clonked down the single step into the noisy, odoriferous main room.

Ouleh the man-killer sat on someone's leg, her Ouleh-stuffed blouse cut down to here, while a homely woman in a long heavy-looking skirt waited tables and a gimp-legged youth bore pottery back to the counter, where a very large man in a linked-chain mail coat was laying a big pickled sausage on a little tray between two bowls of beer. Ever moving, watching his place and his help and his patrons, his eyes did not miss the advent of the gimped old fellow in the wild hat. Besides, he was making enough noise with that outsize staff of his on the floor of oiled wood to make a god cover his ears.

He step-clonked his way to the counter.

"Are you Ahdio?"

The mailed man grinned. "Uh-huh. What do you want me to call you tonight—Notable?"

Under the hat a black mustache moved, but was too full to allow teeth to flash in a rueful smile. "You know everything, don't you? You really a sorcerer, Ahdio?"

Ahdio set a hamlike hand to his chain-scintillant chest and took on a sweet and innocent look—as much of one as that slab of face was capable. "Me? Are you a member of the Hell-Hounds?"

Under the hat, Hanse snorted. "Call me Skarth. I live in the Maze. You've known me for years. Draw me a beer and I'll leave it for Sweetboy."

"Nice of you," Ahdio said, moving for the beer, "but that cat hit a rat like a lightning strike this afternoon and ate everything but the viscera and the contents of its bowels. He always leaves those for me. Cats! Anyhow he's been sleeping it off for hours and probably couldn't even be bothered to stick his tongue into a bowl of beer. How's Notable?"

"Not that sleepy," Hanse assured him, "ever! Thanks." He slid his hand into the handle of the unglazed mug Ahdio set before him, watched a wrinkle or two flake off, and made a snarly noise. "You find out what Strick asked you about?"

"I did. That individual lives in Downwind." Ahdio leaned forward and lowered his voice, although that hardly seemed necessary, in the lowest and noisiest dive in the city and probably on the planet. "Brick, painted blue maybe twenty years ago, four stories high, on Happiness Street. Backs up to an alley just across from a small barn that looks more like a stable and used to be. He goes to sleep to the sound of goats, I reckon. His room's on the fourth floor, in back."

"Perrrfect," Hanse purred. "Top floor rear, hmmm? Just perfect. Look around, Ahdio. You see anybody who looks trustworthy?"

Starting to look, Ahdio snapped his gaze back to the man in the hat. "Where do you think you are, the Golden Oasis?"

Hanse chuckled. "Put it this way, then: I need someone

who's strong enough and willing enough to help me with some night work and who I can trust to keep his mouth shut at least until tomorrow.''

Ahdiovizun was frowning. "You aren't thinking of killing a man, are you, Hanse?''

"Absolutely not." A wrinkled brown finger rose between them, wiggled. Ahdio leaned closer to listen to what Hanse did plan to do. Suddenly every ounce of flesh on the tall, heavy man's form was jiggling with his seismic laughter. He was at least a minute letting that laugh run its course, and easing his belt, and wiping his eyes.

"Skarth, that—that's irresistible." Ahdio glanced over and called his limping helper, too often called "the Gimp" and supposedly Ahdio's cousin's son from Twand. "Throde! C'mere a moment, lad." Ahdio lifted his head. "Frax! Come 'ere a moment, will you?''

Thus it fell out that Strick's bodyguard served as manager of Sly's for a few hours, while Ouleh and Nimsy helped Ahdio's wife tend to business, and Hanse, with a cloaked and hatted Ahdio and Throde, drifted down into that lowest of low ghettos of poverty and stench, Downwind. There the other two learned that under his robe Hanse wore black, black, black, and knives. Both of them recognized the working clothes of the cat burglar called Shadowspawn. He had a lot of good strong rope, too.

Shadowspawn and Throde, wall-climbers both, had to work together: although Ahdio was mighty big, they got him up the side of the building.

Linza was the best thing that had happened to Tarkle in years. He could never understand why he wasn't more popular, among people of both sexes. Oh, no one had ever told him he was handsome or cute either, but what were looks after all when a man was bigger than big and could handle anybody, anybody at all, and really did try to be likable? He had bought beer, ale, even wine for more than one girl and a couple of women, but somehow or another before That Time of Night came around he had somehow or another alienated them and they somehow or other abandoned him to go home alone. Tonight he counted himself really lucky. Oh, true,

Linza's eyebrows met in the middle about like those of that
bastard Hanse, and under those brows—or that brow—one of
Linza's eyes looked ahead and one sort of looked off to the
side, and her nose wasn't so good (but only when looked at
from the side) and she sure wasn't fussy about washing her
hair either, or doing much of anything with it. And he wasn't
too crazy about her voice. But after all what were those; just
imperfections. The point was that she had a really good body
and was willing to share it with Tarkle. That was what
counted, after all.

Besides, she had run out of any kind of wherewithal whatever and didn't have anyplace to stay tonight.

So, holding her close as they climbed the stairs and sort of
letting his hand slide up under that big soft bosom of hers so
that he could feel the restless pendulum's warmth on the edge
and back of his hand, he escorted her to his place and up the
three flights to his room. They didn't talk much, but Tarkle
wasn't too good at talking anyhow and by now Linza was
lurching quite a bit from all those mugs of beer he'd bought
her at the Vulgar Unicorn. This was a wonderful night, he
thought, as he steered her leftward at the top of the steps, and
it was going to be even wonderfuller. Plenty of bed-bouncing
tonight! He was about to drown—happily—in big soft restless
pendulums!

He knew Linza would like his room. Tarkle was big enough
so he didn't have to worry about anything even in this neighborhood, but the fact that his room was on the fourth floor
would make her feel safer. He had a pretty good chair and
one not quite as good, and two rugs, and that nice piece of
wood on the wall, and a good big window—with curtains,
even—and a good large, padded sleeping pallet, and a table
and even a washbowl. All that luxury was in addition to the
two beer barrels he had stolen and cut in half, so that one
made a lamp table and the other a nice seat or footrest or
whatever it was a person might need. His clothing and the
few valuables he kept here were in the big heavy press
standing in the far corner.

"Ah, locked up tight," he said, and Linza with her arm
around him squeezed his waist and made a sound somewhere
between a giggle and a chuckle and a hiccup, and Tarkle

congratulated himself on his good fortune and again counted himself really lucky to have her here with him.

He got the door unlocked and, with a sweeping gesture, pushed it open and swung his arm wide in welcome.

Linza started into the moonlit room, and shivered against him. "Quite a breeze comin' in that window," she said. "You ought to have curtains—hey! Is this a joke er somethin'?"

Tarkle was staring into his room. His whole stomach felt as if it had sunk into his crotch but a great big lump had come up in his throat and despite the draft from the curtainless, open window he was hot, hot, prickly and sweaty in the armpits.

His room was empty.

No curtains. No rugs or cut-down beer kegs. No table and no chairs. No sleeping pallet. No piece of wood nicely mounted on the wall. No lamp and no washbowl. This was impossible; he'd had to plead and bully the aid of two other strong men to wrestle the big tall and *very* heavy clothespress up here and into his room, and even it was gone!

It simply was not possible. He was staring into a bare room without even a scrap of string. It looked larger, empty this way; and so lonely, so pitifully bare, so clean; and as a matter of fact even the floor seemed to have been *swept* clean.

One article, one of all his worldly possessions save what he wore and carried, remained. A pair of winter leggings lay neatly arranged on the floor with the bottoms of the legs pointed neatly toward the doorway where he stood. The legs were well apart; the leggings had been sliced all the way in half right up the middle, right up the crotch.

It just wasn't possible, Tarkle thought, just as his knees buckled.

They celebrated relatively quietly in the back room of Sly's Place, whoever Sly was or had been. Ahdio's wife Jodeera was not happy with some of what she heard from him and the other two jovial triumphants; she muttered, "Boys, just big overgrown boys," now and then, and gave her husband dark looks. Others were directed at that bad influence named Hanse and called Shadowspawn. Yet now and again she had to laugh along with this trio of night-stalkers who couldn't stop talking about what they had done tonight.

"Like to ha' killed all three of us," Ahdio laughed, slapping his belly and reaching over to pour another mug of his better beer.

"Well, I told you we should have moved the clothespress when we first got there and weren't already tired," Shadowspawn said, and Throde chuckled.

"Should have seen it," Ahdio said. "You should have seen it!"

"The gods know I've *heard* enough about it," Jodeera said.

"Not enough," he said, and laughed anew. "Never enough!"

"I druther see the look on that bullying shithead's face," Throde said, staring wistfully into his severalth beer.

"Like to killed all three of us," Ahdio said, "boosting and pulling and grunting that huge press out the window and up onto the roof! These two were pushing and grunting and cursing and I was dragging and sweating and grunting—and cursing, pulling it up with the ropes . . . That damned press is bigger'n I am."

"You could have hurt yourself," Jodeera said.

"Arrr, m'gal, your husband's big enough to handle a little moving job for a friend," Ahdiovizun said, shaking as his voice rose into another laugh.

It kept rising, and Ahdio kept shaking, and the tailless cat named Sweetboy scuttled with a sulky look as the big man nearly fell out of his chair laughing.

"Besides, I had that dry-tack glue on my feet," he said. "The stuff Hanse got from Cholly. It made it easy for me to go up that wall—almost as well and easily as these two wall-climbers." He beamed at his employee and his friend the cat burglar. "Come on back, Sweetboy. Here, I'll pour you a tot."

"But what if someone had seen you?" Jodeera asked.

"Some—who d'you think might've seen us?"

"Someone walking along the street—" she said, and broke off to glance at Hanse, who had snorted.

"We was down in *Downwind*," Throde said. "Up a wall

above an alley. *No*body walks down alleys in Downwind, day *or* night!''

"Oh," she said. "I've never been . . . well. A mean trick on a mean man," she said, and again she could not hold back a smile. "D'you think Tarkle will ever find his things?''

"How?" Throde said. "Nobody but Shadowspawn 'n' me could get up on that roof to see all that stuff!''

Despite the impolite noises Sweetboy was making lapping beer out of his bowl, they all looked at Hanse, who had been nursing one mug of beer for a long, long while. He was not laughing, or even smiling, and he spoke to his mug.

"So much for Tarkle," he said grimly. "Now for that swine Marype.''

Ahdio's face went serious. "It's time I told you something Throde heard that little piece of excrement Hakky say the other night.''

Hanse turned his dark-eyed gaze on Throde.

"Somebody was talking about you seeming to drop out of sight again," Throde told him, "and Hakky told him—quietly, grinning—that Tarkle told him Amoli had hired him to get rid of you, and even told him how to go about it.''

Ahdio snorted. "He said that she said that he said that I said that she s—''

"Who's Amoli?" Jodeera broke in, and Ahdio had to laugh.

"Not someone you'd be likely to know, sweetheart. She's the proprietor of a whorehouse called the Lily Garden.''

The homely woman blinked. She looked at Hanse. "But why—what*ever* have you done to offend a ho'house madam, Hanse?''

But Shadowspawn was staring at Throde. His face registered astonishment, or perhaps it was revelation. Whatever it was, his eyes showed that he had gone back inside himself, where he was deep in cerebration, and calculation, and machination.

Abruptly he rose and left. The other three stared at the doorway through which he had departed their company. Ahdio gave his head a shake.

"And good night to you too, Hanse," he muttered.

*   *   *

Hanse returned to his room long enough to don his padded vest, collect a delighted Notable, and, once they were outside, wait without patience while the cat relieved himself. He was walking away before Notable was satisfied with his ritual sniffing of his urine. The cat snapped his tail to attention and hurried after him, making a complaining noise.

"Be quiet, Notable," Hanse muttered. "We're on business."

Notable replied with a small burbling sound from the throat. It became a hissy noise while he bristled at the dark-cloaked figure that moved toward them just as they stepped out onto the street. When Notable bristled he became about twice as big as he was, which was large enough to frighten big dogs and bigger humans. Yet the smallish approacher took no note, but moved almost stiffly toward Hanse with fixed purpose. Shadowspawn saw, too, and although he made no sound a knife appeared in his left fist too fast for him to have drawn it. But he had.

"*Hanse,*" Mignureal said in an intense tone, "*Hanse!*"

"Easy, Notable! Jileel—what are you doing here at this time of ni—" Hanse's nape bristled and he broke off.

He had heard Mignue's voice, and knew it was Jileel, and yet he had heard more, too: it was that *strange* voice he had heard from Mignue, on a few occasions. Always when he was off on business; always when she had no idea as to his intent, much less his goal. He stepped leftward so that she had to turn. That way a bit of light from a window up the street showed him her eyes. Yes, and that eerie feeling enveloped him. Her eyes were all fixed and starey, really looking as if she weren't at home in there.

"*Hanse—be sure to take that knife with the silver blade.*"

Hanse shivered. O Father Ils! Jileel had it too, then! The S'danzo Seeing ability. And it was as it manifested itself in her older sister, rather than in their murdered mother and indeed any other S'danzo Hanse knew or knew about; Jileel and Mignue didn't have to be given anything, didn't have to *try* to See. They just did.

His voice a little shaky, he was putting away his knife as he said or started to say, "I have it—" and another, taller figure in a cloak came up, and the cloak's hood was up, and this one had two others behind it/him/her, and the sticker was right back in Shadowspawn's hand.

"My hands are in plain sight and you will not need the knife, young man. Do please calm that huge dog as well."

"Termagant!" Hanse said.

"Termagant?" Jileel said in a more normal voice, although it sounded weak. She was reeling, and the tall woman swung an arm around her.

"*Mrrrraowww . . .*"

"A *cat*?!"

"No, Notable: Easy. No danger." And to the much respected Old Woman of the S'danzo: "What are you doing here?"

At the same time Jileel was saying, "What are we doing here?"

The tall older woman tore her gaze away from the astonishing cat. "I think this wants an explanation, young man."

"His name is Hanse. What are you doing here, Hanse?"

"I have a name, old woman. My name is Hanse."

Blinking in surprise and some confusion if not quite revelation, the Termagant looked down at the girl. "No, Jileel, that is the wrong question. What are *you* doing here?"

"Uhh . . . out . . . walking with you? I feel a little funny . . ."

"Termagant," Shadowspawn said in a quiet and decisive voice that commanded the gaze of all eyes. "Those are your bodyguards?"

She seemed to grow taller. "*Escorts.*"

He nodded. "Uh-huh. Jileel, you just had a fainting spell. Take it easy, but step over there with the *escorts* while I have a few words with the Termagant. Careful, now."

The confused Jileel allowed herself to be eased away by one of the two tall cloaks, while Shadowspawn never took his black-eyed gaze off the senior S'danzo.

"Is this where you live, Hanse?"

"Yes."

"And how is it that Jileel knows where you live?"

"Termagant, I swear to you that she does not. You just heard her ask what I'm doing here. She came to warn me without knowing where I was going or where I live." Seeing her lips part, he raised a hand. "Wait. Listen a moment."

He told her about Mignureal, and how she had more than once warned him, as if with a knowledge she could not have. "But did, Termagant, did," he said. "And now Jileel's done it, just like her sister."

She looked surprised, but not as much as she might have. "I know the truth of that about Mignureal," she said. "Her mother told me of it. It is part of the reason I have been interested in Jileel beyond my usual concern for a blooming young woman of my people. Girl, girl," she corrected herself, too hurriedly.

Hanse knew she was reminding herself to keep reminding him that Jileel was only a girl. *And keep your thieving* un-S'danzo *paws off 'er, streetboy,* he thought, but showed nothing.

"Did what she said to you make sense?"

"As it did with Mignue. Once she just seemed to appear—as Jileel did just now—to warn me to be sure to take the striped bowl. It was true I had one, but she had never seen it. It contained lime. If I had not had lime with me that night, I'd have died of Kurd's sorcery."

"Kurd!"

"Another time she bobbed up to warn me to 'take the big red cat.' She had never even seen Notable—this big red cat, here."

"Big, indeed."

"But if I'd not taken him along, I'd have died that night of a Stare-eye snake. A Beysib's, uh . . . ."

"Beynit," she supplied. "You do live an exciting life, young m—Hanse. That monster, Kurd. I think I'll just not ask about that occasion. And on neither occasion Mignureal knew where you were going?"

Rather than risk an error in deciphering that question, Hanse nodded. At least he'd blocked an older person's snotty habit of saying "young man" and "young woman" by the trick of calling her "old woman." He said, "Both times she had no idea. And other times, up in Firaqa."

"And tonight . . . ."

"I assure you, Termagant, no one knows where I am going. A very bad man tried to have me sold as slave, and I think he has already profited from the sale of many others. I intend to stop him.''

"Please . . . would you please say to me her words to you? Jileel's, I mean, tonight.''

"Right after you tell me what you are doing here—I mean, did you follow her or go out walking and lose her, or what?''

It took her a moment to digest the fact that he was as demanding as she, even with *her*. If she found that indigestible, she at least packed it away somewhere in a corner of her craw.

"I was visiting her home. Suddenly she rose and left the room without a word. That is not like her. When we saw her slip out, very hurriedly and cloaked, I counseled her father to silence and I and my two escorts followed her. We followed not as spies, but as protectors, but we did not need to be stealthy; she seemed aware of nothing. She just hurried, hurried. Now I know why—I suppose. Hers and her sister's powers transcend even mi-most.''

"Spies can be protectors,'' he said, letting her know that he knew when a person told a little lie, even the Termagant. And he answered her question: "She stared odd, just the way Mignue does. Did. Her voice was odd, too, just the way Mignue's was. She said my name two or three times, and warned me to take the knife with the silver blade.''

"You have such a knife?''

"I'd show it to you, but I wouldn't want to upset your *escorts*.''

She did not smile, but her eyes did, or nearly. "Now, Hanse . . . can you imagine why such a knife might be of value to you this night?''

"*Will* be, Termagant, will be, if Jileel has the same power as her sister. You know about silver and sorcery.''

Her little sigh was almost inaudible, but she let exasperation color her tone. "I know about silver and sorcery, Hanse.'' He said nothing; she started to speak; suddenly her eyes widened. "Don't tell me this very bad man you mentioned is a *sorcerer*.''

"I hadn't intended to tell you, Termagant.'' When she stared without speaking, he told her. "He is.''

She heaved a sigh, shook her head, glanced over at Jileel, looked back at the youthful man all in snug black.

"Hanse: A few days ago I referred to your reputation. Perhaps it is a bit more than it should be . . . or a bit less . . . well, perhaps those who talk do not know quite all there is to know about this Hanse person."

"No one does, Termagant, believe me."

"I promise not to try to learn more than you want me to know. Will you come and see me, Hanse?"

"Not tonight!?"

"No, no, not tonight, Hanse. At a reasonable time of day when this night's work is done and you can come and visit me in the next day or three, will you do so?"

"Termagant, I will."

"Good," she said, with an exuberant nod. "Then when you come to see me, Hanse, bring me this." Her long-fingered hands came out from within her cloak, and in an instant she had draped a piece of cord over his neck. Something thumped his chest and he looked down.

He was more than surprised. "You give me an amulet, Termagant?"

"I loan you a keepsake, Hanse."

"I thank you, I think. Uh—is it all right if I tuck it inside my tunic?"

For once, she chuckled. "Yes, Hanse, that will be all right."

He nodded, one sharp brief bob of his head. "Good. Thank you. I am glad to know that Mignu—that Jileel is in good hands. The Termagant herself, and two *big* escorts."

For the second time he had made her chuckle, even while she rankled at not having terminated their conversation before he did. A very nervy and decisive young man—and didn't he just love and perhaps live for danger and excitement! No tools or concentration were necessary for her to see that, not her. She well knew that her own abilities were almost equal parts intuition, and observation, and the S'danzo ability.

"Good night, Hanse, and good fortune."

"Notable, we have to be on our way. Good night to you, Termagant, and Jileel, and to you too, you great big pair of escorts, you."

With tail high Notable moved along beside his human, who almost at once took up his nighttime habit of keeping to shadows and alleys. Notable saw quite well in such environs at night, and surely gave no thought to the fact that the black-clad man moved just as unerringly. As a matter of fact Hanse was moving almost without seeing. His brain was busy, working to match Jodeera's information with what had happened to him.

Any city such as Sanctuary had its share of whorehouses: good ones, low ones, and intermediate. True, Sanctuary probably had *more* than its share, particularly of low and intermediate houses. That described the one owned and operated by Amoli: the Lily Garden was not far from the Maze and yet not within those low and dangerous precincts. Thus it was one of the respectable brothels in the town called Thieves' World. Amoli had been friend to the drug dealer Lastel, who had disappeared. Shadowspawn knew of the tunnel leading from Amoli's house-not-home up to the fine home that had belonged to Lastel and was now owned or at least occupied by Marype the mage. In fact Shadowspawn had made use of that tunnel. His nocturnal visit to Marype's den had saved the life of a client of Strick's; in gratitude the fellow had sold the Vulgar Unicorn to Strick at a decent price. Unfortunately that same visit had resulted in Marype's taking vengeance on Thieves' World's thief of thieves. Shadowspawn was sure of that. Yet one aspect of the affair had nagged at his mind: how had Marype known who had been in his lair?

So it was Amoli who sent Tarkle after me. So Tarkle works for her? Or she and Tarkle both work for Marype—or she and that slimebag mage are partners or lovers or both. And the moment I visited his house I was brilliant enough to let her know! Damn! Stupid, Hanse, stupid! Two minutes after I left her that night she must've been hustling her hippy self along the tunnel to tell Marype!

"What we ought to do," he muttered, "is shave some of that fat off the bitch and feed it to her!"

"Mmmaw?"

"Hush, Notable, damn it, I told you to be qui—oh. I thought aloud, didn't I?"

Notable made no comment. He was only an unusually large

and unusually smart cat, although once he had been a man.

Abruptly his human seemed to disappear, and in some shock the cat had to spend a second or three finding him. He blinked pupils gone huge and round as a pigeon's eggs as he stared up at the lean man in black, who was ascending a brick wall in a way that could have been used as training for frightened kittens. Unfrightened, Notable followed. He was almost as quiet, almost as competent at wall-climbing. Almost.

Shadowspawn paused on a ledge formed by a set-in second floor.

"Here," he whispered, "you're too slow. Get on my back."

Notable let him know he'd rather just do his own climbing, but he went along. Resentful, he sank his claws well in. Hanse didn't mind; that was the reason he had so recently acquired the padded vest—black. With Notable riding his back without the hint of a purr, Shadowspawn went on up and onto the roof.

Notable might or might not have been capable or willing to make the necessary jump across the long black rectangle that was an alley, but Shadowspawn did not consult the cat. He gathered himself, crouched, measured, shifted to allow for the change in balance caused by the cat's weight on his back. He did reach back with one hand to press and stroke, once, while he murmured a friendly sound. Then he jumped.

Notable made no comment. He just clung, and clung tightly—meaning deeply. Had it not been for the vest, Hanse might well have been wearing several claws to a depth of a foot or so. Again he reached back to give him an encouraging stroke and tried to press his face against Notable's.

Notable moved his head and averted his face.

"Goo-ood Notable," Shadowspawn whispered.

His miffed rider did not deign to acknowledge those sounds he had come to know and love. He began wriggling, preparing to jump down. Shadowspawn pressed harder.

He murmured, "Just hang on, Notable. See, we cross this roof—uh." He broke off while someone passed on the street or "street" below. "Then we break into a trot an'—"

He jumped again, pouncing more as Notable might have done than in the way of a man. He landed almost noiselessly on another roof with his knees bent nearly up to his chest. This roof sloped and Shadowspawn dropped both hands to it, and pressed. He remained in that position long enough to be sure he was not going to lose footing.

Notable meanwhile drew in all claws, gathering himself, then shot out the rearward ones long enough to leap past this maniacal human's head and onto the roof. He ran right up and stopped only when he was on the ridgepole, which was not so narrow as the pointed-wedge sort. Tail lashing, he pretended to have been solely interested all along in gnawing a particular place in his coat. He peeped around casually to see Shadowspawn sitting athwart the ridgepole, unraveling a slender and expensive rope from around his waist.

"If you don't climb on me," he muttered over his shoulder, "it'll be a lot harder for you to get down."

He followed that with a kissing noise. Notable's tail moved restlessly in indecision but he pretended to have something caught in his paw that needed gnawing out. Another glance showed him that the human had tethered his line and was letting himself over the edge of the roof. Trotting along the ridgepole as if it were a broad meadow, the big cat paused to lower his head and stare into Shadowspawn's eyes. Shadowspawn made another kissy noise. Quite delicately for one his size, Notable stepped onto the black-clad shoulder and leaned against the youthful face. He rode down.

Not far. Amoli liked to sun herself, which was why she had caused the little railed balcony to be constructed just outside her window. To her, it was useless at night. Not to Shadowspawn. He whispered, "*We're there,*" and moments later was preparing to enter the darkened room. It was all as simple as that . . .

Except that just as he was about to swing over the sill the door opened from the corridor, and light from ensconced lamps as well as a carried one burst into the room.

"—as soon as we have accumulated enough money from the slave business," a voice was saying, and it was the voice of Marype, who was just behind Amoli, who bore the lamp, and in those few words he had told Hanse everything Hanse had wondered about; everything he wanted to know.

Cat and cat burglar crouched low in the darkness outside

the window, with black-haired tan hand pressing red fur in an
urgent request for motionless silence. As he had learned to do
long ago from his mentor Cudget, the superb thief called
Shadowspawn did not try to see, or to hold his breath; he
controlled his breathing while he listened. He heard the door
close. He didn't have to look to be aware that the light
remained within the chamber. He didn't hear the chest being
opened, but he heard the jingle and then the sound of a lid
closing. A key turned in a lock.

"Always a pleasure," Amoli said.

". . . business with Tarkle," the voice of Marype muttered, and the door opened again, and closed. The light
remained. Shadowspawn stayed where he was, crouched. His
head was cocked so that he could stare up at a slow-moving
cloud, gray against midnight blue and black. When he decided that it had moved enough, he rose and entered Amoli's
private chamber.

She sat before her little table a couple of feet from her bed,
gazing into the costly electrum mirror she had propped up
while she adjusted her high-coiffed hair. With eyes much
larger than the gold coins called imperials, she stared at the
dark-clad reflection of the young man behind her. The elbow
of his upraised left arm pointed at her; the hand was just
beyond his ear. Amoli's eyes flared and her mouth began
widening.

"You try yelling or reaching for anything untoward and I
throw," he told her quietly. "I know who told Tarkle what to
do to get rid of me. I know who pays Tarkle. I know what
you and Marype are up to. I know you told him I'd been there
that night, almost the moment I left here. Also, I just heard
you two. Amoli, open that chest."

She stared at him in the mirror. "I—he took the key."

"In that case we just ruin the lock. I'm no beginner at
that."

Slowly, she turned. Slowly, she rose, all prosperously
plump and soft in silk and lace of rose and pale blue, scattered with jewels and a wetly glistening string of fine pearls.
Only then did she notice the great big red animal.

"Oh!"

Notable replied with a long *r*-sound.

"Easy, Notable, she's too smart to try anything stupid with two of us armed with all these sharp things." He showed Amoli a clear-eyed gaze. "You remember I told you about my attack-trained watch cat? Did you think I was joking?"

"You intend to take the money, Hanse? Rob me?"

"I forgot to mention, don't try any dumb words to persuade, either," he told her in that same soft voice. "We all know where that money came from. Even my price is in there—the price the slavedealers paid your lackey Tarkle for me. I have to pay Jubal rather more to be able to call myself free again; he *bought* me, Amoli, old friend."

She was shaking and her eyes continued wide and glassy as her earrings. "I'll give you—"

'You'll give me the pearls, Amoli, and six hundred pieces of gold. Just six hundred."

"Oh, not the pearls!" Her hand went to them.

He knew at once that it was just as he had supposed; they were indeed good pearls, and they meant more to her than the gold. Hanse was pleased. He said, "Yes, the pearls."

She made a sobby sound. Seeing his implacable stare, she heaved a great sigh and brushed clothing off an apparent low table. That revealed the table as a long, good-sized chest. After a hesitation and another sigh, she squatted beside it. He watched her extract the large black key from her bosom.

"He made me, Hanse. I didn't—"

He moved a couple of paces to be nearer her, and between her and the door. He had relaxed his cocked arm, but made sure she could see the flat, hiltless throwing knife between his fingers. "Your luck is that you're not lying there wearing this sticker in your key-nook and staring straight up at nothing while *I* open that thing," he told her. "Don't just blabber and make me mad, all right? Both you and Marype are leaving this town. I hope you don't love him, Amoli. I had decided to let you walk out."

She heard his gentle emphasis on the words "had" and "you," and again a shiver rustled her silk.

"I don't love him," she said. "He isn't even M—but damn it, I do love these pearls."

He smiled. Her words and tone told him that she had resigned herself, made up her mind to stay alive and safe. She was going to do it. He watched her lift the lid of the short coffin. She took out the several bags tucked inside and commenced counting out gold coins into one of them. To Shadowspawn the clinking noises were as perfumed lips whispering sweet anythings in his ear.

"Sure a lot more than five hundred imperials in there, aren't there?" he said conversationally.

Either Amoli considered it wiser not to reply—or perhaps too distasteful to think about how much was here and how much of it was about to depart her company.

"What d'you think five hundred imperials weigh?"

"Not nearly enough to be so important," she said.

"Amoli," he said, in a dangerous voice, "I asked—"

"A few pounds. Three or four."

"When you've counted five hundred into that bag, just pop in the pearls and count the rest into another."

"Oh, Hanse, my pearls . . . oh, I'm so sorry . . ." She began to sob.

"Well, I could let you keep the pearls, but they'd probably just take 'em away from you."

"Wh—who?"

"The fellows on the next ship bound for Bandara, after I sold you to 'em."

This time her sob was louder and her shiver a real bosom-rocker.

"Or Kadakithis's dungeon guard, once I'd turned you over to him," Hanse said, in that same soft and perfectly equable tone. "Did you know I spent a whole night tied up inside a big-but-not-big-enough sack in the hold of that damned ship, Amoli? Hmmm? Oh, I did a lot of thinking—I had a *lot* of time to think, Amoli."

Weepily she braced herself and lifted both hands to remove her pearls. Resembling a mother bidding a last goodbye to a darling child just deceased, she moved her hand very slowly to the gold-laden bag. Lovingly, regretfully she deposited the necklace inside. And sniffed loudly. To Hanse's expert eye it looked as if she might be stiffening a bit, maybe preparing for a sudden movement.

"I am so grateful you decided to be smart, Amoli," he reminded her. "I am not fond of killing, but when I throw a sticker at someone, I usually aim at the brightest part. You know, the eye.''

The gemmy pendants from her earrings tinkled with her shudder. She sniffed again, jerked her head to clear tears, and shuddered again when that afforded her a sideward glance of a prowling, improbably red cat of a size sufficient to give pause to demons. She wiped her eyes with her fingers, which she wiped on her skirt where it stretched taut over her thigh. And she began counting gold coins into another draw-mouth bag of soft leather.

''Forget about turning me over to the prince or the slavers,'' she said quietly without looking up, ''and you can have all of it.''

''Then I'd be rich and probably start thinking stupid thoughts about stupid things like maybe trying to take over Sanctuary. And what's a thief without a reason to go out at night? It's my main enjoyment in life. No, I have a better use for all that gold.''

''—nine, one hundred,'' she said at last. ''There.'' She looked up. Her tears and the lead sulphide preparation she used around her eyes had left dark streaks on her plump cheeks. ''Why two bags?''

''Just pass that one to me. I'm going to hand it back to you. For the sum of one hundred pieces of gold, and good imperials at that, I am buying the Lily Garden. You write that out, Amoli. I'll bet the deed's in the bottom of that chest, right?''

''A hun—'' She clamped her lips.

''Yes, I know,'' he said. ''I'm worth more than you got for me, too. As a matter of fact I'm also worth more than those five hundred I'm going to sling through Jubal's window one dark night! Just write it right, Amoli.''

Working her bejeweled fingers down into gold and wiggling them about with care, she fished out the little oilskin packet and extracted the deed. She was just beginning to write on it when someone knocked at the door. She jerked hard, then looked at Hanse. He lifted his left hand for an exaggerated inspection of his knife, and gestured loosely with the right.

Amoli twisted half around on her backless chair and spoke

to the door. "I do *not* want to be disturbed," she snapped. "See that you tell everyone else that. *Everyone,* Vissy."

"But ma'am—" a voice began; the voice of one of the girls.

Hanse made his voice as deep and growly as it would go, and tried to add a lazy-sleepy note. "Shall we include her in our bondage game, darling, or d'you want me t'just go carve out that little bird-turd's blabbery tongue for you?"

No further sound came from beyond the door. Amoli returned to printing words on the bill of sale. She signed it; she used her stamp; she twisted around again to look at Hanse.

"It's done. You want to put your mark on it?"

"Kneel there on the floor, Amoli. That's a safe position, while I *sign* that document."

She knew very well that he could not write or read, but had not dared try to trick him. Nor did she snort at his words. She assumed the position she had taken many times in her line of work, and waited while he made far more marks on the deed than he needed to make an X; a dozen or so. She was beyond surprised to see that he had printed five rather crudely formed but clearly recognizable letters:

H A N S E

"Now I tell you what, Amoli," Hanse said, slipping the document back into its packet and the oilskin down into his tunic. "I'm going to make you a guarantee. I'm going to visit Marype. You put your hands back and cross 'em, and I swear to come back and let you and that bag of a hundred imperials see just how fast you can get yourself out of Sanctuary."

"Whe—where am I going to go-o-o," she whimpered, while he tore cloth and bound her wrists with care to pull the strip of silk between as well as around them.

Suddenly the dark, hawk-nosed face of the sinister night-worker called Shadowspawn came over her shoulder. About an inch from hers, it stared with eyes black as the bottom of a well at midnight.

"You can go straight to any hell you care to, you rotten swinish seller of people," he told her in a voice suddenly quivery with malice, "or just make up your mind to shut up and head for Suma or wherever the next caravan is going. You'll have a hundred fine Rankan imperials, sure!y ninety percent gold, to get you started in the business you know best.''

She swallowed and clamped her teeth, not to mention her lips.

"That's good. Now open wide. *Wider,* damn you!''

He left her lying on her side and half curled on her bed, facing the wall. Her wrists were crossed and bound behind her with a linking line to her ankles, which were also united and pulled up to the backs of her thighs. A lot of silk crowded her mouth and propped it open; a broad violet sash held the gag in place. A broad and folded strip of cotton blindfolded her. Hanse let her hear him close the chest.

"All right, Notable," he said, picking up the cat, "now you just sit right here on this chest and keep an eye—no, both eyes on that tired old whore. If that fat butt moves, hit it with claws 'n' teeth both!''

While a new shiver ran through the bound, blind, voiceless package on the bed, Hanse departed. Carrying Notable.

Using the back stairs he knew Amoli reserved for the use of herself and special clients only, he descended to street level and below, and in short order was moving once again through the dark tunnel that connected Amoli's house with Marype's home—that is, the house that had belonged to Lastel.

"Last time we came along here a large rat attacked," Shadowspawn remarked. "A *very* large rat, and I was fool enough to think it was illusion. Remember, Notable? Notable? Ah, you remember—how charming you look pacing along three feet behind!''

In reply he received a low-voiced *r*-sound.

They went carefully. Shadowspawn liked the dark right enough, but not dark tunnels. He had spent too much very unpleasant time in that maze under Corstic's manse up in Firaqa, accompanied only by the Eye. This time there was nothing. They were not assaulted, either by things sorcerous or un-. Likely Marype's attention had been on his "business with Tarkle," rather than arming the musty old secret entry to his keep in the way he knew best. On the other hand the sorcerous attack on Hanse and Notable had come *after* their previous visit to Marype's den; perhaps the mage left the way clear for Amoli and maybe Tarkle, but something actuated defenses against someone leaving. Unless Marype somehow temporarily suspended it.

Once again a living shadow and an alert yet purring cat came ghosting into the dark-halled home that had been Lastel's and was now Marype/Markmor's. This time they paced the dim corridors, soft-soled buskins as silent on good carpet as the cat's pads, without pausing to peer beyond the closed doors they passed. Seeing no one, hearing no sound and making none, man and cat went directly to that room containing a worktable and things that made the hair twitch on Hanse's nape. Nor was Notable happy to approach the tall door. Once again of many times the walking shadow could not avoid the thought of how despicable sorcery was to him.

And this time . . . this time the people-peddling slime is here!

Reason enough to be more than cautious. Shadowspawn moved close to the big paneled door and pressed against the wall beside it. He listened. He heard sounds, right enough, within the chamber of Marype's sorceries. *O Father Ils and all gods, how I hate sorcery and those who practice it!* And: *He's home, all right. Now should I just—*

His heart leaped and adrenaline surged when something bumped his leg. He released his breath and concentrated on careful breathing: he had felt Notable, of course. Hanse moved his leg slowly in a return caress/scent-sharing.

Why am I doing this? Why don't we just forget this? he mused. *We could go do something fun and less dangerous, like climbing to the top of the governor's palace and jumping off, or lying down for a nap in the stall of an unbroken horse, or—*

The handle clacked and an instant later the door opened. Light burst into the corridor. For once Shadowspawn was not happy to have Notable as company; Hanse might well have stood as he was and let the mage pass. That was not the way of a startled cat. Notable hissed and spat. Just as startled, the emerging Marype reacted automatically with a curse and a kick. His boot made a *whump* noise in the furry side of a large target and the cat sailed several feet down the corridor with tail all abristle and legs flailing—twisting in air to land on all four feet.

Standing beside Shadowspawn without seeing him, a no longer silver-haired Marype cursed again, stared at the cat, gestured at him, started to mumble . . .

Shadowspawn hit him hard in the stomach, backhand in passing, and pounced three feet backward to spin and come down in a crouch facing the sorcerer. Soft, silent buskins alit almost on Notable. The cat made his spit-sputtery sound again and leaped away; the human was silent and went motionless save that one hand snapped back past his ear. The mage gasped, doubled partway, hands to his middle. He straightened and his mouth snapped wide open to yell. That created a target that was a large one, for Shadowspawn. His arm rushed forward, a long swing with long follow-through, and the dagger streaked. It streaked into the target: the open hole between Marype's nose and chin. The silver-chased blade pinned Marype's tongue to the back of his mouth. He made a gargly sound and both hands rushed to his mouth. Meanwhile he staggered back into his sorcerous den.

"Wait!" Shadowspawn called, but Notable was barreling past him after the man who had dared kick him and, in a far more important offense, embarrassed him by taking him by surprise.

"Notable!" Shadowspawn charged after the cat.

Inside the chamber a hideous feline yowling mingled with the hideous gargling sounds Marype made around a mouthful of knife and blood. Hanse rushed in to see the cat looking even bigger because he was all abristle. Yet he was moveless, held in frozen motion by some gesture and gargly mumble of the mage, Notable's stiff, extended tail resembling a steel-spined red brush.

"Here, sorcerer, have another knife!"

The wounded, horrified Marype should not have been able to move as fast as he did; fast enough to dodge the rushing blade. Yet in hurling himself aside he hit the edge of his big table, which teetered with a screech of its legs on the floor. Its litter rattled and toppled. Marype stumbled away, and in desperation now he was able to commit the horrible act he had been trying to gain nerve to accomplish; he dragged the knife back through his tongue and out of his mouth. Meanwhile various tools and uglinesses of his trade went scattering onto the floor from the rocked table.

That included a very pretty cage containing a small furry animal. The cage hit the floor with a rattly bang that dented and bent the bars of soft metal. It rolled noisily. In terror the small furry animal squeezed out and bolted. A large furry animal, no longer held by the sorcerer's spell, became pure cat and pounced. A moment later he was crunching. His mouth trailed the stubby little tail of a vole.

And Marype who was Markmor screamed, a high-pitched wail that diminished rapidly—as he did. Marype was gone, dead; Markmor occupied that body while his own soul reposed in the body of the vole. The vole was eaten. Marype's body was neither occupied nor alive. It began to deteriorate, hurrying to catch up to several weeks' delayed putrescence.

The sight was ugly, horripilating; the stench was beyond horrible.

"Gahh!" Shadowspawn grabbed his nose with thumb and curled forefinger hard enough to hurt. "Notable! Out of here! Gahh!"

And he fled, a huge red demonic *thing* racing after him as if in chase, trailing a straight-out tail like a red bristle-brush. They raced through the house and down to the concealed entry to the old tunnel and along it, and neither stopped running until they were re-entering the Lily Garden.

While he was freeing Amoli of gag, blindfold, and bonds Hanse told her of the horror he and Notable had just fled. "Marype just . . . just . . ."

"That was not Marype," she managed to say, having worked up a little moisture in her dry, dry mouth and licked her lips many times. "Marype is dead. He was stupid enough to bring back Markmor, and Markmor rewarded him by murdering him. Your cat killed Markmor and you watched what happens to a dead man weeks after he died. And I'll tell you, Hanse, Shadowspawn, thief and mage-killer and probably hero too— you've done me a favor tonight. I've got a hundred imperials and my life and I am very, very glad to get *out* of this town!"

And she went.

Next day Hanse, undisguised, visited Strick to advise that

he had found the perfect disguise and a fine business venture for Taya. Strick did what he could and sent her to Ahdio for a more permanent spell. She emerged still shapely and still attractive, but no longer Taya, former prince's playmate. She was Altaya, proprietor and Strick's partner in ownership of the Lily Garden.

That afternoon two men in Strick blue delivered to the palace the jingly contents of Amoli's and Markmor/Marype's chest, to be used in the continuing reconstruction of the city. "To make it Sanctuary's work for Sanctuary," the message signed by Strick and by Hanse read, "independent of Ranke."

Hanse was meanwhile presenting the father of Mignureal and Jileel with a bag containing fine and far too valuable pearls which he had not stolen. He strongly suggested that Teretaff cause the pearls to be made into ear-drops for his several daughters, and "bury the rest under the floor or someplace."

He left without Teretaff's knowing of the sack of gold pieces Hanse had secreted in his shop-home, for safekeeping.

A few hours later in the Vulgar Unicorn, Hanse slipped a lot of golden imperials to the serving girl Silky, and bought drinks for the house until the Vulg grew so boisterously noisy he couldn't stand it, after which he ambled around to Sly's Place. There he bought drinks for the house, but left when the place grew so noisy he couldn't stand it. He went home with a large bucket of beer and enjoyed watching Notable get thoroughly drunk. Watching a cat stagger was more fun than Hanse could remember.

A week later he traded with Cholly the gluemaker for a dagger he recognized: a handsome affair. True, its hilt was marred, but who could resist that nice silver-inlaid blade?

THE INCOMPETENT AUDIENCE

Jon DeCles

ACT ONE

"I don't *care* if he is the new Emperor's cousin!" cried
Feltheryn the Thespian, brandishing a paper broadside that he
had just ripped off a wall before its glue could dry. "If
Emperor Theron *liked* him he wouldn't be in Sanctuary!"

"My darling," said Glisselrand, her fingers flying amidst
many-colored yarns, "there is a difference between liking
one's relatives and wishing them harm. Remember that Emperor Abakithis sent our darling Kitty-Kat here to Sanctuary,
presumably because he thought him a threat. Nobody has any
doubt that Abakithis wanted Kitty-Kat out of the way, but
neither does anybody doubt that he would have dealt severely
with anyone who spilled the royal blood."

"I wasn't suggesting that we *murder* Vomistritus," said
Feltheryn, frustrated by his lady's calmness.

Glisselrand laughed.

"If not, my pet, then he is the first critic ever to escape
that suggestion after giving you that kind of review!"

(Yes, it was *true*! The very vilest villain of all had slunk
into Sanctuary, a creature so reprehensible as to make all
previous contenders—with the possible exception of Roxanne—
pale. It had been written—long before the fall of Ranke, long
before the fall of Ilsig, long before the first settlers had put

down roots at the confluence of the Red Foal and the White Foal rivers—that the appearance of criticism portended the first sign of maturity in an art form. But for his part, Feltheryn rather thought that the appearance of *critics* was the first signal of total social decay, a sign that people had lost control of their own minds and tastes and had therefore to resort to the opinions of others.)

"And rightly so!" Feltheryn growled. He then waxed pedantic: "A critic is one who espouses the idea that one must divorce one's self from emotional involvement in a work of art in order to apply unchanging standards to all such works and thus render a judgment on the individual work based on a reasoned measurement made against those standards. Yet a work of art, by definition, is a thing which directly engages the emotions, carrying feeling *through* what is only, really, a cold construct: a channel by which the heart of a perhaps long-dead artist may touch the heart of a living perceptor!"

Glisselrand looked up at him from her knitting, today a series of small orange, purple, and red squares which would later be assembled into a folksy quilt that would even later give someone a headache. She raised one elegant eyebrow in question, prompting him to continue.

(There had been a point, perhaps thirty years earlier in their romance, when he wondered if, at such times, she really understood what he was saying, really cared; or if she was just humoring him. It no longer mattered to him, for the essence of the situation was that she wanted him to continue, and he wanted to continue, and, after all, it wasn't going to change anything.)

He took a deep breath and delivered his conclusion: "*That* of course means that a critic is someone who is congenitally *incapable* of appreciating art!"

Glisselrand stopped knitting for a moment and considered his thesis. Then she smiled and her fingers once again flew, gnarled but fast.

"Now that you mention it," she said, "it did seem that way in Ranke. They spoke a great deal about form and structure and style, but I am not sure I ever met a single critic who I felt *really* understood what he was talking about. Flash without fire, as the poet says. But looking back at our years in Ranke, I do believe we can be grateful that Sanctuary has only *one* critic, even if he is an especially bad one, and even if he is the Emperor's cousin.''

Feltheryn growled again and Glisselrand wondered if perhaps he was thinking of producing *The Cowslip Flower,* a play in which he was magically transformed into a camel.

"With all the faults this town has," Feltheryn continued, "with all the horrors it has endured, yet the old adage about Sanctuary has proved untrue. It was *not,* after all, the one place you could find the worst of anything. Stinking Sanctuary could still hold high its head on that one point, and I think it could have got along just fine without *ever* having acquired a damned *critic* of its own!''

"Well, my dear," said Glisselrand, "I quite agree with that. I just wonder that the people of Sanctuary have fallen for it.''

"It's the economics of the thing, of course!" Feltheryn continued to rave. "It's not cheap to come to the theater, because producing theater costs so much, even with the generous patronage we've got here. That's all the opening a vulture like Vomistritus needs! A little clever writing, a wicked turn of phrase, he hires a couple of scribes who can copy neatly if not well, pastes these broadsides all over town to gain an audience, and then the people will spend a copper to read what he has to say before they spend their soldats to come see the play. And the most insidious thing about it is the smug satisfaction of those who have *never been* to see one of our performances, yet who feel competent to discuss them!''

"How long have the broadsides been up?" Glisselrand asked, stopping her work once again and fixing Feltheryn with a look not unlike the one she gave the crooked bailiff in the great trial scene of *The Merchant's Price.*

"Well, the paste was still wet when I pulled this one down," said Feltheryn. "It cannot be too long.''

"Very good!" said Glisselrand. "Then we shall set Lempchin to running around town today pulling them *all* down. Better still, we shall give him a chance to practice his performance (he wants so much to go on stage!) by going in disguise, and thereby not making it obvious that we are the ones responsible. Unless Vomistritus is very well off, he won't be able to have his scribes keep making copies as fast as we can take them down. Perhaps he will get tired of being a critic and find some other way to annoy people!''

Lempchin was called, Glisselrand cozened the chubby boy neatly into disguising himself in the interests of the theater troupe's welfare, and Feltheryn was shortly back to preparing the script for *The Chambermaid's Wedding,* the next play the company was to produce.

Their current production, *The Falling Star,* was doing well enough, but Feltheryn was not fond of playing the villain and Glisselrand was waking each morning after the performance with aches and pains brought on by the finale, that desperate scene in which the actress who was the ''star'' of the title hurled herself from the castle walls rather than face the charge of murder against her from Act Two.

Of course as the villain Feltheryn got that wonderful scene in the second act in which he soliloquized about the joys of lust: and the scene that followed was not without satisfaction as he got to order the torture (horrible, but off stage) of Snegelringe, who would soon *deserve* torture if he didn't stay out of the bedchambers of some of Sanctuary's better class of bored ladies. Rounsnouf, the company comedian, got to play the torturer and he was quite good at it; although one had to keep an iron hand on his performance or he would chew the scenery to such a degree that the audience would begin to laugh, and *that* was unforgivable in a play of such passion and violence.

It was a good play, no doubt about that! But Feltheryn would have preferred to delay his own murder to the last act. As it was, he lay dead in a puddle of pig's blood at the end of the second act, and there was naught for him to do for a full third of the play but sit backstage in his costume and makeup waiting to take a bow at the end. And he had a sneaking suspicion that the applause he got would have been considerably greater if the audience had not had time to forget how good he was when Glisselrand plunged the knife from the supper table into his throat.

But enough of that! It was time the company took on a comedy, and *The Chambermaid's Wedding* was probably the best comedy ever written. Tragedy was all very fine, and it inevitably drew a crowd, but Sanctuary was a town with plenty of tragedy of its own; Sanctuary could use a few laughs, and Feltheryn intended to provide them.

There was only one small difficulty, and that was the lack, in the troupe, of a third-string female. Glisselrand would of course play the Countess, and Evenita the title role of the Chambermaid. But there was Serafina, the Schoolgirl, to cast as well, and one needed a strong actress for that because there were a great many lines, a song, and most of the time on stage the school*girl* was disguised as a school*boy*. That was because she had a schoolgirl crush on the Countess and, in an innocent schoolgirl way, wanted the Countess to make love to her.

They had tried doing the play with a boy in the part and it had proved a disaster. That was before Lempchin had joined the company. If they were forced to use Lempchin it would be *worse* than a disaster! Besides which, audiences loved to see a pretty young girl dressed up in tight pants pretending to be a boy. It was traditional, and even a bit erotic.

No, Feltheryn sighed to himself as he sat at the kitchen table looking at the script; they would have to find another female, that was all there was to it. And the best place to look for women was in the Street of Red Lanterns, at the Aphrodisia House. Myrtis had helped them before, she might be able to help them again.

He went upstairs to where Glisselrand was preparing for an afternoon nap, explained carefully what he had in mind, and got her blessing. Whatever else might be thought of *The Chambermaid's Wedding*, it was the one play in which all the sympathy and love went to the older woman, not to the younger title role; and Glisselrand was of an age to appreciate that.

Feltheryn would of course play the Count, who was also in a way a villain; but at least he would be on stage right up to the final curtain.

His trip to the Aphrodisia House was despoiled only by the presence of the offending broadsides distributed by Vomistritus. Apparently Lempchin had not yet got to the Street of Red Lanterns. Feltheryn pulled a few down as he passed them, but the glue was beginning to dry and it was difficult to get it off his hands once it was on. He had to beg pardon at the door when he finally arrived and ask for a basin and then, as the glue was much tackier than he had thought, he had to ask for help from one of the ladies of the house.

Feltheryn was not beyond appreciating the charms of the lovely young woman who helped him, nor was he in the least insensitive to the fine-tuned professionalism of her performance, displayed in even so humble an activity as helping him get his hands clean. The world's oldest profession was at least eighty percent theater, he recalled from his wild and reckless youth. Any woman could offer sex for money, but it took *talent* to make that sex so desirable that the audience returned again and again for the show.

And it *was* a show: the act itself was only the last curtain of an evening compounded of beautiful costumes, exotic perfumes, graceful movement, tantalizing conversation, stimulating music, and a setting that was a marvel of womanly design. To visit the Aphrodisia House was to enjoy a show with only one plot but a constantly changing cast of characters: and it was that fact which made the difference between Myrtis's elegant courtesans and the sad and desperate women who walked by night in the Promise of Heaven.

"There now!" said the young woman, drying his hands with an embroidered towel. "We've got it all off, Master Feltheryn. I'll clean up this mess, and you can go talk with the madam. Do you know the way to her room?"

"No, I am afraid I have not had that pleasure," Feltheryn answered in his most courtly fashion as he stood from the little table.

"Then I'll have one of the girls show you," she said, beginning quickly to clean as she had said she would. "Shawme! Shawme, would you please show Master Feltheryn up to Myrtis's room? I sent word up to her that he was here."

Shawme, a mere child whose blue eyes held inordinate pride, smiled at Feltheryn and led him up the stairs. A moment later he was seated in a small parlour, explaining his needs to Myrtis, the proprietrix of the Aphrodisia House, and sipping the blackberry tea she provided.

"—so you see, lovely lady," he finished, "she must be

talented and willing to learn to act if she cannot, and reasonably beautiful, but she must also have the sort of figure which
lends itself to wearing men's clothing. For most of the play
she must be disguised as a man, and it must not appear
laughable that she is so disguised. The audience will suspend
its disbelief to see a young girl in tight pants, but it will not
accept a full-blown womanly figure in the same outfit. I very
much want to do the play, but without your help I fear I
cannot."

Myrtis laughed.

"My dear Feltheryn! The fact is, there are plenty of people
running around this town in the clothes of the opposite sex,
and most of them are women. For some strange reason they
assume cross-dressing to be the one way in the world they can
protect their precious chastity. Not that I am in any wise
tolerant of any man abusing a woman, mind you, but *really*,
there are so many other and better ways of preventing rape!
Why, you will never find a softer, more engagingly feminine
roster of ladies than reside within my walls; but any one of
them could tell you a dozen ways to keep a man in place if he
tried to take something that wasn't his. Yet it is not the
lovely, soft, delicate ones who worry, and who sometimes
should. It is those hard, intolerant women: the ones with
some kind of chip on their shoulder. They never in their lives
have tried to make themselves attractive to men, yet they
assume they are irresistible to anything on three legs. Ha!
They should try working here, coaxing some poor merchant
to arousal who is more worried about whether the money is
well spent than whether he is having a good time! But beyond
that, these women have gone to extremes to make themselves
less than attractive to men, have often learned some devasta-
ting martial art in response to their fear, *and* they have
acquired manners that would get them *barred* from *my* house
if they were men; and still, they go through life assuming that
rape is around every corner! So they disguise themselves as
men, and spend most of their life energy worrying about
whether they will be found out. It saddens me deeply. A
woman should live her life going forward at full charge, not
cringing back in fear of something that may never happen."

"But Myrtis," said Feltheryn, "some women do get raped."

"Well of course they do!" said the madam. "And some get murdered and some get robbed and some get tortured and a great many are beaten by their husbands in the cozy confines of respectable marriage. By far the greatest number of women die in *childbirth*! But life is about *living*, Master Player, not about the piddling little moment at the end when you die. Oh, some of these fearful women are dear friends of mine, and I try to understand. But it does seem foolish to put such a high value on rape when a woman in this town is far more likely to be robbed or murdered. What a rapist seeks to take he really *cannot*, unless the woman lets him; and that is not her body, but her *dignity*. She may not like the physical part, it may sit with her like a canker for her lifetime if she lets it; but frankly, *nobody* can use *my* body to humiliate *me*. I am flesh, but I am *more* than that. I am a *woman*, and inordinately proud of the fact, and neither pain nor humiliation can touch that. Besides, men get raped too, so it's not much of a disguise in the long run. In fact, in Sanctuary, disguising yourself as a goat wouldn't be much better!"

"I had heard that goat rape was up," Feltheryn said.

"Only since the influx of all those foreigners who are working on the walls." Myrtis smiled. "But getting back to the point, I do believe I have someone in mind who might fill the bill. Her name is Sashana. Her family was killed by Raggah in the desert. She hid among the dunes, and then, being very young, managed to pass as a boy with the next caravan that came by. It was sensible in those circumstances, but now she lives and dresses as a woman. In fact, such a charming woman that I have often wished her fortunes had been a little worse when she came to Sanctuary. She would have made me a bundle! I'll give you her address, and a letter introducing you. She does not disguise herself anymore, but she doesn't take any chances, either!"

It was too late in the day to pay a call on Sashana when Feltheryn left the Aphrodisia House. There was to be a performance, he had to get into his makeup, and before that he needed a little rest. It was not as if he were a young man. He noted, as he left the Street of Red Lanterns, that all the broadsides were, if not gone from the walls, at least defaced

enough to be uninteresting to the passersby. He made his way
back to the theater, went up to the room he shared with
Glisselrand, and lay down on the bed next to her.

For a moment the stimulation provided by Myrtis's elegant
environment caused him to think about waking his leading
lady for an afternoon tryst; but thinking about it led quickly to
dreaming about it, and in his dreams he was more the man
than even he used to be. He had discovered, with age, the one
truth a young man dare not face: that dreams are *always* better
than reality.

The *Lady* Sashana lived in a small but well-appointed
house in as good a section of town as Sanctuary had. She
employed few servants but they were all strong and healthy
and Feltheryn suspected, as he waited in her parlour, that they
could double as bodyguards. There were shelves in the parlour, and on them manuscripts: beautiful volumes bound in
fine leather. Reading the titles, Feltheryn understood exactly
why Myrtis had sent him to Sashana. Most of the manuscripts
were plays, and those that were not were tomes of tales of far
lands and enchantments. There were even some he had not
read!

Lady Sashana entered the room with a graceful but firm
step, the tilt of her fine chin bespeaking confidence and the
clarity of her green eyes revealing intelligence. Her hair was
chestnut brown, not long but coiffed with beads in a manner
that gave the impression of controlled luxuriance. She wore
an emerald satin gown with a mauve chiffon overdress, colors
which enhanced her beauty even more in the environment of
rubbed woods and buff and cream velour that was her parlour.

"Myrtis's letter intrigues me," she said, taking a seat and
gesturing that Feltheryn should take the one opposite.

Her voice was rich and dark and naturally vibrant. Without
further consideration Feltheryn knew that she was precisely
the woman for the part, if only he could persuade her.

"I am glad of that," he said, "for now that I meet you I
see that Myrtis's praises were not half what they should have
been. To be brief, I note by your library that you hold an
interest in the theater. I note also that you own a copy of *The
Chambermaid's Wedding*, and are therefore familiar with the

part of Serafina. It is that part which I would like you to play, if you would consider the prospect of performing a play in public.''

Lady Sashana laughed, a deep, throaty laugh like the songs of large warblers from the forest.

''Master Feltheryn, can you imagine the scandal it would cause in Ranke if a woman of my position and breeding were to appear on stage? Oh, I should be barred from every respectable house and exiled from court for years! But this is not Ranke, Master Feltheryn, this is Sanctuary, and here I am in little danger of being forced to live the dull, constricted life my mother lived before her untimely death.''

She stood and clapped her hands together with all the strength and deliberation of a potter about to assault a new lump of clay.

''Of course I shall do it, if you will promise to teach me all the things I need to know!''

She strode to the shelves and Feltheryn was delighted to see in her walk that she was already transfiguring her body language to that of the character she would play. She would need little coaching for *this* part, he thought as she removed the blue-bound volume from the shelf. She turned to him and held the heavy tome against her breasts with both arms, like a sacred treasure.

''Oh, I *love this town*!'' she cried, her eyes glittering with delight.

The *next* morning the broadsides reappeared on Sanctuary's buildings, but with an improvement: they were put up with a different kind of glue.

The glue that had stuck so tenaciously to Feltheryn's hands was nothing compared to the stuff that caused Lempchin to cry and babble as he returned to the theater from his rounds, his hands, face, and clothes plastered with pieces of paper bearing the offensive criticisms. He had become, in less than an hour, a miserable little walking billboard, and nothing they tried could make the stickum dissolve.

''Well,'' observed Rounsnouf as he gnawed on a piece of cold fowl he was having for breakfast, ''nothing sticks to an actor like criticism!''

"Rounsnouf, that is *not* funny!" scolded Glisselrand, who was dressed in her best and most dignified clothes for a day of canvassing contributions. "Can't you see the poor child is terrified?"

"It would be worse if the glue had been applied to the rim of his chamber pot," Rounsnouf said. "As he didn't get around to emptying them this morning he would be in dire straits indeed!"

This caused Lempchin to howl all the worse and rush toward Glisselrand for comfort; but she dodged him deftly, and he stumbled instead into Rounsnouf, thus gluing himself firmly to the fat little comedian in a way that made them resemble a globular waste receptacle.

"*Enough!*" Feltheryn cried, now thoroughly distracted from both his breakfast and his script. "Lempchin, stop that caterwauling! And you, Rounsnouf, you've got what you deserve for goading the boy. You're stuck with him, at least until I can get you both down to the Street of Tanners. That glue is a nuisance, but I doubt that it is fatal. It was no doubt made by Master Chollandar, and I am sure he has a solvent for it. It will take time, but you will both be free soon enough to cause me other problems. Perhaps we can also get enough of the solvent to take down those damnable posters, while we are at it!"

"Well, thank the gods!" said Glisselrand, clearly relieved that *she* would not have to accompany anybody to the Street of Tanners. "If that is settled, then I must be off. Goodbye, my sweeting! Be sure and get your nap if I am late."

She kissed Feltheryn on the cheek.

"Don't be *too* late, my love," said Feltheryn, kissing her cheek in turn. "You need your beauty rest as much as I do, with that dreadful leap at the end of Act Three. And don't stray into any streets that look more dangerous than others. Remember that the folk of Sanctuary have very little in the way of money to contribute, unless they are truly wealthy."

"I know, I know, my dear." She smiled. "But there are a *few* people of wealth and position we have not yet visited, and it is my intention to correct that. Goodbye now, and take care."

She exited through the kitchen door.

Glisselrand never merely *left* a room. She always *exited*.

Had anybody but Rounsnouf been glued to Lempchin, the journey through the streets of Sanctuary would have been a mortifying experience for the boy. But Rounsnouf being the comedian he was, the trip proved to be an amusing one. When people pointed and laughed, Rounsnouf turned their jibes back on them:

"Don't laugh, lady, I can see the man *you're* stuck with!"

"If you think this is bad, you should have seen me last night before I sobered up!"

"I told the tailor there was room enough in this outfit for two, so he put somebody else in here with me!"

"This isn't what you think! I'm really Enas Yorl's twin brother. Both of me!"

It was in this manner that Feltheryn led his two charges into the miasma that permeated the Street of Tanners, past Zandula's tannery, and into Chollandar's Glue Shop. A lanky boy with a mop of golden hair asked them to wait and a moment later the master gluemaker emerged from the back, wiping blood from his hands.

Feltheryn wasted no time in explaining the predicament of his comedian and his factotum, adding at the end: "There are also the broadsides. I shall have to purchase some of the solvent for taking the miserable things off the walls of this fair city as well as for removing it from Rounsnouf and Lempchin."

Chollandar grimaced and leaned on the counter of his shop.

"Master Feltheryn, you have been a good customer, buying all the glue for your stage constructions and the like, but . . . Well, I *cannot* sell you the solvent for that glue."

"Why not?" asked Feltheryn.

"Because Vomistritus paid me an unconscionable amount *not* to sell it to anybody. I didn't know at the time I made the agreement that there would be problems like this . . ." He indicated the squirming bundle that was Lempchin and Rounsnouf. "But the contract was quite clear. He said he had trouble with vandals, and I assumed he was going to use it to put up some sort of protection. It will hold wood, metal, anything you can think of; and of course, human flesh as well, but I never expected . . ."

The gluemaker lapsed into a troubled silence, his eyes cast down on the counter.

"Perhaps I could cancel that contract," suggested Feltheryn, "by simply offering you more."

Chollandar laughed.

"I don't think you *can*!" he said. "The amount he offered me was so large I thought he was joking. He said I was welcome to check his credit with Renn, which I did, and frankly, Master Feltheryn, I wonder that there's any money left in Ranke at all. If you was to ask me, I'd say the new Emperor is cleaning out the treasury and storing the loot in his cousins' pockets. First Noble Abadas moves in and hires a house full of Ilsigi servants, for the gods know what purpose, and makes it clear that the Emperor has some very nice relatives. Then this *not*-noble Vomistritus moves in and shows how *un*pleasant the Emperor's relatives can get. If I was Emperor Theron I'd call Abadas and his family home and cut off the purse strings to old Vomit-breath, as his servants call him. But I'm not the Emperor, and I'm not in a position to just cancel my agreement with one of the Emperor's cousins. Still, it does seem a little inhumane to leave these fellows . . ."

At that moment a commotion in the street interrupted the discussion and a boy no less pudgy than Lempchin, but with olive skin, came rushing in.

"Master, master!" he cried. "There's a whole *army* coming down the street!"

"Is that so, Sambar?" Chollandar asked. "Then we must dispose ourselves to defend the fort, eh, Master Player?"

They all went through the front door of the glue shop and saw, if not an army, at least an irate war party. Pages, foot soldiers, and an unnerving number of gladiators. At the front of this column strode an older man with a look like storm clouds on his countenance. In the center of the column eight gladiators carried a veiled sedan chair, and from the sedan chair came the terrified shrieks of a woman having hysterics.

"Oh, dear," said Rounsnouf quietly. "It's Lowan Vigeles, and he seems to be upset."

"Who is Lowan Vigeles?" asked Feltheryn, just as quietly.

"He's Molin Torchholder's half-brother," explained Rounsnouf.

"Then why haven't we seen him at the theater?" asked Feltheryn.

"Possibly because they're estranged," said Rounsnouf, "and possibly because he keeps to his estate at Land's End, training gladiators, and possibly because . . ."

Rounsnouf stopped explaining as Lowan Vigeles came to a halt in front of the glue shop.

"So, gluemaker, I see by the company you keep that you have already run afoul of your formula's success!" announced Lowan Vigeles.

Chollandar let out a huge sigh, and began once again his explanation of the arrangement he had made with Emperor Theron's cousin Vomistritus; but the Rankan nobleman cut him off.

"I care nothing for what that pretender's petty relations may offer you in the way of riches! The plain fact is that my sister-in-law, the Lady Rosanda, has got herself as stuck up in this mess as have that man and that boy!"

With that he pulled open the curtains of the sedan chair to reveal the Lady Rosanda, who did not have as much paper glued to her as Lempchin and Rounsnouf, but enough: enough to set off her hysterics again.

"Now, gluemaker, you *will* get a bottle of solvent, and you *will* release the Lady Rosanda from her humiliating predicament, and *then* we will consider the situation of your contract with Vomistritus."

Chollandar threw up his hands in a gesture common to persons of business throughout the world, a gesture indicating a hopeless situation, a gesture indicative of profits down the drain. He headed into his shop, but a gesture from Lowan Vigeles gave him the company of two gladiators, just in case he should try to proffer some other solution to the problem than the solution which had been demanded.

In a very short while the Lady Rosanda was free of the glue and papers and secure once again in the seclusion of her chair. Chollandar applied some of the solvent to Lempchin and Rounsnouf as well, freeing them from both the offending broadsides and each other.

There was then a lengthy discussion between Lowan Vigeles, Chollandar, and Feltheryn concerning the doom that had descended upon Sanctuary with the arrival of Vomistritus. It was revealed that the Lady Rosanda had merely tried to bring home one of the broadsides for the family to read; and that her sympathies, formerly opposed to any operation which had her estranged husband's blessing, were now definitely with the theater. It was also revealed that Lowan Vigeles was a profoundly level-headed man when not provoked by the screams of his sister-in-law, and further, a man well versed in law.

Unfortunately, after careful consideration of the situation, Lowan Vigeles could not think of a legal and legitimate way of breaking Chollandar's contract with Vomistritus; at least not one that would keep the gluemaker both alive and adequately reimbursed.

The subject of murder was skirted with the greatest delicacy, and clearly left as a last contingency.

"After all," Lowan Vigeles said, sighing, "that usurper, Theron, would like nothing better than an excuse to send his army down here to crush Sanctuary and sow it with salt. But enough! I must take Rosanda home. I will see to it, Chollandar, that it is made clear you had no choice but to use the solvent on my behalf. Yet we must all of us think, and think hard, on some way to undo this Vomistritus before he undoes us!"

"Perhaps," suggested Feltheryn, "we might discuss the matter again after a performance, perhaps over a late supper? I trust that we will see you and the Lady Rosanda at the theater in the near future?"

"Oh, most definitely!" said Lowan Vigeles. "Most definitely!"

Back at the theater, Feltheryn felt ready for his afternoon nap; but Evenita reminded him that he had asked Lalo the Limner to come by regarding the sets for *The Chambermaid's Wedding*, so he went instead to get his script and the rough sketches he had made, which the master painter would turn into fine drawings and, eventually, stage pieces. Evenita had also taken the trouble to prepare a lunch for Feltheryn and Lalo in Glisselrand's absence, and as she served them he was once again glad that he and his lady had accepted her petition to join the troupe.

There had been many, many such petitions over the years, from young women and young men of greater, lesser, or equal beauty. And many had made those petitions from similar motives: the desire to leave an unbearable life and the hope of some measure of glory. But most of those petitions had been rejected. Those might be admirable ambitions, but they were not what made an actor or an actress. To join the theater for those reasons was as foolish as getting married for those reasons!

But Evenita's tale had been so piteous, her life so fragile at that point, that they had relented and accepted her and taken her safely away from her hometown, hoping perhaps that along the way they might find her suitable employment. She had repaid their kindness with a diligence and a show of talent that was quite unexpected, even spectacular, and now she was one of the minor jewels of their little crown. Her dark hair and warm brown eyes, her round face and full lips, were of a kind of beauty that contrasted greatly with Glisselrand's patrician features and auburn hair. And she could cook, as the little spiced clams she was serving them for lunch attested!

Lalo asked a number of pointed questions, made suggestions (most of which Feltheryn accepted), then packed up his sketchbook and bade goodbye. Feltheryn considered the bed which invited his company upstairs, then remembered a detail of the set (a door which *had* to be real, which *had* to open and close) which he had not mentioned to Lalo, and so he was off running after the painter. By the time he had found him (at the Vulgar Unicorn) and set the matter straight, and got back to the theater again, it was time to get into makeup and run lines.

And as if all the previous excitement of the day were not enough, Glisselrand was late in returning from her canvassing! Feltheryn continued to dress and prepare, but as nightfall came on he worried more and more; and was on the verge of calling the performance and sending out a search party when the door opened and his leading lady rushed in and started to dress.

"My dear, you have no *idea* what an exciting day it has been!" she said cheerfully, slipping out of her clothes and into her costume.

"I might guess," Feltheryn responded as he applied his lip rouge with a tiny brush of camel's hair.

"You know," she babbled on, "everyone has told me, again and again, that I must stay away from that shabby little house down on the White Foal, but something inside me, some *instinct*, said to me that anyone who grew such lovely flowers—you've seen them, haven't you, the black roses? —must be a very nice person indeed! Well, after visiting *three* homes where they clearly had plenty of money but no taste, and getting not a single contribution, I decided to follow my instincts!"

Feltheryn stopped working on his makeup and sat stock-still, his brush not moving at all. He knew full well who lived in the house on the White Foal River. The hair on the back of his neck began to rise.

"Naturally enough," she continued, "I was not so foolish as to attempt to violate the wards on the iron gate. People don't put up wards for nothing, you know. Instead I went up and sniffed the roses. They have a *lovely* fragrance. That was sufficient to get the attention of the lady of the house without giving her the feeling that I was being pushy, or violating her privacy. When I neither left nor tried to pluck the blooms, her curiosity was whetted and she came out on the porch. I waved hello and complimented her on her roses and asked if there were anyplace I might purchase similar plants. She smiled at that, with just a touch of contempt I think, but I didn't let it bother me. I told her how much they reminded me of the ones we have to make out of paper when we do *Rokalli's Daughter*, and that of course let her know that I was with the theater. —Would you help me with the corset, dearest?—Well, the gate swung open and she invited me in for tea! That is one of the nicer things about being in the theater, don't you think, Feltheryn? Almost anyone is glad to receive a player into their home, perhaps out of the sense of celebrity. Except of course that time in Sofreldo when the whole town censured the baron and baroness for inviting a mere *actress* to break-fast; but then, that was a frontier town, after all. Well, anyway, you cannot imagine how delighted I was to see the inside of her house. Feltheryn, it was like being back *home* again. It was a gorgeous riot of color! Silks, satins, velvets, everything strewn about with the gayest, wildest abandon! I showed her my knitting, and I think she was very pleased. And I gave her a little bag of one of my tisanes, you know, the ones I take along as a gift for people who contribute more than their share to the theater? The poor dear, she seems so shy, really. I don't imagine she has many women friends. She's exceptionally beautiful, and you know how that makes many women jealous. I have suffered enough from that myself, all these years. There now, I think I'm ready!''

Feltheryn swallowed hard.

"Did she then make a contribution?'' he asked, opening the door of the dressing room and offering a silent prayer to whichever deity was responsible for the safe return of his lady.

"Well, no,'' said Glisselrand sheepishly: a very unusual mode of response for her. "She said that at the moment she had nothing suitable in the house. And . . . Well, I hope that you won't be too upset with me, Lamby, but, well, I . . . I told her I would leave her name with Lempchin out front, so that she could come to see a show for free. Her name is Ischade, and I am sure that when things look up for her, financially, we'll see her in the audience all the time.''

And as if the previous week's ordeals weren't enough, the morning after Glisselrand gave Ischade a free pass to the theater, Lempchin brought home a *dog,* a scruffy little bitch with a disturbing gleam in her eye and a glittering nimbus of *something* about her that made Feltheryn loath to say *no* when the boy proffered the usual tale of having been followed, and could he keep her?

"If you can teach her tricks!'' the master player said. "And if you name her *Beneficence.*''

"Master Feltheryn,'' said Lempchin, with a worried but reasonable look on his pudgy face, "you can't go out and call a dog: 'Here, *Beneficence*!' Everyone will laugh, and besides, it won't carry!''

"You are right,'' said Feltheryn. "But when I was a boy,

before I became an actor, I had a dog named *Beneficence* and we called her *Benny,* which will carry quite well, don't you think?''

"Oh, *yes,* Master Feltheryn, yes! Thank you!" cried Lempchin.

The small dog looked up at Feltheryn with an expression of scandalized horror, and for a moment he thought she understood exactly what he was saying. She backed away and let a low growl escape her lips.

"I am afraid it is that, Benny, or find another home," said Feltheryn firmly.

The dog hesitated, as if she would do *just* that rather than answer to her new name; but at that moment Molin Torchholder entered the back of the theater and headed down the center aisle, and *that* seemed to change everything. She looked at Molin, looked back at Feltheryn, did three neat back flips in the air, then disappeared into the scenery before Molin got to the stage.

"A born actress," Feltheryn said, and rumpled Lempchin's hair before turning his attention to his patron.

"I have heard," Molin said, without preamble and *with* embarrassment, "that Rosanda will be attending the theater. Could you keep me advised of the nights you expect her, so that I can absent myself?"

ACT TWO

As if by divine edict (and in Sanctuary, it seemed the only way that it could happen) things began to go well. Vomistritus's broadsides stayed up, but his poisonous commentary failed to cut too deeply into the theater's receipts. Those who took the critic at face value and stayed away were balanced by those who were intrigued by his acerbic pen into coming to see what could possibly be so bad.

Lalo delivered final sketches for *The Chambermaid's Wedding* and they proved to be his most inspired designs to date. The flowery pergola for the wedding scene was of surpassing loveliness, and construction of the costumes and properties was begun with much enthusiasm by all concerned.

Lady Sashana proved not only beautiful and enthusiastic, but an apt pupil as well. Glisselrand actually blushed when the disguised Schoolgirl sang her the serenade, and that was no small tribute from an actress who had played the part more than fifty times.

As for Myrtis: she was pleased to contribute the talents of some of her younger protégées to the production, and the girls themselves were pleased and delighted (and amused) to be playing the Chambermaid's virgin bridesmaids.

"The only problem," Myrtis commented, "is that song in which they sing about being pure and chaste. Some of their customers may be in the audience, and if the poor men laugh, their wives will figure it out!"

Lempchin discovered that his new dog could learn any trick with the greatest of ease. It was not long before he had persuaded Glisselrand to sew a fluffy collar for the mutt, and not much more time before Benny had got a role in the show, doing tricks for the Countess in the wedding scene.

Master Chollandar stopped by the theater to deliver some glue and related how Vomistritus had demanded half the enormous payment for exclusive rights to the solvent returned on the basis of the one unauthorized use in freeing Rosanda, Rounsnouf, and Lempchin.

"I argued with him," said Chollandar, "but in the end I figured I would have to give him what he wanted. And that's not so bad, because it was really a *lot* of money that he paid. But I made him print, on each broadside, that the glue was dangerous and might not be removable. And I told him that if he didn't print the message on the poster, I would not be responsible for the consequences."

"Did he accept that?" asked Feltheryn.

"Oh, yes," said Chollandar. "I think he enjoys the idea of spreading something dangerous around Sanctuary. It makes him feel sinister, maybe."

Near the closing of *The Falling Star* a small purse appeared on the table in the greenroom, directly after the performance. Although Lempchin did not remember admitting her, a note within the purse identified the gold it contained as a "small" gift from Ischade; and Glisselrand commented that she was happy the dear shy woman had not only fallen upon better times, but, it seemed from the size of the gift, now reveled in them.

Glisselrand finished the red, purple, and orange quilt, and one day when rehearsals had gone especially well presented it to Sashana: who accepted it gracefully and in the spirit in which the gift was intended. Sashana then asked Evenita (in private) if she had anything for a headache, and Evenita, who also possessed a quilt, rushed to an apothecary for some of the little leaves whose crushed essence was palliative for eyestrain.

The Falling Star closed, there was the usual closing-night party for the cast and a few friends, then the serious business of preparation for the next play began. Old sets were torn down, wood and canvas cannibalized, and the theater rang with repeated speeches and reeked with the smell of paint.

Lowan Vigeles and Lady Rosanda sent their regrets that they had not managed to see the recently closed play, but with their regrets they sent a request for the best seats in the house for opening night of *The Chambermaid's Wedding*. This presented a problem, as the best seats in the house were those in the royal box, and they would surely be occupied by Prince Kadakithis and the Beysa Shupansea, who, Rounsnouf assured Feltheryn, were not the favorite people of the Rankan household at Land's End.

Feltheryn asked Glisselrand's advice in the matter (which was his usual procedure in such thorny circumstances) and she quickly composed a note to Lowan Vigeles expressing regret that the best seats were those in the royal box, which had been flocked at the expense of the prince and the Beysa, who would most surely be in attendance.

"Do you think it wise to say that?" Feltheryn asked as he read the note.

"Read on," his lady commanded.

The note further expressed regret that the theater did not have a second box of equivalent splendor, and noted that in Ranke the company's theater had possessed three such boxes: the royal one at the center, and the two at the sides of the stage which allowed the attendance of visiting dignitaries and guests of the company's director. The note then politely asked whether Lowan Vigeles would like to have the royal box on the second night or a lesser box on opening night, and appended the opinion that many attendees *preferred* the second night, as the initial nervousness of the performance by then had dissipated.

Feltheryn smiled.

"I see you are angling for more pomp and flocking," he said; and Glisselrand grinned.

"It couldn't hurt, my dear," she said.

Rehearsals continued, the costumes and sets were finished, and in no time at all it was opening night. Lowan Vigeles and Rosanda elected the royal box on the second night, Molin Torchholder accompanied the prince and the Beysa for the first night, and everything went as smoothly as melon with custard. In fact, by the end of the first act the impossible seemed to be taking place.

"Yes, that's *him*!" said Rounsnouf, who was playing the servant who turned out to be the father of the bridegroom, who was played by Snegelringe. "That laugh is unmistakable. Look out through the peephole! You see, that big, fat, ugly man? That's Vomistritus, and he actually seems to be *enjoying* himself!"

Feltheryn looked, saw, and had to agree that Vomistritus was big, fat, and ugly. His face was like a cantaloupe about to spoil. He had sagging chins aplenty and a grayish tone to his skin that made one wonder if he coupled regularly with corpses. His stubby fingers rested wetly on the rail and his bulgy eyes were bloodshot. His mouth was slack; Feltheryn wondered if he drooled as well. His teeth were snaggly when he smiled, and his smile was not unlike that of a shark. He wore loose robes of goose-turd green that failed to conceal his corpulence.

The young woman who sat next to him was pretty, and obviously paid for her participation.

"Suppose he turns out to be an *honest* critic?" asked Lady Sashana, stunning in tight blue satin breeches and a white brocade coat.

"An honest critic?" asked Snegelringe, standing close to her but as yet unable to affect her with his charms (she knew his hairline was receding under the wig).

"Yes," said Sashana. "Suppose he is actually doing what

he *thinks* he is doing. It may be that tomorrow morning we
will awake and find a good review glued all over town.''

"Such things have occurred, my child," said Glisselrand,
"but rarely. I don't think it is that critics go to the theater
hoping to see a bad play so much as that they have seen so
many plays they are numbed to the experience. I suspect they
are like courtesans: always hoping for the exceptional and
most of the time disappointed.''

"That," said Feltheryn, taking his eye from the peephole
that allowed the actors to see the audience without being
seen, "and the fact that it is easier to cut a thing to ribbons
than it is to imbue it with life.''

"That's from *The Choice of Mages,* isn't it?" Sashana
asked.

"Yes." Feltheryn smiled. "When Demetus realizes that
even a child can kill, but that he, the greatest of magicians,
cannot give life to the dead; not true life. That's when he
abandons the warrior's path.''

Sashana sighed. "I'd *love* to play Retifa!" she said.

Glisselrand's eyebrows shot up and for a moment Feltheryn
wondered whether the company would make it to the second
act of tonight's show. Retifa was one of Glisselrand's favorite
parts.

"Of course," Sashana continued, "I'd need about thirty
years of experience on the stage before I'd attempt it. And
then I just might not have the talent. It takes a truly great
actress, like *you,* Glisselrand, to carry off that part. Have you
ever played it?''

Feltheryn relaxed, assured that equilibrium had been re-
established: and then it was time for the second-act curtain.

By the end of the play everybody in the cast was ebullient,
and when the bows were all finished they were giddy with
mutual congratulations. It was agreed that *never* had the town
of Sanctuary known so much laughter, so much sheer good
feeling. They all hurried to the greenroom and took seats
behind the table, backed by big jardinieres full of flowers and
potted palms, and soon the room was filled with people
congratulating them.

The prince and the Beysa came first, then Molin Torchholder, then several noble families responsible for various aspects of the production. It was a shock to Feltheryn when he looked up and saw the doorway filled with goose-turd green, but he took it in good stride when Vomistritus waddled forward and began to congratulate them all.

"Never seen it so good!" the critic burbled in a loud but ill-supported baritone voice. "Such finesse! Such style! So much tastier than that tawdry tragedy you did last time! My compliments! You may be sure my broadsides will read in your behalf on the morrow. You, Madame Glisselrand, were superb! I was fare to weeping when you contemplated the Count's infidelity. And you, Master Feltheryn, were such a masterful buffoon; how *did* you manage that last scene, apologizing to her on one knee? One would have thought a man of your age would have difficulty with so much spriteliness. Ah, but my greatest accolades are for you, Lady Sashana! Your step! Your song! Your amorous elegance! How could anyone resist your entreaties? Why, I must confess, I thought the Countess to have a heart of stone when you pled your case! And if *I* felt so, then rest assured, *all* your audience must surely have felt so! For is that not the purpose of a critic? To stand in for the whole audience? To try and *feel* the play, not merely as he would alone, but as each and every viewer would feel it? Not so different from a director's job, is it, Master Feltheryn? Only *you* try to stand in for the audience *before* the play is played, and *I* try to stand in for them once you have prepared it. To see whether what you saw is what they see. You see? See! Saw! Ha ha!"

And thus he went on, for considerably longer than was seemly for a man at the head of a queue, and in considerable contradiction to the tenor of his previous tone regarding the troupe. When finally he left, and the rest of the well-wishers had paid their respects and departed, the whole company was exhausted. They repaired to the kitchen, where Lempchin had broken out cold pasties, and when they had finished rehashing the night's triumphs and restoring the energy expended by acting, they all went to bed, happy: and wondering, each in his or her private way, if perhaps the slight magic resident in the play had wrought some change in Vomistritus.

* * *

The second night was as glittering a triumph as the first. Not only did Lowan Vigeles and Rosanda attend, they brought with them enough gladiators that there was barely enough room in the theater for seating. The gladiators were all dressed in their most elaborate noncombat gear, so the candlelight flashing off gold in the audience was very near distracting from the spectacle on stage. Only Lady Rosanda outshone them. She had dressed in High Rankan style in a way that was quite as impressive as the formal *cosa* the Beysa had worn the night before.

Except, of course, that the Lady Rosanda kept her nipples covered.

By the third morning Vomistritus's review was plastered all over town, and it was gushing with praise for the production and everyone in it. If any unreasonable prejudice could be found in his words (Rounsnouf noted over a breakfast of hot lemon-grass tisane and egg bread fried in bacon grease) it was the opulence of his praise for Sashana.

"No doubt she's wonderful," he mumbled as he chewed. "Just not *that* wonderful!"

Thus it came as a surprise when, on the fourth morning after the play had opened, Lady Sashana arrived at the theater with her bodyguard servants and declared her intention to kill the Emperor's cousin, and the price be damned.

"My poor child!" Feltheryn exclaimed, pulling a chair out from the table so that she could sit down and noting that her face was bruised. "What on earth has happened?"

Lady Sashana clenched her fists on the table before her and tried to speak, but her breath was coming hard and the emotions that stormed across her face were too varied and confused for articulation. Feltheryn looked to the bodyguards and noted that they also bore bruises; and cuts and abrasions as well. Worse, each cast his eyes to the floor as Feltheryn looked at him, and the red burn of shame colored all their features.

"He—" Sashana began, but she choked on the words.

Glisselrand came into the kitchen, saw Sashana, and immediately put a cup of hot tisane before her. Myrtis entered behind Glisselrand and froze, her face going professionally blank.

Sashana drank some of the tisane, coughed, then tried again.

"Last night after the performance I received a note from Vomistritus. It said that he was having a small supper party and requested my attendance. After all the nice things he said about the production, and about my performance, I decided to go."

"At that hour of the night?" asked Glisselrand. "In Sanctuary?"

Sashana smiled ruefully.

"I am not a fool; at least not a *complete* fool! I took along my bodyguards, with the very good excuse that it would be unsafe for me to travel the streets that late without them. Vomistritus met me at the door himself and seemed more than pleased to admit my men. He ordered his servants to provide them with wine and meat, then led me to the upper chamber where the party was."

She took another sip from her cup.

"At once I divined my state, for the room was set for supper for only two. I turned to go, but the door had been locked from the outside. I demanded that he open the door, but he laughed. I used the best voice that you taught me and called for my men, but there was no response. Then Vomistritus went to the table and sat down to eat, uncovering dishes and behaving as if the battle were won. Then, *then* that overbred imitation of a downwind *pud* had the colossal gall to quote *your* speech at me, Master Feltheryn, the one from the second act of *The Falling Star!*"

"Men call me venal, yet they do not know, the depths of my depravity and desire . . ." Feltheryn began.

"Yes, that one!" Sashana cut him off. "Can you imagine it? And he delivered it *badly!* Well, of course I took my cue and went to the table, but Vomistritus is not *that* much an imbecile. There were no knives. The whole repast was finger-food, and none of it very good-looking, either."

"He might at least have had a decent meal prepared," said Glisselrand.

"How would a *critic* know the difference?" Rounsnouf asked.

"I told him I would as soon couple with the corpse of a

poxed leper,'' Sashana said coldly. Then a burst of bitter
laughter escaped her lips. ''I should have known coarse language would inflame him! He rose from the table and came
after me, exactly as in the play. But he had not counted on
my regular wariness, nor on the dagger I keep in my stock-
ing, under the skirts of my gown. I slashed for his throat, and
by the gods, my cut *should* have killed him!''

Her green eyes flashed like demon fire.

''What happened?'' asked Feltheryn, by habit and nature as
good an audience as he was an actor.

''I cut, but his damned fat saved him! He yowled, blood
spurted, but my dagger didn't reach the vein. At that his men
rushed in and seized me. I think one of them is missing a
finger, at least, but there were too many and they got me
down. Then things got worse.

''He wrapped a linen round his throat and his eyes bulged
all the more, and his servants brought in my bodyguards, all
stripped and bound. My men were held and forced to *watch*
as he . . .''

Once more Sashana's voice broke, and rage and desperation and horror all warred for supremacy on her face. One of
her servants wept.

''He . . . He quoted more of the play,'' she said at last.
''How I do love to break the tigress of her fight . . .''

There was a cold, horrible, quiet moment. Then:

''He raped you,'' Myrtis said quietly.

It was the cue Sashana needed.

''Yes, the bastard *raped* me!'' she cried, and in a swift
moment she was on her feet, her dagger in her hand and
somehow the delicate cup from which she had been drinking
smashed against the opposite wall. ''And I *will kill him*!''

Myrtis alone of the company was able to move, able to act
against the icy tide of horror and anger which engulfed them
all. She moved to Sashana and took her in her arms, where
Sashana finally was able to let her tears come, her sobs break.

After a while Sashana quieted, then whispered again, against
Myrtis's breast: ''I will kill him.''

''No, child,'' Myrtis said. ''You will not kill him. If you
kill him then it will be over for him, and you will be left with
this pain and no place to put it.''

"What do you mean?" Sashana asked.

"I mean that justice is a matter of balance," the madam said. "He did not take *your* life, so taking *his* life is an inappropriate punishment. We must seek instead to take exactly the things he took from you. We must seek to relieve *your* pain by putting it upon *him*."

"Are you talking *magic*?" Feltheryn asked. "Or . . ."

"Myrtis," Glisselrand said, "I don't think we will find anyone who will want to rape Vomistritus."

Myrtis snorted in a very uncourtesanly way.

"This is Sanctuary, Glisselrand," she said. "That would be the least of our difficulties. It is not the sexual part of the crime with which I am concerned, but the violence and the humiliation. And more than that, a means by which we may mete out this villain's punishment without bringing down the town around us."

Sashana drew away a little.

"Oh, he is very aware of that!" she said. "When he was finished he said that I was powerless to gain revenge because if he was harmed the Emperor would tear down Sanctuary and decimate the population. He was very proud of knowing what *decimate* meant. He joked about it, asking me which friend out of each ten I would like to see murdered before my eyes!"

"My lady!" cried the servant who had wept, "let *me* deal with him, and after I am done I will give myself up to the prince for execution! That will save Sanctuary and revenge us *all* as well!"

"Nobly offered, Miles," Sashana said. "But I cannot sacrifice you in exchange for a creature so far beneath you in worth."

"Lady Sashana," Rounsnouf said, and for once his comic's voice was pitched in dead seriousness. "If I might offer a plan?"

Sashana turned to him. She still trembled, but the prospect of some action, *any* action, seemed to calm her. "Yes?"

The comic addressed the madam: "Myrtis, how well do you know the proprietor of the House of Whips?"

"Well enough," Myrtis answered.

"There is a small courtyard in that house, with stocks,"

said Rounsnouf. "It was a popular place when the Stepsons were here, or so I am told, but now its fortunes have declined; especially since that goat farmer . . ."

"Yes, yes!" Feltheryn interrupted, beginning to see the drift of what the comic was saying. "About the stocks?"

"They seem a gentle torture to anyone who has not endured them," Rounsnouf said, "but in fact being forced to stand bent over at the waist, one's head and wrists through the board and one's rear end exposed, can be an agony. The back hurts first, then the muscles of the shoulders, the legs, and so on. They ache, they cramp, and by the end of the first day one is willing to do *anything* to escape. And that even without the assistance of the patrons of that particular house, many of whose chief pleasure lies in the infliction of various other tortures upon a bound victim."

"A good beginning," said Lady Sashana, now regaining some of her composure. "But we are not discussing some attractive slave, we are discussing Vomistritus."

"My lady," said Rounsnouf, his little eyes beginning to glitter with creativity, "the courtyard is there for that special taste of public humiliation. There are windows round it from which one may watch what transpires without being seen. That too is a taste to which the house caters. One could stand thus concealed and drop a soldat or two to anyone who gave an especially fine performance. And I am sure there are many in the Downwind who have never been able to afford a night in the Street of Red Lanterns, many whose tastes might be beyond our darkest imagination. Word could be dropped with the Beggar King, Morruth, and who knows what might transpire? Though you might not guess it, there are those in Sanctuary who are even less attractive than Vomistritus!"

Sashana took one long breath and her shuddering stopped. Her proud chin lifted, but still she looked to Myrtis for some council.

The smile, and the nod, that Myrtis gave might have frozen even mighty Tempus with fear.

"It were best," said Glisselrand, her rich voice suddenly an emblem for reason, "that none involved be recognized. Moreover, what is to stop Vomistritus from announcing himself to his tormentors and offering more money than any of us possess for his freedom?''

Rounsnouf giggled.

"That very glue by which Lempchin and I were bound shall be brushed across his lips," the comic said. "Before we deliver him to his particular purgatory he shall be prevented from praying his way out!"

"Better!" said Sashana.

"And Master Feltheryn," Rounsnouf continued, "we have not performed *The Fat Gladiator* for some years; can we perhaps use the demon costumes from the last scene? We shall wait, and we shall lure him to the woods with some sort of tryst, just as in the play, and there he shall be set upon by horrors, bound up, his mouth glued shut, and he will not be able to swear who it was who delivered him! Then we can burn the costumes, eliminating the evidence."

They all looked to Feltheryn, but Feltheryn did not answer at once. That they were asking to destroy some old costumes was nothing. Neither did he mind the risk. Of course Vomistritus would recognize the plot of *The Fat Gladiator* at some point in the proceedings and understand that it was the theater troupe taking revenge upon him; that didn't matter, for the critic could not have them *all* killed. Emperor Theron would not tolerate that, not even from his cousin. And the criminal in such a case would be obvious to all.

No, Feltheryn hesitated for Sashana's sake. If he approved the plan he would be putting her into a position wherein she inflicted such cruelties as she felt she had endured. Wherein she could achieve a catharsis, but at what cost to her? She was a fine-born lady; but she had also survived the murder of her parents and the rigors of the desert. How might this chance wind twist the very finest sapling?

But then, how had it already been bent?

Feltheryn nodded.

"But still," the master player added, "there is an untied string. We may prevent Vomistritus gaining any evidence against us, but he will *know*, and he will try to take a counter revenge if I am any judge of him. We need some sharp and terrible sword to hold over his head, that he may never come back against us again."

There was another silence in the room, then a quiet cough sounded from the doorway. They turned to look and there stood Lalo the Limner, his ginger fringe of hair awry, his fingers stained with paint where he had come early to adjust a few things about the set with which he had not been satisfied.

"I believe I can help with that," Lalo said.

Thus it was that in a strangely deserted park called the Promise of Heaven, a heavy man dressed in goose-turd green was assaulted by demons. He cried out, but his minions were appalled, when they rushed to his aid, to find their way blocked by a contingent of gladiators from Lowan Vigeles's school at Land's End. The cries of their master soon ceased, or at least became muffled, and those minions (having only the loyalty born of cash) quickly retired from the fray.

It was not the first time that park had played host to demons; but later on, the ladies too much enslaved to krrf or too ill featured to work in the Street of Red Lanterns returned, their time well compensated.

It might have been noted that for a few nights the School-girl disguised as a Schoolboy (in *The Chambermaid's Wedding*) was a little less springy of step. That perhaps the play took on a tenderer note than it had shown on opening night. That certain aspects of the ensemble were sharpened while others were softened.

It might have been noted, but it was not, for in Sanctuary few people came to see a show more than once. And there were thenceforth no critics to be concerned.

For to be a True and Just Critic is a risky business. One must have standards against which one measures, but one must also become submerged in the emotions of the work. One must, like the director, be able to see the play from the point of view of an entire audience. One must, in fact, *be* an entire audience.

Yet an audience does not simply *observe* a work of art. An audience participates. If a play is performed perfectly, but with nobody to see it, it is not a play. A painting unseen does not exist, not even for the painter; for the purpose of art (and of everything else of value in life) is communication. A tree falling in the forest does *not* make any sound. At least, not any sound that an artist could understand.

An audience does not merely *come* to the theater, it *brings with it* Observation, Participation, Response. If the audience comes unwilling to submerge itself in Feeling and Understanding, then it is like a lover who merely lies there, waiting to be acted upon.

It is the difference between those sad women who walk the paths of the Promise of Heaven and the beautiful ladies who sail the satin sheets of the Aphrodisia House. The difference between a courtesan and a whore.

In short, the audience unwilling to act its part is incompetent, and nothing in the performance, nothing in the painting, nothing in the book, nothing in the music will alter its state; and the critic stands in for the audience.

A rain came, brief but enough to wash the ink from the broadsides that defaced the town's walls. On the back wall of a closet in the palace a new portrait appeared, one which Prince Kadakithis was pleased to receive from Lalo the Limner but which he did not desire to display in public, as it showed, with the preternatural accuracy of Lalo's brush, the True Soul of a naked ugly man in the stocks at the House of Whips. It was a portrait which might be of use to the prince should the new Emperor plan another visit to Sanctuary, and its subject knew the prince possessed it.

A small dog had to be told *point-blank* not to do so many tricks, as she was stealing the scene in which she appeared from the star.

And one night, when the actors all repaired to the green-room, the jardinieres were filled with fragrant black roses.

OUR VINTAGE YEARS

Duane McGowen

Rumor had it that some measure of prosperity was once again gracing the streets of Sanctuary. The reign of terror that had lasted since the False Plague Riots had abated, as the various factions which had fractured Sanctuary into warring districts crumbled in upon themselves or left town for new frontiers or more profitable battles. The streets seemed to be peaceful and relatively calm recently, and business seemed to be returning to normal. "Seemed" being the operative word on both counts.

There could be no doubt, however, that commerce was on the up-and-up these days. Beysib and Rankan invaders alike seemed to favor diplomacy over military action and turmoil. Terrorist activities by the PFLS, which had all but brought the business world to a standstill, were on the decline. If one were inclined to believe the wildest rumors, it was said among some that Zip, the former PFLS leader, was now in charge of assuring peace on Sanctuary's streets. Though many shook their heads in doubt at this bit of highly speculative information, there could be no denying that the nights were now free of terrorist raids, and that young toughs no longer came to the merchant stalls by day to collect "protection" money from bullied peddlers.

"Sanctuary is finally what Sanctuary should be," the merchant class agreed. For they were making the most profit out of the town's newfound prosperity. The masons, workers, and craftsmen who had poured into town to build the walls commissioned by Molin Torchholder were now plying their respective trades in the city at large. The enriched artisans increased the wealth of the local merchants as buying and selling became the backbone of Sanctuary's upward-rising economy. The most shrewd entrepreneurs were looking into the future for wise and lucrative business investments. The town that had once been considered "the anus of the Empire" was now a place for people of that broken and war-torn Empire to come and rebuild their lives.

This was true of many refugees from troubled Ranke, who paid the caravan-masters handsomely to bring them across the desert to the port city under the rulership of the Rankan Prince Kadakithis and his Beysib consort, Shupansea. Some of these refugees had relatives in the Rankan populace who took them in and gave them shelter and comfort. Others, like Mariat, were not so lucky. Having no one else to turn to, Mariat had brought her three grandchildren, the surviving remnants of her once powerful and affluent family, to Sanctuary to rebuild their lives from scratch. With only her own determination and wit to rely on, she was still optimistic about the future.

Mariat drew her wagon to a halt at the entrance to the Bazaar. Behind her, the other wagon driven by her eldest grandson, Keldrick, also came to a stop. Keldrick and his sister, Darseeya, kept an alert watch to make sure that no one approached the two wagons without warning. Though the boy was only fourteen and the girl twelve, the events of the past year had matured them beyond the normal bounds of childhood. They knew that no unscrupulous eyes should be allowed to view the contents hidden in the two covered wagons. For there lay the future of Mariat's family.

While her two older grandchildren kept watch and the youngest one slept in the back of her wagon, Mariat scanned the Bazaar for the safest, least crowded route through it to the residential parts of Sanctuary. Her little troupe formed an island of motionless calm in a sea of swirling activity. Around them danced the brightly colored skirts of the S'danzo. Merchants cried their wares and buyers bought them. Garrison

soldiers strode boldly through the crowd with the seeming, if
not the actuality, of purpose. Here and there, beggars begged
and pickpockets dodged artfully from purse to purse. The
bleating, baying, and neighing of the animals in their pens
were almost indistinguishable from the noises made by the
buyers, sellers, and thieves of the Bazaar.

It was not the first time in the past several months that
Mariat realized she was out of her element. She passed a hand
through her gray hair which had rapidly been turning white as
the days dragged by since her former life had come to an
abrupt and bloody close. It never even occurred to the middle-
aged woman to dye her hair to the color of youth, as many of
the women in her former social sphere had done. She bore her
gray hair as a badge of honor which should rightly come with
age. And her determination and positive outlook kept her face
and bearing young and graceful, despite the horrors she had
suffered recently.

She was a tall, stately, slim woman in her mid-fifties. Her
posture was straight and perfect, and she exuded the cultured
mannerisms and grace of a woman of station, which she had
indeed been scant months before.

Mariat had been impressed with her first sight of Sanctuary: the city's tall new walls shining in the morning light.
Now she was once again faced with nagging doubts, which
nibbled like little demons at the back of her mind, as she
surveyed the chaos and pandemonium of the Bazaar. It was
an environment alien to a woman from the upper strata of
Rankan society.

"Ah, there you are, madame," called a friendly and pleasant baritone voice which Mariat had come to love during her
journey to this place.

She turned and saw the minstrel Sinn heading toward her
through the crowd. As he squeezed between two fat merchants haggling over the price of a chicken, his hand deftly
intercepted a street urchin reaching for his purse. The bearded,
brown-haired bard looked at the quaking youth with mild
amusement. The young beggar and thief was astonished at the
quickness with which the man had caught him, and now fully
expected to be turned over to the watch for due punishment.
But Sinn merely smiled, and forced the boy's palm open. The

minstrel inserted a silver piece into the urchin's hand, then closed the boy's fingers over it.

"Off with you now," the bard said, "and don't be telling any of your friends that I'm an easy mark, or I'll find you and nail your hide to the city wall."

As the minstrel let the boy go and watched the urchin disappear into the crowd, Mariat smiled and thought how typical such generosity was of the man called Sinn. She and her grandchildren had come to know and love him as he traveled with them in the caravan from Ranke to Sanctuary.

The bard had taken a liking to the three children, and had played with them and sung them to sleep every night. Mariat was glad, for he was the only positive masculine influence that the children had had since their own father, her son, had died suddenly and violently. For some reason, Sinn had attached himself to her family and looked after them during their caravan journey.

Now the bard approached her wagon. After giving the horses a reassuring pat on the nose, he turned and smiled up at the woman who held their reins in her hands.

"I believe I have found us suitable accommodations, madame," he said politely and cheerfully. Though Mariat could no longer make claim to her aristocratic station, Sinn still treated her with the grace and respect due a lady of substance. This not only endeared the charismatic minstrel to her even more, but was a constant source of strength and reassurance to her, planting and nurturing the seeds of belief in herself so that she could accomplish the task she had come to Sanctuary to fulfill.

"Come up then, friend," Mariat said, offering him the seat beside her on the wagon. "And lead us to the place you have found. I am parched and travel-sore, and I wish to take a decent bath and eat a decent meal."

"You shall have both and more," Sinn answered, laying his mandolin carefully between himself and Mariat to make sure it came to no harm. The instrument was, after all, the tool of his livelihood. Then he directed Mariat out of the Bazaar towards the inn he had located, and Keldrick followed behind with the other wagon.

*   *   *

Much later that night, Mariat relaxed on a comfortable bed in her own private room. It was the first real respite she had had in many weeks. The establishment Sinn had discovered for them was called the Warm Kettle. It was a quaint and charming inn, located in a decent part of town. "Decent" meaning it was not in Downwind or the Maze. Having only been in town one day, Mariat had already learned that honest people avoided those two thief-infested rat holes like the proverbial plague.

The proprietors of the Warm Kettle were a pleasant, elderly Ilsigi couple. Shamut and his wife, Dansea, had been in operation long before the Rankans took over, and their business went on undisturbed for the most part by any of Sanctuary's troubles. This was mostly due to the fact that they minded their own business and ran an honest establishment.

The couple asked no questions of their clients, and they expected no trouble in return. Shamut had been more than helpful in assuaging some of Mariat's foremost anxieties. The contents of her wagons, which she had guarded preciously across the mountains and through the desert, were now safely housed in the locked vaults of Shamut's cellars. The Ilsigi innkeeper had also been able to recommend merchants and tradesmen she could contact about business investments. Lastly, he had provided her with the name of the man to whom she would have to go to find out about the availability and price of land around Sanctuary: the city's foremost bureaucrat, Molin Torchholder—Rankan priest.

With her goods and her grandchildren safe for the moment, Mariat sought her first night of true, peaceful rest in months. However, as she unwound and let the sweet winds of sleep carry her into unconscious oblivion, the ghosts of her recent past were resurrected and met her on the threshold of nightmare.

She drifted back to her life of nine months ago. Her husband, Kranderon, had run the most successful and respected vineyard in all of Ranke—the Aquinta Winery. Aquinta was a western province of Ranke, and its soil yielded the most suitable grapes for fine wine. Kranderon's family had built a mercantile empire on their vintage, which was considered the finest, most superior wine in all the lands. It was the nectar of emperors and kings, and people of cultured tastes lauded its praises from as far north as Mygdonia to as far south as Sanctuary.

Mariat, who had come from a minor noble house of Ranke, had married the dashing young Kranderon, heir to the Aquinta wine empire. For nearly forty years her life had been easy, cultured, and aristocratic. She was accustomed to the finer things of life, to hosting balls and dinner parties and wine-tasting extravaganzas. The former Rankan Emperor, Abakithis, had visited their estate often to personally survey their stock for his own wine cellars. The Emperor had held Kranderon and Mariat in high esteem.

But, unfortunately, emperors have a way of dying and empires do change hands. The new Rankan Emperor, Theron, though a brilliant military strategist, had little appreciation for the finer points of culture and etiquette. His taste ran more towards large quantities of ale than the refined delicacies of vintage wine.

And Kranderon, though farsighted in business ventures and money-making opportunities, was shortsighted in the political and military arena.

As the Rankan Empire began to crumble in upon itself with intrigue, upheaval, and treachery, the former allies and friends of Abakithis fawned upon Theron, assuring him of their loyalties and declaiming any allegiance or respect for the previous Emperor who had once embraced them as friends and peers.

Kranderon was not so quick to desert the memory of his old friend Abakithis. The wine merchant openly criticized Theron's administration, and insinuated that the new Emperor had committed treason in playing a part in his predecessor's assassination. His loyalty to the murdered Emperor cost Kranderon dearly.

As Ranke fragmented and languished in turmoil, many outlaw bands began to scourge the outlying province. Theron found excuses to conveniently withdraw Rankan troopes from Aquinta. Kranderon was not worried, however, for he felt that he and his men could hold their own against undisciplined outlaws and brigands.

One night nine months ago, however, a suspiciously orderly group of brigands attacked the estate. Though wearing

the apparel and brandishing the weapons of outlaws, the men
who raided Aquinta fought with the discipline and tactics of
seasoned soldiers and veterans of many campaigns.

Kranderon and his men were overrun. The squire of Aquinta
saw his only son fall, fighting valiantly to protect his young
wife. Kranderon himself was taken prisoner, and forced to
watch as the soldiers disguised as outlaws had their sport with
his daughter-in-law, the mother of his three grandchildren, in
view of her fallen husband's corpse. When they had finished
with her, one man held her head back by her hair and slit her
throat. The raiders laughed as her life's blood shot high into
the air.

They slashed and burned a large portion of the vineyards,
and they broke into the cellars and smashed open the aging
vintage. Kranderon watched as a fortune in wine spilled
across the floors of his home and mingled with the blood of
its fallen defenders. Then the raiders hung the squire by the
neck with one of his own supple young grapevines. As
Kranderon slowly strangled, they fired arrows into nonvital
parts of his body to increase his agony. Then they rode into
the night, taking no plunder with them as brigands were wont
to do.

The message was clear to all the other squires in outlying
areas. Theron's wrath was keen and swift to vengeance. The
other estate masters flocked to Theron's court to join the
ranks of sycophants clinging to the last shreds of a rotted,
corrupt Empire.

But the sacking of Aquinta had not been complete. Mariat
had cloistered herself with her grandchildren—Keldrick,
Darseeya, and five-year-old Timock—in the secret vaults hidden beneath the wine cellars. Those gloomy catacombs were
known only to Kranderon and Mariat. It was there that they
wisely hid their finest, most expensive vintage. Mariat's quick
thinking saved herself and her grandchildren from the mael-
strom of violence which descended on Aquinta that night.

The four surviving members of Kranderon's family left
their hiding place and crawled through the wreckage of the
once formidable estate. In the throes of initial shock, Mariat
was able to organize the remaining servants and bury her
dead. Over the next few days, she denied herself the luxury

of grief, for she knew that she must act quickly to assure her family's survival. She retrieved her husband's cache of money (which was not small by any means) and arranged for a caravan to take her south, out of the reach of vengeful Theron.

Mariat loaded one wagon full with her husband's finest vintage. The bottles of wine which would have purchased a small kingdom before were now made priceless because Aquinta was no more. The tragedy which had devastated Mariat's family had also placed a fortune in the woman's hands. The irony was not lost on her.

In a second wagon she loaded the few possessions her family would take with them, along with a secret she and her most trusted servants had worked far into the night to harvest. This secret of Mariat's was her key to rebuilding a viable future for her family in Sanctuary.

So now she was here in the city of new hopes and opportunities. As dawn broke through the window of her room in the Warm Kettle, Mariat threw off both the bonds of sleep and the chains of the past. She refused to let self-pity or grief deter her from her course. It was a new day in Sanctuary, and time for new beginnings.

In fact, Mariat thought, it would be a lovely day to take the children outside the city's walls for a picnic in the open lands.

It is often thought, but entirely untrue, that evil and ugliness always go hand in hand. In Bakarat's case, however, those two nonvirtues blended together in imperfectly perfect harmony.

He was called "the Toad" by his associates and others (though not to his face). One look at his person would abate any suspicions as to the veracity of the nickname.

His buttocks and gut were mammoth in proportion. Those who dealt with him often wondered if they would have to widen the doors of their business establishments to admit him. Atop those heaps and rolls of quivering flesh sat a hideous apparition of a head. As if in mockery of manly features, Bakarat's neckless head looked as though some insanely humorous god had sculptured in living flesh the likeness of a toad made human.

But Bakarat's mind was by no means as sluggish as his wobbly gait. The Toad was known as the most successful merchant and entrepreneur in Sanctuary. Though all found the vision of his person revolting, none could afford to offend the wealthy merchant.

The Toad had not attained his exalted economical status by entirely honest means, either. Next to the legendary Jubal, he ran one of Sanctuary's most sophisticated and complex information and crime networks. In fact, it was rumored that the only reason Jubal had not eliminated this potential rival was the fact that Bakarat paid him well to turn a blind eye to his clandestine endeavors.

But Bakarat was also known for his expertise and shrewd deployment of business ventures. And this was why Mariat had arranged an appointment to see him the day after she took the children outside the city walls.

It had been nice to get the children outside the city and into the clean country air for a while. But the day had been profitable in more ways than one for the wine merchant's widow. For the land she saw about Sanctuary pleased her very much, and she was certain that much that had lain untouched for many years could be put to good use.

Now the realities of the business world had brought Mariat reluctantly to Bakarat's doorstep. The disdain she felt for the sniveling excuse for manhood which offered her a chair in his office was expertly hidden behind her facade of genteel grace. Mariat was far too good a socialite to let her feelings and emotions show in her demeanor.

Bakarat was also unreadable as he sat down across from her at his desk. When she had asked his scribe for an appointment the evening before, the Toad had immediately put his information network into action to find out all he could about the Rankan woman. After all, it was not often a woman of her apparent stature would condescend to deal with a "Wriggly" merchant such as Bakarat.

What he found out, he thought he could put to good use to serve his own greedy interests. He now knew, through his grapevine which reached even into honest establishments such as the Warm Kettle, that Mariat was the widow of the famous and recently departed Kranderon, squire of Aquinta Winery.

This meant that the woman was perhaps well moneyed, and Bakarat's mind whirled with the possibilities of cheating her out of her fortune. It was also a safe assumption that, like most Rankan women of station, Mariat was not the keen business person her husband had been. The Toad relished the idea of taking advantage of the woman's plight.

"Now, what may I do to serve you, madame?" the Toad intoned, being sure to address the woman according to her former station and thereby hopefully gain her trust. He had to make Mariat believe that he was concerned with her best interests in order to take full advantage of her.

"I have a proposal for you and your friends," Mariat said, coming straight to the point.

"Friends?" the fat man queried. "What friends are those? I am afraid I don't know what you are talking about." He smiled, approximating a look of ignorant innocence admirably.

"Come now, good sir, if we are to quibble over the realities of your business dealings we shall be here all day," Mariat countered, blunt but still pleasantly sociable. "And believe me, sir, with my busy schedule I do not have time to argue over trivial matters at the moment."

"But of course," the Toad said, beginning to re-evaluate the woman's business savvy. "However, I fail to see what my fellow merchants can help you with that I cannot. Perhaps you should tell me a little more about exactly what it is you are proposing?"

"Fair enough," Mariat said, relieved at getting the conversation back to the business at hand. "I want to make you and some of your trusted merchant associates an offer to take part in the most successful and elaborate business venture to take place in Sanctuary in recent years."

Bakarat raised a suspicious eyebrow.

"Really," he said with a slightly sarcastic drawl. "That is quite a grandiose statement. I trust you have some means other than high-flown words to persuade my associates and I of the soundness of this proposal?"

"Indeed," Mariat said, and she reached in her carrying bag and produced a corked and sealed bottle, which she placed delicately on the desk in front of the merchant. She carefully turned the bottle so that he could view its rich, red, full-bodied contents, and she made sure the label pointed in his direction so that he could read it.

The Toad looked even more like his namesake as his eyes bulged when he read the label. It was a bottle of Aquinta's finest vintage; ten years old and oak-barrel aged. Before the sacking of the vineyard, it would have brought at least a hundred gold pieces in the wine market. Now, being part of a limited edition of wine (the vineyard no longer being in operation), it might draw at least ten times that much in auction.

"Huh—uh—how many of these do you have, my good lady?" the fat merchant stammered. Mariat smiled, pleased at having taken Bakarat by surprise and gained the upper hand in negotiations.

The Rankan widow had not spent forty years as the wife of Ranke's foremost wine merchant and learned nothing. Her husband had taught her well the trade of doing business.

"Let us just say that I have enough to interest you and your associates. Perhaps now you would be so good as to arrange a meeting with them tomorrow afternoon in the common room of the Warm Kettle. I have rented that room from Shamut the proprietor, and he assures me that no one will disturb our business meeting."

She paused, smiling at the Toad's gaping maw. Bakarat was utterly surprised by the woman's quick-dealing business manner. However, he soon got control of himself as the engines of his devious mind went whirring into action, calculating how he could best turn this deal to his advantage.

"I believe I know of five men who will be most happy to hear your proposal for the sale of this fine vintage. However, if you will permit me to act as your agent in this endeavor, I will be happy to relieve you of the unpleasant tasks of business arrangements," Bakarat said, conveying himself as the soul of virtue and goodwill.

"I thank you for your generous offer," Mariat replied just as sweetly, "but I really could not burden you with so weighty a responsibility on my account."

She rose quickly, holding up her hand to stop any further objection.

"Enough of these pleasantries, though," she said, collecting the bottle from Bakarat's desk and replacing it carefully in her carrying bag. "I have other things to attend to today. Thank you, good sir. I look forward to seeing you and your friends tomorrow at the Warm Kettle."

With that she took her leave from Bakarat's establishment, and he attempted to delay her no longer. He had already formulated his plan for handling this upstart Rankan bitch. He would show her the cost of doing business in Sanctuary, and he would by all means maintain the upper hand in the distribution of the wine.

"Bartleby," the Toad called his scribe into his office.

"Yes, sir," the thin, weedy, long-nosed scrivener whined as he entered his employer's domain.

"Get me Madame Mariat's itinerary for the rest of the day," the fat merchant ordered. "And then contact our good servant, Master Mange, and tell him to meet me with his associates at the Vulgar Unicorn tonight at dusk."

Bartleby swallowed, knowing that the name of Mange meant some skullduggery was afoot. He hastened to comply with his master's wishes.

Molin Torchholder was a very busy man. Over the past years since coming to Sanctuary, he found that most bureaucratic matters had fallen squarely upon his shoulders, and that many of the more mundane governmental duties had become his responsibility. This was primarily due to the fact that Prince Kadakithis could not be bothered with such technicalities. The youthful prince was far too busy pursuing his idealistic dreams for the unification of Sanctuary's varied peoples, not to mention his ongoing "task" of keeping the Beysa occupied, mollified, and satisfied.

However, when word came to the Rankan priest that a woman named Mariat wanted to see him, he put aside his scheduling and planning for the rebuilding and continuing edification of Sanctuary to arrange an appointment to see her. The Torch had known her husband by reputation and had even met Mariat once or twice back in the heyday of Ranke's splendor. He had heard of the tragedy which had struck Aquinta, and he was now curious to find out why Mariat had come to Sanctuary, and what possible business she could have with him.

A soft knock came at Molin's door. It was Hoxa, his secretary, letting him know that Mariat was there to see him. The priest nodded for Hoxa to let the woman into his office.

"Greetings, madame," Molin said, rising and coming to meet her as if she were an acquaintance he had not seen for many long years. In actuality, that was the case, though he had not known her well back in Ranke.

"Lord Torchholder." Mariat curtsied as the priest kissed her hand. "It has been far too long since I have had the pleasure of your company."

"Please accept my deepest sympathies and condolences on the recent deaths in your family," Molin said with unfeigned concern. "Kranderon was a fine man and an astute business-man. He will be sorely missed by all who knew him."

"My thanks for your kindness and thoughtfulness," Mariat said, as she accepted the seat Molin offered her. He himself chose a seat next to hers, rather than returning to the chair behind the desk which he had occupied before her entrance. The priest did this as a show of respect, treating her as a peer rather than a subordinate.

It also occurred to the Torch that the woman had been speaking the finest Court Rankene since she had entered his office. She spoke it so naturally that he had slipped into the court language himself without even realizing it. It was going to be a pleasure to hold discourse with someone so cultured and polite.

"And please accept my sympathies, for I believe that you lost your beloved wife not too long ago," Mariat continued.

"Yes," the Torch replied. "But my wife and I had been estranged for some time. Even still, I believe that we can both understand the poignancy of grief which death can bring."

Molin paused, and then continued, trying to get the conver-sation away from the intensely personal subject at hand.

"To what do I owe the pleasure of this timely visit?" the priest asked, broaching the subject as politely as possible.

"I have heard so much about you, Lord Torchholder, since I entered Sanctuary. People say that you have done wonders for this town, rebuilding the city walls and restoring order,'' Mariat began, smiling sweetly and demurely.

Looking into her face, which was very handsome for a woman of her years, the Torch realized that it had been a very long time since he had exchanged pleasantries with a woman so near his age and station. This interview was turning out to be an enjoyable interlude for the worry-laden priest.

"You are most kind, madame. I have labored to bring this thief-ridden town up to some measure of respectability. Your kind comments are a tribute to what little success I have had,'' the priest said modestly.

"It's been more than a little success from my vantage point, my lord. Why, I have even heard it said in some parts of the Empire that Sanctuary is a place to come to start life anew,'' Mariat returned, maintaining the air of grace and decorum.

"Is this your intention, to start your life over in Sanctuary? I am sure that Kranderon has left you sufficiently provided for. Perhaps a retirement to one of the uptown estates would be of interest to you. I am sure I can arrange a lease for a reasonable price, between friends.'' Lord Torchholder was finding himself hoping that the woman would indeed move uptown and become a part of his social sphere.

"Actually, I had something more audacious in mind, my lord,'' Mariat said, flirting gingerly with the priest. "In fact, I am formulating a business venture which will benefit Sanctuary's economy considerably.''

That statement took even conspiracy-seasoned Molin by surprise. He blinked at her incredulously.

"What do you mean?'' he asked.

"I think perhaps you would like to have your secretary join us, so he can take notes on what I am about to propose,'' Mariat said. Suddenly but smoothly the courtly lady transformed into a businesswoman.

The Torch rose and crossed over to the door of his office.

"Hoxa,'' he called. "Would you please come in here and bring pen and parchment?''

As the priest's secretary seated himself, Mariat laid out her plan for the future. Skeptical at first, Molin soon lost his cynical outlook and was drinking in her plan wholeheartedly. Hoxa was so dumbfounded by the brilliant simplicity of the plan that he stopped taking notes several times just to listen to the wine merchant's widow. Then, of course, they had to go back over the points he missed so they could have them recorded.

After obtaining information and the answers to certain questions from the priest, Mariat left Molin Torchholder with the latter's assurance that he would be in attendance at the merchants' meeting in the Warm Kettle the next day.

As Mariat left the palace complex which housed the priest's office, she felt light on her feet and much younger than her years. Everything seemed to be coming together beautifully.

Back in the Torch's office, Hoxa also commented with optimism, "I think she can really pull it off. She actually sees Sanctuary as a place to build, not to tear down." He turned to his superior and asked: "Could it be that this is no longer the same city you came to years ago?"

Molin Torchholder sighed and said, "Perhaps we have done some good after all."

As the stranger entered the Vulgar Unicorn, he took in the scenery with one sweeping glance. Though he had been in his share of dives and bars all across the Empire, never had he seen so despicable an assemblage of depraved and unsavory individuals. The denizens of the Vulgar Unicorn made the street slime of the Bazaar look like saints and princes in comparison. There was not an honest face or an untainted soul in the place.

The stranger made his way over to one of two free tables against the barroom's west wall. He sat down and waited to be served. He shivered as he contemplated the night dangers of the Maze he had just braved to come to this place.

He did not have long to wait, for soon the barmaid made her way over to his table.

"What'll it be, luv?" she said, with a disinterested glaze in her eyes. Those eyes widened in disbelief at his answer.

"Just a cup of boiling water, if you would be so kind, my girl," the stranger said. "I have some herbal tea which I think I'll take before sampling your establishment's finest."

"Water costs the same as ale," the barmaid said tartly. "That's the rule of the barkeep, Abohorr the One-Thumbed."

"Please be so kind as to tell that august personage of monodigitation that I will pay just such a price," the stranger retorted with a sophisticated air.

He watched bemused as the wench tried to work out the meaning of the words.

"That means I'll pay!" he said in mock exasperation. "So just bring me the water, and make sure it's boiling hot."

As the barmaid left to fulfill his request, a heap of filthy rags detached itself from the bar and shambled in the stranger's direction. As it approached his table, the man saw that the rags housed the even filthier body of a wizened old man. Out from the cowl peered a withered and ruined face, across which a deep and ugly scar cut diagonally, in and out of a black and dirty patch over the unfortunate's right eye.

"Spare a few coppers for a man down on his luck," the old beggar wheezed, blowing a noxious fume in the other man's direction.

The stranger, however, proved to be no soft touch or easy mark. He pulled his cloak aside to show not a purse, but weaponry that had heretofore remained hidden. At his side was a stylish, basket-hilted short sword. Across his left breast was a belt housing several feathered, steel darts.

"If you would like to eke out the rest of your miserable existence, I would suggest you move along. Otherwise, I could arrange for you to make an early withdrawal from this hellhole." The stranger was being sarcastic, but there was enough menace in his eyes to warn the old beggar off.

As he returned to his place at the bar, the old man muttered under his breath, "Gettin' pretty damn difficult to earn a decent living these days. Nobody respects the beggin' class anymore."

The barmaid brought the stranger his boiling water, and he brewed himself a cup of tea with it. It was a special krrf derivative which would enhance and heighten his artistic senses, though it would dull his practical perspective somewhat. The drug was often used to supplement the working of his trade, that being the singing of songs and the weaving of tales.

As the stranger sipped his tea, a more familiar figure waddled into the Vulgar Unicorn. It was Bakarat, called the Toad, one of the most affluent men of Sanctuary's merchant class. The fat man waded through the crowd to the remaining free table on the west wall. As he seated himself, ignoring the stranger at the next table, three other seedy characters left their stations at the bar and slid (or more appropriately slithered) into the seats opposite the Toad. They began their devious conniving, trusting the noise of the barroom to cover their clandestine plan-making.

"I have a job for you, Mange," Bakarat said, addressing the oldest of the three men across the table from him.

Like the Toad himself, the man he spoke to fully warranted his nickname. Mange was a bounty hunter. And on one too many nights of sleeping on the forest floor of the swamps, he had picked up a rare scalp disease which caused his hair to fall out in patches. Hence the unkind name "Mange."

"What is it?" the patchy-headed man replied. "The boys and I are always happy to be of service to you."

Mange referred to his two companions. Bakarat knew their reputations from his previous dealings with Mange. The big, muscle-bound, lantern-jawed oaf was named Wik. He was the bounty hunter's muscle. Wik continued drinking ale, paying little attention to the bantering of Mange and the Toad. Decisions and plan-making were the work of those better suited for it mentally. Wik was happy to take his orders and spend the money he got buying a few moments of even more ignorant (if that were possible) bliss in drunken stupor.

The third man was a skinny, snotty-nosed youth named Speido. He aspired to the thief's profession and had a particular talent for stabbing unarmed and unsuspecting people in the back.

"Listen up, we don't have much time," Bakarat ordered his three companions. Then he laid out the plan that they were to apply their special talents to.

"An old woman named Mariat will be returning to her rooms at the Warm Kettle shortly. She'll be bringing her three grandchildren with her, and they will be returning from

an interview at the Scholar's Guild where she was hiring the
kids a tutor.''

"How do you know when she'll be getting back to the
Kettle?" Speido sneered. "Surely she won't be walking the
streets at night with those brats."

"I have paid to have her delayed," the Toad replied in an
aloof manner. "My connections in the Scholar's Guild will
make sure she leaves at the time appointed."

Mange smiled as the merchant put Speido in his place. The
young bravo had a lot to learn when it came to dealing with
men of Bakarat's caliber. It never occurred to the bounty
hunter to question that what the fat man told them would
transpire exactly as planned.

"You three are to kidnap the children," Bakarat continued.
"And make sure that you do not harm them. Then take them
to the normal holding place and wait for further instructions."
Bakarat finished his orders with giving the men Mariat's
description. Then the trio of bandits rose and left the Vulgar
Unicorn to fulfill their errand.

After they left, Bakarat called one of the local harlots over
to his table. As the fat man was distracted with her attentions,
the stranger seated behind him slid off his chair and wove his
way through the crowd to the door. Progress was slow and
cumbersome, due to the crowded conditions, the krrf tea the
man had drunk, and the anxiety which was quickly overcom-
ing him.

As he moved through the room, his cloak fell to one side,
revealing a mandolin which was slung across his shoulder.

Seeing it, one of the tavern patrons cried for the minstrel to
give them a song. Although the man had originally come to
this dive in hopes of such employment, he turned it down
now as a far more important matter possessed his mind.

He reached the door and miraculously avoided any brawls
caused by bumping into the Unicorn's uncouth clientele. He
escaped into the night and paused briefly to breathe the
unpolluted air outside. Of course, the three men he was
looking for had already disappeared.

Taking a deep breath, Sinn took off in a run to make his
way out of the Maze.

*   *   *

As he wound his way back through the alleys and twisting turns of the portion of town called the Maze, Sinn cursed his krrf-muddled senses.

Part of his success as a minstrel was due to the fact that he etched every detail of everywhere he went indelibly into his mind. Now, however, he was in a state of panic, fearing for the lives of his friends. And the drugged tea he drank was no help as he struggled to remember the course out of this rat hole. His heart sank as he realized that the thugs would probably reach the Warm Kettle long before he would have a chance to get there and warn Mariat of her danger.

He swore for the one-thousandth time to kick the habit of taking krrf. This time, he had an impetus which he felt might make his oath stick.

The bard skidded to a dead halt at an unfamiliar intersection. He looked around him bewildered, his heart leaping up into his throat and its very beat screaming accusations of ineptitude at him.

Then he spotted a familiar landmark, a house with red-painted shutters down the right-hand road. He took off again and passed through a shadowy lane. His hopes were just beginning to rise when a figure leapt out of the shadows. Catching him by the arm, it spun him around to face the bare steel of an unsheathed stiletto.

"Since you're in such a hurry," the thief whispered, his rank breath rich with garlic and beer, "you won't mind if I relieve you of the heavy burden of your purse. That way, you can get where you're going much faster." The thief sneered as he motioned with the knife for Sinn to give him what he wanted.

The sudden shock of the confrontation cleared the bard's head. As the drug's effects dissipated, he drove the reason-freezing panic from his mind.

Sinn nodded condescendingly and reached slowly into his cloak. The thief licked his lips, expecting a nice haul from one so richly dressed as the minstrel was.

To his surprise, the thief suddenly found himself looking down the blade of a fancy short sword. The moonlight gleamed wickedly off its sharpened edge, promising death.

The minstrel's quick and deft movement had been a single

blur of motion. Now Sinn had the upper hand on the situation.

"Out of my face, damn you," the bard cried. "Or I'll nail what little brains you have to the back of your skull!"

The thief gulped, turned, and ran, disappearing quickly into the shadows of the Maze.

Sinn forgot him instantly and took in his surroundings. He was now completely disoriented and had no idea as to which way he should go to get out of the Maze and make it back to the Kettle.

With a silent prayer for inspiration and direction to whatever gods would listen, the bard fled up the street and into the night.

Mariat let out a gasp of relief as she rounded the street corner and saw the friendly, familiar lights of the Warm Kettle just ahead. It was neither wise nor safe to be walking the streets at night, even in this relatively calm section of Sanctuary. The empty streets and sidewalks she had traveled on her way from the Scholar's Guild attested to that fact.

She cursed those idiot scholars and their paper-shuffling nonsense. She would have had the children home long before dark if they had not batted her around from person to person, like a ball in some children's game. After the runaround she had received, she would have walked out on them, were it not for the fact that there were not too many educated people in Sanctuary. Her grandchildren needed tutors, and they deserved the best. She would simply have to overlook the inconvenience caused by the inept clerks.

The Kettle was only four blocks away when a man stepped out of a dark alley and blocked her path. Mariat drew back suddenly and pulled the children close around her.

"What do you want?" She fought to keep fear from showing in her voice. Being an educated woman, she knew that animals were more likely to attack when they sensed fear. And men who harassed women and children were no better than rabid animals.

The man was peculiar-looking. His head looked as though his hair had been torn out in patches, rather than balding naturally. He smiled luridly.

"It's not safe for a woman of quality to be walking the

young lads and lassie alone at night with no protection," he
sneered. "Perhaps you'll allow me to be your escort."

"I recommend that you step out of our way and leave us
alone," Mariat said, addressing the ruffian in such a way as
to put him in his place. "I will call for the watch if you do
not leave us immediately."

"Oh, now, that ain't polite," Mange drawled, "nor is it
particularly wise. My friends behind you might do some
injury to your kiddies before those sleeping dogs on the watch
got here."

Mariat now whirled and looked behind her. Sure enough,
two more figures detached themselves from the shadows and
moved to block her retreat. One was a large, hulking brute.
The other was a slim, sinister youth. Both looked like they
would just as soon slit her throat as talk to her.

"Now," continued Mange, "the boys and I will just take
these beautiful children to a place of"—he paused and winked
at her—"safekeeping. Later on you'll be notified as to where
you can pick them up, and how much their room and board
will cost you."

"Kidnapping," Mariat whispered, under her breath. "And
ransom . . . who is putting you up to this?" Her voice rose as
anger began to take possession of her.

"Shhh. Quiet, Madame Mariat," Mange said, and smiled
when he saw the shock register in her eyes as he used her
name. "We wouldn't want to wake up the good people of this
neighborhood, would we? My, but that could turn into nasty,
bloody business, couldn't it, boys?"

Wik and Speido snorted in amusement.

"And some little children might not get to grow up,"
Mange concluded menacingly. "Wouldn't that be a shame,
Grandma?"

Mariat swallowed, and the paralysis of fear and panic crept
slowly through her body. In all her scheming, she had never
planned on the life-threatening situation which now faced her.
She had been hoping to avoid the more unsavory aspects of
living in Sanctuary altogether. Now she knew that was not
possible, and some things never changed. Though more prosperous, Sanctuary was still a thieves' world. She hoped that
this schooling would not cost her the price of her grandchil-

dren's lives. They were the only family she had left. They were her only reason for living.

"That's better now," Mange was saying as he moved forward. "Nice and compliant, like a good old Rankan bitch."

What happened next caught everyone by surprise, including Mariat. Incensed with rage at hearing his grandmother addressed so, young Keldrick broke free of his fear. He leapt forward with a kick, putting all the weight of his body into it, which slammed with a sickening thud into Mange's groin.

The bounty hunter screamed in surprise and pain, and fell to the ground, rolling in agony and clutching at his crotch.

Wik grabbed hold of Keldrick and lifted the boy high into the air, shaking him. Speido sprang forward and backhanded Mariat across the face, knocking her to the ground. Then he scooped up Darseeya and Timock into his lanky arms.

Suddenly, the feathered shafts of two darts sprouted from Wik's right shoulder. The big oaf bellowed and dropped Keldrick to the ground. Then Wik spun around tugging at the hated sting in his back.

Sinn came roaring out of the night like a demon released from hell. Behind him ran the street urchin to whom, two days before, he had given a silver bit in the Bazaar. The boy, named Jakar, had seen Sinn wandering lost in the Maze and had returned the bard's generosity by leading him out of the tangled streets and to the Warm Kettle.

Speido dropped the children he was holding and pulled his dagger. Mariat staggered to her feet and screamed.

"Murder! Murder! Help!!" She prayed desperately for the watch to hear and answer her cry.

Sinn pulled up short and drew his weapon on Speido. When the sniveling youth saw that his dagger was facing a short sword, he lost all heart for the fight and tried to turn tail and run for it.

Speido only made it a few feet before Keldrick threw himself across the thief's path. Speido tripped and sprawled headlong on the ground, and Jakar leapt immediately on his back and battered the thief into unconsciousness with a small cudgel.

Mange was still lying on the ground clutching himself and watching the world spin around. But Wik, having pulled the darts from his shoulder, roared like a bull as he plowed into Sinn, bowling the minstrel over with the sheer bulk of his weight.

As the giant pinned Sinn to the ground, the bard felt his breath quickly leaving him. He worked his sword arm free and slammed the flat of the blade against the big man's skull. Had he known Wik any better, he would have aimed for a more vital part of the man's anatomy.

Wik rose from the ground like the personification of wrath. In his upraised hands, he lifted the man who had interrupted a simple, uncomplicated assignment. The big brute ignored the old woman and children clinging to his massive frame who were trying to deflect him from his purpose. He hurled the minstrel at the nearest wall with all the force he could muster.

Sinn felt some of his ribs crack and give way as he slammed into the building. As he crumpled to the ground in a mangled heap, he strove to fight off the darkness which was insisting on overwhelming him. He could not leave Mariat and the children undefended.

But as he lost his grip on the conscious world, he heard at last the unmistakable voice of the watch.

"Halt in the name of the prince!!" they cried.

Then oblivion took him.

Bakarat shifted his massive bulk uncomfortably in his seat. He looked disdainfully at his five fellow merchants seated in the common room of the Warm Kettle. The chairs Shamut had provided for the meeting were quite comfortable for them, but a man of the Toad's prestigious girth needed something more accommodating to his size.

He was about to call for Shamut to give him something more comfortable, when Mariat made her entrance into the room.

The fat merchant regarded her with hate. Somehow, she had made his plans last night go awry. He had learned from his underground network of informants that Mange and his cohorts had failed in their task. Bakarat did not worry about them implicating him. He had too many friends in high places. But he was exceedingly aggravated at having to enter this meeting without leverage over the woman Mariat.

The Rankan widow cleared her throat and called the meeting to order.

"Gentlemen," she began. "My thanks to you for taking time out of your busy and pressing schedules to come to this little get-together. I promise you I will make it worth your while."

Bakarat smiled to himself as he glanced at his business associates and saw the skeptical looks on their faces. Although none of them would ever sink to the depths of criminal intrigue at which the Toad operated, they were all shrewd businessmen who looked cynical of the fact that a woman could have something of interest for them to consider, other than her body.

"First," Mariat continued, "allow me to make two special introductions."

As she spoke, a young boy in his early teens entered the room. He brought with him a clean slate upon which he began to draw a map.

"This is my grandson Keldrick, who has recently proved himself man enough to take part in this assembly."

The merchants shifted uncomfortably, not quite understanding what she meant. Bakarat was becoming more and more agitated as the scene developed according to Mariat's plan.

"And may I also introduce Lord Molin Torchholder, who has come to hear and appraise our proposal as well."

Now the men in the room were absolutely stunned. They sprang to their feet, knocking over some of their chairs, in order to give due deference to the Rankan priest whom all knew by reputation. Bakarat was embarrassed to find that his chair followed him when he stood up to bow to the Torch. With his fat rump squeezed against its sides, the chair had a grip on him like a vise.

"Please be seated, gentlemen." Lord Torchholder waved all of them back to their chairs. "Let us hear what Madame Mariat has to say to us."

The merchants sat themselves down and now gave their alert attention to the Rankan widow. The presence of Lord Torchholder gave immense credibility to Mariat. Now they were willing, even eager, to hear what she had to say. All of them except the Toad.

"Thank you, my lord," Mariat acknowledged Molin's statement. "And now to the business at hand."

"All of you are aware that Aquinta wine was the most sought-after vintage in all the Empire. In fact, I have been informed by Lord Torchholder that only the wealthiest of Sanctuary's elite have ever been able to sample its famous bouquet."

"That's true," said one of the merchants, "but what is that to us? We have all heard what happened in Aquinta. There will be no more wine forthcoming from those fields."

"That is sadly all too true," Mariat continued. "But I have called you gentlemen here today to inform you that I possess an entire wagonload of Aquinta's finest vintage, and I have it safely housed right here in Sanctuary!"

The implications of the announcement were not lost on this group of men. Being merchants, they all knew that one or two bottles of the precious, now priceless wine would bring an unbelievable price at auction. To tell them that an entire wagonload was available was like telling someone that a mountain of gold is waiting in his backyard, ripe for the taking. Even Bakarat, who knew the purpose of the meeting (or so he thought), was taken aback.

"So you're coming to us to back the auction of your merchandise?" one of the other merchants asked hopefully.

"Yes, but that is not the end of it," Mariat said. Now was the time to present her plan—her whole reason for coming to Sanctuary. She said a silent prayer as she prepared to reveal her proposal to these men of business and profit.

Bakarat was feeling increasingly uncomfortable. First the woman had thrown in an ace in the hole by inviting the Torch. Now she was introducing an entirely new scheme. He felt control of the meeting slipping from his already shaky grasp.

"Just a moment," the Toad objected. "Either you want us to help you sell the stuff, or you don't. Which is it? I wish you would get to the point because our time is very valuable."

"Very well," Mariat replied, staying calm and showing much more common sense than the fat merchant was displaying.

"The prime vintage was not the only treasure I have brought to this city." Mariat paused. She had them completely in her grasp. They were all wondering what else could possibly match the revelation of wealth she had already made. All of them were on the edge of their chairs, except for the Torch, who already knew of her plan.

"In another wagon, I brought with me five hundred saplings of my hardiest vines from Aquinta. They have been stripped and prepared for travel, but within six months of their planting they will yield fruit from which we can begin pressing wine. Within three years, we will have the first fine vintage ready. In the meantime, we will slowly auction off the wine I have brought from Aquinta for capital."

She paused to let her proposal sink in. The Torch, she knew, was already willing to back her. The other five merchants were looking at each other thoughtfully. But the Toad was shaking with beet-faced rage. He looked like he might literally croak. He could not accept the fact that he was being outmaneuvered by a woman.

"You're insane," he said, rising and knocking the chair off his huge butt. "And the rest of you are insane if you're going to seriously consider this cockeyed plan. She wants you to pour your money into this ridiculous scheme of hers, and for what?" He turned to Mariat again. "What do we get in return for our investment? Three years of waiting and then nothing when it falls apart!"

"Please, To—I mean, Master Bakarat, calm yourself. My plan is as wise an investment as most. I am putting my entire life's savings into this venture, and I am opening up this proposal to let some of you in on it from the beginning. All I need is the capital to buy the land, the proper equipment, and hire the laborers. I supply the vines and the supervision of the vineyard. I offer the investors a forty percent share of the first five years' profits, after the wine becomes sellable. In the meantime, I offer the same percentage for all the existing wine we sell over the next three years. Gentlemen, you cannot lose."

"What makes you think you're qualified to run a vineyard?" Bakarat exclaimed.

"The fact that, with my husband, I operated the most successful vineyard in the Rankan Empire—the Aquinta!" Mariat countered the fat merchant. "Who do you think helped my husband all through the years with the operation of the winery? I even ran it alone when he was gone for long periods on business.''

It was obvious that the other merchants were rapidly becoming convinced.

"This is madness, I tell you," Bakarat continued, oblivious of all reason himself. "There is no place to plant a vineyard in Sanctuary!"

"No, not in the city proper," Mariat agreed. "But outside the walls there lies tillable land that has lain fallow for years. I have examined the land and the soil, and found plots in the hills and the upper swamps which will be suitable for grapes, given the proper drainage and irrigation."

She pointed to the maps that Keldrick had drawn, and showed the men where she planned to set up the winery.

"That's government land," the Toad shouted. "You won't be able to buy that for the price of your entire stock of vintage!"

"As a matter of fact," Molin Torchholder interceded, "she will be able to purchase it for the price of its back taxes. As the minister in charge of land development, I see no reason why this land should be unused. I have heard Madame Mariat's proposal, and I am ready to enter into an agreement with her on behalf of the prince. Who is with me?"

The merchants all stood and shouted their willingness to participate.

Bakarat was absolutely livid.

"I warn you," he threatened his associates, "if you enter into a pact with this woman, you will regret it."

"Master Toad," Mariat said in disdain. The merchant whirled on her, not believing that she would dare to address him so.

"This brings me to a bit of unpleasant business which I had hoped to delay until after the meeting. However, your arrogance and threats leave me no choice."

She opened the door and called into the hallway.

"Commander Walegrin, would you be so kind as to step in here, please?"

Mariat played her final card as the officer in charge of the city garrison strode into the room. Walegrin was followed by two of his men, one of whom was supporting the weak-looking figure of Sinn the minstrel.

"Commander, please perform your office." Mariat stepped back as Walegrin approached the completely dumbfounded Bakarat.

"I hereby place you, Bakarat the merchant, under arrest for conspiracy to commit kidnapping and extortion."

Fear struck the Toad for the first time.

"You can't do this to me," the fat man whined and objected. "You've got no evidence, no proof."

"Master Sinn," Walegrin asked, "would you be so kind as to affirm that you witnessed a conversation between Bakarat and three ruffians we now have in custody, in which the said Bakarat contracted their services to kidnap Mariat's grandchildren?"

"I do confirm it." Sinn managed to grate out the words between pain-clenched teeth. Though his broken ribs had been set and taken care of, he was not supposed to be up and about for another few weeks. He had insisted on coming, however, to play his part in the Toad's arrest.

Bakarat finally realized he was beaten, for the moment. He bowed his head in silence as Walegrin's guards bound his wrists. But as he left the room, the Toad lifted his ugly head to give Mariat one final, withering look of hatred and malice.

His glare said better than any words that he would not rest until he had paid her back for this indignity.

"Don't worry about this dung heap, madame," Walegrin said as he shoved Bakarat out of the room. "He's going to be keeping the rats in the dungeon company for a very long time. I hope they won't be offended by his moving in on them."

Walegrin and his men left the room with their prisoner, and Dansea, the innkeeper's wife, came in and helped Sinn back to his room.

Mariat turned to the merchants.

"Well, friends, are we ready to drink a toast to the Aquinta Cartel?"

They all agreed heartily. Darseeya and Timock came in on cue, bringing a bottle of fine Aquinta vintage, and the pact was sealed with a drink. Later, Lord Torchholder witnessed

the more formal written agreement as the merchants signed
their names to support Mariat's proposal.

And so the Aquinta Cartel was formed and officialized.

It was a beautiful day in the spring of Sanctuary as Mariat
and her three grandchildren overlooked the land recently purchased by the Aquinta Cartel.

"There is so much work to be done," Mariat said to
Keldrick, Darseeya, and Timock. "And we must never shirk
from hard work. For on this land, we will build the new
Aquinta."

"Keldrick," she said, bringing the boy around to face her.
"You are the man of this family now. You must learn to lead
as you have learned to be a man. I know you can, for you are
the true son of your father and grandfather."

She paused and looked down at the run-down farmhouse
which would soon be refurbished to be their home on the
winery, in addition to the uptown mansion Lord Torchholder
had arranged for them.

"Children, this is home, where we will spend our vintage
years. This is where we build anew, from the ground up."

It was an entirely new kind of day dawning in Sanctuary. A
day of hope.

QUICKSILVER DREAMS

Diana L. Paxson

"Aglon! I thought they'd killed you!"

He stands in her doorway, a pale figure in the moonlight that filters through the gauzy curtains, but no other man she knows has such fine shoulders or such a head of dark curly hair.

"I'm suprised they let you come up to me at this hour—were you off on some mission? Why did they tell me you were dead?" Joia sits up in bed, throwing the covers aside in welcome. It must be late indeed, for the Aphrodisia House is silent.

He does not answer. Shadow veils him as he comes towards her. Then he's by the bed and once more the light falls across him. She sees him pale as a marble statue of a god—all except for the black gash in his throat where the blade went in . . . She opens her lips to scream, but his touch freezes her.

Cold! He is so cold . . .

"Eshi's tits! Joia, you gone crazy?"

The sharp slap was muffled by bed-curtains. Still whimpering, the girl fell back against the silk cushions. A dark figure moved; light sparked from the flints and a wavering spark of lamplight firmed and grew.

"You're not Aglon!"

107

"Aglon's dead! You little bitch, have you had so many men you can't even remember?"

"Ricio . . ." The name ended in a little catch of the breath. The girl pushed herself onto one elbow, brushing tumbled auburn curls away from her eyes. "Thank the gods! I thought Aglon's ghost was . . . after me! I was so afraid."

She reached out to him, but he shrugged away her hand. He was very young, and the welts where she had scratched him were already rising red on his chest.

"Ricio, sweetest," whispered Joia. "You're not going to get mad just because I had a little nightmare? Look, I'm awake now. Don't want to waste the rest of the night, do you?"

"What's the use, if every time I touch you, you think I'm Aglon! I suppose all us garrison men are alike to you!" He sounded sullen, and she hid a smile.

"Oh, Ricio, it was a *nightmare!* He didn't mean anything to me once I met you!" This time he did not brush away her caress, but he was still frowning. "Look—this is the only thing he ever gave me—" Lamplight played like quicksilver on the glimmering surface of the ball the girl took from the night table. His belt pouch was hanging on the bedpost, and she dropped it in. "You take it, Ricio. I don't need it anymore!"

Despite his pique his body was responding. Joia's hands grew bolder.

"You scratched me . . ." he said hoarsely, turning at last.

"I'll kiss it better, so?"

The guardsman groaned and eased back against the cushions as she bent over him.

"He came to me—last night. It was terrible . . ." Joia took a very small sip from the porcelain teacup that Valira pressed into her hand, then set it down again. Valira sighed. She was only twenty-two; even at the Aphrodisia House that was not yet old. The careful bleaching that lightened her Ilsigi-dark hair into something nearer gold hid no grey. Perhaps it was having a little daughter of her own that had made the other girls think of her as motherly.

"You were with Ricio?"

"He paid for the whole night," explained Joia. "In my

nightmare I thought he was Aglon and I woke up fighting. And then he got jealous when I told him what was wrong.''

"Puppy—" said Valira, resting her elbows on the inlaid wood of the table. It was new, like most of the furnishings, like most of the facade of Sanctuary—a glossy surface to hide the fact that underneath, not that much had changed. "You'd think he would sympathize. Aglon was his comrade."

Joia shook her head. "Ricio is very young." Her hennaed curls hung limp, and the violet shadows around her eyes owed nothing to the paint pot. "I told Ricio that I never loved Aglon, but it wasn't true. Oh, Valira, I fought him, but I wanted him. He was like ice inside me, and he just kept on. And now I can't seem to get warm."

Joia was wrapped in a fluffy shawl of silk and wool which had probably been looted from some northern valley, and Valira felt the smooth skin of her own forearms pebble with chill despite the sultry heat of the day. One of the new girls came into the breakfast room, heavy-eyed and abstracted, nursing her own cup of tea.

"I wanted him," said Joia, "and now I'm afraid."

"Did you have a nightmare?" asked the other girl. Flaine was new, and pretty in a kittenish sort of way, another escapee from the streets of Sanctuary.

"I hope that's all it was!" muttered Joia.

"I had bad dreams too—" said Flaine. "They must have been dreams . . . he promised me—" Her pouting lips closed tightly.

"Something pinched me all night!" said another girl. "Couldn't sleep a wink, an' when I woke I felt all black-an'-blue!"

Valira raised one eyebrow. The child looked hagged, but she could see no marks on the dark skin.

"We seem to have an epidemic—"

"If Lythande were still in town I'd ask Myrtis to talk to him," Joia said suddenly. "Do you know anyone in the Mageguild who'd take out the price of his help in trade?"

Valira laughed. "When a wizard gets horny all he has to do is summon up a few succubi! Anyway, I've never seen any of that crowd here."

"But you grew up in Sanctuary!" said Joia. "You must know someone!"

Valira frowned, remembering a little man with ginger hair whose painting had shown her her soul. He had recommended her to Myrtis, had taught her that even a half-penny whore from Sanctuary's waterfront could have a future. And when his wife, Gilla, stayed here during the False Plague Riots a few seasons back, she had been kind.

"You do know a mage!" exclaimed Joia, watching her. "Please help me, Valira—I'm afraid!"

"Lalo is not exactly a wizard . . . and his wife is more than enough woman for him," Valira said slowly. "I don't know if he can help. But I'll take you to see."

"Go back to the Mageguild if you want formulae!" Lalo exclaimed. "I've told you—I don't work that way!" He pushed the diagram back across the worktable to Darios. His easel was waiting beside the window with the finest imported paints beside it. Why was he wasting the morning light talking?

"All arts have rules. Can it hurt you to try and think systematically?" the young man asked patiently. "Why do you think the gateway you visualized to reach my spirit when my body was walled up in that vault worked so well?"

"Because I'd painted the thing in the first place—" Lalo began.

"You didn't make up the design!" Darios shook his head. "The details you remembered so clearly came from S'danzo tradition. Without those symbols the Otherworld would be impossible for the human mind to comprehend. The images let us focus our perception of reality, just as we control our emotions through words." The young mage paused for breath. "Look—here is the first plane—that's the world around us, the world you know—" He tapped the crudely drawn diagram.

Lalo glared at him. The boy was unnatural. Lalo was the one who should have been making the careful explanations, complaining about hotheaded youth when his apprentice protested as his own master used to do. But it was only a fluke of fate that had made the mageling his student at all.

"You're wasting your time, Darios. Why don't you go

back to the Mageguild? Now that things have settled down, they're trying to rebuild the school,'' Lalo exclaimed. It was not yet noon, but the day was hot already. He could feel perspiration adhering his thin tunic to his skin like one of Cholly's glues. "What in the name of Ils do you think you can learn from me?''

"The things that no one at the Mageguild knows.'' Darios combed his fingers through his curly black beard. Young as he was, it flowed across his chest like a master's. Gilla's feeding had filled him out. He took refuge sometimes in a dignity that gave him the air of a much older man.

"You can kick me out, but no one can force me to go back there. Even in the old days wizards like Enas Yorl and Ischade could go their own ways, and now Markmor is back, and there are half a dozen other independent operators trying to hide the fact that there's precious little of the old magic left in this town.''

"Well, if my magic has survived because it's different,'' Lalo said triumphantly, "why are you trying to change me?''

"Because magic draws magic,'' Darios replied. "You've got it, and you can't get rid of it—wouldn't if you could—'' The dark eyes lifted, and Lalo grimaced, remembering the days when he had thought both mortal and magical sight lost. He knew better now. Even if fate should blind him again, he could see in the Otherworld.

"Randal tried once to recruit you, and as things calm down, others will be after you—others who fear you and want to get you out of the way. Or who want to use you, as Molin Torchholder is using your paintings of Sanctuary's past to shape the future. Don't you wonder about some of those symbols he's having you put in? Here's the key to them—'' He tapped the diagram. "I'm just trying to help, you know. Molin or Randal or anyone else with knowledge can use you as you use your own paints until you learn!''

Lalo covered his eyes. His head still hurt sometimes since the concussion that had temporarily blinded him. There was a pounding in his temples now—if he was going to have the headaches, he might as well start drinking again!

"The second plane,'' said Darios implacably, "is the sphere of the moon. It governs all things fluid, both the ocean and the astral sea. A good source of symbols for operations involving the Beysib, wouldn't you say?''

This afternoon, thought Lalo, *Darios is going to practice drawing until his fingers wear away!*

They had reached the fourth sphere when the sound of feminine laughter from the kitchen broke Darios's concentration.

''I doubt I'll remember even what we've done so far—'' said Lalo, taking pity on him. He could hear Gilla and their oldest son, Wedemir, but neither of the other two voices sounded like the girl with whom both Wedemir and Darios were in love. *Darios can't hear the difference,* he realized. *Maybe I do know a few useful things after all.* He opened the door.

A wave of chypre scent tantalized his nostrils even before he saw the two women who were eating Gilla's Enlibar orange nut cake at the new kitchen table. Gowns of sheerest gauze struck a compromise between Sanctuary's minimal demands for decency and the unseasonable heat. They were a strange sight in Gilla's kitchen, brightened though it was by the burnished copper pots and bunches of peppers that hung from the beams.

Parasols of painted silk leaned against the whitewashed wall. One of the women had a tumble of garnet curls dressed high through a circlet of pearls. The intricately knotted dark braids of the other seemed dusted with gold. It was only when she turned to face him that the sophisticated veneer vanished and he saw the bright spirit within, as he had seen it once through garish face paint and the pinched face of poverty.

''Valira! You're looking well!''

Darios, following him through the door, stopped short, staring.

''Joia and Valira are from the Aphrodisia House,'' said Gilla, suppressing a smile. ''Ladies, this is Darios, my husband's apprentice.''

''He's wearing a mage-robe—'' said the second girl. Her voice was strained.

''He used to study at the Guild,'' explained Gilla. The girl looked up then and Lalo recoiled, seeing the naked face of fear.

''Sabellia be praised. Perhaps they can help me!''

Darios sent Lalo a glance in which panic and professional interest warred. The limner found himself relaxing. Magic might still frighten him, but mere physical beauty had no power over him now. Wedemir leaned back in his chair and grinned at the mageling's discomfort.

"Have another slice of cake," said Gilla. "You girls worry about your figures too much to eat properly, but troubles are best faced with a full belly. We'll get some real food into you as soon as the sausages are done."

Valira set down her teacup and laughed. "I remember—you used to feed half the neighborhood when I was a child."

"It's not food I need, but sleep!" said Joia.

Lalo cleared his throat. "Neither of which I can help you with. So just what is wrong?" Joia wiped away tears without smudging her eye paint and began to tell her tale.

"And Joia is not the only one," said Valira when they had finished. "Doree has been having nightmares too, and some of the others. Well, after the past few years there's hardly a one of us who hasn't lost someone she cared for. We're supposed to be professional, but when a man has been kind to you, it's hard."

"I wanted Aglon *alive*! Why is his ghost trying to kill me?"

"His ghost, or is it something else, taking that form?" asked Darios.

"A demon lover?" Wedemir laughed. "At the Aphrodisia House?" He sobered as Valira glared at him. "Sorry, lass—but you have to admit—"

"I hope Aglon's ghost comes to the barracks to haunt *you*!" Joia exclaimed. "You were his friend!"

"Aglon—" said Gilla into the strained silence. "The name sounds familiar. Did we ever meet him, dear?"

"He was one of the lads who helped me dig out Darios," Wedemir said bitterly. "Got knifed in a little cleanup action Downwind a few days ago."

"He was a lovely boy when he was alive—" sniffed Joia. "Always gentle with me; he used to give me things—"

Lalo sighed. "I understand your sorrow, but what can I do? If you want an exorcism, perhaps Darios—"

"Oh, I'm just a pleasure-girl, a hysterical bit of fluff! Of

course you don't believe me! Joia began to cry in earnest now
and Wedemir gallantly offered her his military scarf when her
wisp of a handkerchief failed. She accepted it with an automatic flutter of her lashes, but Lalo did not think she really saw.

"I have been certificated as an exorcist by the Mageguild,"
said Darios stiffly. "I would be willing to conduct a purifica-
tion of your chambers tomorrow if you desire."

Joia opened her eyes at the polysyllables and Valira's lips
twitched. "Well, Joia, at least *he* is taking you seriously,"
the older girl replied. "Why don't we let him try?"

"Now on this panel," said Molin Torchholder, "I want
you to paint a design of crossed swords and spears on the
border of Lady Daphne's gown."

"Hakiem didn't mention that detail," said Lalo, looking
from the design he had already roughed in on the plaster to
the drawing again. He pulled his straw hat forward to shade
his eyes. It was another in the string of very hot days that had
been baking Sanctuary, and sunlight blazed back from the
white wall with a painful glare. He supposed that he should
be grateful he was not working on the new walls outside the
city, as had been at first proposed. It was the newly resur-
faced wall around the palace that Torchholder had decided
should display Lalo's skill.

"Hakiem isn't paying you," said the priest. He stepped
back from the wall, and the servant who held the broad
parasol moved with him. That was a good idea, thought Lalo.
They had already put up hoardings to protect the unfinished
work from curious eyes. Maybe he could get a portable
canvas sunshade as well. Torchholder turned. "I was there
too, remember. Are you doubting me?"

The limner frowned. He had sketched from the storyteller's
descriptions without thinking, and as Hakiem spoke he had
seen, as if the images were flowing directly from the old
man's memory through his fingers onto the page. Those
scenes had felt right. What Lord Torchholder was telling him
now did not. And this was not the first time.

The picture of Prince Kadakithis's first entrance into the
city showed a rising sun haloing him with gold. But the
prince had actually arrived through the north gate. Along with

most of the rest of the population, Lalo *had* been there to see him ride in. He had made the change in the picture, but it had rubbed him the wrong way. Like this. Now he began to wonder about the devices he had been told to paint on the parade shields of the prince's guards. Unimportant details, he had thought them, but what if they were something more? He shivered a little despite the heat of the sun. Darios's warnings were beginning to make more sense to him now.

"If I'm going to make a change in the design, I want to know what it means—"

"What it *means*?" Torchholder stared at him. "Why should it have to mean something?"

"In that case, I think it would be more aesthetic to give her gown a pattern of eagles with outstretched wings. In gold, since she comes of noble kin."

The priest's gaze sharpened. "Limner, you presume! You are only a tool in my hand, and you will do as I say!"

"No." Lalo held out his paintbrush, then laid it down. "*This* is a tool. It has no choice but to do my will. But though you can put me down and hire another painter, you cannot force me to work for you. And there is no other artist in Sanctuary who can do what you really hired me for, is there, Torchholder? There is no one else in the Empire, perhaps in the world . . ."

The silence stretched out between them. Beyond the hoardings he could hear a beggar cursing two soldiers with demon-haunted sleep as they ordered him to move on, the whining song of the water seller, a distant scream—all the normal sounds of a Sanctuary summer day. Finally the priest grimaced and looked away.

"Don't argue with me, limner," he said. "Don't meddle with things you don't understand."

Lalo started home down the Wideway as dusk began to shade the streets and the sea breeze lent a welcome coolness to the air. In the end he had agreed to paint the gown as Torchholder had ordered it—for now. It had occurred to the limner that Gilla was a crony of Glisselrand, and the prima donna of Feltheryn's company seemed to be on good terms with the people at Land's End. If he wanted to know what

Daphne had really worn that day, he could ask. But the priest had a point. Even Darios must agree that there was no use in standing up for a principle he did not understand.

He felt exhausted. He wondered how Darios's day had gone—Lalo's lips twitched as he visualized his apprentice trying to maintain his dignity in the Aphrodisia House. He would have to keep a straight face tonight when he asked him how the exorcism had gone.

"Lalo . . ." The croak of a call came from close behind him.

Lalo stopped short in the street, then whirled, hand going to the hilt of his dagger as someone stumbled into him.

"Cappen Varra!" Lalo stared. "Where in Shalpa's name have you sprung from? It's been years!"

"You recognized me!" The minstrel straightened, pushing back the hood of the extremely tattered cloak that covered disreputable breeches and a tunic scarcely less worn.

"Of course—" the limner began, then flushed, realizing which kind of sight he had been using, for such a getup was inconceivable garb for the dapper musician he had known. Only the battered harp case was the same. "But this is no place to stand talking. You look thirsty, man, and here's the Unicorn—let me buy you some beer!"

"I'm not going to tell you where I've been," said the harper when they were settled in a back booth with two big tankards of brew. It was early yet for the Unicorn; except for two guardsmen they had the place to themselves, and a slatternly girl was still wiping down the bar.

"You don't want to know, and I don't want to remember. Not sure it's safe to tell you anyway." For a moment the minstrel's fingers closed over the silver amulet at his neck and his gaze went inward. "All I'll say is that when I walked through the gates this place really did look like a sanctuary."

Lalo stared. "Well, it's true that things here have finally settled down. Trade's reviving, too."

"*Your* trade is prospering, I can see!" Cappen Varra surveyed Lalo's smock—stained now with paint and perspiration, but good linen, and new. "You never used to offer to pay for the beer!"

Lalo took a long draft and grimaced, wondering whether

this batch was a little off or he was losing his taste for the stuff.

"A lot of things are different now, including me," he agreed. He looked at his old friend, wondering if here was someone who might understand.

"You haven't—*made*—anything else, have you?" whispered Cappen Varra. Involuntarily they both looked at the blank wall where once Lalo had drawn the accumulated evil of the Vulgar Unicorn and breathed into it a soul.

"No. I wear a mask over my mouth when I paint these days so that I won't breathe life into anything by chance," said Lalo. "But I've learned to do a few other things. Sometimes it's hard to tell the difference between imagination, or art, and what's real!"

"I understand—" The harper held out his tankard to be refilled. "I nearly got lynched once when I sang a story I thought I'd made up and it turned out to be true."

"How can that happen?" exclaimed Lalo. "When I paint, or you sing, are we spying on reality without knowing it, no more to be blamed than a mirror going down the road that reflects both the sky and the mire, or are we shaping it somehow?"

"Do the stars or the cards create our futures, or does the person who reads them define what will be?" echoed Cappen Varra. The beer had put the sparkle back into his eyes. "That's a question for the Mageguild, not for me!"

"Not the Mageguild!" Lalo shuddered. "They'd look for a way to sell it. I only ever met one mage who cared for magic more than money. He was the Imperial Magelord, and he taught me how to seek truth in my painting. But that was years ago. He's probably dead by now."

"Got a theory—" said Cappen Varra, whose tankard had just been refilled for the third time. "Reality's not solid. 'S like clay, but most people don't have th' strength to mold it, or know how. The gods can. Mages can shape it with their spells, 'n' artists, sometimes—" he gazed at Lalo owlishly over the rim of his tankard, and the limner realized abruptly that after Cappen Varra's privations, even the Vulgar Unicorn's sour beer had been too much for him. And evening was coming on. The limner could not possibly leave his old friend alone and incapable in this part of town.

"Gilla will have dinner ready by now—" he said briskly.
"Why don't you come along home with me?"

Cappen Varra grinned. "Think I'm drunk? Maybe so.
Easier this way. I know about changing things, see—I sang a
door open to th'other world, sang up a crowd o' demons to
kill the folks who'd captured me. Killed everybody. Just like
th' Black Unicorn—" His eyes filled with tears. "Even th'
children!"

Lalo cast a swift look at the wall. As the lamps were lit he
seemed to see that demonic form still shadowed there. But he
had banished it! And after that they had scraped down and
replastered the wall!

"Come on! We're getting out of here!" He tossed some
coins on the table and grasped his friend's arm. Why had he
started asking these questions? The concept of an unalterable
fate was bad enough, but the idea of a malleable reality at the
mercy of anyone who could master it terrified him.

"Were the girls at the Aphrodisia House *very* beautiful?"
Latilla stared into Darios's face earnestly.

"Yes, of course." The young man blushed, and Lalo hid a
smile. "But some of them were very silly as well."

"And so are you," said Gilla repressively. "Eat your supper, Tilla, and let the poor boy tell his tale."

The color faded from Darios's face and he turned to Lalo
again. "I wish you had been with me, sir. It was hard enough
to do the exorcism with them all chattering around me like
magpies, but I managed to complete the ceremony. I don't
know if it will do any good, though. Each dream I heard from
one girl seemed to inspire the next to tell of something even
more terrible. By the time I got through, the girls were all
hysterical."

"Did you sense anything demonic?" asked Cappen Varra
curiously, pushing his bowl away. Drunk or sober, Cappen
Varra retained his good manners, but the last of the beer
fumes seemed to have worn off.

As usual, Gilla had risen to the occasion. After a disap-
proving sniff at their breath, she had ladled out enough fish
stew with rice and red peppers for everybody. And the minstrel had eaten with an appetite that endeared him to his

hostess, who beamed upon him now. She had even agreed to let him stay in Ganner's old room for a while.

Darios shrugged. "The atmosphere was upset, but that's only to be expected. I couldn't concentrate well enough to say."

"I can add some more cream sauce if the stew is too hot for you," said Gilla, eyeing his plate.

"What?" Darios looked down and took another spoonful. "No, it's wonderful mistress—I was just distracted."

Cappen Varra cleared his throat and began a long and convoluted story about a camel drover, a prostitute, and a priest of Anen.

He was just finishing when the door swung open and Wedemir strode in.

"I've sewn the new insignia on the tunic you brought me, dear. Have you eaten? I can make up some more pilaf—" Gilla began, but Lalo motioned her to silence. Wedemir's eyes met his gratefully.

"I need to apologize to Valira," he said. "Whatever is wrong at the Aphrodisia house is catching! Last night half the men woke up shouting about demons!"

"What do you mean—what exactly did they say?" Darios asked.

Wedemir's face grew grim. "Valira told us that the girls dreamed of lost lovers. Well, the bonds between fighting men are just as strong—and our losses—you know how many have died these past few years!"

"Are their ghosts returning?" whispered Gilla. "Are the dead going to walk among us again?" Lalo shuddered, remembering that terrible time.

"It would be impossible," said Darios. "That kind of manifestation requires a power source of a magnitude unavailable in Sanctuary anymore!"

"They are not returning in their bodies, thank the gods!" exclaimed Wedemir. "But there's enough magic coming from somewhere to power these hauntings. The lads feel they're being watched, things break, they have stupid accidents. The amulet sellers in the Bazaar are doing a brisk trade!"

"Perhaps the exorcism you did at the Aphrodisia House today will stop it, Darios—" suggested Lalo.

"I'll have you up to the barracks tomorrow to repeat the process if it does!" said Wedemir. "Another few days of this and the men will be no use at all!"

But Darios was still looking worried, and that night Lalo's sleep was haunted by memories of the Black Unicorn. In the morning they were awakened by a messenger from the Aphrodisia House, bearing a chypre-scented letter from Myrtis herself begging Lalo to come to her.

"A four and a three!" cried Ricio as the dice bounced across the wooden floor. "I'll stake you my new saddlecloth you can't better that, Ottar!"

Wedemir looked up from his tally sheet as the voices rose. There was no rule against dicing among his soldiers as long as it stayed friendly, but for a moment there had been a disturbing sharpness in the boy's tone. He knew already that Ricio couldn't carry his wine, but all they had here was thin beer.

There was a murmur of agreement from the other man. Once more the dice cup rattled, he heard a shout from the kibitzers as the cubes fell.

"He's taken you proper, Ricio, lad—" said someone. "Better call it a night, now. I know for a fact that you've lost all your pay, and it's against regs to wager your gear!"

"I'm *not* rolled up!" said Ricio. "Got this!" Laughing shrilly, he held up a shimmering silver ball. "Love gift from a lovely lady. Ottar! Stake you this for all you've won and your back pay!"

"Give it up, Ricio!" called his friends. "Your luck is out. What's Joia gonna think if you lose that too?"

He rounded on them, waving his tankard so that the liquid inside splashed his friends. "Shut up, you! Don't you say her name!" He turned back to Ottar, who was watching him speculatively. "You 'fraid to try again? You 'fraid my luck'll change?" Ottar shrugged fatalistically. Ricio laughed, shook the dice cup, and threw. "Five and five!" he cried, slapping the cup into his opponent's hand.

"Hey!" cried one of the others, licking his wet hand, "he's got brandy in here!"

As Wedemir got to his feet he heard the click of dice across the floor.

"Six and six," said Ottar, reaching for the silver ball.

"No!" shrieked Ricio. "You barbarian swine!" Wedemir took another step towards him, and then everything changed. The room was filled with pale-haired northerners, waving bloody knives; Wedemir smelled smoke. He started to turn, saw Ricio's knife flash. Instinct took over and his callused fist connected with the boy's jaw.

There was a sudden silence. Wedemir blinked and rubbed his fist, staring at men who looked back at him with equally astonished eyes. Where had the barbarians gone? No one made a sound but Ricio, who moaned as the silver ball rolled from his hand, and Ottar picked it off the floor.

One of the other men sniffed at Ricio's tankard. "Well," he said sadly, "there's nothing but beer in here now."

"Lalo my dear, surely you understand that this has got to end!" Myrtis poured fragrant spice tea into a cup and handed it to him. "The worst of the nightmares seem to be over, but the girls are haunted by their memories. It is bad for trade."

Lalo shifted uneasily on the overstuffed cushion, hoping he would not slide off and spill tea all over the ivory satin brocade. He was a little unnerved by Myrtis's trust. Even Darios, sitting quietly behind him, wore an exasperating expression of calm expectance.

"My pictures won't be what the girls expect, you know—"

"I've told them it's for publicity," said Myrtis. "They'll come in one by one, and you'll draw them. If I don't like the results I don't have to use them, you know."

Lalo put down his teacup and picked up his drawing pad, and Myrtis rang her little bell.

The Aphrodisia House accepted only the most beautiful. Darios's flushed face showed Lalo what it was like to look at them simply as a man. No wonder the lad had found his exorcism hard going. But the limner saw them with other eyes. As he began to work, outer awareness fell away.

Not many had spirits as beautiful as Valira's, but in several he found depths of faith and fortitude that would have astonished their customers. He saw on their souls the scars of neglect and cruelty and despair. In many he found jealousy or greed. In almost all of them he saw fear.

"Afraid?" Myrtis laughed bitterly when the last girl had gone. "Of course they fear. Age, illness, poverty—all they have is their beauty. Every one of them fears what will happen when it is gone. The attention their lovers pay them is their reassurance. But you should look again, Lalo—that's not all your pictures show."

Blinking, he focused on the shaded backgrounds with which he had surrounded his sketches, and realized that they were more than random lines. It was not only the portraits that showed fear—the fears themselves were pictured on the page. He shook his head in pity, understanding now what had made the faces that way.

"There are your hauntings, Madam Myrtis," said Darios.

"Destroy them!" she exclaimed.

"I cannot—" said Lalo. "They are not my fears. But perhaps I can change them." A sweep with the eraser and a few deft strokes transformed a demon to a godling, emaciated old age to serenity. Another change took the lines of discontent from a pretty mouth, put hope back into sullen eyes. The sketches had been simple. Altering them into something the girls would be flattered to hang in their bedchambers did not take long.

"Let us see if this improves the atmosphere—" He handed the pictures to Myrtis.

"But that's not what you saw!" objected Darios.

"No, but when Madam Myrtis gives these sketches to her girls, perhaps this is what they will see—and believe—and believing, make it so," answered Lalo, remembering what Molin Torchholder had asked him to do. "I only wish I knew what it was that suddenly gave their fears such power!"

"My lady Kurrekai is one of the great ones that attend the Beysa herself"—the palace maid laughed at her soldier—"with a serpent for a neckpiece an' all. She has a different head-dress for every day of the week, an' she's generous. What do I need with presents from you?"

"Even this one?" growled Ottar. He pulled something from his pouch and offered it shyly. The girl exclaimed as the

wrapping fell away and the sun glittered on the silver ball.
"Pretty, huh? Does your lady have one o' these? You come
out with me and I'll be generous too!"

The girl gave him a calculating glance. Ottar wasn't bad-
looking, really. He pressed a wet kiss into the palm of her
hand and she felt a warm glow.

"Tonight, then?"

She nodded, laughing, and dropping the silver ball into the
pocket of her apron, skipped away. She had scarcely turned
the corner before her swain was forgotten. The silver glittered
so charmingly. She could hardly keep from pulling it out to
fondle, even when she was working.

That night she dreamed of riding in a gilded litter borne by
matched slaves, while a whole troop of barbarian warriors
who looked like Ottar marched behind. But the litter turned
into a darkened alley. She screamed as it was set down
roughly, but no one heard. And then hard hands were pulling
her out into the street, tearing at her clothing. Hard bodies
thrust against hers.

The next morning, she was clumsy as she served breakfast
for her Beysib lady, who was on duty with her mistress that
day. As she started to pass a basket of oranges, she tripped,
and the silver ball fell out of her apron and rolled across the
floor.

"How lovely!" said the Beysa, and held out her hand.

Lalo laid in the undercoat of color for the background with
long, smooth strokes of his brush. He knew that Molin
Torchholder was watching him, but he continued to paint
tranquilly. It was mindless labor, but the durability of the
final product might depend on the care he took now. At least
there was no way the priest could quarrel with him about this
part of the job. The air was beginning to heat as the day wore
onward, but it was still reasonably comfortable beneath the
awning's dappled shade. He painted quickly.

"You're not stupid, and I know you don't lack imagination," said Molin Torchholder suddenly. "I don't understand
how you remain so calm."

The brush splattered paint across white space, and Lalo
reached for a rag. He finished wiping the color away, then

turned to stare at his patron, his own self-mockery deepening as he realized that Torchholder had not even noticed his clumsiness.

"Other people wear me out with their pleas for place and position, or their accusations against those to whom I've given them. Other people wear themselves out suspecting each other of exotic forms of treason. But not you, Lalo . . . why?"

Lalo washed out his paintbrush, considering the question. "Perhaps because I want different things?"

"Ah—" The priest nodded. He did not look as if he had slept well. "And what are your ambitions, Master Limner?"

"To feed my family . . . to paint the truth . . . to stay alive . . ." Lalo said slowly. "That's seemed ambition enough, these past few years."

Molin Torchholder answered with a snort of laughter.

"I envy you. The palace was a madhouse this morning . . . a madhouse. Two people came to tell me that someone had bribed the workmen to leave weaknesses in my walls. One thought it was agents of the old Emperor. The other was sure that it was the new one, setting things up so that he can attack Sanctuary. Vashanka's rod! If Theron showed up right now I'd hand him the keys!"

Lalo suppressed a smile. In the Aphrodisia House they had demon lovers. In the palace it stood to reason that they would have nightmares about intrigue.

"Somebody else said that the prince had been poisoned, and just as I was escaping from him, one of the astrologers came running up with some tale that a piece of the Nisibisi Power Globe had been found! No truth to it, of course. I checked. But that one had me remembering when staying alive was almost ambition enough for me!"

Lalo dropped his brush.

I'm calm, he told himself. *I'm calm. Torchholder just said so.* But the priest's words reminded him uncomfortably of what Gilla had said.

He straightened slowly and found that the priest was staring at him.

"Now why, I wonder, should that news trouble you?"

"No one wants those days to come again." Lalo dipped his

brush in the paint and carefully stroked along a borderline. "Some of the girls at the Aphrodisia House were having bad dreams too. I drew pictures of them, changed the pictures a little, and the trouble seems to be going away. I'm sure there's no connection, though."

"Of course not." Molin Torchholder rose to his feet and stood looking over Lalo's shoulder. "But you didn't do badly, Master Limner. You learned a lot in those days. You want to paint the truth, you say. But we both know that you already can. I keep wondering when you're going to do something with that power."

And with that parting shot he moved onward, leaving Lalo staring unseeing at the wall.

The dead man gets to his feet grinning, his skin still the color of a fish's belly from the beynit venom in his veins.

"You betrayed me!" The Beysa takes a step backward, aware of the muscular grip of her serpent around her upper arm as its head darts forward defensively. "I killed you!"

"Yes . . . yes." The creature grins. "And how many more? You killed your own people, Beysa! Their blood cries out for revenge!"

"But it was my duty!" Dimly she remembers that this has happened to her before. She must deny it, but it has never been so real! "And for you above all to betray me . . . I let you love me, Tovek—you were a Burek man!"

"The killing went on too long . . ." He comes towards her with outstretched hands and the beynit hisses angrily.

"I stopped it," she cries. "House Burek fled the Empire. Why are you haunting me? We live now in another land!"

"Beysa, you will bring destruction to all who love you. You cannot escape the past!"

Tovek's hands close on her shoulders, cold, slippery with blood, but she cannot get away. The beynit strikes at him and he laughs. And now his face is changing; alien features writhe beneath the pallid skin. She sees fair hair and light, astonished eyes that harden as they focus on her. Then the serpent strikes again . . .

"Ki-thus! Kadakithis! No!" Her shriek tears the heart from her breast.

Hissing—the beynit's hissing roared in her ears. Her fingers tightened on muscular coils that constricted beneath smooth skin.

"Shupansea! My lady, be still now—it was a dream . . ."

"The prince—" she whispered.

"He is here."

The Beysa's eyes flew open. His hair was still tousled with sleep, his eyes alarmed, just as in her dream. For a moment she thought she saw that other figure too, shadowy, already fading away. As the prince started towards her, Lady Kurrekai stepped between them. The Beysib woman's arm already bore the twin puncture marks where the beynit had struck her. Her own snake coiled around her neck protectively, tongue flickering as it tested the air; the bite of the Beysa's would do her no harm beyond a little dizziness, but Kadakithis had no such immunity!

"Kurrekai, keep him away from me!" He looked hurt. She choked back a sob.

"Wait a few moments longer, my lord," Lady Kurrekai said quietly. "When she is fully awake the serpent will calm itself. Then you may come to her."

Shupansea lay back, breathing deeply. It had been a dream. Of course it had been a dream. Tovek's bones were dust in the earth of the Glorious Home, and she was safe in Sanctuary.

"And this was not the first nightmare?" the prince was saying now.

"There was only one yesterday," said Kurrekai, "but this is the third tonight, and it is not yet dawn. She will not let me try to drug her, but she must sleep. Perhaps she will listen to you."

The Beysa pushed herself upright against her cushions with a sigh.

"Shu-sea, love, what were you dreaming of?" The prince settled himself carefully on the foot of her bed and took her outstretched hand.

"A man who betrayed me before I ever laid eyes on you!"

"The traitor Tovek . . ." said Kurrekai bitterly.

"Holy Mother Bey," whispered the Beysa, "did you see him too?" Aroused by her emotion, the beynit lifted its head, then settled between her full breasts again.

"And before that it was two of those Stepsons," said the lady-in-waiting implacably, "marching bold as brass down the hall! The guard saw them too, but he thought it was his own nightmare!"

"Lock the snake up and sleep with me!" cried the prince. Both women stared at him. "I know you don't like to leave it, but you have to rest!"

"Kadakithis, I could kill you . . ." Shupansea said slowly. "Even without the beynit. My blood is poison, Ki-thus! Oh! If you were Beysib you would understand!" They gazed at each other across a chasm of race and culture that mocked their clasped hands.

"I understand that I love you," he said finally. "And I am still prince in Sanctuary. If you cannot rest, then no man of learning in this town is going to sleep either until you are free!"

"Another week and I should be able to get rooms of my own," said Cappen Varra, handing his empty plate to Gilla for a second helping of pie. "Playing during the intermissions at Feltheryn's theater may not be exactly what I would have chosen, but the work is regular!"

"You're welcome to stay on here," said Gilla.

"Well, I need more privacy to practice, you know—I don't like to think I'm disturbing you!" Cappen's glance caught Lalo's in warning, then flicked away again.

"But who could mind listening to your music?" Gilla exclaimed.

Lalo suppressed a smile. He suspected that it was not the practice of music that the minstrel had in mind. Feltheryn had hired a new actress for their latest production, and Cappen was already courting her.

Replete, they were all pushing their plates aside when there was a knock on the door.

"Open up! Lord Torchholder's orders—open up in there!"

Latilla, too young to remember the times when a knock on the door was a signal to hide, was already scampering to obey. Lalo opened his mouth to call her back, then shut it again. If they were Torchholder's men he had nothing to fear. Did he? He fought back memories of the night when Coricidius the Vizier had sent the Hell-Hounds to pluck Lalo from his bed. Surely the priest who had been the closest thing he ever had to a patron could mean no harm to him.

"What does Lord Torchholder want with me at this hour?" he asked as the guardsmen pushed into the room.

"Didn't say. You're to come with us, bring your drawing things."

"He can't be wanting Lalo to draw a picture for him at this hour!" exclaimed Gilla. The man shrugged.

"Got my orders. That's all I know."

It had to be more than artwork, thought Lalo, gathering up his things. Suddenly he remembered his conversation with the priest the previous morning. Darios was watching him, a little pale, biting his lip as if he wanted to speak but was not sure—

"I want to bring my apprentice with me too—" Lalo turned, satchel in hand, and Darios stood up eagerly.

"Got no orders—" the guard began.

"Oh, what does it matter!" exclaimed one of the other men. "He said to get the limner quickly. Can't hurt to take two!"

They moved quickly through the streets of the city. Even in the Maze folk got out of the way of a well-armed troop who seemed to know their business. Lalo had never gone across town so fast. But it was only as the guards conducted him up the broad staircase towards the royal suites instead of downward to the Hall of Justice lockup that he realized how great his fear had been.

The air in the upper corridor was heavy with the scent of incense and expensive perfume. Embroidered hangings glowed on the walls and Lalo blinked, seeing with doubled vision the flicker of lamplight on figured tapestries and the glimmering afterimages of richly robed courtiers and armored men.

He took a deep breath and closed his eyes, opened them abruptly as he heard a low laugh and saw before him the agile form, the sardonic grin, and the gleaming knife of the assassin Zanderei.

"Watch out!" He stopped short and the guard behind him bumped into him, swearing. "He's got a knife!"

"Who? Where?" Swords flared from their sheaths and Lalo was thrust hard against the wall. "You fools, jumping at shadows! There's nobody here!"

Lalo blinked. There was no one now, but he had seen *something*, or why should he suddenly think of a man who had been dead for years?

"They're all jumping at shadows here, if you ask me," muttered one of the men as they started forward again.

Darios pressed close to him, twitching like a nervous horse. "I thought I saw my old master," he whispered. "But maybe it's the incense—Lalo, somebody has been doing exorcisms here!"

Why? wondered Lalo, unless . . . Before he could follow that thought to its conclusion the gilded doors at the end of the hall were pushed open and they were thrust into the presence of the prince and the Beysa and their attendants. Lord Torchholder was brooding like a thundercloud by the window. As they entered he turned. A gesture sent the soldiers away.

"You told me that you cured the bad dreams of the girls at the Aphrodisia House with your drawings," the priest said abruptly. "I want you to do it again!"

"For you?" He stared around him. Molin Torchholder simply looked angry, but the Beysa appeared haggard, and even the prince was pale.

"For everybody—" said Prince Kadakithis. "It started with the Beysa's nightmares, but everybody's seeing things now. Damn place is haunted! Can't go on like this, you know."

Lalo nodded. Zanderei was his own personal nightmare, but the potential number of specters who might haunt a prince boggled the imagination, especially in Sanctuary. But it was one thing to see, and to alter, the simple secrets of girls in a house of joy. The hidden fears of princes might recall deeds that for the safety of the city must not be changed! And even if that could be accomplished, how could they allow the man who had seen all their sins to live?

And it might not work anyway. He had not painted living nightmares, but memories.

"Are the dreams all that is wrong?" he asked carefully, playing for time.

"No!" exclaimed the Beysa. She toyed nervously with the silver ball on the table. "There's a feeling of pervading dread! Even waking, I see shadows . . ."

Lalo shivered. Even as she spoke he could feel it, and knew that this was something worse than his own fear. He felt Darios trembling beside him. He had to do something to distract them—he remembered what Cappen Varra had said about the power of people's minds.

"Darios—" As he spoke, the boy's gaze came back to him gratefully. "It's time to use some of that training you're always talking about. I want you to think of something simple— think of a color, I don't care which one. Think of those hangings changing, that's right—" He paused as Darios's face creased in concentration. "Even the lamplight is that color, everything is—"

Then his breath caught, because everything was turning blue. The Beysa's nictitating membrane came down, her piscine heritage unmistakable in the undersea light.

"You can look now . . ." he said softly, enjoying the way Darios's eyes widened as he saw the change. He trembled on the brink of understanding. If he was right . . . Tensing with excitement, Lalo summoned up the memory of crimson, and visualized the blue shifting into purple that continued to warm until swirls of ruby lapped across the carpet towards Darios.

The young man's eyes danced. A deeper blue flared suddenly between them. Lalo refined his focus and the glow disappeared in a burst of flame.

"*Master* Limner—" Molin Torchholder's voice broke their concentration. Blue light and red pulsed for a moment, and then they were gazing at the peach and gold hangings of the Beysa's suite once more. "Just what was that demonstration intended to prove?"

"That the palace is not haunted . . ." Lalo answered him. "Don't you see—it is not only your fears and nightmares; *any* thought, projected strongly enough, will be amplified—"

"That's it! A psychic amplifier—" exclaimed Darios. "I was so sure that everything of that kind had been destroyed— but I ought to have thought of it before! They were made by the Guild in imitation of the Nisibisi globes, but of course they possessed nothing like the same degree of power.''

"But we had a Hazard," began Prince Kadakithis. "Why didn't he find this thing, if it exists?''

"It could look like anything—a toy, a jewel," answered Darios. "A mage shielded against hauntings might not be able to tell.''

"Can you tell?" asked Lalo, blessing the thought that had prompted him to bring his apprentice along.

Darios frowned, and half closed his eyes. They all fell silent as a sphere of pale light appeared before him. "Lalo, watch and tell me if it gets brighter when I move around." Slowly Darios began to circumambulate the room.

"What's that?"

The sphere was blazing. Lalo pointed to the point of light that reflected it from the silver ball in the Beysa's hand.

"I . . . got it from my maid," said the Beysa, dropping it. Lalo picked it up as it pooled silver light across the floor, and felt his fingers tingle. It was so innocent a thing to have caused such suffering . . . He could breathe life into the things he drew, but the silver ball could take anyone's thought and make it a reality. And all those symbols Darios was trying to teach him—with this they could be as real here as in the Otherworld. It occurred to Lalo that such a thing might be more convenient than a pad and pencil, and he thrust the thought away.

"I suppose we will have to call the Hazard back to destroy it," Molin Torchholder said into the silence.

"They'll want it, but not to destroy," said Darios. "And I think it must be done away with—the violence it has seen has soured it. I think that only a mage of great strength and purity of spirit could use it for good now!''

"I don't like the thought of those fellows getting their hands on anything like this again," said the prince. "Just when we've got them under control . . ." All eyes moved back to the quicksilver glitter of the thing the limner held in his hands.

"Perhaps there's another way," Lalo said then.

"It was all your fault, you know," said Molin Torchholder. Lalo lifted the brush with which he was filling in the ground color for Prince Kadakithis's robe from the plaster and turned to stare at him.

"We've traced that wretched mage-toy back from the Beysa's maid to a soldier in the garrison, who won it from another lad, who got it from his girl at the Aphrodisia House. And she got the thing as a gift from one Aglon, who picked it up when he was helping *your* son dig *your* apprentice out of the ruins of the Mageguild not so long ago." His expression was hard to read in the dappled shade.

"Then it's just as well I showed you how to get rid of it, isn't it?" Lalo answered calmly.

"How did you know that if we all closed our eyes and visualized the amplifier vanishing it would disappear?" asked the priest curiously.

"It had no power of itself. Amplifying images and emotions was all it could do—it seemed worth a try."

With an effort Lalo kept his features impassive. Better not reveal how terrified he had been that his plan would not work, or backfire. But that was over. Now his thoughts were quiet, like the city as it forgot its nightmares and returned to life's waking dream.

"You've changed. You would never have dared to suggest such a thing nine years ago."

"Changed?" Lalo began to laugh. "Who hasn't changed? Including you. And what's the use of it all if we don't learn anything?"

"What have you learned, limner?" Molin Torchholder watched him curiously.

"That I am not a silver ball, to be used or misused at will," Lalo replied. "I'll paint the truth you show me, Torchholder, but don't try to make my magic tell lies."

For a moment the priest looked at him, then he shook his head with a short laugh and turned to go.

Lalo watched as Molin Torchholder made his way around the curve of the wall to return to the palace again. Then his gaze came back to the rough outlines of the mural before him. That lower left-hand corner needed something—some detail to balance the rolling storm clouds on the right. His lips twitched suddenly, and he mixed a little white and black together to produce a silvery grey.

Kneeling, he drew in the outline of a ball between two stones. It must be done now, while he remembered the weight and size, the slick feel of it in his hand. A touch with some other colors reproduced the rainbow glimmer it had mirrored in the Beysa's room. As Darios had said, it was a shame to waste it, but where could they have safely kept such a thing?

It would be safe here. Perhaps no one would notice it. Even if they did, no one could use it—no one but him. *I hope I never need to breathe it into life again—but if I have to, I will,* thought Lalo as he added the last sparkle of silver and sat back on his heels. *Molin Torchholder asked me what I'd learned.*

I'm beginning to discover the answer now . . .

WINDS OF FORTUNE

C. J. Cherryh

Clouds of steam. The horse stood still while Strat washed it down with rags and slopped water onto the stableyard dirt—a completely ordinary horse except the thumb-sized patch on its rump where there was simply—nothing. It angered Crit that Strat spent excessive time on the creature, but, unlike Critias, acting commandant of the Stepsons, Companion to the God— his partner Straton had no fear of the undead.

The horse had died under him—once. It had come back from Hell for him. It had rescued him from enemies. Straton returned that loyalty.

That small patch was the necessary Flaw—in a creature Hell had given up. But it in no wise flawed courage, or faith.

Better than men, Strat thought. Better than the love of women, who had proven, overall, faithless.

Critias had saved his life multiple times, too; and Strat had returned that favor, such as he could—but Crit was Crit—the ultimate pragmatist. There was only one creature in all the world that a man could believe in to such an extent, and trust absolutely; it stood with eyes shut—enjoying the warmth of life—

After the cold of Hell.

It came to Strat that he had known too much of that cold himself—that if he had any hope for himself he had to shake free of such influences.

134

There had been, above all, a woman—a sorceress who haunted his dreams.

Be rid of her! Crit said.

But one's dreams did not forget . . .

A quiet tread scuffed the dirt of the yard, stopped, at Strat's back. He looked behind him, saw his partner standing there fists on hips, saw Crit frowning at him.

"You're on duty," Crit said. "Dammit, Ace—"

Strat thought back to the morning, recollected a promise—to spell Gayle at a problem uptown, night duty, when they were so damned short-handed. He dropped the sponge into the bucket and faced Crit with a shake of his head. "Sorry," he said. "I'll get up there right now."

Crit walked closer and blocked his path to anywhere. "Strat—"

"I forgot, all right?"

Crit hit him on the shoulder, held that same shoulder, compelled an attention he did not want to give. "Forgot?"

"I said I forgot. I'm sorry." He moved to break away, but Crit tightened his grip, jerked him around again for a look straight in the face.

He dropped his eyes. He had no idea why, only that Crit's stare was unbearable—no matter that Crit had pulled him out of situations a sane man would not contemplate, no matter that he owed this man who was closer than a brother. That look on Crit's face wanted more from him than he had left in him to give, more of his soul than he was going to have again in his life, and though he knew it—Crit had yet to accept that fact.

"That's the bad shoulder," Strat said, deliberately pitiful; and tried with a shake of his head simply to go his way, and not to fight with Crit.

But Crit slammed him around against the corner of the stable. "Where in hell is your head?"

Another man he would have taken into bare-handed combat. But he owed Crit too much, and there was too much he'd fouled up on, like this, too much Crit cared about he didn't care about at all.

"Are you seeing her?" Crit shouted into his face.

"You know I'm not," Strat said. "I'm in barracks every night!"

Crit grabbed him by the throat. If Crit strangled him that was all right. He hardly cared. That was the trouble. That was what maddened Crit.

Crit shook him, Crit slammed him back against the post. Strat only stared, short of wind, and said, "Better if you hadn't pulled me out of that cellar . . . Better you'd left me there."

In some part he hoped Crit would give up finally, let him alone, simply let him coast into oblivion.

Or hit him and give him cause—some cause, any cause to fight for—

But Crit, who had killed more men than anyone could remember, some of them piece by piece and slowly, looked at him as if he was feeling that kind of pain himself—as if someone hurt him and made him crazy, and he loved that someone too much to do what he would do to anyone else in the wide world who crossed him as far as Strat had.

"What's the matter with you?" Crit asked quietly. "What in hell's—the matter with you?"

One dreamed, that was all.

"I'll kill her," Crit said.

Strat grabbed Crit by the sleeve, hard. Maybe it was a measure of how far he had come that it was Crit's danger he thought of most acutely. It was all right for him, he didn't matter, he had stopped mattering; but Crit, he thought, Crit had no logical part in this, and Crit, who had come alive through coups and assassinations and battles, had no chance at all against Her. "Crit," Strat said. "Crit, I'm going to the damn palace. I'll be there, I'll be there, all right?"

Crit didn't say anything. That scared him, and got his attention, when damned little else could.

"I'll get up there," Strat said. "I'll do the damn duty. —Crit, I'm *through,* you hear me? I'm through with her, I'm not going back, I promise you."

Crit still said not a thing.

That scared Strat—more than any threats Crit could have made.

Night, more than night, in days of slow business and unseasonable weather, an exhausted, weary town—those hours when even the inns, even in Sanctuary, began to give up their last customers and throw out the drunks—and the bar help went home, some two by two, some not . . .

A woman screamed in an alleyway near the Vulgar Unicorn, a small yelp of a scream, cut off of a sudden, followed by a grunt of pain—the Unicorn's barmaid knew where to put an elbow and a heel. But the man was big and he was gone on krrf. A thump! followed, then a slither—of a light body hitting a brick wall and slumping to the trash at the bottom of it.

The rapist liked that fine. He liked it so well he grabbed the woman up by the hair and kicked her, which it took, besides the krrf these days, to get him excited—

But in the interval of a kick and the body hitting the pavement, the rapist heard another step on the dusty cobbles, a soft, stealthy step behind him.

He let his victim lie, facing—it was incredible to him—a cloaked, aristocratic woman, here, in these streets, in this alleyway.

He heard his earlier victim crawl aside, scrabble in the trash trying to escape, but this hooded, this incredibly elegant slut—amazed him—

Amazed him so much he was not expecting the sudden crack of a brick across the back of his skull . . .

Ischade faced the bloody, panting barmaid across the body—in a desire both dark and frustrated by the assistance. "Thank you," Ischade said with irony, wrapping her cloak about her for the sensuality of it; and shuddered at what it stirred. "Do you live in this alley? No? I'd seek lodgings on the Unicorn's street—if I were in your place. Too far to walk—at this hour."

"Who *are* you?" the barmaid asked, it not being incredible to her, perhaps, that a woman in silk and velvet knew her nightly route. Perhaps it frightened her. Perhaps it told her she might have escaped the rat to run straight-on into the cobra's sliding coils—

But: "Go home," Ischade said. "Don't linger here. What's one more body—in Sanctuary?"

The barmaid caught a breath, looked at Ischade a moment longer, as if the spell touched even her—

It might. The curse was never specific. Only Ischade's personal taste was—and Ischade felt nothing but frustration and a rising anger at the girl's very existence, and at her courage—in a world where help was scarce, and no one cared. Perhaps she saw Ischade for what she was. But few did. Few—hearing of her—understood. People looked for vampires.

"Go," Ischade whispered, and the barmaid turned and ran, limping, for the end of the alley.

Ischade followed her—hoping—in case of some other trouble that might be drawn like predators to a crippled fish. She saw the young woman haul herself up a rickety steps in the alley next, saw the door shut; and eventually saw dim light from the shutter seams, the woman having, after some effort, Ischade supposed, gotten a lamp lit.

One remembered such necessities. Dimly. Long ago.

She had her own necessities—deadly, urgent necessities, since Strat had left—since she had broken the ties that held him. She had lives to hunt, to sustain her own; and she had her preferences in victims.

She walked on her way, walked the roughest areas of Sanctuary, that region south and harborward of the Unicorn. It was a thief who accosted her finally.

"I've nothing for you," she told him, having some conscience, at least, or having acquired one from her associations. He was very young, he had offered her no violence—and perhaps there was something in her manner that warned him, made him the least bit anxious: he looked behind him and to either side, as if suspecting some sort of ambush in which a woman obviously out of place in these alleys—might be the bait.

He seemed to decide otherwise then. He whipped out a knife, advanced a step or two as if she might leap at him—or someone might pounce from the shadows. He demanded money.

It was the knife that decided the question. She put back her hood, she caught his eyes she said, in a low voice, "Are you sure you want what I do have?"

The robber hesitated—the knife gleaming uncertainly in the dark. "A whore," he said, "a damned whore—"

"I know a place," she said, because now she had a look at him he was handsome, if he were washed, and he had a wit that might save his life—a few days, at least; and longer, if he would listen.

He came with her to the house on the riverside, that house which passers-by somehow failed to see, or, seeing, failed to notice—a house lost in hedges, behind a low iron gate, behind overgrown grounds and half-dead trees—

She wanted light—and light blazed from candles and from lamps, bright, so bright her young thief flung up his knife-hand to shield his eyes—he had never put the weapon away—and swore.

Taz swore again once his eyes had cleared and he had gotten a look at his surroundings, an untidy tumble of silks and satins, garish fabrics, costly furnishings—in a house which had ways of looking much smaller outside than in.

A nook and a silk-strewn bed—she never made it, only tidied it occasionally. She dropped the cloak like a spill of ink on the bright rugs, the busy fabrics. She was all in black, a necklace like drops of blood—a dusky skin, straight hair black as night, eyes—

Eyes that every man in his youth knew were waiting for him, somewhere, somewhen, if he was man enough. . . .

He forgot about his thieving. He forgot about everything except this woman, never even took offense that she *insisted* he go into the back room and bathe. One could hardly take it amiss, since she offered him a gentleman's clothes, the kind of perfumed soap the gentry used, and trailed a finger along his neck and said, softly, smelling of foreign spices and musk—

"Do everything I tell you and you'll be here more than tonight, you'll be here many, many days and nights—do you like that idea? You won't have to steal again. You'll have everything you could want—does that appeal to you?"

He could not believe this was happening. He only stared at her, with the soap in his hands, and said, "Are you a witch?"

"Do you think so? —What's your name?"

It was dangerous to answer that with witches. He had heard so. He looked into her eyes and found himself saying truthfully: "Taz. Taz Chandi."

Her finger traced his chin. "How old are you, Taz?"

He said, lying, knowing she was at least older, but he had no idea how much older, "Twenty-two."

"Nineteen," she said, and he knew he had been dangerously foolish to lie: he was afraid then. But she kissed his lips gently and sweetly, and left him to his bath and his anticipations . . . which were for the first time since he was twelve—outlandish and hopeful and full of delicious dreams . . .

Til he heard the front gate squeak and, with thoughts of returning husbands or ogres or Shalpa only knew what sort of interruption in this lovenest, hastily dressed in what the lady had provided.

Crit trod the garden path most warily, with an eye to the front door. He was sure the vampire knew he was there. He had his hand on his sword for all the good it would do, tramping through the weeds, under dead trees, up the rickety steps.

The door opened as he had thought it would, since he had been unblasted by magics getting this far; it opened the instant he trod on the last step, and she came out—wrapped in black and glaring at him with the warmth of an adder.

"What do *you* want?" she asked. "Am I not through with Stepsons?"

He kept his hand on his hilt, like a religious talisman. He said, "Evidently you aren't through with my partner. I'm here to ask you to leave him alone."

He was not a man who found asking easy, and all but impossible when it sounded like empty-handed begging—because he had no negotiating points and there was not a damned thing he could do to the bitch, not a damned thing he could do to save his life if she took a notion to do to him what she had done to Strat, and so many, many others.

In point of fact he knew he was a fool to come here, but he had gone in under fire for Strat before, and more to the point, Strat had gone in for him; at times he had wanted to beat Strat senseless for his foolishness—once he had even done it; and once he had thought he had a chance of shaking Strat back to sense. But Sanctuary had dealt hard with them both, as it dealt with everyone who came here. It was a sink that drank down lives. And Strat's seemed to be the price it wanted.

So he came here, unarmed as witches and wizards reckoned such things, and looked up at the witch, and said the only thing he could say: "Let him go."

Ischade held her door in her hands, a shadow against the lamplight slanting past her and reflecting off the boards. She said, "I *have*, Crit."

"The hell!" He came up that last step onto the porch, where he towered over her. "Stop playing games!"

"I assure you." She left the door standing half-open and came closer, holding her cloak about her, black velvet about bare shoulders, a whisper of silk, a waft of musk. He was sure she was naked under it—some other tryst, some other damned soul. "Leave! Now!"

"Name your price. A favor. A disappearance. I'm not particular. You want some pretty boy, dammit, I'll *buy* you one, just leave my partner alone."

The shapely chin set, eyes hooded like a snake's. "What about *you*, Crit?"

He glanced away quickly, but not quickly enough.

"Look at me," she said, and he had to, knowing it was a slide over the brink, knowing there was no way out. Her hell-burned eyes had no bottom, except Hell itself, and there was no looking away. But he could still *want* to be off the porch, down the walk, and out the gate, that was the bad part—he could still want escape.

"Bargain?" he said. When he had begun to deal with her, maybe he had known that. Maybe that was why he had ditched Strat and come here, stupid as it was, because he was out of answers, and he finally cared about something again, and hated his helplessness.

"Get out of here," she said, and shoved him without laying a hand on him. *"Get out of here, dammit!"*

He caught his balance at the bottom of the steps, he caught his breath there, staring up at cold rejection of himself, his offers, his stupid hope of weaseling himself and Strat both out of this situation—a hope of escape for both of them . . . in a

day that Ranke was falling and they were posted here behind
the lines, no use, no future, no damn use to anyone including
themselves. Strat could not leave this city. Take him out by
force and he would escape and ride back to it, that was how
bad it was—and he had known that, had not objected over-
much when Tempus had left them here in command of the
rear guard.

He had hoped to solve this—cure Strat and get him away
from this woman.

"Out!" she said, and that voice went through brain and
bone.

He heard the door slam before he got to the gate.

He had thought about killing her—but that thought had
completely fled him when he stood in front of her. His hand
had been on his sword all the time, for all the foolish good it
had been: he had not even been able to think of it in that
context when he had been close enough.

He flung open the low iron gate, heard it clang shut behind
him.

"Ma'am," the boy said tentatively, with his knife in hand—
With a thief's knife, a gentleman's clothes; and a staunch
resolve on a fresh-scrubbed face. "M'lady?"

Ischade gazed at this chivalry in the light and the heat of
the candles, heat so intense it made sweat run, light that
blinded and blazed white—and a fool of a thief stood there
with this mooncalf look and a knife for their mutual defense—

"He could spit you like a pig," she spat at him. "That
man's the garrison commander, that's a Stepson, thief!"

One was my lover. One was.

Gods, she thought, dropping her eyes against her hand,
shaking her head, *I sent him away. I broke the spell, dammit,
I set him free, there's no more spell, dammit to the hells!*

But it was not Crit she was thinking of.

"M'lady?"

It was an anxious voice. The lights had dimmed. She
looked at her young thief and saw still the scrubbed, frightened face—the knife clutched in a white-knuckled fist.

"What are you doing with that?" she demanded.

He looked less and less certain—even what he was doing

here. He tucked that hand behind him, said diffidently, "In case he was comin' in here, m'lady."

"What, to defend me?"

He shrugged, twitched the knife-arm shoulder, looked abashedly at the floor and up again.

Gods.

She held the cloak about her, she beckoned him closer, she looked at a face that looked so very much different than her unkept thief.

A pretty boy, Crit had said. When she wanted Strat, who was not a boy, who was most certainly not a boy—

She touched his face, worked a small sorcery, brushed the hair from his brow. He tried to put his arms around her, jerked her close—

She pushed him away, both attracted and repelled—for all the wrong reasons. She said coldly, "There's clothes, there's money, take what you want and get out of here. I'll call you on another night. For your own sake—listen to me now."

His jaw set. He prepared some foolish argument, some protestation of his manhood, his impatience.

She waved an arm and the door banged open, disturbing all the candles and the lamps. She let go her spell . . .

He stayed for nothing. He ran. She heard the gate, let him past her wards, and banged that shut and the door, clang! boom! after him.

She was shaking after that. She dropped her head against her hand and tried to forget the lust that was her curse, that at times and by the pull of the moon was stronger than reason, stronger than love—

The desire that killed—killed everyone but Strat. Strat had found a way to survive, until things changed, until Strat turned moody and sullen and the anger grew in him—the anger to invoke the curse and kill him.

So she had driven him away, given him back to Crit, given him his freedom from her ensorcelments—

Crit, tonight, came here to offer stupid bargains, with no knowledge whether she would even keep her word—Crit was not lying, he could not be lying, under those terms, there *was* still some attraction; and that fool boy, the thief—with a knife, ready to use it if Crit had burst through the door—

For what, she asked herself, for what, except male stupidity?

For what reason in hell, except a man would not hear No. . . .

For what reason, gods, except Strat was a fool and Strat did not understand her.

Like the boy who thought he was going to be a hero. Like Strat—who did not know how to lose and did not know how to retreat from what he thought was his right and her obligation to him.

Who—gods!—had been with her too long, had been too close to her not to know what she was and who should have, for once in his stubborn, prideful life, run the way the boy had.

But Strat did not understand that.

She looked up at the ceiling, at the blaze of lights that glittered in her eyes.

And stopped what she was feeling, shut it off cold, because love was the killing-urge, it was all mixed up with tenderness, it wound all through it, because when a man intimate with her started making up his own mind what he wanted, and once frustration became force, that someone died; and it was pleasure and it was anger at a fool and it was pain and revenge all wrapped together.

"Damn!" she cried, to any god who might be listening, and to the thrice-damned and very dead mage who had set the curse on her. Lights blazed about her, candles unconsumed.

Like her endless, deathless life—no less now than it had been a hundred years ago . . .

And so many, many dead to her account . . .

Crit came quietly into the stableyard of the safe-house, threw the reins over his horse's head, and led the horse through the gate, quietly still, figuring Gayle must be upstairs— not that the commander needed an excuse for late-night exits and entrances—whether from some night business at headquarters or a late night on the Street of Red Lanterns; they had all been working odd shifts, they were still cleaning up paperwork and dealing with files, and whatever sleep Gayle or Kama was getting was hard-won.

He walked the horse quietly to the stable door, and turned

suddenly, with a reach at his sword, because of a step alongside the stable in the dark, a large shadow.

Shepherd.

The big man said, "Strat hasn't gone uptown, he's gone to see Randal."

"For what?" Crit demanded in his frustration. He had no difficulty believing Strat had gone off somewhere—Randal was hardly where he would have guessed, but he had no reason to doubt this uninvited visitor. Shepherd—came and went like a ghost, him and his outmoded leather armor and that big clay-colored horse of his, with the panther-skin shabraque; reins of woven grass, the scent of the marsh about him—a spook for sure if Crit had ever seen one—came in when the Riddler had left with most of the forces, and talked about Debt and the Honor of the Corps, and things that the last guard was too out of sorts to hear these depressing, final days. . . .

Shepherd shrugged, casting a large shadow in the stableyard lamplight as he stood aside. "Your partner's in trouble. But you understand that. Make no bargains with the witch."

"What do you want?" It bothered Crit; it had been bothering Crit ever since this man had showed up, the way this man moved in claiming to be a merc, assumed so much, came and went as if the rules meant nothing to him; and why in hell Crit let him get away with it Crit himself had no idea—

Except there was a great deal in this man that reminded him of the Riddler.

"Go to Randal," Shepherd said, and when Crit started back to the stable, caught his arm. "Be surprised at nothing. Your time here is coming to an end."

"Hell!" Crit stalked off a few paces toward the stables and stopped abruptly to ask, "Whose time? Who told you?—What's Strat up to, dammit?"

But Shepherd was gone.

Ischade had left the river-house, walked the pre-dawn streets of Sanctuary with no destination in mind—thinking about Crit, thinking about what existed between those two, and what a fool Strat was—

She would have made him commander over Sanctuary—

she might have, if Tempus had not stepped in to redeem his
man, and put Crit in command in Strat's place.

She would have made him more than that, if that had not
happened; she would have made him more than a lord of the
Rankan Empire—if Tempus had not stepped in, if there had
not been the war, and if there had been some hope of Strat
continuing to be for her what he had been—

But all those things had turned dangerous, and impossible;
and she found herself tonight, having rejected Crit's desperate
move, having thrown her young thief out of the house, walking the warehouse district near the river and toward that street
uptown that led to the hill—

And thinking of things that might have been—in these
strange days of peace in the ravaged streets of Sanctuary; in
these strange days of war in the very heart of Empire.

She found herself on the high street, in the midst of which
a house stood with boarded windows and bars on the doors—

And downhill—and over a street or two, in an area not so
rich and not so poor—there was a house she also knew . . .

"What is it?" Moria asked, when Stilcho waked sweating
in their bed, in this fine house they afforded these days.
"What is it?"—holding to him; but he would have none of
it—some times he would not, some nights he could not.

This time he sat, naked and shivering on the side of their
bed—and stared into the dark. "Light the lamp," he asked
Moria. *"Light the lamp!"*

And Moria, born Ilsigi, born a thief and a daughter of
thieves in this city, scrambled for straw and lamp and the
coals in the hearth, to produce that little flame that shed light
on the modest rooms and drove away the visions of Hell—

Because her husband (so she called him) had died once in
the hands of the beggars of Downwind—and all of him the
witch had gotten back but his eye, wherefore the scars on his
body and the scars on his face.

That eye was still in Hell, where he had been until She had
called him back; and when there was no light to distract the
living eye it sometimes, even yet, looked into Hell—

Where he saw the dead in their torments, and saw demons,
and saw the demon that still lurked in Sanctuary, demon of all

the wicked desires that had ever existed in human hearts . . .

"Stilcho," Moria said, putting her arms about him, pulling the sheet up around him, against the night chill. She kissed him and he was still cold—

Because She had used him for her emissary to Hell—so many times. He had been Her lover, and died as her lovers must die; and always she had had that mystical string on him that drew him back to life . . .

"She's calling me," Stilcho whispered, reaching for Moria's arm, holding to Moria's warmth, when the chill of the grave got to him.

Moria held to him. And all the time that they had lived, they, Ischade's fugitive lover and her fugitive servant, on Ischade's stolen gold—had been poised on a knife's edge; and now—now he waked in sweats and *heard* Her calling him very clearly:

I need you, She was saying. *Come to me.* . . .

"I hear her too," Moria whispered. "Oh, *gods*, no—don't go!"

Haught, the ex-slave, the dancer, the mage—stirred in his sleep too, in a barred boarded house—stirred at the side of the creature with whom he shared his exile—got up from bed and walked to those windows, feeling—something finally, be it only the threat of Hell and death.

He looked out from those windows and saw, with a most curious frisson of fear, the black-cloaked shadow standing in the street—

Saw that hooded figure facing him and looking—he felt that stare go straight to his gut—with full cognizance that he was watching Her at that moment.

"Mistress," he whispered, longing for the safety She might offer—arrogant Haught, who had been Her apprentice, Her most disobedient apprentice. He found himself shivering—but it might be the cold—and with a certain weakness in his joints—it might be hunger: it was only sorcery had sustained him in this boarded-up mansion, past the stores buried in the cellar, which were long since depleted.

It seemed to him—he hugged himself, shivering more and more in the predawn chill—that he heard her voice speaking

to him very clearly, telling him if he would serve her again—he
might be free.

And magician and sorcerer that he had been, he was only a
prisoner now, of something much worse. It was not nails and
boards on the windows that kept him in—it was powerful
wards; and it was not Tasfalen he lodged with, but an undead
housing something that had been Roxanne the witch—a presence which made terrible demands of him and which bided
asleep, but not asleep, not ever quite asleep; it drank down
vials of dust he found for it, of its shattered Power-globe—
and it only grew more malevolent and more bitter and more
dangerous and demanding.

He longed for Ischade's house. With all his heart.

I'm here, he prayed, looking out that shutter, hoping that
She would hear that thought as She heard so much that passed
in Sanctuary, *I'm more than willing, mistress, if only you'll
forgive me, mistress, I'll not make those mistakes again. . .*

He caught his breath, the impression was so strong—of
anger, of summons—he trembled, he began, against his own
better knowledge to consider which of the doors and windows
he might pry open to admit Her—

To admit Death Herself—or willingly to go to Her. . . .

Zip poured blood over the stones of the little altar he had
made—blood he had let from his own veins, there being no
better to hand. He had served the Revolution, he had let
blood enough of Rankan overlords, he had done all manner of
things and killed more Rankene pigs than he could remember—
but it had not brought forth his god, the god that was going to
liberate the town. The Revolution had died—or won—or
things had simply changed beyond a need for the Revolution
or a hope for its success. Somehow things had gotten mud-
dled for him, because he had begun sleeping with a woman of
the enemy—Kama, Tempus' daughter, of all people, on the
outs with her father, but still one of the foreign Enemy—

Perhaps that was the reason his god failed to answer him.
He had found the old stones of this altar on the river-shore,
and set it up there during the witch wars and fed it during the
Revolution; and he had moved it to this sacred street—stone
by stone, until he began to build again in the Street of

Temples, well, if not *on* the street, at least in an alley next the great shrines of Empire and of the quisling Ilsigi gods—

And he had failed at first to find the shape of the ancient altar—he had piled up stones only to see them tumble, or to have pieces left over.

But a stranger had come along at the depth of his frustration and told him—*told* him without hesitation!—what stone to place on what stone, and lo! the altar had taken shape, firmer than before—

Zip knew that this stranger, with the clay-colored horse, the woven reins, this strange, old-time warrior—had to be special—was perhaps numinous, because the hair still rose on his neck when he thought about it. He made his offerings, he hoped for another such manifestation—

But the stranger appeared elsewhere in the streets of Sanctuary, these days. Zip had seen him by plain daylight, the stranger had turned up riding in the lower town, by noontime; or around the Garrison by moonlight; sometimes one saw him riding by the river-shore, in the night—as if he were searching for something lost in the marsh—

The stranger's name was Shepherd, so the rumor was in the streets, and once Zip had seen him stop at that house in the Shambles where the Stepsons lodged, and ride through that low gate that let him into a certain yard—

Where the Stepsons kept their horses in a ramshackle stable.

That association was what gnawed at Zip.

He poured blood from his own veins over these ancient stones, hoping for an Ilsigi god. Even an Ilsigi devil would do—something of Sanctuary's own people and not the occupation forces.

And something, finally, finally glowed within the crevices of the stones—glowed and winked out again.

"What do you want?" he cried, kneeling on the dirty cobbles, pounding his fists on his knees. "What do you want me to do?"

There was silence, and in that silence he heard the slow, hollow ring of a horse's hooves out on the Street of Temples—in this hour just before the dawn. For some reason that leisurely advance seemed ominous to him, the most dangerous, the most fatal thing in the world, and he knew that rider would

stop and that shadow would loom in the alley-opening, saying
to him, in a deep voice.

"Boy, what are you praying to?"

"I don't know," he confessed, on his knees before that
mounted shadow, and felt cold, cold as the dead in the White
Foal.

"Boy, what are you praying for?"

"For—" But revenge was not it, not exactly; and it was
dangerous, to say something too quickly or to say it wrong,
Zip sensed that, he sensed he was in the greatest danger he
had ever been in, that—

God, he slept with a Rankan woman, he had started out
wanting revenge on Rankene pride, started out sleeping with
her to screw some enemy woman and ended up sleeping with
her because it was someone to sleep with, and somehow he
got to looking for things from her, like—the way she wasn't
at all like the rest of her kind, she was good, she could be
rough as a dockside whore and gentler than his dreams, she
became—an addiction with him, an unpredictability, he never
knew what she was going to be, or why he felt the way he
did—but it excited him, *she* did, and he had to have her—

He was filth before his god. That was all he was, and the
questions shot straight to his heart.

But a second time: "What are you praying for?" the
stranger asked—it was Shepherd himself. There was a waft of
chill swamp air about him.

"I don't know," Zip confessed, and knotted his fingers in
his hair, head bowed. "I just don't know anymore . . ."

"Never go to a god," Shepherd said, "with preconceptions."

"Pre—what?" He squinted up at the mounted shadow, saw
the red gleam of the eyes of the panther-head on the horse's
chest.

"I'll make it easy for you," Shepherd said. "Wrongs set
right. Problems solved. Lives set in order. Is that what you
want? Go to the market: fortune-tellers charge a copper for
promises like that. Much cheaper than blood."

The stranger was making fun of him. Zip stood up with his
hand on his knife, with all the old, foolish anger rising up in
him. A man could take so much, but not laughter at his
expense.

"Wrongs set right," the stranger said in a deep voice. "But what if *you're* one of those wrongs—what if that anger of yours and that hate of yours *had* no Rankans to turn to? Can you imagine your life then?"

He could not. He did not know where he would be or what his life would be for, if not Ranke; and Ranke was falling on its own, without any need of him . . .

"You sleep with Ranke," Shepherd said. "You *need* Ranke, boy, you need it to live, because when it's gone, there'll be nothing left of you. You've had your answer. Quit praying."

Zip's hand fell. He stood there in that cold that came of hearing the truth and knowing everything Shepherd said was true.

He was still standing there when the rider shouldered past him, slow clatter of hooves down the alley and into the dark of the shrines on either hand.

The light was gone from his altar. The very air felt cold. And the stones of that altar suddenly tumbled apart, scattering across the cobbles of the alley.

Taz the thief stood on the corner of the river-road in the dawn, sullen and out of sorts and watching the house the way he had been watching when Ischade had come out of it and when she had come back and when other men had come to it—well-dressed men, mostly, and one woman and one limping beggar. Taz failed to understand, but curiosity gathered his courage toward the dawn, never having seen her return—he came up to the iron fence himself, and laid a hand on that gate in the hedge.

He yelped in pain, recoiled with a shivering cold up that arm.

But the gate, glowing blue as Shalpa's ghostfire, unlatched itself and swung inward on its own. Taz stood there somewhere between shock and a terrible compulsion to walk that path and, thieflike, prudently, something whispered to him, persuasive as temptation to sin, to reconnoiter the place—himself in the fine clothes she had given him; and with all these other finely dressed folk—did he not belong here? Why was he excluded?

Come ahead, something said, come ahead, come ahead—

He took the first step, he took the second, not really

wanting it, but he felt his hand brush the gate, felt it leave his hand—

He walked the path and ducked aside into the weeds and into the hedges, where a crack in the shutters gave forth a seam of light into the brush; he worked his way most carefully into this hedge against the house and rose up beneath the window, carefully, carefully to peer into the crack—

Into a room where the witch sat in the glare of countless candles—on the floor, on a bright array of discarded silks. Her face was white, her eyes were shut, her strange guests stood as shadows in the background of this cluttered room.

It was witchcraft he spied on, Taz was sure of it, it was most real and dangerous witchcraft, of a sort he had seen in the skies and in the streets of Sanctuary in recent years, when the dead had walked and lightnings and whirlwind had warred over the harbor. . . .

A thief knew when he was out of his league. Taz was easing backward in the brush when there was a sudden clap of wings, air against his neck, a raven's harsh cry—

And the shutters banged open in his face, inside and out at once, setting him face-to-face with a startled man: he swore, Taz yelped, and Taz was off through the bushes and for the only way out he knew, the front gate—

But it clanged shut and glowed blue and perilous in front of him, and he whirled around at the creak of the front door behind him.

He walked toward that door—not that he wanted to, but his body moved, and the distance between him and the porch steps grew less and less.

A man stood in that doorway, a one-eyed man who met him as he came up onto the porch, who set his hand on his shoulder and said, half sadly, "You should have run when you had the chance, boy."

But he went inside. He had to. He took his place with the others, a bearded, foreign man, a beggar with the remnants of handsomeness—a Rankene lady, the pale, one-eyed man who had snared him on the porch. . . .

She had never moved. She sat in the midst of this goings-on with her hands open on the knees of her black gown, her eyes shut, her lips moving in a constant murmur.

* * *

"Randal—" Strat felt uneasy on the steps of the Stepson-mage's apartment, uneasy in being in the mage-quarter in the first place, in an area where Rankan personnel were less than welcome, especially these days.

He felt uneasy in the second place because one had no knowledge what sort of wards an anxious mage might set; and Randal, with his enemies, had every right to be anxious.

And he felt that unease in the third place because he had had enough of dealing with wards and with witchery in all its manifestations, and he was disgusted to find his knees all but shaking as he stood on Randal's second-story landing, under a night sky and in a rising wind, and hammering away with more noise than a body ought to have to use to raise a mage out of sleep.

"Randal, dammit, wake up!"

A dog barked. Strat looked over the rail and down, and saw a black cur in the shadow down there, next the bay horse—

Someone sneezed, and instantly where the dog had been was Randal, in a night-robe and bare feet, wiping his nose.

"Damned allergies," Randal said. "I thought—"

"Thought what?" Strat came hastily down the steps, no little annoyed for the public scene.

"Thought—I smelled an associate of yours about you."

That was not what Strat wanted to hear. No. He grabbed Randal by the arm, hauled Randal into the privacy against the bay horse's side, and said, "I want you to come with me. I want you to talk to her. . . ."

Randal sneezed again, wiped his nose with the back of his hand. "For what? What good can I do? The woman's doing nothing against the Guild, and alone—"

"Talk to her," Strat said, holding his arm so tight Randal flinched and physically began to pry loose his fingers. He realized that and let go, took a grip on Randal's shoulder and kept that lighter, with a mortal effort. "I can't sleep, I don't rest—"

"I don't think it's sorcery," Randal said.

"What do you mean, 'don't think it's sorcery'!" Another effort to keep his voice down and the grip gentle. "Man, I'm forgetting things, I don't know where I am half the time, I *think* about her like I was some damn fool kid with his first lay—''

"It's not witchery."

"Damn if it isn't!"

"Has it dawned on you, Ace, that all of that equally well describes a man—in love?"

Strat stood there with his hand on Randal's shoulder and stared at him before he gave him a shove against the horse. "I came to you for help, Stepson!"

"That's what I'm telling you. I know spells. I know bewitchment. You've had it, but you haven't got it—that horse has, but you haven't." Another sneeze. "She cut you loose. The ties that've been on you—aren't. But you keep thinking about her. You can't sleep. You can't eat. You wake at night thinking about her, wondering who she's with—"

"Damn you!"

"So what else is it—but love?"

"You're useless!" Strat said, and picked up the bay horse's reins. "I'm going to have it out with her!"

"Don't!" Randal said, catching at the reins as Strat threw himself into the saddle. "Strat!"

But Strat pulled up on him, reined aside, and the bay took out at a run—with a black dog loping along: Strat saw it when they turned the corner and the dog got into the lead, running right under his horse's feet.

The bay horse shied up then, screamed and shied as the dog jumped at its throat, and Strat felt—

—nothing under him. Simply nothing stopping him from flying through the air and landing dazed on the cobbles.

He scrabbled for his knees, bad shoulder stunned, knee and hip paralyzed—he fell on his face again, somewhere between pain and numbness, and stopped caring whether he lived or died—because the horse was gone, and all there was in the world was Randal sitting on the filthy cobbles beside him, saying to someone—"I sent it away. I don't know if I should have done that—"

And Crit's voice saying: "You damn fool!"

As someone gathered him off the pavement and cradled his

head in his lap—someone familiar, over a lot of years, someone who kept saying, "Ace, gods, I'm sorry."

The horse was gone—turned to air beneath him. It was the
last gift she had given him. And it was gone. His friends took
it from him. Or she did. There was only the taste of blood in
his mouth.

She did not know *why* she did what she did—it was only
the night, and the feeling of change in the wind, and the
feeling of things slipping away from her. She murmured,
though perhaps none of her folk could hear her, "Protection
for my own is all I can do now. But that I do, as best I can."

She wanted her own with her tonight. Behind her closed
lids she saw the dying of altar fires, she heard the stirring of
gods in their shrines—she gathered her forces on this night
and she wove spells to protect this place, such as she could.

Against all wisdom to the contrary—she drew her servants
around her, revised the lines of her power—drew them from
all over the city to protect them on this night: she felt Haught's
battering at the wards that held him, felt the pleas he flung at
her, like a moth battering at the glass—

But one face she saw more than all the rest, one touch she
wanted most, and, dyed by a thousand murders and a thousand more black sins, she tried to stop thinking about him,
telling herself no, let him go, stop the anger, stop the wanting—

He could be in Hell itself and she could draw him to her:
pyromant, necromant, she could still raise the dead—singly
and with effort, who once had summoned legions out of
Hell's long patrol and set them to march against her rival—

She had lost a great deal—she had blown a great deal of
her power away on the winds, had seen the dust of a shattered
Globe of Power settle like a dream over Sanctuary, making
mages of beggars and diminishing the power of the mage-
born irrevocably: if that were not so she could lift her hand, raise
the lightnings, change the wind—*take* the failing Empire,
make herself that power that would shake the world.

As it was, the Empire would fail and fall, the greatness
would slip away from Ranke, and the marbles crumble and
the decline, centuries long, bring new powers, new mages,
new wizardry—

She was done with dreams of power. She let Ranke enter its long, lóng slide to destruction, she listened to the rising of the wind, the echo of that wind in empty fanes and altars, she said softly, ever so softly,

"Goodbye, Strat."

Knowing they would not meet again, even in Hell—her curse being immortality.

"Damn you!" Strat said, when they had gotten him onto his feet. But Crit held him there, in the cold, dusty light of dawn, a stinging wind skirling through the streets of Sanctuary, Crit had his arms about him, held him like a brother.

There was no sign of the bay horse. He ached from head to foot. His knee and his elbow were bleeding, and would stiffen.

"Get up on my horse," Crit said then. "We'll get you another."

He looked from one to the other of them in this beginning of dawn—Crit and Randal, and it was strange, as if having lost everything he had, he could feel so free—

So damnably nothing-left-to-lose—except Crit, standing there holding him on his feet, Randal supporting him from the other side.

He let them help him to the saddle, he let Crit and Randal lead him through the first stir of morning in the streets. He listened to Crit telling him how Shepherd had told him where he had to search, he listened to Randal saying there was something strange in this wind . . .

Shepherd met them at the turning. Shepherd said—leaning on the saddlebow of the big mud-colored horse, and looking straight at them, "Our service is done. Time we were moving on."

A gust of wind rocked at them. A flash of light hit their faces. Crit's horse shied and stood with its ears back, Crit and Randal holding it while Strat held on—and whatever had been Shepherd became a burst of light, a grim figure on a dark horse; a rising whirlwind, and a boy's voice saying,

"Follow the Shepherd. . . ."

"Abarsis . . ." Strat had no idea which of them had said it, or whether his eyes really remembered the figure in the light.

Follow the Shepherd. . . .
Time we were moving on . . .

Winds out of the desert battered at Sanctuary's shutters, swirled stinging clouds of sand and dust against a brazen sun.

Something fled shrieking on that wind, unbound—a witch's disembodied soul skirled three times about the towers of the Lancothis house, skimmed forlornly along the river and flew—formless and lost—before the gale.

So Haught reported, arriving wind-scoured and dusty at the river-house that day. It was a much-chastened Haught who kissed the hem of Ischade's black robe and begged shelter from this wind.

Ischade considered this contrition. "Don't trust him," Stilcho said coldly, Stilcho being at least the most privileged of her servants, and Haught's logical rival.

"I don't," she said plainly, and picked up her cloak and put it on. "Stay here," she said. "You'll be safe, at least, whatever happens. . . ."

She left then, took to the winds herself, and lighted in raven-shape by the city gate, where a sullen, closely wrapped crowd had gathered—a crowd through which she moved as a black-cloaked woman, willing no one to see her, or if they saw—to forget that they had seen: that gift she still had undiminished.

She came on the rumor Haught had brought—was there to see the last of the Rankene forces ride through the streets, out the gates.

They were very few—amazingly few, the crowd murmured, wondering if there were not more to come.

A handful of mercs; the few remaining of the 3rd Commando; and last to leave, the Stepsons, Randal the mage; Critias . . . with Strat beside him, on a tall dun horse, no banners, no haste. Strat did not even turn his head as he rode past, near enough she could have touched him.

The riders passed the gates, in blowing dust so thick it made shadows of them, made them nothing more than ghosts in the golden light.

For a moment the crowd began to drift—but one left the gate, one went out leading a mule, quickly lost in the dust.

Some said it was another merc; some said it was one of the rebels—looking for revenge, perhaps, Sanctuary's last violence aimed at Ranke.

Ischade knew that boy-almost-man—a scoundrel named Zip, or some such, servant of a god inimical to her: she felt that presence strongly when he passed, before the crowd began to disperse.

After that was just the dust, just the ghosts of buildings in what should have been bright day, the hill lost in haze and dust, yellow sand skirling along the streets.

Roxanne was gone, to heaven or to hell or whatever demon wanted her. The gods of Ranke deserted their shrines. Sanctuary was falling away from the Empire, the forces that had sustained Ranke were leaving and she might have followed them—but could not, not as far as they went, and not where the god might lead them. She was always a creature of the shadows, and of candlelight, and needed lives to sustain her life—

Except his.

She cherished that one claim to virtue.

THE FIRE IN A GOD'S EYE

Robin Wayne Bailey

The shallow waters of the White Foal glimmered blackly in the late night, purling with a suspiciously sweet rush and gurgle over its stony bottom. It whisper-whispered, as if it ferried secrets; deepening, as it went south between its inauspicious banks toward Sanctuary and Downwind and beyond to the sea. Sharp as a razor's cut was the line where the water touched the land at the fording point between Apple Lane and the Generals' Road, but looking far up or down its course there was no telling the river from the sky. For all that a fanciful mind could guess, it might have flowed down from a source somewhere in the dark heavens to touch the earth only briefly, here at the end of the world, before it plummeted over the edge and on, to the underworld. This river, with all the detritus that it carried, with all the dead who had washed up on its shores, with all the souls who had given themselves in despair to its waves, this river would make such a fitting link.

But the lone rider, who sat quietly astride a huge gray horse in the middle of the ford, watching the water foam and rill around the animal's fetlocks, was no poet, just a soul weighed down with weariness and burdens of the spirit. Such thoughts were only the shrapnel of too many sleepless nights, easily kept at bay by drawing a dusty cloak tighter around the shoulders, and pulling a dusty hood closer to shadow one's face.

Sabellia, too, Bright Moon-mother, had shadowed Her face
this night, turned away from the world below, and surren-
dered the world to the darkness. Even the stars, those myriad
sparkling tears She had shed for Her heavenly children and
for the children of the earth, those, too, were hidden behind a
thick, cloudy veil.

The rider's gaze turned away from the sky and toward
Sanctuary. At a nudge, the horse moved up the muddy bank
and turned down the Generals' Road, its hooves clip-clopping
smartly on the brick-and-stone paving, ringing even more
loudly on the wooden planks of the tiny north bridge that
crossed Splinter Creek. The rider halted briefly. Off to the
left stood the charred ruins of the house of the dead vivisec-
tionist, Kurd. Next to it, though, stood a new house, shoddily
built from scavenged lumber and stones. Lamplight shone
through the cracks of hastily constructed shutters, and gruff
voices echoed through the door. There was the smell of lime
and sand about the place, and unfamiliar tools leaned against
the outside walls. Some itinerant workers on the city's new
fortifications probably had decided to stay, though the work
was done.

Suddenly, the door swung open a crack, and someone
peered around the edge, alerted, no doubt, by the hoof-sounds
on the bridge. They watched warily as the rider passed by.
Obviously, they had quickly learned the ways of this city, this
thieves' world.

Off to the left stood the high, stark silhouettes of the city's
granaries, barely discernible in the night, though they towered
above the new wall. Nearer burned the lamps of the Street of
Red Lanterns, where scented women plied special delights
and special tortures, according to the appetites of their customers and the weight of their coins. Special effort had been
made to extend the new wall around the granaries, while the
brothels were left outside in its shadow.

The rider thought about that, then shrugged. In Sanctuary,
one might have expected just the reverse.

After a massive construction effort that had been the talk of
the Empire, the new wall was finished. It encompassed the
entire city now. Atop the huge edifice, watch fires burned,
and shadows moved about in the flickering glow. The new,

iron-banded doors of the great Gate of Triumph stood open, but a pair of garrison sentries stood at the duty post just inside.

"Whoa, there!" one of them called, coming forward as he curled one hand almost casually about the hilt of his sword. "What kind of foreigner comes visiting our town at such an unholy hour? Come out from under that damned hood. Show your face there."

The sentry's hair and clothing exuded the odor of smoked krrf as he came as close as the rider's knee, and his eyes sheened with drug-glaze as they caught the torchlight from the duty post. His jaw hung just a bit too slackly, and his motions were languid. An addict, probably.

The rider wanted no confrontation, so pulled just a corner of the concealing hood back and glared at the sentry, who backed up immediately. "My apologies, Lady!" he mumbled. He took his hand quickly away from his sword's hilt, and shot a fearful glance at his partner. "We didn't know it was you. Of course, you can pass. Welcome home!" He made a deep bow, and the rider passed him by without a word.

Caravan Square was abandoned this time of night. So was the Farmer's Run, though one could never be too sure there, for it was too close to the Maze, and every shadow and dark cranny was to be watched. Governor's Walk was also quiet, and the sounds of the horse's hoof-falls cracked with uncomfortable volume on freshly repaired street cobbles. Even in the darkness the work on the smaller, inner wall that enclosed the palace was evident. The rider continued straight ahead, following that wall.

At the place where West Gate Street joined Governor's Walk, a city watch patrol, six uniformed men, suddenly blocked the way. The oldest of them, a man whose graying curls spilled out from under his steel cap, and apparently the captain, held up a lantern and shined it on the rider.

The light glimmered on a sleeve of metal rings that covered the rider's left arm and the hand that held the reins. It fell, also, on the hilt of a sword, whose tangs were shaped like the wings of a bird. As the rider shifted in the saddle, the cloak parted slightly.

"Why, if it ain't the Daughter o' the Sun, 'erself, it is!"
The old man laughed unpleasantly. "Come back to stir up
more trouble, have ye?"

A much younger watchman stepped up to his captain's side
and grinned. "You know," he said nastily, "I had a cousin
killed in that PFLS ambush she set up last year. I can tell it
straight, I was glad to hear somebody fixed her . . . !"

The old man gave his subordinate a sharp elbow in the ribs
and scowled. "Shut yer mouth, Barik!" The scowl turned
into a twisted little smile that showed several missing teeth.
"Can't ye see she's just on 'er way home after a long while
gone?"

The younger watchman gave his captain an insubordinate
look as he rubbed his side. "Yeah," he said sullenly. "I
guess I can see that."

"Then bid 'er good nightie, boys, an' let 'er pass!" He
motioned all his men back and made a deep, sweeping bow
that was pure mockery. "Welcome home, Lady Chenaya!"
he said grandly. "Our regards to yer noble Rankan family!"

Chenaya was tired and rode on, forgetting about the watch-
men and their meaningless taunts. But when she reached the
Processional she stopped again. A wind swept up Sanctuary's
most famous street, bringing with it the sweet tang of the
salty sea, and there, in the silence, she thought she could just
hear the rush of the breakers and the rocking creak of the old
wharves at the Processional's farther end.

Gods, it was good to be home, and it would be good to rest
soon. She wanted to sleep, sleep for days, and wake up to the
faces and laughter of those she loved. She had seen too much
in her time away from Sanctuary, learned too much, perhaps
dared too much. All she wanted was to close her eyes and
forget it all.

She rode on along Governor's Walk, past the park called
the Promise of Heaven, until she reached the Avenue of
Temples. She saw no one else in the streets as she went, and
reflected on that. Sanctuary had quietened in her absence.
From the park, it was only a short distance to the Temple of
the Rankan Gods.

Chenaya dismounted and dropped the reins of her horse.
She gave it an affectionate pat along the withers before she

turned toward the temple steps. The animal was war-trained,
bred in the finest stables of Ranke's capital. It wouldn't
wander away while she was inside, and she pitied the hapless
fool stupid enough to try to steal it, horse bites being a
difficult thing for any physician to treat.

She climbed the twelve marble stairs and passed between
the columns that formed the temple entrance. A pair of oil
pots burned there, providing light, for adherents were welcome at any hour. On either side of the temple rose the great
stone images of Ranke's lost war-god, Vashanka, and Sabellia,
the moon-goddess. Streamers of incense wafted up around
them from circles of tiny holes cut into the floor about their
feet. The sweet smoke curled and swirled, and rose out
through round, open skylights.

Between those two deities, though, was the great altar of
Savankala, overhung with its massive golden sunburst and
ringed with burnished oil pots, whose flames sputtered and
danced. There was no statue, no image of Savankala, save
the symbolic sunburst. Who, after all, could look on the face
of the sun?

Chenaya knelt wearily before the sun-god's altar, made
proper obeisance, and fished out from inside her garments a
heavy leather purse that hung on a thong around her neck.
Loosening its strings, she poured into her hand an egg-sized
diamond. It was warm with the heat of her body, and as she
opened her fingers wider, its perfect facets caught the firelight
from the oil pots. A rainbow of rays shot about the temple.

The stone tiles of the floor vibrated suddenly, and the very
air grew taut with an unutterable tension. Above the altar,
Savankala's sunburst began to burn with a potent white light,
until all darkness fled His temple, and the shadows shriveled
into nothingness.

Chenaya curled into a ball around the diamond, and trembled. The light stabbed her eyes, though she flung up her
hood to hide her face and squeezed her eyes shut with all her
strength until they leaked thick tears. She did not cry out,
though, or call her god's name.

Slowly, the light subsided. Chenaya put the jewel back into
the purse and hid it in her clothing again. She rose, then, to
stare at the sunburst. It no longer burned with the Bright

Father's essence, nor did the temple stones. Yet, in her soul she felt Him near.

She lifted one of the many oil pots, taking care not to drown the wick, and set it in the middle of the altar. Next, she drew a small dagger from her boot. The silver blade shimmered. She raised it quickly and cut a long blond lock from her hair and held it in the wick's flame. It went up in a flash. The singe-smell and the smoke curled upward as Chenaya left the dagger as a further offering on the altar next to the pot. A moment later, she turned away and left the temple.

Her horse snorted when he saw her coming. She gathered the reins and mounted, ready to go home to Land's End. Before she got far, though, something caught her eye, a gleam of metal lying on the ground by the outside corner of the temple. She cast a glance over her shoulder. No moon in the sky, no stars, nothing to cause such a glitter. Cautiously, she dismounted again.

It was her dagger, point down, stuck in the earth. Her jaw gaped as she bent closer. No mistake, it was hers. She rose again, and peered suspiciously up and down the street. No one, not even the best thief in Sanctuary, could have got into the temple, snatched the dagger from the altar, and gotten out again without her notice. Even if such a thief lived, he wouldn't have been so clumsy as to drop it making his getaway.

She frowned and thought about the gleam that had caught her eye. There was no such gleam now from any angle as she moved around it. The damn thing was barely visible in the temple's shadow.

She was too tired for such puzzles. The hour was late, and home was near. If Savankala didn't want her offering, she wasn't going to just leave it in the dirt. It was a good blade. She bent down and grabbed the hilt.

Her senses reeled suddenly, and the earth seemed to yawn as she fell crazily into a great black hole. A scream formed, burbling in her throat. She bit her lip, though, and clenched her jaws tight, refusing to give it voice. Down she tumbled into the strange darkness, deeper and deeper, until somewhere far below, or far ahead—she could no longer tell direction— she saw a greenish glow and a form like a body in its shroud cloth. It, too, was falling, falling toward her at fantastic speed, coming closer. Now the shroud slipped away from its head, and she saw a pallid, horrible face with no eyes rushing at her.

Chenaya threw up her arms, on the verge of releasing the pent-up scream. She mustn't, she knew. But she couldn't help herself!

Then, as she opened her mouth, she found herself outside the temple again, and the world was the world she knew. She collapsed back against the temple wall, gasped for breath, and slowly fought down the panic that had filled her. There was no hole, no corpse, no greenish glow. Just the dagger at her feet.

She stared at the blade. Whatever had just happened, the dagger had been the trigger. Her fingertips had only brushed the hilt, and the world had lurched.

Of a sudden, she kicked the dagger, sending it flying end over end into the middle of the street. Nothing happened. She folded her hands over her mouth and trembled. Maybe it had been an illusion, a standing dream. No, make that nightmare. She was so tired, but she had to master herself, had to keep a tighter control.

She picked up the dagger and thrust it into its sheath in her boot and mounted her horse. It was just a short ride now to Land's End. She would be there soon, and she could rest, though not sleep. That would come later. At least, though, she'd be home. It would be good to see her father and Dayrne.

But when she made the turn onto the short road from the Avenue of Temples that should have taken her to her father's estate, she found herself at a dead end, staring at the cold stone of the city wall. Damn it! The wall's course had effectively cut off Land's End, and all the other estates, from the rest of the city. No doubt, Uncle Molin had chuckled about that. Hell, he'd probably planned it.

Frowning, she turned her horse around, rode back down the Avenue of Temples to the street called Safe Haven, and from there, to the Wideway, which ran along the wharves. There, the rush of the breakers, the humming of ships' guy wires, and the creaking of old timbers made a magical music, and the smell of the salt sea blew inland, overpowering. Unfortunately, so was the smell of fish. She turned her gaze away from the beautiful sea and concentrated on the road, setting her mount to a gallop until she came to the Gate of Gold, so named because in former times, when the caravan trade came this far south, it marked the way to the lucrative trade in Ilsig.

Two more guards stood at the Gate of Gold's duty post. They moved into the middle of the road, blocking the way, when they heard a rider coming. Chenaya slowed to a walk, then stopped. One of the men recognized her at once. "Lady!" he said with genuine politeness, inclining his head, then coming to attention. "Glad we are to see you back, though it could be under more pleasant circumstances."

The other soldier also inclined his head. "Many of us respected your father," he added gently. "And his accomplishment at this year's Festival of Man . . ."

Chenaya's eyes widened at mention of her father. *Respected? Past tense?* Forgetting the guards, she spurred her horse suddenly, filled with a dreadful apprehension, and left the gate swiftly behind. There was no road north outside the wall. She rode overland at breakneck speed, pushing her mount, heedless of the dangers—the unexpected trench, the patch of slick grass. She bent low over the horse's neck. Its mane lashed her face as she sought to outrace the fear the guard's casual words had put into her.

She passed Sanctuary's southernmost estate. It was supposed to be abandoned, but above its private walls, lamps burning in some of its upper windows said differently. She had no time to worry over that, though. She used the reins to whip her horse, driving it faster as the ground rolled up and down.

At the main gate of Land's End, she jumped to the ground, ran, and seized the gigantic iron knocker. Thrice, she slammed it against the metal plate, and thrice more, before a small square portal of wood in the gate's door slid back and an unfamiliar face peered out at her.

"What do you want?" the face snapped. Dark eyes stared warily at her. "It's late."

Chenaya froze, incredulous, then glared angrily. It was her

luck that the gate would be guarded tonight by one of Dayrne's recruits. This fool didn't know who she was! She grabbed the knocker and smashed it down again and again with all her frantic might, raising a terrible noise.

The gate jerked open suddenly. Curses pouring from his lips, a huge figure stepped outside. Despite his size, he was cat-quick. He caught her hand and pulled her away from the knocker. "There's people sleeping!" he grumbled. "That's enough of . . . !"

Chenaya seized his wrist and twisted hard. It didn't budge the giant, whose size and strength were obviously far greater than her own, but her mere attempt surprised him enough to let her move slightly behind him. She drove her heel into the weak area behind his knee, evoking a startled cry, and slammed her elbow into the side of his head just behind the ear. She didn't bother to watch him fall, just left him lying in the dirt, as she pushed the gates wide and rushed into the courtyard.

Two men, half naked, but with swords bared, came rushing out of the house.

Chenaya stopped and waved her hands desperately. Dismas and Gestus were old friends. They would know her.

They stopped as recognition dawned in their eyes. "Mistress!" Dismas shouted excitedly. "You're back!" He turned immediately to his partner. "Gestus, go wake Dayrne. Tell him she's come back. Wake everybody!"

Gestus muttered an incoherent welcome in broken Rankene and ran back into the house. Chenaya whipped off her cloak. When Dismas reached out his hand to clasp her arm in a gladiator's greeting, she threw the cloak over it and dashed after Gestus. "Mistress!" Dismas called in surprise, then he hurried after.

Dayrne was halfway down the great staircase when Chenaya reached the main hall. Wrapped only in a brief kilt, he stopped, stood there a moment, and looked at her. Then he rushed down the stairs, only to stop suddenly again. His eyes peered into hers, darted away momentarily, then drifted back. She read so many things in his eyes, things she had seen there before. She knew how Dayrne felt about her, had known for some time. But never had she seen his joy turn so abruptly to pain and hurt.

He reached out and clasped her arm. "Cheyne," he said quietly, using the nickname he had given her years ago. "There's no way to soften it. Lowan Vigeles is dead. So is your Aunt Rosanda."

Stunned, Chenaya could only look at him.

Dismas and Gestus were with them now, and they gathered close in a circle and put their arms around each other. The giant she had beaten at the gate rushed into the room, sword drawn. Immediately, though, he grasped the situation, looked shamefaced, and put down his blade.

"My apologies, Lady," he said sullenly. "I didn't know who you were, and you didn't say anything."

Dayrne started to turn and answer, but Chenaya's unyielding grip made him hesitate. She clung to him, grasping his arms, pouring all her strength into her grip. *Hold on,* she told herself desperately, locking his gaze. *Here's your anchor!* She felt Dismas and Gestus, their arms around her, too. *Here are your anchors!*

"It's all right, Dendur," Dayrne said over his shoulder. "Have someone see to her horse, then go back to your post."

The soft closing of the door as Dendur departed made a sound that touched Chenaya with its symbolic finality. She let go of Dayrne and slipped free of Dismas and Gestus. Slowly, she climbed the staircase and went to her father's room. The door was closed, but she pushed it open. Everything was just as she remembered it. Nothing had been disturbed. She walked to Lowan's sturdy chair by the fireplace. There was no fire, for it was too warm to need one. She unfastened her sword belt and let it drop to the floor. Then she sank down in the chair, just as her father always did, with the same languid motion, pushed her feet out, just as he always did, and stared into the hearth, the way she remembered him doing.

Dayrne came into the room and closed the door. She looked up at him, and loved him for the concern he wore so plainly on his face. He knelt down beside her and laid his head on the chair's carved armrest. She rubbed her thumb over his brow, over the lines of his hurt, before her own pain became too great, and she turned away to gaze back into the cold fireplace.

"Cheyne?" he said, looking up. He repeated it. "Cheyne?"

He leaned closer, trying to make her look at him, but she wouldn't.

"Chenaya?" He shook her arm, rising to his feet, the worry on his face transforming to fear. "Please, talk to me!"

She clutched the diamond hidden in its leather purse under her tunic, and twisted in the chair to avoid Dayrne's face. She drew her legs up—her father's chair was big enough for that—and curled into the crook of its great wooden arm. Tears streamed suddenly down her cheeks; she couldn't hold them back any longer. She hugged herself, and cried and cried.

But though she cried, she made not a sound.

Dayrne paced about the peristyle, the large central room of the Land's End estate. It was also half garden, and the gray, depressing half-light of the Sanctuary morning streamed in. Though it was spring, there had been so little sunshine of late. Rashan, the high priest of Savankala, and friend of the family, sat motionless on one of the marble benches. Daphne, recently divorced from Prince Kadakithis, now a permanent resident of Land's End, tapped a dagger blade idly against one palm as she watched Dayrne.

"Word's out all over town that she's back," Daphne said with a wicked smile. "Word also has it that Zip decided hiding wasn't good enough. The little coward sneaked out of town before dawn this morning." Daphne flipped the dagger in the air and caught it by the point. "Anyone disappointed?"

Dayrne was disappointed. His hands clenched into fists. He'd have much preferred to find Zip and all the rest of his little PFLS rats and do to them what he'd done to their comrade, Ro-Karthis. He tried. His gladiators had torn up the town looking for piffles, but they'd all burrowed too deeply into the earth after Lowan's murder.

He'd made an example of Ro-Karthis, though. The people of Sanctuary had never seen a *Bhokaran ferryboat*. Few living in this hellhole even knew of that country far to the west. The sight had impressed them, though. He, himself, had fired the ship as it floated from the harbor with a living, screaming Ro-Karthis crucified on the mast with Lowan Vigeles and Lady Rosanda laid in regal splendor at his feet. Dayrne

could still hear Ro-Karthis's shrieks, see the smoke and sparks
rising on the wind while the flames burned all. A *ferryboat*,
they called it in Bhokar. Two souls ferried to heaven, one to
eternal hell.

It had been too good a death for Lowan Vigeles's murderer, but it had made a point. The few remaining members
of the so-called Popular Front for the Liberation of Sanctuary
had reportedly crept out of town one by one. Zip, supposedly
reformed from the PFLS after being made one of the city's
three commanders, had crawled into a hole so deep no one,
not the prince, not Molin Torchholder, not even Walegrin,
knew what had become of him.

Now, Daphne claimed, even Zip had gotten away.

Dayrne blamed himself. He should never have let old
Lowan talk him into taking so many men north to the annual
Festival of Man. Oh, they'd done well in the games. Spectacularly well. Twenty-five death matches and only two losses.
The Empire's greatest gladiatorial schools had been not just
defeated but humiliated by an unknown school from Sanctuary, of all places. It had driven the odds-makers and the
bet-takers crazy. Ranke would be talking about it for years.

But while he and the best men from Land's End had been
up north, Ro-Karthis had used iron claws to scale the wooden
stable gate, crept unseen into the main house, and murdered
Lowan and Rosanda in their sleep. The gods alone knew who
might have been next if Daphne hadn't discovered him. Against
orders, she'd been out after dark working the training machines alone—angry, no doubt, because he'd refused to take
her to the games.

She'd just come back to her own quarters when Ro-Karthis
emerged, bloody knife in hand, from Rosanda's rooms.

Daphne had damn near killed the bastard, and frankly,
Dayrne marveled at the self-control she'd shown by sparing
Ro-Karthis until his return. Of course, Daphne's idea of
self-control had been to hamstring Ro-Karthis and sever the
tendons in his elbows. It probably hadn't taken her more than
the necessary four quick strokes with her sword, either. Then
she'd staunched and cauterized the blood flow to save his life.

Of course, long before Dayrne had gotten home she'd
extracted from the stupid fool the reason for his crime—to

revenge the PFLS for the damage Chenaya had done to their organization.

"What I can't figure out," Dayrne snapped suddenly, smacking his fist against an open palm, "is why she can't talk! She won't make a sound!" He turned toward Rashan. "You should have seen her last night. She cried and cried, tears enough to put Sabellia to shame, if hers could hang in the sky. But not once did she so much as whimper!" He shook his head as Daphne came to his side. "I tell you, it's weird!" She touched his arm, and he met her gaze worriedly. "It's got me scared," he said, no easy admission for a man like Dayrne.

Rashan rose to his feet and he, too, began to pace. "Could it be shock? Maybe you should have told her more gently."

Daphne snickered and shot the priest a scornful look. "Chenaya?" she said with a sneer.

Dayrne frowned and shook his head vigorously. "She beat poor Dendur up, rather than tell him her name," he reminded.

Daphne's eyebrow went up in mocking surprise. "*Poor* Dendur?" she muttered. "He's almost seven feet tall and thicker than the city gates!"

"You're not helping, Princess!" Dayrne shouted abruptly, using her title as an insult, as he did on the training field to make her work harder.

But Daphne was having none of it this time. "How can I help?" she answered sharply. She waved the dagger under her trainer's nose. "Chenaya's in one of her moody snits, and that's understandable, if you ask me. Just leave her alone. She'll pull herself together."

Rashan folded his hands into his voluminous sleeves and gazed toward the ground. "Could it be a spell?" he wondered aloud. "Or some curse? We don't know where she's been the past seven months, or what she's been up to."

"Knowing Chenaya," Daphne offered as she turned away, "only trouble."

"Don't you have a home of your own now?" Dayrne said irritably.

She gave him the kind of smile an adult loves to give a nasty neighbor child just before knocking it back on its side of the fence. He knew well enough she now owned the southernmost estate next to Land's End. It had been part of her divorce settlement from Kadakithis, that and half his treasury.

"It's full of your gladiators, remember, teacher?" She gave him a pouty look. "You couldn't let good men sleep in those drafty, leaky barracks you made them build, forever. They're gladiators, not carpenters. They'd have turned on you at the first sign of spring rain." She tilted her head playfully and winked at him. "I probably saved your life."

"It *could* be a curse," Rashan mumbled to himself.

The peristyle's doors opened, and a tall, blond man, clad in a brief red kilt and a gladiator's broad leather belt stepped across the threshold. He stopped there and called out to Dayrne, beckoning as he nodded greetings to Daphne and Rashan.

Dayrne walked over to him. "What is it, Leyn?" he said quietly.

Leyn kept his voice low. "Molin Torchholder is here," he said with a look of warning. "He heard Chenaya was back. You know what he wants."

Dayrne nodded, frowning. Someday he'd drive a sword through that old schemer's gut, even if Molin was Chenaya's uncle. The human weasels of the world just weren't to be tolerated by honorable men, and there were far too many such in Sanctuary. He knew what Torchholder wanted, all right.

"You kept him in the courtyard?" Dayrne asked.

Leyn pursed his lips and nodded.

"I'll take care of him," Dayrne answered, ushering Leyn out and following him. He paused long enough to close the doors. He'd explain to Daphne and Rashan later. "I'm beginning to get irritated with Lord Molin," he added as he and Leyn walked side by side.

"He is a bit of a pimple in the crotch," Leyn agreed.

Dayrne went out into the courtyard and paused long enough to glance at the steel-colored sky. On such a gray day bad news just had to come calling. And there had been too many gray days, lately.

Molin had come with an escort of three garrison guards. Two stood just behind Molin, while the third remained beyond the gate with their horses. Dismas, Gestus, Ouijen, and Dendur stood on the opposite side of the courtyard and scowled unpleasantly at them. Leyn went to join his four friends and added his scowl to theirs.

Dayrne went straight up to Molin Torchholder without giving so much as a glance of acknowledgment to the two nervous guards. "This is not a good time, Molin," he said sternly.

Molin Torchholder was unruffled by the use of his first name without the use of his title. "I've come to talk with my niece about Lowan's estate," he said evenly, taking care to maintain his dignity in the face of Dayrne's deliberate affront.

Dayrne glared into the other man's face, then down at his sternum just under the breastbone, imagining he could see the spot right through Molin's robes. Yes, there he would put his blade cleanly. It would make a soft, squishing sound, steel and flesh, and Molin would give a little moan as he rolled his eyes. Someday.

"She's resting," Dayrne finally answered. At least, he hoped she was resting. Chenaya was almost hysterical about not falling asleep. No sleeping, no talking. *What was happening to her?*

Molin Torchholder regarded Dayrne stiffly and lifted the point of his nose a bit higher in the air. "I've come twice now," he reminded Dayrne. "We've got to get this business settled."

Dayrne almost reached for his sword then and there. Instead, he clenched his fist. "You pompous bureaucrat!" he hissed, making the effort to keep his voice under control. "Lowan Vigeles wasn't dead a day before you showed up to claim his estate."

A low chuckle came from behind Dayrne. "Daphne threw him out on his ass," Ouijen remembered aloud as he idly twisted the long braided lock of dark hair that draped over his shoulder.

Dayrne ignored the interruption. "Now, Chenaya's not back a day, and here you are to press your claim again. What's the matter, Molin? Doesn't Kitty-Kat want you at the palace anymore?"

The insults were beginning to take effect on Molin Torchholder. His cheeks had reddened at Ouijen's remark,

and now a second time, Dayrne had addressed him personally, and in such a mocking tone. His eyes burned with
suppressed anger. "It is not a claim," he stated starchly. "It
is a fact. Land's End is mine. Under Rankan law, daughters
do not inherit their fathers' holdings. Lowan was my
brother . . ."

"Half-brother," corrected Daphne, coming out the door
and joining the gladiators behind Dayrne. She smiled at Molin
and blew him a kiss, all the while tapping the dagger on her
palm as she had done in the peristyle.

Molin deigned to acknowledge her. "Princess," he said
with a nod. "Nevertheless, I am Lowan's closest surviving
male relative. The fact is indisputable, and the law is the
law."

Daphne, Dismas, Gestus, Leyn, Ouijen, and Dendur all
crept forward until they stood in a semicircle on either side of
Dayrne. They were all tapping daggers on their palms now,
and they were all grinning unpleasant little grins, winking at
one another, and giving tiny provocative nods and suggestive
tilts of the head to the garrison guards, who began casting
nervous glances toward the open gate at their backs.

"When the Lady Chenaya is ready to discuss it," Dayrne
said, emphasizing her title this time, "I'm sure she'll send for
you." He glanced meaningfully at his companions and back
at Molin. "Meanwhile, occupation is nine-tenths of the law."

"And armed occupation is the other tenth," Daphne added,
wearing her favorite smile again, the adult one.

Molin Torchholder knew the better part of valor. "Very
well," he said finally. "Give my niece my regards, and tell
her I'll call on her again in three days' time in the hopes that
she'll be feeling better. Meanwhile," he added, putting on a
smile very much like Daphne's, "try not to damage or scratch
anything." He spun about and motioned his escort out the
gate.

The gladiators closed ranks around Dayrne. "He's going to
be trouble," Leyn said, watching the three departing men
mount horses just beyond the gate.

"I could speak to Kadakithis," Daphne offered.

Dayrne's mouth drew into a tight line. "No," he said
finally. "Technically, Molin's right, and we can't hold him

off forever. Sooner or later, Chenaya's going to have to deal
with him. Where is she?''

Gestus answered in his fractured Rankene. ''Sees Lady
sunrise down by hers temple giving worship.'' He glanced up
at the sky and shrugged his shoulders. ''Precious no sun to
worship lately.''

Ouijen had more recent knowledge. ''I saw her just a while
ago in the aviary. She was feeding Reyk. I tell you, though,
she looked like hell. I don't think she's slept or eaten for days.''

''I'd better have a talk with her,'' Dayrne said. ''Somebody close the gate.'' He let out a heavy breath and looked
around suddenly. ''And what are you all doing here? Who's
running the training drills this morning? This is a school,
remember?''

He left them then, and went to look for Chenaya. He would
check the aviary out back in case she was still there with her
pet falcon, but first, since it was closer, he'd check her room.
In the main hall he started up the great staircase. Then,
remembering Rashan, he happened to glance down the hallway to the peristyle and glimpsed his mistress just going
through the doors. Dayrne turned and hurried after her.

A strange scene greeted him as he entered. Chenaya shot a
look his way and swiftly closed her hand around something
she'd been showing Rashan. The priest's face was white as a
virgin's wedding sheets. He stared fearfully at Dayrne, as if
he'd been caught in a criminal act.

Obviously, Dayrne had interrupted something. Chenaya
walked a few paces away from the priest and tried to act
nonchalant while she slipped something into a small bag that
hung on a thong about her neck. Rashan licked his lips, his
eyes darting every which way. Dayrne thought he looked like
a mouse suddenly come face-to-face with a very big cat.

Dayrne was in no mood for games. ''What is it, Cheyne?''
he insisted. ''What have you got there?''

Chenaya gave him a stubborn look and dropped the purse
down the front of her tunic. Rashan wrung his hands. ''I've
got something to do,'' he said suddenly, and he headed
toward the door.

Dayrne caught the priest's wrist as he tried to go past.
''Oh, no you don't!'' He gently but firmly pushed Rashan

back. Then he turned again to Chenaya. "You've never kept anything from me, Cheyne, not since we were kids. Don't start now."

Chenaya bit her lip, her face mirroring some inner struggle. She clutched at the bag under her tunic, but her hand hesitated there, and she said nothing.

"Let me help, damn it!" Dayrne shouted suddenly. His frustration and worry built past the point of control. He wanted to reach out and rip the purse from her neck, or grab Chenaya and shake her, or, gods help him, just wrap his arms around her and hold her close until she broke down and told him everything. That last, he knew, would never happen.

Chenaya gave him a doubtful look. Dark circles ringed her puffy eyes, and her cheeks were gaunt. Dayrne realized then that she had not even taken off the armor she had worn last night. Even her garments were the same.

He met her gaze, and this time his eyes did the pleading.

It was enough. Slowly, Chenaya pulled out the purse again and poured the huge diamond into her open palm for him to see. It drew the weak light in the room like a sponge and gave off fantastic flashes of fire in exchange. Dayrne caught his breath.

"It's called the Fire in God's Eye," Rashan said in a worried voice as he came to join them. He lifted his own hand over the stone, as if warming his fingers before a fire. Tiny dazzling points of light reflected on his skin. "There's another jewel just like it," he continued in a bare whisper. "A twin. Sometimes, they're called the Savankala's Eyes, because they're mounted in the holy sunburst in the great Temple in Ranke."

Dayrne had heard of the stones, of course. He looked incredulously at Chenaya. "You stole it?"

She nodded slowly.

"Just the one," he pressed, "or both of them?"

She tapped the diamond with a finger, indicating just the one jewel.

"And this has something to do with why you can't or won't speak?" he asked again, and again she nodded.

Dayrne began to pace. He was doing a lot of that lately, it seemed. He knew of the stones, but he'd never seen them.

Until recently, he'd never been much of a god worshipper, and he'd never been in the Great Temple at Ranke. He turned to Rashan as Chenaya put the diamond back into its purse once again. A sudden suspicion flared up within him. "What do you know about this?" he said to the priest. "You're Savankala's high holy-holy in this city. Is this why she left Sanctuary? Did you send her to steal this?"

Rashan wrung his hands, and he gave Dayrne a look of pained offense. "No! No!" he protested. "I wouldn't have dared! She didn't say a word to me before she left town!"

Dayrne caught the priest by the sleeve. "Then why was she showing it to you?"

Angrily, Chenaya knocked Dayrne's hand away from Rashan, and she stepped between them. Then her expression softened, and she eased the priest back toward a marble bench and motioned for him to sit.

Rashan folded his hands in his lap to keep them still. "Each jewel is invested with a portion of Savankala's power," the priest went on in a rush. "They were the god's own gift to the Rankan nation, given generations ago when the Empire was young, as His personal sign of divine favor."

"They're magic?" Dayrne grumbled. He turned to Chenaya again. "Then you are cursed?"

She shook her head violently.

"Maybe this will help." Daphne sauntered into the room, bearing a flat, brown box, which, when its hinged lid was opened, exposed a smooth sheet of soft, wax tallow, and a delicate bone stylus. She offered these to Chenaya, along with a smile of welcome. The two women exchanged embraces and stood apart again. "Just because she can't talk doesn't mean you can't still get some answers." She continued lightly. "Personally, I think I prefer her this way."

Chenaya ignored Daphne, took the wax tablet, and began to write in the soft substance with the point of the stylus. A moment later, she showed the box to Rashan. It was not writing at all, but a drawing of a sunburst.

Daphne raised an eyebrow. "She's no Lalo," she commented.

The priest peered closely at the wax. "The holy sunburst in Ranke," he said, squinting.

Chenaya shook her head and drew the symbol for Sanctu-

ary beneath the sunburst. Then she pulled the purse from
around her neck. Without removing the diamond, she thrust it
down in the center of her drawing.

Rashan's face turned a new shade of pale. "Mount it in our
sunburst?" he exclaimed with sudden comprehension. "This
is stolen! God would strike me dead and destroy the temple!"

Chenaya shook her head emphatically and scrawled on the
tablet, *His permission.*

The priest's expression underwent a slow transformation.
His eyes filled with a queer light, and he rose to his feet.
"You've accepted it, then. You've spoken with Him again."
He reached out and grasped Chenaya by the shoulders. "You
are truly the Daughter of the Sun!"

Dayrne watched as Chenaya's face crinkled with irritation
and she brushed the priest's hands away. It was an old
argument between Rashan and Cheyne. It was no secret that
Chenaya was favored by the Bright Father, but the priest had
been possessed of a strange fanaticism for some time now that
she was, in fact, the sun-god's true daughter. Rashan had
even tried to convince Dayrne, and with the help of an even
stranger painting, which hung in Chenaya's rooms, he'd almost succeeded.

Chenaya rubbed the heel of her palm over the wax surface,
wiping away the old markings, smoothing it again for more
writing. With hasty precision, she carved two smaller sun-
bursts side by side. Under one, she put the symbol for
Sanctuary. Under the other, the symbol for Ranke. Then she
wrote, *Savankala's will.*

Rashan's face transformed. His look of worry turned to
determination and excitement. "One in Ranke, and one in
Sanctuary," he cried. "Then we must do it immediately."
He spun toward Dayrne, gesticulating, his hands aflutter.
"This explains the sky of late," he said. "Savankala has
risked much to send us this prize. This jewel has traveled
without the proper consecrations. Until it is safely mounted in
His temple, He is half blind." He touched Daphne's arm as if
the two of them were close friends, something the princess
would have adamantly denied. "It's just as I've suspected
recently. One by one, the gods are turning away from
Ranke."

"But why can't she speak?" Dayrne said insistently. "What's this jewel to do with that?"

Chenaya bit her lip, and the stylus remained still above the wax tablet, though her gaze flickered over all their faces, imploring.

Finally, Daphne tilted her head and shrugged. "A girl's just got to have her secrets." She went to Chenaya and took her by the arm. "At least, let me clean you up and get some food down you while Rashan makes his preparations," she suggested with her usual sarcastic lilt. "I know priests and priestly ways. Something this important will take at least a week."

Chenaya looked genuinely frightened. Frantically, she scrawled across the tablet. *Tomorrow*. It was the only symbol she made, and she drew it again for emphasis. *Tomorrow*.

A platter of cold roast pork, the two turnips, and bits of cheese and bread had lifted Chenaya's spirits considerably. The mug of milk laced lightly with amber-colored vuksebah, a very expensive liquor, had done even more. She couldn't quite remember when she had eaten last. Sometime in Ranke before she'd stolen the jewel, she assumed. Once that was in her possession, she'd ridden hard for Sanctuary, killing one horse on the way, avoiding all towns, stopping at one noble's isolated estate long enough to sign her desire to buy another mount. There'd been no time for eating, and little to drink.

A serving woman, under Daphne's orders, had brought the food to Chenaya's rooms, and that had surprised Chenaya. Except for Aunt Rosanda, Daphne, and herself, there had never been any women at Land's End. Daphne, apparently, had taken it on herself to change that. There were just over a hundred men on the estate now. Someone had to launder their clothes and do the cooking and marketing.

Daphne had mentioned hastily that, in Chenaya's absence, she had shared some adventure with the poor women who sold their bodies in the Promise of Heaven for coins to feed their children and to keep some kind of hovel's roof over their heads. With her own money, which was quite plentiful thanks to her settlement with the prince, Daphne had hired some of those women, taken them out of the park, and given them decent jobs as household staff.

Chenaya wasn't about to object. Two of those women had just bathed her and dried her with soft towels and combed out her tangled hair. She felt better than she had in days as she dressed in a clean white chiton, fastened her broad leather belt about her waist, and laced on a pair of sandals. That done, she fastened her short sword to the belt, and hung the small bag containing the diamond around her neck once more.

Fed and dressed, she started to leave her rooms. Near the door, though, hung the painting of her, which Lalo the Limner had executed. She stopped before it, feeling the arcane heat that radiated from it, staring at an idealized image of her face with shining blond hair that swept outward and upward and became flame. It had been this portrait and what it portended that had driven her, half mad, from Sanctuary, that, and the very unpleasant ending to her business with Zip and the PFLS.

Only, it hadn't been an ending. She had fallen in love with Zip while setting her trap for the piffles, and instead of killing him when she should have, she'd saved him for prison, instead, and turned him over to Walegrin. Devious were the minds of Sanctuary's politicians, however, and somehow, with her gone, Zip had been released and made one of the city's military commanders, along with Walegrin and Critias. No doubt, she had Uncle Molin to thank for that. And Kadakithis, once her favorite cousin, could not be held unaccountable, either.

They all had played their part in Lowan Vigeles's death. Ro-Karthis was not the only one who had cut her father's throat. Zip, Walegrin, Uncle Molin, Kadakithis. Not one of them was innocent.

She brushed her fingertips gingerly over the portrait. The paint and canvas were warm, almost too hot to touch. It had frightened her that night, watching Lalo, at her insistence, paint it. It had terrified her. His particular magic had revealed the truth she had been unwilling to accept, that she was bound body and spirit to the sun-god. In her fear, she had fled like an unreasoning child.

Seven months had changed that. She clutched the jewel called the Fire in God's Eye, without taking it from its bag. There were more changes yet to come, changes for her and changes for Sanctuary. But first, she had to survive another night, and she feared, for she could feel herself weakening. More than anything, she wanted to sleep.

But she had to check on Rashan and his progress at the temple. When the diamond was safe in a consecrated mounting, then she could rest, then she could mourn her father and Aunt Rosanda properly, then she could contemplate a new direction for her life.

She left her rooms and passed through the upper hallways, refusing to let herself even glance toward the door to her father's rooms, putting his death out of her mind for now. She went downstairs, nodding curtly to a pair of unfamiliar women who smiled at her from their work in the kitchen, and stepped out into the rear grounds near the aviary. There were a dozen cages there, each home to a fine raptor, and a large cabinet built on a post, which contained bells, jesses, and proper gloves for handling such birds.

Chenaya took a thick leather glove and a jess from the cabinet and went to Reyk's cage. The falcon fluttered its magnificent wings in greeting as it climbed onto her arm, and she slipped the jess onto its right leg. Reyk was excited to see her and he flexed his talons in the glove's quilted leather. They'd been apart too long, she and this bird.

From the aviary she could see the training fields. Scores of men were hard at work on the great wooden machines and in the sand pits. Beyond were the old, hastily built barracks, no longer in use. Beyond that rose the private wall that encircled Land's End. Opposite the training field, against the southern wall, were the stables. She headed there at a brisk walk.

A large man, unfamiliar to her, bowed when she approached. "Lady Chenaya," he said in a gruff but courteous voice. "You honor us." She nodded and gave him a brief smile, the only response she could make. He had the look of an experienced stablemaster, and she assumed Dayrne had found him somewhere. Indeed, the stables were as clean as any part of Land's End. Fresh straw had been laid, and the horses stood contentedly in their stalls.

With the stablemaster in tow, she went to the stall where
her big gray stood. He had been well groomed this morning,
and his mane had been freshly clipped close to his neck. He
had carried her well the past few days. Chenaya led him from
the stall by his halter and informed the stable master through
hand signals that she wanted him saddled. He fastened a lead
to the halter and led the gray toward the tack room.

Chenaya wandered toward the far end of the stables, where
those horses were kept that were either too young or not
properly broken for riding. There she found the colt that she
had such hopes for, the product of a god-blessed union between Lowan's snow-white mare and Tempus's full-blooded
Trôs horse. She gazed at the young animal with pleased
wonderment. Its coat was a golden color she had never seen
before, its mane and tail flaxen. It had the Trôs fire in its
eyes.

"He grows rapidly, mistress. I've never seen one like
him."

Reyk's wings beat the air, and he gave off a shrill cry of
menace. Chenaya had not heard the stablemaster come up
behind her. The man stepped quickly back, eyes widening,
bringing a hand up to ward off an attack. Chenaya grinned to
herself. He knew a lot about horses, that much was plain, but
he had a lot to learn about birds and how to approach them.
She gazed toward the stable entrance. The gray stood saddled
and ready for her.

There would be time later, she hoped, to play with the colt,
but there was business to attend to now. She calmed Reyk by
stroking the crown of his head with delicate touches. Perhaps
she should have hooded him this morning, but she never
hooded him. He was just excited to see her.

The stablemaster hurried along ahead of her and set down a
step stool so she could mount the gray with Reyk on her arm.
When she was settled in the saddle, she leaned down far
enough to touch the stablemaster's shoulder. It was the only
thanks she could offer. Then she turned the horse from the
stable and waited while he opened the southern gate for her
and closed it after.

Chenaya looked at Reyk and stroked his head again. *Ready
for some exercise, pet?* she thought silently. She made an

upward motion with her arm, letting go of the jess at the same time, and Reyk soared upward. She watched him as he circled higher and higher in the slate-gray sky. Then she started off, knowing he would follow.

She rode toward Sanctuary's great wall and followed it south to the Gate of Gold, retracing the path she had made last night. The falcon beat her to the gate and perched atop it until she caught up. Then, calling to her, he took to the sky again. Two sentries at the duty post watched as she trotted through. They made no effort this time to delay her.

The Wideway was full of carts and people coming and going about their morning business. Some glanced up with smiles and watched her go by. Others pointedly ignored her. She didn't care. She drew a deep breath of the lively salt air. Far out on the sea, the white sails of the fishing fleet and the Beysib treasure ships knifed through the ashen clouds.

Safe Haven Street was also crowded, and that surprised her. Sanctuary seemed to have gained populace in her absence. The roadways teemed in marked contrast to their dead-of-night emptiness. She was forced to slow her mount to a walk as she turned up the Avenue of Temples.

Suddenly, her head swam. She clutched at the hornless rim of her saddle and wrapped her legs around the horse's barrel chest to keep from falling. A queer darkness surrounded her, filled her, though she was sure her eyes were open. Out of that blackness, tumbling end over end, came the same shrouded corpse she had thought was a dream the night before. Straight for her it flew, and the cloth parted from its horrible face. Its eyeless gaze met hers.

The blackness and the vision exploded in a shower of red sparks, and pain shot through Chenaya's body. She opened her eyes slowly and found herself on the ground. She had fallen off the horse after all. A throng of people quickly gathered around as she tried to draw a decent breath.

An old woman, whose brightly dyed red hair sprouted in all directions about her head, set aside her marketing basket and bent down beside Chenaya. Her wrinkled old face was twisted with narrow-eyed concern. "Are you all right, honey?" she kept repeating, taking Chenaya's hand in her own.

Chenaya's eyes snapped wide suddenly at the old woman's

touch, and her gaze swept the sky, spotting Reyk already in his killing dive. "Get back!" she shouted, pushing the woman away. Barely in time she got the thick leather glove up and gave a sharp whistle. Reyk's weight hit her wrist like a rock, but she caught his jess and held him securely.

She looked at the old woman then, sprawled beside her. "Sorry," she said with a sigh of relief. "He thought you were attacking me."

The old woman put on a dazed smile. "S'all right," she muttered, staring at Reyk as others in the crowd helped her up. "S'all right. You folks at Land's End been right good to some of us," she said to Chenaya. "I knowed who you were when I saw you fall . . ."

Suddenly, Chenaya clapped a hand to her mouth. She'd spoken! She hadn't meant to, but the deed was done. She glanced fearfully up at the sky. Its gray color was already darkening. One hand felt for the diamond in its purse under her clothing. It pulsed against her skin with a steady, inaudible thrumming that unnerved her.

She grabbed the old woman by the shoulder with her free hand. "Get to your homes," she said urgently to everyone. "Shutter your windows, and don't look at the sky! Believe me! Go!"

The crowd stared uncertainly for a moment, no doubt wondering if she hadn't fallen on her head. Reyk beat his wings as if to drive them away, but still they hesitated. Then, as if sensing her urgency, the old woman made a quick curtsy and hurried away. It was enough to break whatever spell held the crowd. They looked at the sky, at Chenaya, then hugged their baskets to their bodies and hurried away.

Chenaya whirled around and found herself staring at the cornerstone of the Rankan Temple. Here, almost on this same spot, she had found her dagger point down in the earth the night before, and here, she had had her first vision of that deathly hurtling specter. Now she had had the second.

"Up, Reyk!" she cried, releasing the falcon. Her horse stood still, waiting, as it had been trained to do. She left him there and ran inside the temple. Rashan and a dozen other priests were hard at work, lowering the sunburst on the great chains that held it suspended above Savankala's altar.

"Rashan!" she called. There was no point in keeping silent any longer. The damage had been done. She could feel the diamond's pulse against her chest. Rashan saw her and came running as fast as his old legs would allow. The others stopped their work to see what transpired.

"Your voice . . . ," he started, but Chenaya waved an impatient hand to shut him up.

"The diamond is in danger," she told the priest hurriedly. "We all are!" She licked her dry lips and swallowed, getting control of herself. "First, though, tell me. Is there something buried under the cornerstone of this temple? Don't lie, and be quick!"

It was Rashan's turn to swallow. "Every Great Temple is consecrated with a sacrifice," he told her.

"A human sacrifice?"

He nodded again. "It was done on the night of the Ten-Slaying in honor of Vashanka some years ago. He requires such sacrifices."

Chenaya cut him off. "Vashanka is lost," she snapped. "Remove his image from this place. But right now, put half your priests to work digging that thing up. Dispose of it. Whatever it is, it is repugnant to Savankala. It pollutes his temple."

Rashan looked indignant. "How can you know these things!"

She caught him by the front of his robes and glared. "I am the Daughter of the Sun, old man!" she said, setting him down roughly. "You and the Bright Father both wanted a high priestess. You've preached my heritage all over town, don't deny it! I don't any longer. In the desert far from here, Savankala came to me, and I acquiesced." She pulled the purse from under her clothes and squeezed it in a fist. The thrumming was stronger now, more desperate. "That's why I have the Fire in God's Eye. He asked me to steal it and bring it here!"

"But it's a public street!" Rashan cried, protesting. "If we try to dig it up, Walegrin's men will surely stop us!"

Chenaya grabbed his sleeve and drew him outside. "Look up!" she shouted in his ear.

The sky had taken on the color of a deep bruise. Clouds of

purple and yellow rolled in from the north. Only the palest
hint of the sun showed through the infrequent gaps. A wind
swept down the streets, blowing thick dust and refuse. Sanctuary's citizens went running in the gale as their garments
whipped about them.

Rays of rainbow radiance began to leak from the purse
about Chenaya's neck, giving her face an eerie, up-shadowed
appearance. "This is my fault!" she shouted over the rising
wind. "While I kept silent the high priests of Ranke could not
find the jewel." She clutched at the small bag again. The
light from it was bright enough now to show the bones of her
fingers through the skin. "I didn't even sleep for fear of
crying out in my dreams. But I broke my vow to save that old
woman's life. The priests of Ranke still wield considerable
magic. They know where I am now. The sound of my voice
alerted them, as God, Himself, warned me it would, and they
want the diamond back!"

"But Savankala wants it here!" Rashan answered, his
voice rising in pitch, like the wind. He wrung his hands.
"What can I do?"

She grabbed the front of his robes again and pulled him
close. The wind was screaming now, as if it were trying to
drown her voice and stop her words. "Dig that thing up!"
she ordered. "The Bright Father rejects it. The Fire in God's
Eye can't dwell in the same house where it's buried. Purify
this place. Use every priest you have. And prepare the mounting as swiftly as you can!"

"How much time?" Rashan wailed.

Chenaya gazed at the festering sky. "Very little," she
answered with a cold shiver. "Do what I tell you," she
charged. "The diamond must stay with me until you're ready.
I'll send Dayrne and some men to help with the digging.
He'll act as a messenger, also. Send him to me at the private
temple by the Red Foal River as soon as you're done!"

Rashan ran back inside to organize his priests, and Chenaya
ran to her horse. There was no sign of Reyk. The dust stung
her eyes as she leaped astride her mount and raced away. The
streets were almost empty, but still she nearly rode down an
unwary pedestrian. He cursed, and she cursed, and then she
raced on.

People were huddled in doorways, in nooks and alleys, under carts, behind barrels and crates, all cowering down, faces half covered with shawls or cloaks or collars. On the docks, ships and timbers groaned and creaked. Sails snapped like angry whips, and riggings hummed wildly. Rising white-caps danced on the surface of the sea.

Chenaya sped through the Gate of Gold, at last catching sight of Reyk as the falcon followed overhead. In no time she was at the southern gate of Land's End. She pounded furi-ously on it with her fists. "Let me in!" she shouted. "Let me in!"

The stablemaster opened the gate for her. She raced past him without explanation and rode for the training fields. There she found Dayrne running his gladiators through drills even in the face of a budding storm. He brightened when he saw her, but she had no time for friendship.

"Take as many men as can leave right now!" she told him loudly enough for everyone to hear. His jaw dropped when he heard her speak. Then he snapped it shut. He knew her well, and he knew by her face alone when she was deadly serious. "Take shovels and do what Rashan tells you." She started to turn away, then paused long enough to add, "Some of you may have to hold off Walegrin and his men. Don't let him interfere."

She sped away, taking the memory of Dayrne's sudden grin as she crossed the field and pulled up before the armory. She dismounted. The door was unlocked. Rushing past the racks of wooden training weapons, she drew down four good swords with sheaths, whose weight and balance suited her. With the one she wore at her belt, that made five. She prayed they would be enough.

Carrying the swords under one arm, she mounted clumsily again. Reyk sprang from the armory's roof edge and screamed shrilly to let her know he was still with her. She rode off, weaving among the banks of huge training machines, casting a glance toward the stables, pleased to see Dayrne's force already assembling there.

At the east wall of Land's End was another double-doored gate with a wooden bar. Without dismounting, she wrestled with it, nearly dropping her armload of weapons, but managing. She sped through, leaving the doors to bang in the wind.

The waters of the Red Foal lashed the shoreline furiously.
She paid little attention, but rode straight for her private
temple to Savankala. It stood, white and beautiful and open-
roofed, a circular arrangement of eight slender columns, just
above the shore. She jumped off the horse, clutching her
swords.

The sky churned above her, as if she were the center of a
great disturbance. It was not her, though. It was the diamond.
Forces were marshaling, forces that would steal the diamond
back or destroy it. The priests of Ranke had not suffered the
magic-stealing destruction of the Nisibisi Globes of Power,
which had robbed Sanctuary of so much arcane vitality. Their
magic was still quite formidable. Already, in the strangely
colored clouds, she could feel things probing, searching,
taking shape.

Here, at her own temple, she stood the best chance of
facing whatever shape their magic took. Also, out here beyond
the city wall, there was far less threat to the townspeople.
Chenaya ran up the three steps, across the round marble floor,
to the small altar. Twin braziers stood at either end, kept
always burning, tended each day by Rashan. She laid her
swords down upon the altar and added to them the one she
wore. She cast away their sheaths, exposing the bright blades.

Chenaya lifted each blade and prayed over it, then shoved
it deep into the coals of a brazier. There was a small chest
near one end of the altar where Rashan kept the fragrant
incense, *kasabahr*, favored by the sun-god. She scooped two
bountiful handfuls and cast them on the coals. Smoke and
sweet scent rose swirling up, and she prayed again, consecrat-
ing the blades in the heat and fumes, and with her prayers.

The air screamed suddenly. Out of the vortex of clouds, a
pair of demons came shrieking down, the vanguard of an
army taking form in the demented sky above the temple. The
demon's eyes burned redly, and they reached for her as they
dived, slavering, fanged mouths yawning.

Chenaya gave a scream of her own, snatched one of the
swords from the coals. The blade shone, endowed with a
white heat the braziers alone could never have achieved. It
trailed smoke and light as she swung at the first demon. A red

flash erupted, the demon wailed in pain, darting aside, and the blade's light dimmed a little.

The second demon flew at her. Again she swung, striking at the neck as she sidestepped, and again there came a red flash as sword touched demon flesh. Twice more she chopped. Each time the flash nearly blinded her, and the sword dimmed a bit more. The demon emitted a piercing cry of pain. It seemed no more to the eye than a creature of gas and cloud, but Chenaya felt the impact of her blows. It clutched its vaporous body suddenly, and with taloned fingers, as if to end its agony, it ripped itself apart and discorporated.

Chenaya had no time to cheer her victory. A rain of demons fell upon her then. She swung her blade in a dazzling arc, driving them back, striking a clawed hand, severing it in a red flash. It dissolved into nothingness before it hit the ground, and the demon wailed. Others pressed her, and her sword dimmed, each blow having less and less effect.

Abruptly, the glow wavered and faded from her blade altogether, and it was just a sword again, its metal scorched and blackened. Before she could react, a demon sprang at her. One hand tangled in her hair, and she screamed with pain, while its other hand ripped open her chiton and closed on the purse and the diamond within. Chenaya tried to push it off, and though her fists beat on nothing tangible, still it struggled and clung on, grappling with the leather thong about her neck.

Then a sword swung down, passing harmlessly through the creature's skull. Chenaya twisted enough to see Daphne, crouched on the altar and swinging ferociously, but ineffectively, at the hideous shapes that swam around her.

"The consecrated swords!" she cried to Daphne. "Use those!"

Daphne understood at once. She drew a blade and swung it in one practiced motion, and a burst of scarlet erupted over her head as a demon died. The red glow reflected spectacularly on the silver links of the manica she wore on her sword arm. "Nice!" the princess muttered. With a weird smile she chopped at the demon wrestling Chenaya, slaying it.

Chenaya spun toward a brazier, grabbing a pair of swords. She whirled them twice, sectioning a creature as it reached for her. Cold hands raked suddenly at her back, and she cried with pain and despair as the severed thongs gave way, and the purse fell to the floor. The diamond spilled out, glowing like a compressed beam of sunlight.

A demon dived for the jewel, but a golden brown streak beat him to it. Reyk climbed again, clutching the Fire in God's Eye in his razor talons. Immediately, the demons forgot Chenaya and Daphne and swept up into the sky after the falcon.

Daphne wiped the sweat from her brow. Blood flowed from a trio of lined cuts on her unarmored left arm. She glanced down from the altar where she stood. "You'd better have a damn good explanation, mistress," she said with her usual mocking lilt on the final word.

Chenaya ran out between a pair of columns to follow Reyk's darting flight. The demons were too close, too swift, and too many for Reyk to avoid very long. She gave a sharp whistle. The raptor folded his wings tightly and plummeted earthward, momentarily leaving the demons behind. Chenaya held out her gloved arm, and Reyk landed, dropping the jewel. Immediately, she sent him up again, set down one of her blades, and grabbed the diamond from the floor.

"I wish you hadn't done that," Daphne muttered, glancing at the charging demons and, briefly, at her sword. Its light was almost gone. Still, she struck fearlessly at the first to come near enough.

Then Dayrne was there, too. Picking up the sword Chenaya had set down, he lashed out, cleaving a demon in midair. "Rashan's ready!" He shouted, shielding his eyes against the unexpected flash. "Go!"

Chenaya threw down her blade and grabbed another from the brazier. Daphne did the same, taking the last of the consecrated weapons. "We all go!" Chenaya called back.

"I don't have a horse!" Daphne cried. "Go on!"

Chenaya ran toward her own mount, clutching sword and jewel. "Ride with Dayrne!" she ordered, throwing herself into the saddle. "If I go down, one of you get this thing to Rashan!"

She rode as fast as the horse could carry her, swinging her sword wildly at the pursuing demons. The air shimmered with flashes of red as creatures swarmed around her and tried to drag her off, caught her reins and tried to tear them from her hands or gnaw them in two, as they ripped at her hair and clothes. She felt blood trickle down her back. Though they were physically weak, their claws were sharp.

The guards at the Gate of Gold saw her coming and flung themselves into the ditches on either side of the road. She risked a glance over her shoulder as they scrambled up, shouting curses. Dayrne and Daphne were right behind her. The demons had no interest in them at all. It was the jewel they were after.

She raced up Safe Haven Street and onto the Avenue of Temples. The way was suddenly blocked by gladiators and priests all clustered at the corner of the Rankan Temple. At her cries they turned, dropping shovels and tools, and scattered out of the way. A wide, black pit yawned before her. Even as her eyes widened in surprise, she felt the horse's muscles bunch. She hugged the animal with her knees as it leaped the pit and crashed to the other side, its great hooves hurling dirt.

All the way up the steps of the temple, she fought demons, until the fire faded from her consecrated blade. She threw it down, screaming with frustration, and clutched the diamond to her breasts as the demons swarmed around her. But Dayrne and Daphne were swiftly at her side, their blades still bright and glowing. "Get inside!" Dayrne shouted, pushing her toward the temple entrance. "Rashan's waiting! We'll try to hold these things here!"

Chenaya ran inside. A pair of young acolyte priests heaved the great doors closed behind her. It did no good. The demons followed, passing right through the heavy wood, like ghosts.

"Here!" Rashan called from the altar at the front of the temple. Savankala's sunburst had been lowered on its golden chains until its points touched the floor. Rashan stood before it, waving frantically to her. A half-dozen priests waited on each chain to hoist it aloft again.

"Hurry!" Rashan urged as she reached his side. Demons flew down the aisles toward them. "Place it right in the center," he instructed, pointing to a position on the sunburst.

"Where?" she cried in confusion, staring. Only a couple of grooves and notches had been carved into the metal, far too wide to hold the Fire in God's Eye. "There's no mounting!"

Rashan snatched the diamond from her and held it to the sunburst. Then he took something from his robe pocket, slammed it over the diamond, gave it a twist, and stood back.

Within a strange bubble of translucent blue, the Fire in God's Eye began to shine with a greater light, igniting the sunburst, itself. As it had last night when she first brought the diamond, the sunburst exploded with a pure white luminescence that filled the temple. The priests cried out, shielding their eyes, falling to the floor to hide their faces. The demons, too, shrieked with despair. As the light touched them, they broke apart like brittle things, and the pieces wafted away into nothingness.

When the last demon was gone, the light from the sunburst ebbed. All that remained was a soft golden glow that issued from the sunburst's heart.

Chenaya rose to her feet and helped Rashan to his. "What was that bubble?" she asked breathlessly. "That thing you put over the diamond?"

A rare small grin broke over Rashan's face. "Beysib glass," he answered. "It's something new they've started making while you've been gone. There wasn't time to sculpt a proper mounting into the metal, so I improvised."

Chenaya raised an eyebrow in amazement. "A bowl?" she said.

The old priest shrugged. "It worked, didn't it?" He turned and gazed at the sunbrust. Tentatively, he reached out and touched it with his fingertips. It was more than a symbolic image now. It was holy. It contained a fragment of the sun-god's power. "The Rankan priests will try to seize it back," he murmured lowly so his fellow priests wouldn't overhear.

Chenaya shook her head. "No. Since I was successful, they know it is Savankala's will. They still have the twin stone. The Bright Father has not forsaken Ranke, but now his favor also falls on Sanctuary."

There was a heavy, frantic pounding on the temple doors, and shouts from the other side. At Rashan's nod, the acolytes nearest drew back the bar and tugged them open. The entrance immediately filled with gladiators ready to do battle. When they saw that the fight was already over, they lowered their weapons, looking almost disappointed.

Daphne sighed. "Well, since there's nothing more to do in here," she said to Chenaya, "you should come see what they dug up from under the cornerstone."

They all backed outside. On the ground near the pit lay the shroud-covered form from Chenaya's visions. She bent down and lifted the cloth slowly from its face. "Ugh!" was all she managed. She moved quickly away, scanned the sky, and whistled Reyk down. She wrapped his jess around her hand and gave him a soothing stroke.

"Looks a lot like Kadakithis the morning after our wedding night," Daphne said. She nudged Dayrne in the ribs. "I was kind of hard on him his first time."

Dayrne's expression betrayed nothing. "I should hope it was the other way around," he answered.

Leyn gestured for some of the gladiators to carry the thing away. Then he turned to Chenaya and Rashan. "It wasn't a body at all," he explained. "Rather, pieces of many bodies all stitched clumsily together to make a simulacrum of a corpse." He rubbed the back of his head. "For the life of me, I can't figure why someone would go to that kind of trouble."

"To pollute the temple," Rashan answered, his eyes filling with a sudden understanding. "Vashanka demanded a human sacrifice to consecrate this place. It was to become one of the Great Temples of the Empire, but from the beginning things kept going wrong in the construction. Rooms collapsed, ceilings leaked, columns cracked, and it never quite seemed to get finished." He folded his arms into his sleeves and stared into the hole they had made in the road. "But this was not a proper sacrifice at all. There never was a consecration. Whoever put this *thing* here saw to that." He clapped his hands with new joy. "We must have a new consecration! A celebration!"

Chenaya caught Rashan's sleeve. "No sacrifices," she told him. "The barbarous Vashanka is forever lost. Savankala frowns on such practices. This will be a Great Temple now, but only if you heed Him."

Rashan looked at her for a moment, then made a deep bow. "I heed the word of Savankala," he said reverently, "and I heed his true daughter."

Chenaya looked at him piercingly. She turned to Dayrne and touched his huge arm. Then she turned back to Rashan. "I lied to you about that," she said abruptly, "to convince you to follow my orders. In the desert, I made a pact with the sun-god. There is a bond between us, yes. One that you do not understand and that I will not explain. What transpired is very personal and very private." She looked at Dayrne again, reached out for his hand, and interlocked her fingers with his. "In any case, He has a sincere desire to spread His worship here. Ranke has become moribund. It's an empire without a future. However, in exchange for my bringing the Fire in God's Eye to Sanctuary, the Bright Father has agreed to stay out of my life. My fate is my own again."

Dayrne stared down at the hand he held, so small against his own, yet filled with strength. "What does that mean?" he asked, his confusion plain.

She smiled at him. "Don't worry. You and I will discuss it over the days and nights to come." She let go of him then, catching the gleam in Daphne's eyes. "But not now. Right now, I think we'd better refill this hole before Walegrin comes along."

"So you see," Chenaya said frankly, standing before a full court in the Hall of Justice, meeting the hostile gaze of Molin Torchholder who stood at the side of Prince Kadakithis's great chair as her cousin squinted over the document she had given him. "I did not inherit Land's End. Knowing the Rankan law, my father left it to Dayrne. You know Lowan's writing. You have his seal."

Kadakithis looked utterly uninterested. He handed the document back to Molin and folded his hands in the lap of his expensive silk robe as he gazed down at Dayrne, who stood just behind Chenaya. "Then why didn't your man simply explain this to Molin when he came to visit?"

"Because it's a forgery!" Molin Torchholder muttered, casting the document to the floor. It slithered down the few steps of the dais from the throne to Chenaya's feet. "A clever forgery!"

Chenaya declined to pick the document up. She merely smiled patiently at her uncle. She liked to see him twitch. "Because he didn't know about it. Father told only me where he kept his will, and as you know, cousin"—she nodded to Kadakithis again—"I've been out of town."

Kadakithis waved a hand under his nose as if to shoo away a fly. "Well, it all looks legal to me—the signature, the seal, the whole business. It is a prime piece of real estate, Molin, and I don't blame you for trying. But I'm afraid it belongs to Dayrne now."

Dayrne stepped forward, the smug glee on his usually stern face almost enough to make Chenaya chuckle. But now wasn't the time for that. "No," Dayrne said gruffly. "It belongs to Cheyne. Rankan law says she can't inherit property, but it doesn't prevent her from owning property. I sold Land's End back to her this morning"—he looked straight at Molin—"for a single gold soldat." He pulled the gold coin from his waistband and held it up for all to see. A murmur of restrained amusement ran around the court while Molin fumed.

Dayrne and Chenaya turned as one and marched from the Hall of Justice, across the courtyard, and out into Vashanka's Square where their friends and comrades were waiting. "Well?" Ouijen said eagerly. "What happened?"

A slow grin spread across Chenaya's face.

"You should have seen Molin," Dayrne whispered, drawing them all closer.

Daphne clapped her hands and laughed. "It worked!" she cried before Gestus shushed her.

Dismas sighed with melodramatic relief. "Thank the gods!" he said. "I practiced all night on that signature. I didn't think I'd ever get it right!"

Chenaya's grin brightened into a smile as she reached up and rumpled Dismas's hair. "You?" she teased. "The best thief and forger ever sentenced to an arena anywhere?"

They walked across the square and out the Processional Gate. The clouds over Sanctuary had vanished. The sky was a wonderful blue, and the sun shone warm and golden. A fresh wind blew up from the sea. Chenaya stared that way, watching the tops of the masts of ships rocking to and fro along the wharves where she had sat two nights ago and thrown a painting into the water.

"You miss him, don't you?" Dayrne whispered in her ear.

She thought of her father, calling up all the good memories of times they had spent together. "I'll always miss him," she answered quietly.

"But not today!" Daphne snapped. "No morbid moods today." She pulled a fat purse from her belt and tossed it in the air, catching it again before Leyn could snatch it. "It's the Maze for us, my brothers, and a few drinks at the Unicorn. That's as good a place as any to spread the word and let this city know." She waited, looking at them and finally winking.

"Chenaya's back in town," she proclaimed. She turned then, tossing her raven hair over her shoulders, grabbing Leyn's arm, and pulling him along as she led the way.

"Somehow," Dayrne muttered with a weak half-smile, "I think it knows."

WEB WEAVERS

Lynn Abbey

Sanctuary had been quiet since Theron's loyalists pulled out. A hundred people, certainly no more than two hundred, had straggled through the new gates to begin the long journey back to Ranke. The ordinary citizen of Sanctuary didn't miss a single one of them. The ordinary citizen of Sanctuary hadn't yet guessed that the city had been cut adrift, to sink or swim on its own strengths. Men and women who had spent their lives complaining about the Empire scarcely noticed it was gone.

For the undermanned garrison, the calm was a blessing. They desperately needed time to reorganize, to recruit new men, to train them, and to test their informant networks in the absence of the Stepsons, the 3rd, and the Mageguild Hazards. A week passed, and another. A storm rolled in from the sea. It rained for three days running, and when the skies cleared, the towering yellow-grey clouds above desert had collapsed. Farmers came to the temples with their thanksgiving offerings.

Walegrin had been brevetted to full commander of the garrison in Critias's stead. It came as a surprise to him. He expected that dubious honor to fall on Zalbar's shoulders. Zalbar hadn't taken a drink in over a year, and he was much more familiar with the corridors of power than a shag-officer like Walegrin, who had spent his life on duty in one imperial backwater post after another. Walegrin was no happier about

spending his days in an airless room hearing reports and
giving orders than Critias had been. Whenever the opportunity arose, he assigned himself to a street patrol.

An opportunity arose when the square sails of a Beysib
merchanter were sighted beyond the arms of harbor.

Sanctuary's harbor was its hope for a prosperous future.
Some ancient, forgotten god had amused himself (or, perhaps, herself) removing great bites of continental rock. The
anchorage was deep and calm within the tricky rip-current
that carried away the Red and White Foal sediments on every
tide. Since the days of the Ilsigi settlers, seafaring men had
shaken their heads: such a beautiful anchorage, and no good
reason to use it.

Then Shupansea and her fellow exiles began tortuous, ongoing negotiations with their enemies back in what they
called the Glorious Home. Progress was slow, all could not
be forgiven, but—if the exiles longed for the luxuries of their
past—a merchant or two could supply them.

The local merchants scented a fortune or two in the crates
and coffers piled on the wharf for the staring Beysib clientele.
They desperately wanted to want what the fish merchants
were selling, but trade was proving difficult to establish. To
mainland eyes, Beysib wares were strange, not intriguing;
weird rather than exotic. Fortunately the urge to bargain
transcended cultural, linguistic, and monetary boundaries. Each
successive Beysib merchant vessel carried more cargo for the
mainlanders to examine; each vessel was greeted by more
mainland merchants.

They were lined up along the wharf before the Beysib ship
cleared the offshore current. A sharp-witted merchant hoped
to make a fortune before noon. Walegrin and Thrusher mingled with the noisy throng to make sure those fortunes were
honest—merchant honest.

The Beysib ship came into the harbor with her galley oars
shipped and her rust-colored sails stretched tight. She rode
low in the water, but her lines showed speed despite her
heavy holds and metal-clad bow. A catapult rose from her
stern; she'd burn the sails of anything foolhardy enough to
chase her. The exiles insisted that the ship, and her sisters,
were their homeland's cargo vessels—lumbering relations of

their warships. It might be that the fish-folk were lying
through their staring eyes, but no Sanctuary sailor felt the
urge to challenge them.

"Pirates each and every one of them. Barbarians," Thrusher
muttered as Beysib sailors swarmed over the rigging as the
ship drew alongside the wharf. "They think we're animals,"
Thrush continued. "They think we've got no souls because
we don't have fish eyes like them. Don't think they've made
a square deal with us since their first ship put in here. Stealin'
us blind is what they're doing. I'll bet they're selling us
garbage."

Walegrin grunted noncommittally; he wouldn't take his
friend's bet. For all that he'd been born a thrall, Thrusher was
a snob. As far as the commander could tell, the Beysib were
getting insect egg cases, uncured pelts, and barrels of swamp
beer for such goods as caught a mainland eye. The Beysib
might be selling garbage—Walegrin couldn't be sure—the
Sanctuary merchants definitely were.

The two soldiers broke up a fistfight between Beysib sailors and Sanctuary laborers. They fished a careless merchant
out of the harbor. A red-haired Ilbarsi offered them a bribe of
pickled passion fruit. A Rankan offered them pearls if they'd
guard a certain triple-locked chest against all comers. They
took the fruit, and took the Rankan to the palace lockup for
stealing. The carnival was still going strong when they returned to the wharf.

A woman with a donkey cart blocked their way. The wharf
could support a three-horse dray, but there were drainage
gaps between the diagonally laid planks. The donkey was
sweating in its harness; the woman was pulling the donkey;
and the wheels were wedged into the gaps.

Walegrin nudged Thrusher. The woman had to be new in
town. Only a stranger would lead the donkey along the wharf
rather than across it, much less own a cart that could get *both*
wheels stuck.

"I don't understand it," the woman explained as the two
men made a barrier between her and the unamused crowd.
She was almost as frantic as the donkey.

"We'll get you out of here," Walegrin muttered. He took
the woman's shawl and wrapped it over the donkey's eyes.

Donkeys were smarter than horses, but not by much. "Never done this before, have you?"

"Why, no . . . When the other ships came in, my brother-in-law was home . . ."

Walegrin walked away to exchange places with Thrusher. He got a firm grip on the single axle, then nodded his head, lifted, and scuttled sideways as Thrush got the donkey moving.

"No! No! Not *that* way. I've got to get out to where they're unloading."

The two men exchanged an evening's conversation in a glance. The cart settled back onto its axle, free now, but still blocking traffic.

"The length of an axle is set by the prince's decree," Walegrin recited to the woman, who was, by then, in tears. "It's matched to the width of these planks and the width of the gap between them." He handed the shawl back to her. "This cart gets stuck out there and I'll have to impound it. I'll have to take it to the palace and it'll go to firewood unless you pay a fine of two soldats."

The woman's tears ceased; she turned pale enough to frighten the commander. There was no fine for women fainting on the wharf, but he had no desire to have his arms full of drooping femininity. To his immense relief she squared her shoulders and started breathing normally again.

"Is it permitted to tie a cart here—by the cobblestones?"

Walegrin nodded.

"Then I shall carry my goods myself. I cannot risk my brother-in-law's cart. I do not have two soldats."

It was the second time she'd referred to her brother-in-law, and both times she seemed to shrink as she uttered the words. She hadn't mentioned a father or a son, nor a brother or husband; not even a sister's husband. Walegrin looked at her with the beginnings of sympathy. Slaves had more rights than a childless widow cut off from her blood family. "I don't make the laws, goodwife," he said, taking another step toward her. "I'll carry your goods back here for you."

For a moment it seemed she had been too broken by her misfortunes to take advantage of Walegrin's offer. Her eyes widened; they were blue. It was possible that, if she were not so thin and anxious, she'd be a handsome woman. It was hard to tell, and the commander was about to turn away when she made up her mind to accept his offer.

Since the Beysib traders and their mainland counterparts did not share a spoken language, bargaining was done with gestures. Factotums recorded the transaction in the appropriate languages on parchment, which was then torn and divided among the principals. In theory, there was no need for shouting, but the clamor along the wharf was guaranteed to give all but the deaf a headache.

Chests and bales were still coming off the ship, to be opened on the first empty patch of wharf the merchant encountered. There was no such thing as a clear path and the indigenous criminals were having a field day. Walegrin spotted a light-fingered youth in the act of lifting a sizable purse. Their eyes met, and the thief kept lifting. A half-dozen overflowing chests separated the law from the lawbreaker, and even if they hadn't, Walegrin had all he could do to keep up with the woman.

She strode past more gimcrack and gewgaw dealers than Walegrin cared to count. Personally, he saw nothing that would tempt him to crack his nest egg. But he was a soldier; women were supposed to be different.

There was a hierarchy in the disorder. The frivolities which the fish judged most likely to please the natives were crammed together at the landward end of the wharf. The consignment goods destined for the exiles were more carefully displayed closer to the ship. Midway between them three silk sellers displayed bolts of cloth and finished garments.

Silk had been known since the Ilsigi Kingdom. Mainland silks were thick and brittle compared to the fiber the Beysib Empire produced in vast quantities. They took dye poorly and, in any event, not even the Ilsigi alchemists had conjured colors like those the Beysib set in their silks. They shimmered in the sunlight; any fool could see Beysib silks were worth their weight in gold.

Walegrin was not, therefore, surprised when the woman stopped to examine them, although how she thought she could buy silk when she was scared witless by a two-soldat fine was a question he couldn't answer. Why she would buy it was another puzzling question. For all its beauty, Beysib silk was not selling well in Sanctuary. It came in two equally impractical varieties: gossamer sheer that snagged and tore on a whisper and damasked over a horsehair foundation so stiff that the cloth supported itself.

Perhaps in the Beysib Empire, where it was both cool and dry the year around, such cloth could be made into wearable garments. In Sanctuary, a person could be noticed in Beysib silk, but never comfortable. It was comfort, more than any sense of propriety, that drew Shupansea and the other Beysib women out of their bare-breasted costumes and into traditional Rankene gowns.

The woman studied each length of fabric. She twisted it, and tugged it, and got down on her knees to examine the underside. The merchants began to get hopeful, then she started walking again.

"What *are* you looking for?" Walegrin protested as his companion neared the expensive end of the wharf. "It's not going to get any cheaper."

She looked at him as if he'd grown another head. "I haven't seen what I need," she announced, and kept moving.

Walegrin tossed a round-bottom jug back to its owner and scurried to catch up with her. They approached the stern gangplank. Beysibs were buying from Beysibs, wailing in their peculiar language over merchandise only a fish could find attractive. The woman was moving slower now. She stopped beside a greasy man hawking ceramic snakes and indicated that she wished to bargain.

The Beysib was almost as confused as the commander. The woman slashed her hand and shook her head as he lifted one garish reptile after another out of its case. Walegrin had a very crude understanding of the Beysin language, but if he had any hope of getting off the wharf before midday, he was going to have to intervene.

He confined the woman's gesturing hands in his own. "The man's shown you everything he's got. You keep pointing at empty boxes, and he keeps telling you that there's nothing in them to sell."

"You understand him . . . ? Then, tell him I want to buy the dross."

"The what?"

"The dross . . . *Dross*—the packing around his wretched statues!"

"Dross?"

Walegrin shook his head. He knew several fish words for garbage, a few of which would likely turn the merchant's bald scalp a brilliant shade of red. He knew the fish word for purchase—if buying a woman's time at a brothel was the same as buying something from a merchant. He opened his eyes as wide as he could and started talking. If his luck ran true to form he was about to create a scandal.

The merchant roared with laughter. He slapped his naked belly and turned the crimson color Walegrin had so hoped not to see. His eyes bugged out. "You joking."

Walegrin swallowed hard and, adding more gestures than he'd used the first time, tried again. He got the feeling that the greasy fish understood him well enough and that the third and fourth tries were simply for the amusement of the other Beysib who'd wandered over to watch the barbarian make a fool of himself.

The ceramics seller guessed that the game had gone on as long as it could. The gales of laughter ceased; he flashed his fingers twice and muttered *koppit,* which had become the generally accepted name for any of Sanctuary's myriad copper coins.

"Twenty copper bits," Walegrin told the woman.

"Now explain to him that I will pay him forty when he comes back next time, but that I can't pay him anything now."

This time it took no effort at all for Walegrin to show whites all around his green eyes. "Lady, you must be out of your mind."

She was stung by his sarcasm, but clung to her dignity. "I am a weaver. When I have finished with his dross it will be worth a hundred times his twenty copper bits."

Walegrin dug into the pouch at his hip. "Fine. You can owe *me.* I'm not going to make a monkey out of myself telling your lunacy to this fish."

Irregular copper disks rained into the merchant's hands. He poured them into his coin coffer, then demanded a silver coin for the box the dross was in. Walegrin threw the coin so hard

it bounced, and disappeared between the planks into the
harbor. The fish revealed his painted teeth. Walegrin was
more careful with the second coin. Walegrin picked up the
box carefully; it would have cost another five coppers for
rope to bind it shut.

"They throw this stuff into the harbor at the end of the
day," the commander complained. "It's garbage. You've
paid half a soldat for *garbage* you could have fished out of
the water tomorrow morning."

She would have preferred to whisper; she would have
preferred not to reply at all, but he was her partner now and
she felt she owed him an answer. "I know that, but once the
salt water touches the dross, it's ruined."

"Lady—"

"Theudebourga. My name is Theudebourga."

Walegrin scowled. "Lady, how can you ruin garbage?"

Theudebourga proceeded to tell him. The wharf was still
crowded; they had to go slowly. By the time they had returned to the cart Walegrin knew more about the pernicious
effects of seawater on garbage than he'd wanted to know.
Thrusher took one look at the pair of them and instinctively
knew to ask no questions until after the box was loaded and
the woman on her way.

"The Vulgar Unicorn's probably serving by now," the
hawk-faced man suggested. "You look like you could use
something to take the taste from your mouth."

The commander allowed himself to be led from the wharf
in silence. The Vulgar Unicorn was open, but it was undergo-
ing one of its infrequent cleanings. The shutters and doors
were wide open, the common room was awash with sunlight,
and workmen were busily repairing a month of damage. The
two soldiers kept going until they found themselves beyond
the Maze.

Once the Shambles had been as rough a neighborhood as
the Maze, though without the Maze's perverse reputation.
Later it had swarmed with the dead, the half-dead, and the
other assorted leftovers of Sanctuary's magic troubles. Now it
was the quarter where newcomers made their homes in abandoned buildings. It was fractious enough that the soldiers
knew it as well as they knew the Maze, but there were also

signs of prosperity. Well-fed children in carefully mended clothes played games beside their mothers, who created gardens wherever sunlight touched the ground.

Not all these diligent women were from way beyond Sanctuary's newly painted walls. Some had been widowed in the years of chaos, some had seized their opportunity and exchanged the Promise of Heaven or the Street of Red Lanterns for ordinary domesticity. Walegrin knew most of them by name, and a few of them much better, but it was understood these days in Sanctuary that you didn't talk about the past without invitation.

The Tinker's Knob was typical of Shambles taverns: salvaged from the wreckage, it had a lingering charred odor, and a cellar no one cared to enter after sundown. Its sole claim to fame, and the inspiration for its name, came from a hammered plaque depicting the exploits of a singularly well endowed tinker.

Walegrin looked right past it.

"Want to talk?" Thrusher asked, pushing a wooden mug across the table.

The commander shook his head, but the skeleton of the story rose out of him. "What's happening to this place?" he asked rhetorically. "An honest soldier helps a foolish woman buy garbage from a merchant whose ancestors were snakes and fish."

Thrusher shook his head. "You could've left when the orders came. You could still leave," he stated the obvious.

Walegrin drained his mug and poured another from the pitcher. He hadn't seriously considered throwing his lot in with the Stepsons when they left. In three years he could convert his officer's commission into a tidy pile of gold and enough land to support a handful of heirs. All his adult life he'd been planning for that conversion. Yet he stayed in Sanctuary where there was no guarantee the Torch or the prince would acknowledge the years he'd spent in the *Empire's* service.

"Damn your eyes—this is my porking *home*!" He slammed the mug against the table somewhat more forcefully than he'd intended. The entire room went wary. Thrusher sat back in

his chair, taking careful measure of his commander between
cautious sips of ale.

There was no doubt the last few years had aged Walegrin.
Gods knew, those years aged everyone they hadn't killed.
Age had softened the angles of the commander's face, giving
it the semblance of wisdom without compromising its strength.
He was a good deal calmer than he'd been before leading his
men back to the city of his birth with the secret of Enlibar
steel almost five years ago.

Thrusher reckoned he might head north to the capital himself if the haunted, self-cursed Walegrin reappeared—and
with that reckoning, the lieutenant got a handle on his friend's
problem.

"Women, eh? The woman on the wharf?"

Walegrin grunted and spun his mug between his fingers.
He preferred not to talk about women. His father had been
killed because of a woman—killed and thoroughly cursed.
Walegrin wasn't certain that he'd inherited the curse; his
half-sister, Illyra, said he hadn't. But even S'danzo Sight
couldn't say for certain where ordinary bad luck left off and a
curse began.

For Walegrin, the dividing line between luck and curse ran
straight through Chenaya Vigeles. Chenaya was the sort of
woman a poor man dreams about: beautiful and wealthy,
sensual and wealthy, eager and wealthy. When Molin Torchholder
said the palace needed eyes and ears at the sprawling Vigeles
estate, Walegrin volunteered. Even then Chenaya had a reputation that would have given a wiser man pause. And that led
to the question: Was it bad luck or stupidity that catalyzed a
curse?

Chenaya took a fancy to him, much as a breeder fancies a
particular bull or stallion at the stalls. She'd taken him to her
bedroom and given him experiences he could never afford on
the Street of Red Lanterns. For a week, maybe two, but
certainly no more than a month, Walegrin dwelt in heaven.
Then Chenaya figured out just whom her lover worked for.
Molin Torchholder's distrust of his niece was a paltry thing
compared to Chenaya's hatred of her uncle. A lesser woman
might have killed him while he lay defenseless in her bed, but
not Chenaya.

The battle lines were drawn and Walegrin of the garrison was both weapon and battlefield. When Chenaya was finally driven from the city—no thanks to the Torch—Walegrin forswore the company of women. He'd need to take a wife when he converted his commission, but a wife was not necessarily the same as a woman.

She's back.

The word came a month ago, in the midst of the awkward investigation into the midnight assassination of the Torch's estranged wife and Chenaya's father.

Be my eyes, my ears, again.

This time Walegrin risked his carefully nurtured patronage with Sanctuary's most powerful bureaucrat. She'll kill me, he'd argued, which, though true, wasn't the real reason he feared Land's End. He knew he wouldn't mind dying if she took him upstairs first. The Torch hadn't pressed the issue, and Chenaya had yet to cross Walegrin's path, but the commander couldn't talk to a woman without thinking about Chenaya. He was as jumpy as a cat on a griddle.

Thrusher knew about Chenaya. There wasn't a man in Sanctuary who didn't know something about the legendary Chenaya. Thrusher even knew about Walegrin and Chenaya. He'd asked for details at the beginning, and, after receiving a florid description of experiences he would never know himself, lost interest. He didn't know how Chenaya haunted Walegrin's idle thoughts; he couldn't imagine confounding Chenaya with a timid, scrawny weaver.

They finished the pitcher and returned to their patrolling. Their camaraderie was broken for the moment. The afternoon was an endless succession of circuits along the wharf and past the customs and storage houses. The big black ship had pulled in all but one of its hoists. The fish merchants were up at the palace making private transactions, but in general the fish stayed to themselves. Cross-culture brawls were the exception rather than the rule.

The big black ship might stay in the harbor a week or more, but after the first day few paid any attention to it. Walegrin returned to a commander's duties. Once a day he went over to the caravan gate to inspect whomever the other officers might have recruited. Walegrin pointed out that the recruit would receive the same wages as a soldier in the Rankan army—five soldats a month, less expenses—but he never said the recruit was *joining* the Rankan army. Business wasn't brisk, but the ranks were starting to fill. The third watch, formerly made up largely of Zip and his semi-feral commandos, was reinstituted. The two existing watches were reorganized. Thrusher went to the new unit and Walegrin found himself training a wet-behind-the-ears lieutenant named Wedemir.

Wedemir was short and dark, like Thrusher, but with a round face and flat forehead that fairly shouted Wriggly. He gave his age as twenty-two, the same age Walegrin was when he jumped from soldier to officer. Walegrin judged that the man was young for his years. At the very least Wedemir wasn't burdened with the shield of distrust that Walegrin had carried through his teens and twenties. There was no faulting Wedemir's record. He'd been on the barricades through the worst of the anarchy and seen things, no doubt, that he'd never told his close-knit family.

"My father's Lalo, the artist," the boy said defensively as he and Walegrin left the barracks on a get-acquainted patrol.

Walegrin grunted. Wedemir's mother was Gilla. His younger brother died in the False Plague Riots and his sister waited on the fish in the palace. Walegrin knew all that and more from the Torch's dossiers. For the moment, the commander was more interested in the movements of a woman coming from the Justice Hall toward the West Gate. He led Wedemir, still prattling about his family, toward the practice ground where Thrusher was explaining the difference between right and left to the newest recruits.

"I don't think they were ever very happy about me joining. Not that they'd ever say anything outright . . . Well, my mother would, but not my father . . ."

The woman turned. Walegrin caught a glimpse of her profile before Thrush's recruits came between them, not long enough to be sure if the woman was Chenaya or not. Probably not. Chenaya had little cause to come to the palace, and when she did she was usually dressed for war.

"Something wrong, Commander?" Wedemir asked.

Walegrin snapped to attention. He hadn't realized how

much time he spent absorbed in his own thoughts until Wedemir
had been glued to his side. Thrusher knew how to be invisi-
ble; Wedemir didn't. It wasn't the young man's fault, but it
kept both of them from relaxing.

"Wait here, I want to get something from the tower room."

"Can't I get it for you?"

"Gods below, you're not my servant, you're an officer in
the R—" Walegrin caught the untimely word on the tip of
his tongue. Just that morning the prince had proclaimed a
reduction in the hearth tax without once mentioning Ranke or
the Emperor. Whatever they were officers of, it wasn't the
Rankan army anymore. "Just *stay* here!"

Wedemir froze on the spot. Walegrin took the tower steps
two at a time. What he wanted was another glimpse of that
golden hair to tell him which way not to go with Wedemir.
He leaned out over the railing. The men on duty looked with
him and at him. The commander spotted his quarry arguing
with a water seller. The angle was still bad; he couldn't see
her face.

"What're you looking for?" one of the soldiers asked.

Walegrin gripped the rail with both hands and thought fast.
"I was looking to see if there were crowds gathering anywhere. Problems. Disorderlies. Don't want to bore my new
lieutenant."

"It's as quiet as a clam," the second soldier confirmed,
still scanning from street to street. "Just the way you like
it."

"But there's been complaints coming in all day from the
Uptown. Something died, from the sound . . . er, smell of
things. Nothing serious, though, an' it's not going anywhere
so I haven't sent anyone," the first soldier added.

"Something died?" the commander asked.

"We had at least four people come down here since dawn
to say that they can't stand the smell. We got nothing more
than that. Nobody's *seen* what died, they just say it smells
worse than the charnel house going fulltilt."

The golden-haired woman headed west. Uptown was east.

"We'll check it out."

Walegrin would have gone Uptown regardless of the gold-
haired woman. The soldiers in the tower had been recruited

from the men who came to Sanctuary to work on Molin's walls. To them, Uptown was just another quarter.

Wedemir's face tightened when Walegrin joined the words *died* and *Uptown* in the same sentence. Reflexively, the young man checked his weapons; just as reflexively, the fingers of his right hand made an Ilsigi wardsign. The commander didn't blame him, though he had no personal faith in gestures or amulets.

They went through the gate at a twenty-league pace. Urgency radiated from them, and the few people on the streets scuttled under the eaves to let them pass. The stench rose like a wall across Safe Haven.

"What died?" Wedemir asked, for although the odor was unlike anything in his experience it was profoundly organic and decayed.

Walegrin shrugged and adjusted his headband. Safe Haven was empty, all the windows were tightly shuttered. The commander could follow his nose, or he could trust his instincts. He chose his instincts and left the street for an alley and a flight of worn, stone steps. Wedemir was right behind him. Anyone who lived through *that* night would never forget this path.

They emerged in a burnt-out courtyard. The Peres house looked pretty much as it had since it burnt. Storms had tumbled a few more of the beams and a skeletal tree, but no one scavenged here for wood or charcoal. After the False Plague Riots there'd been a dozen burnt-out quarters; now only Peres remained. And would remain at least so long as anyone remembered.

A pillar of fire had surrounded the Peres house that night. It reached from the depths of hell to the heights of heaven. It illuminated a war between gods and demons, if not good and evil. Magic fueled it, and when it collapsed all magic was gone from Sanctuary. No one came straight out and said the Peres quarter was cursed, or blessed, by what happened, but it *was* shunned.

The stench hovered over the ruins, neither stronger nor weaker than it had been on Safe Haven. Walegrin held his breath. He reached into his memory for the tricks of perception every soldier had been forced to learn when magic was rampant. He knelt down and squinted.

Scraggly weeds and nettles with nasty, velvet leaves grew in the ashes, just as a feral sort of magic was creeping back into Sanctuary. Beneath the notice of reputable farmers, or mages, but good enough for the desperate. And not the source of the death stench.

Wedemir hunkered down beside his commander. "Should we have the priests come and burn it off?"

"Probably." Walegrin got to his feet. "Looks harmless enough to me, but what do I know about these things, eh?"

Wedemir was wisely silent. "The other place?" he asked after a moment.

Heavy vines grew across the windows and doors of the home of the missing and presumed dead Tasfalen Lancothis. They reminded everyone who passed that this was a place not to be tampered with. The Peres quarter was where magic died; the Lancothis quarter was where it lingered. There had always been ghosts in Sanctuary. The problem with Lancothis was not that it was haunted, but that it leaked.

Unpleasant faces appeared in the windows of Lancothis. Strange sounds oozed through its crumbling plaster. Flashes of light in colors the mind cared not to remember shot through the holes in its roof. Rumors said the house wasn't haunted; it was a prison for whatever had lost the fight over at Peres. The priests of Ils and Savankala professed not to know the truth. Those who did know hid that knowledge carefully.

"What's that?" Wedemir pointed to a second-story window where a tattered curtain waved in the harbor breeze. The vines around the window were broken. Withered leaves rustled in the breeze.

Walegrin frowned. He'd noticed the rupture right off, and hoped his new lieutenant was less observant. He'd sooner go to hell than into Lancothis. Someone would have to find out what had happened, but not him—not *this* afternoon—because whatever had happened here, it didn't stink. The breeze was clear and lightly scented with honeysuckle.

Gratefully choosing the lesser of two evils, Walegrin led the way back to Safe Haven, where they followed their noses instead of their assumptions. There were more false starts and dead ends, but finally they reached a house that made their guts heave and their eyes water. With one hand clapped over his face, Walegrin motioned for Wedemir to follow him into the courtyard.

The commander expected to see something vast and revolting; what he saw was an unhappy donkey and a high-wheeled cart, both unfortunately familiar.

Wedemir couldn't understand Walegrin's muttering. He lowered his hand from his face. "Wha . . . ? Ough! Gods—" He hastily re-covered his mouth and lurched toward the archway, where he could be heard heaving.

An anger approaching mindless fury kept Walegrin breathing. He strode across the yard to the reeking midden. He kicked aside a bit of straw. His worst suspicions rolled into the sunlight. Filling his lungs with the foul air, Walegrin bellowed her name.

"Theudebourga!"

Silence. Wedemir rejoined the commander. He didn't recognize the name, but he shouted it anyway. The air wasn't going to kill him, and he wasn't going to be able to stop breathing it. The stench wasn't as noticeable now that he'd purged himself, rather like the numbness that follows an injury.

"Theu-de-bour-ga!"

Walegrin grabbed a spar of firewood. He struck the iron rim of the cartwheel with such force that the firewood splintered and both men had to dodge the pieces. When they reopened their eyes a thin nervous woman stood in the archway, flanked by a passel of children and another woman holding an infant.

"What in the names of a thousand forgotten gods are you doing here?" Walegrin pointed the remnant of wood at the midden.

Theudebourga's eyes were as wide as any Beysib's and her quivering voice seemed to come from somewhere in the next quarter. "Schapping."

Walegrin glanced at Wedemir, who shrugged and shook his head. "Tell me that again," the commander said in his best threatening tones. "I didn't understand you."

The woman with the infant looked at Theudebourga, as did the children, then they all eased away from her.

"*Schapping*," she whispered, scarcely louder than the first time.

"Make sense, woman." Walegrin took a step toward her. He'd never struck a woman in anger or the line of duty, but the temptation was growing very strong.

Theudebourga fell to her knees. "Schapping . . . schapping . . ."

Wedemir risked his life and closed his hand over the commander's upraised arm. "Beating her won't help. She sounds foreign. I don't think she understands you."

"She understood me well enough when she got me to buy this witches' brew for her."

Wedemir released him. Sanctuary hadn't gotten so civilized that a man could stand on honor for a stranger. Theudebourga would have to stand for herself, which she did, scurrying over to the midden. She plunged her arm into the mess and came up with a fistful of sticky, stringy stuff. Holding it before her like a weapon or a shield, she advanced into Walegrin's reach.

"To make silk, you must schappe—get rid of the part of the cocoon that isn't silk."

In a corner of the commander's mind there was a mote of dusty knowledge whispering that silk didn't come into being as dyed, woven cloth, any more than wool or linen did. Wool came from sheep, and linen came from a plant, and silk . . . ? Did silk come from a cocoon?

When he thought about it, the garbage they had bought on the wharf did look like cocoons all wadded together. But that goo hanging over her fingers like so much melted cheese or worse . . . *that* couldn't possibly be silk.

"She's trying to make fools of us," Walegrin assured his lieutenant.

Wedemir wasn't so sure. He wasn't an artist like his father, but Lalo had taught him to keep an open mind about beauty. And Gilla, his mother, had taught him to keep an open mind about people. He extended his arm and allowed Theudebourga to drop the mess in his palm. It had a texture appropriate to its smell. Wedemir closed his eyes and remembered the few times he'd encountered real silk. He went past the slime and the stickiness to the fiber itself.

"I don't know, Commander Walegrin, but I think she's telling the truth."

Walegrin was, to say the least, unconvinced.

The other woman eased forward with her children and the infant. "Please, lord, I didn't know. Berge said we could make silk, and silk would make us rich. She said she learned how from her husband's people. I didn't know it would reek like this. It's not my fault. Punish *her* if you must. Take her away before my husband comes back. It's not my fault."

Walegrin didn't doubt Theudebourga was the driving force behind this debacle. Still, families shouldn't cast each other to the winds, or wolves, or soldiers. He scowled down at her, and the infant *stared*.

With a lamentable lack of tact Walegrin stared back. "It's almost a fish," slipped past his lips.

It was inevitable. In all other respects Beysib men were no different from any other. They frequented the Street of Red Lanterns and the Promise of Heaven. The marvel was that Walegrin had never seen a dark-haired, round-faced, *staring* child before.

The woman covered her baby's face with her shawl. Walegrin noticed that none of the other children had Beysib eyes. He looked at everything a second time. That wasn't dirt on their faces. Regrettably, it was all starting to make sense.

"When will your man be back?" he asked.

"Sundown, maybe later."

"Maybe never?"

The woman shook her head. "He'll be back. Dendorat comes back." A world of bitterness underlay her words.

"He'll beat you all when he finds this."

The commander's thoughts turned inward. It was easy to imagine Dendorat, because he could imagine himself feeling as Dendorat must feel. A man leaves his hearth and home to find a better life for them. He comes to the tail end of the Empire and, to his amazement, he finds a better life sweating on the walls of Sanctuary. He sends money to bring his wife and children to the promised land. The next thing he knows she's breeding, and he's the gods' happiest father waiting for a son who will never go hungry. But the son isn't his . . .

What can he do? What else can he do? He turns against his wife. He begins to wonder about the other children hung about his neck like millstones. The doubts gnaw at his gut, driving him to despair. Maybe he never beat his wife before, but he beats her now because she wears the face of his pain . . .

"Commander?"

Walegrin blinked. He wasn't half-S'danzo like his sister; he didn't have the Sight. But he'd wager next month's pay that he had the story right.

"Commander, what are we going to do?"

They were all looking at Walegrin. The commander knew what should be done. Of course, he was condemning these women and the children to misery, not to mention losing the money he had inadvertently invested in this lame scheme.

"You cannot do these things in the Uptown quarters," Walegrin explained apologetically, not meeting anyone's eyes. "Take rooms in the charnel quarters," he suggested, knowing the sorts who lived there. "Maybe they won't mind."

Theudebourga pointed at the courtyard well. "But we need *fresh* water."

She took Wedemir's hardening mess and washed it in the bucket. When she was finished the water wasn't fit to drink, but the white-gold fibers clinging to her wet fingers had begun to look like silk. She rubbed them dry in a corner of her shawl, then held them out for Walegrin to examine. The breeze in the courtyard wasn't enough to rustle a leaf or turn a hair, but it was enough to lift the wisps out of her hands.

"Clean, clear, fresh water," Theudebourga said as her palms emptied. "Anything less—the schappe clings and the silk is ruined.

Wisps tangled in the stubble on the commander's upper lip. He twitched, blew, finally caught them in his fingers. Softer than a whore's breast, soft as silk . . . Walegrin twirled them between thumb and forefinger, and let them spin away. He began to suspect he was throwing away a lot more than a few silver coins.

Wedemir interrupted again. "What *can* we do?"

Walegrin shook his head. The complaints they were getting about the smell would seem trivial when the gutters started running with Theudebourga's rinse water. He quoted from his mentor, Molin Torchholder: "We're guardians of the welfare of the city, not the guardians of any single citizen. There's nothing we can do." He turned to face Theudebourga. "I'm truly sorry, but you can't do this *schapping* here."

"But it doesn't last," Theudebourga insisted. "Only another day . . . Once the schappe is gone we must spun it into floss, then the floss has to be woven. Surely no one would complain about spinning and weaving?"

The commander shook his head. Beneath the tears and the pleadings and the wringing hands, this woman had the same temper as his Enlibar sword. Which, he decided, made it all the more important to stand firm.

"And when the weaving is finished, then you will sell the woven cloth," he continued for her. "And with your profits you'll bargain for more of this *dross* from the fish sellers. Then you'll make a bigger midden . . . and a bigger midden again the time after that. And you'll say at the prince's court of justice that you've *always* done it. The garrison came and didn't stop you . . .

"No, my lady, you won't catch me like that."

"It doesn't have to be like that," Wedemir objected.

"Don't go taking her part in this. I know what I'm talking about. When something's wrong, you stamp it out at the root. The longer you let it grow, the worse it gets." Walegrin continued to watch Theudebourga. None of this would be happening if he'd done his duty and impounded the damn donkey cart when he'd had the chance.

Theudebourga touched Walegrin's arm. "Please, don't abandon us; help us. You *know* I can do this. I learned this in Valtostin from my husband's family before the army came. We gathered broken cocoons in the spring, but the silk we made was never so fine as this will be. You believe me; I know you believe me."

Walegrin twisted away. It was easier to apprehend a murderer, or examine a corpse, than deal with a determined woman. "All right, until sundown tomorrow . . . I can go along with that, but no weaving, no spinning. When I come back here tomorrow night I want to find this place empty. Do you understand, *empty*? If I can't report that I couldn't find a trace of you, I will personally take all of you and your possessions and your silk down to the Swamp of Night Secrets and leave you there. Just one more day to stink up the air and poison the water, and then you're gone, do you understand me?''

Theudebourga straightened her shawl and her back. "We understand."

Wedemir didn't, but he held his peace. He'd been a soldier long enough to know the difference between hard bargaining and an order. Still, when he and Walegrin were through the archway and beyond hearing, he demanded an explanation.

"Do you realize what you've done to them? Do you think this man, Dendorat, will leave because they say so? He'll beat them, if he doesn't kill them. And the silk . . . The silk is *good*, Commander. Don't we care about what is *good*? They told me an officer must judge as well as follow orders. What do I do when I judge my orders to be wrong?''

Walegrin stopped short. There was nothing friendly in his expression when he faced the younger man. "If you're so concerned about right or wrong you should have apprenticed yourself to the magistrates. We're soldiers, *Lieutenant* Wedemir, we enforce the laws—the emphasis goes on *force*. No one loves a soldier. People don't think about us unless there's trouble somewhere. At best, we're useful bullies.''

There was an uncomfortable silence while Wedemir searched for words that would not compromise him, or enrage the commander. "I guess it's a good thing that you've only got a few more years.''

The commander resumed walking. They were at the harbor before he spoke again, weighing every word and hesitation. "It is my silver sitting in that midden, but that does not influence me; I counted it lost the moment it left me. I am not without sympathy. There is no question of the right of what they are doing, only that they are doing it in the wrong place. And I have done no wrong in forcing them to find a better place.''

"What better place? Where could they go where they'd have what they needed, and there wouldn't be complaints? The charnels? Downwind? Could you see those women and children lasting three days Downwind?''

Wedemir thought his questions had obvious answers, but
Walegrin scratched his ear and took them seriously.

"Well . . . They should be downwind, or at least not
upwind . . . They need clear water, but the water won't be
clear when they get done with it, so they need a stream that
goes straight to the rivers . . . That puts them outside the
walls in a villa. They don't have any money and that
Theudebourga, she'd never put her mark on an indenture . . .
A patron. They'd have to find someone with a villa who'd
tolerate the stench for a chance to get a bargain on the
finished silk."

"Which villa would you suggest: Eagle's Nest? Jubal's old
place now that the Stepsons are gone, or what about Land's
End with Chenaya and her gladiators?" Wedemir drawled.

For generations these three estates had marked the end of
Sanctuary and the beginning of the wilderness. Now they
were all being worked again, each in a different way, but the
meaning hadn't changed. At least the meaning hadn't changed
for Wedemir. As far as he was concerned they remained
equally inaccessible; he knew nothing of what had happened
between Walegrin and Chenaya. So when the commander
snarled that he'd see the women in hell first, the lieutenant
knew only that he had crossed into dangerous territory.

"I promised my parents I'd visit them if I came close to
home." It wasn't an absolute lie. Gilla was always glad to
see her eldest son; and he had a sudden need of his family.

Walegrin understood. "I'll go on ahead. No need to catch
up with me. You've learned enough for one afternoon, I
think."

There was an ache in Wedemir's gut, as if he'd drunk one
of Gilla's bitter purges. For a moment he felt cold and alone,
then he headed up familiar streets to the just-barely-respectable
quarter where his family had always lived. He sought a
meaning for the commander's hostility. He was an intelligent
youth with a lively imagination. It was impossible for him to
guess the truth of the matter, but that didn't stop him from
finding a satisfactory explanation: each estate he'd mentioned
was bound to the past or the Rankan Empire. The silk workers would need a different sort of patron. By the time Gilla

heard his thick-soled sandals on the stairs, Wedemir had his plan worked out.

Walegrin, in contrast, had no plan. He checked out the warehouses with a deliberately empty mind. He'd satisfied himself that the onus wasn't on his hands. His shoulders were relaxed when he crossed the empty caravan plaza on his way to the Bazaar. There was an emptiness in his gut—but that could be entirely attributed to hunger, and he knew just the remedy for that.

It was Sixthday—which was easier than remembering that it was also Eshi's Day, Spirit's Day, Sabellia's Day, or Somebody Else's Day—and on Sixthday, Walegrin ate dinner with Illyra and her family. There'd been times when he hadn't felt welcome here at all. Then last autumn, for no apparent reason, Dubro solemnly announced that his wife would be pleased to set a place for her brother at the week's-end table.

Their home had grown considerably over the years: a wall here, a roof there, a second anvil, and, most recently, a rebuilt forge with one bay for Dubro and a new one for his journeyman. Illyra's chamber with tasseled curtains stuck out to one side like an afterthought.

Illyra was happy, Walegrin told himself when he noticed that the curtains were roped tight, happier than she'd been when she sat in that airless room Seeing secrets for anyone who crossed the threshold. Hadn't she always said she couldn't See when she was happy? Illyra was happily surrounded by her family and neither he nor Dubro had to worry about what, or who, she Saw.

Walegrin didn't have to duck his head to enter this room, or worry that he'd break a stool when he sat down. Little Trevya saw him first and came racing across the hard-packed floor, her limp all but vanished. She shrieked as only a two-year-old could shriek when he scooped her into his arms. Trevya had always been fascinated by the bronze band across his forehead, but lately she'd discovered a more intriguing toy: the heavy straw-colored braids the band was supposed to confine.

"Want ride!" she trilled when she'd caught them in her fists.

With a patient sigh he leaned forward and let her pull his head toward the ground.

"Again!" She gave the braids a demanding yank.

This is the last time, Walegrin thought as he straightened up. *The little beggar's stronger than she thinks . . . and getting heavier.* But he was still playing the game when Illyra came through the other doorway.

"Wale—why, you're all covered with spider silk!"

It was a tone they all knew and respected. Trevya dropped silently to the ground. Even the hammering outside stopped. Walegrin dusted his shoulders and arms. There was nothing clinging to them, of course. Against all probability, Illyra was Seeing.

"I stink of it, you mean," Walegrin stammered. "There was a problem over in Safe Haven. Some crazy newcomers fermenting cocoons in their courtyard. That's all."

Illyra gave a little shudder. The image vanished. She cocked her head to one shoulder. The image didn't return; but it had been a true Seeing, however much he wanted her to pretend it wasn't. "It's nothing to worry about," she assured him with an affectionate hug.

That was true. The little impulses that flashed across her mind weren't ominous. They were not always literally true, either—the S'danzo Sight often came wrapped in layers of meaning. Illyra might have let the vision go as both insignificant and obscure, but it meant something to her brother, and *that* had her curiosity aroused. It nagged at her throughout the meal; she was never more than half attentive in the conversation.

"I'm going to go after a crustade for dessert," she announced, knowing that she already had one secreted in her scrying chamber. She took her shawl and a copper half-bit from the pouch hanging by the door. "I'll be right back."

She was silhouetted in the sunset, then gone. The afterimage lingered in Walegrin's mind. Sunset. Sixthday. There wasn't a warm baker's oven in the Bazaar, nor anywhere else in Sanctuary. It took two days to braise a joint large enough to satisfy the men at her table. She never relied on last-minute inspirations or improvisations . . .

Walegrin followed her out the door and around to the back where the ropes across her scrying chamber dangled.

"Tell me what you See."

He took her completely by surprise. The cards flew from her hands. They scattered across the room, onto the floor, and into the powders she used for her essences, but three fell neatly on the table where she did her work.

Illyra blushed; she began to dissemble. Walegrin's features composed themselves into his interrogator's face and she abandoned the effort before a half-dozen words were out of her mouth.

"I was curious," she admitted.

"I'm curious myself. What did you See?"

"I told you what I *Saw*. You were surrounded by spider silk. It shimmered with all the colors of the rainbow—"

"What did it mean, Lyra? What did it mean?"

The seeress looked away and caught sight of the cards on the table. The *amashkiki,* the spirits of the cards, supported her. Eagerly she adjusted their alignment. "Here . . . The Lady of the Forest. The Lady of the Stones. Between them, the Fifth—"

"Ly-ra . . . Do it right."

"No, no, this is right."

"It was an accident."

Illyra hunched her shoulders and thrust her jaw at her brother. "I do not have *accidents,*" she hissed.

Momentarily chastened, Walegrin allowed her to continue with her explanation.

"I See good fortune, easily come by."

"Where? Where do you see that?" He prodded the cards. One Lady sat at a stone-weighted loom, the other was a spirit with cobweb wings, and the Fifth of Air was a scattering of petals floating away from a bouquet. "All I see is something trapped between two women!"

"What do you need me for if you know everything? Go ahead, you tell me what they mean."

"Women surrounding me. Women weaving a web around me . . . a trap. I don't see any 'good fortune' in that."

Illyra squinted. The tip of her tongue poked through her pursed lips. "I suppose . . ." she agreed slowly. "I could See that. There *is* a woman in your life right now, and she is weaving something." She tapped her fingernail on the petals of the Fifth of Air. "But this is not an ill aspect." In her mind Illyra reached for another card; she Saw, and began to giggle.

"What? What's so bloody funny? Dammit, Illyra, this is *my* life you're laughing at, isn't it? You don't do this with your other querents, do you?"

Illyra shook her head and gradually regained her composure. He was right, of course. A S'danzo girl learned early not to laugh at her querents, regardless of their questions or her visions. Giggling ruined the mystery, and it was bad for business. She swallowed her laughter. "If you were one of my querents I would tell you that you must accommodate." She paused and swallowed again. "Yes, *accommodate* your good fortune."

"What's that supposed to mean?"

The seeress lifted the edge of her shawl to cover the lower part of her face. "If a querent asked that, I would say: It will be made clear in time. Accommodate your fate, and you will find good fortune."

"And the women. What of the gods-be-damned women?"

"Woman. There is only one woman, Walegrin, I'm sure of that. I don't know about the woman. She is not here. These are not her cards. I cannot say if she will have good fortune or not."

The visionary spell was broken. The giddiness drained from Illyra's body. She sighed and began to collect her cards. Walegrin could feel the lightning charge dissipate.

"Accommodate," he repeated. "That word is supposed to have some especially profound meaning for me. You're telling me not to fight what happens, aren't you? Don't do anything at all. Don't get involved, don't care, don't worry. What happens, happens—"

Illyra stood up. "I didn't say that. I said accommodate your fate . . . learn to live with it."

"Same difference."

She gathered the last of the cards. The Seeing had become part of memory where it lost most of its power. Nothing was guaranteed; memory could change over time. "Same difference," she agreed. "Will you stay for the crustade?" She lifted the bowl from the high shelf where she had kept it safe from inquiring eyes and fingers.

Like most superstitious people, Walegrin lived in a world where the supernatural tended to confirm, rather than challenge, his prejudices. He was willing to reach an accommodation with his fate, if accommodation meant that Theudebourga, her problems and her silk, could be exiled from his mind without shame or guilt.

The crustade was calling to him. "I'll stay," he said, taking the heavy bowl. "Wouldn't want to see it go to waste."

The heavens had clouded over by the time Walegrin hauled himself back to the officer's quarters inside the palace. A light rain began to fall. Its gentle rhythm on the shutters, not to mention the aftereffects of a huge meal, sent the commander into a dreamless sleep. Godsfearing folk rose early on Seventhday; everyone else slept as late as possible. Walegrin's recent promotion entitled him to lie in bed until sunset if he so desired. He was not pleased when someone came pounding on his door well before midday.

Stark naked and surly, Walegrin cracked the door and braced it against his leg. "This had better be important," he snarled.

The recruit trembled. He restarted his story twice before mustering enough wit to explain that everyone who'd eaten dinner at the garrison mess was huddled up at the latrines. The duty officer couldn't take two steps without retching and there were only a handful of men who could climb the ladder to the watchtower.

"Shit."

"Yes, sir," the recruit agreed.

Walegrin let the door go. When he'd lived in a barracks with nothing but a chest to hold his worldly goods, he'd always known where everything was. Now that he had a square room to call his own, chaos reigned among his possessions. He found his breeches and shirt on the floor where he'd left them, but the sandals . . . Walegrin owned four of the ventilated boots, any two of which would make a satisfactory pair. One was usually visible, while the rest hid in the darkest corners where the commander suspected they consumed his

wrist guards, which, at any rate, had disappeared completely.
The Enlibar sword, at least, was where it belonged.

"Let's go," Walgrin said when he'd gotten the door latched
behind him.

Physicians and mages were summoned to the privies where
they decided that the epidemic had just about run its course.
The afflicted were unimpressed, but Walegrin could see that
most of them, while they'd be useless for a day or so, were
already recovering. Only two men needed sickbeds, and one
of them had been sick for a week.

The cook was dragged from the kitchens. He insisted the
flux couldn't be his fault; the meat was rotten before he
cooked it.

"Why did you cook it, if you knew it was rotten?"

The cook said it wasn't his job to question the meat the
stewards provided. He was a cook. He insisted he'd done his
job well: after all, the men hadn't complained while they
were eating.

Walegrin had him flogged and tied to a post by the stables
where the recovering men could offer sympathy, suggestions,
and the occasional clot of horse manure.

The cook had a point; he didn't purchase the meat. Walegrin
spent the rest of the afternoon looking for the guilty steward.
Shunted from corridor to corridor on a stream of insincere
apologies, the garrison commander was unable to wring a
confession from any of the palace flunkies.

"Somebody paid for a carcass of rotten meat," Walegrin
fumed when, in frustration, he made his way to Molin's
workroom. "Somebody's responsible, and somebody other
than that half-idiot of a cook should be punished."

"Should, should, should," the Torch chided from his chair.
"How many times must I explain to you that *should* doesn't
work in a palace?"

"It ought to."

"Suffice to say, the problem's been taken care of."

Walegrin wasn't grateful to have his work done for him.
"You knew about it?"

"Let's just say it wasn't a single carcass, and I, myself,
spent the night circling my chamber pot and cursing the
stewards."

Molin Torchholder was a powerful man in Sanctuary, but not because he had the ear of his god. Walegrin expressed his skepticism.

"It wasn't difficult. I sent Hoxa down to read the provisions receipts. One of the understewards is already under lock and key, and I've got the name of a place Downwind—"

"You might have let me know, my lord Molin."

Torchholder smiled pleasantly. "I couldn't find you." He pointed to his table; it was apparent that he did not feel up to standing or walking. "There . . . Hoxa wrote it down for you. Take it as you leave."

Words could not adequately express Walegrin's feelings as he crumpled the vellum scrap into his pouch, and gestures would have gotten him hung. The sun was setting. He'd wasted the entire day; it was time to go on duty. Half the men didn't answer the roster call; dinner was predictably awful, then a squall blew up and settled into a steady rain. The only pleasant moment of the entire double-watch came when Wedemir announced that the raid on the Downwind abattoir had been a success. The men were drawing lots to see who would question the prisoners.

Wedemir lingered in the doorway. "Sir? About yesterday . . . ? The silk workers, remember? I used your name—"

Walegrin paused and remembered. "Don't worry about it."

"Did you go to see them?"

The commander shook his head. "If there's ever another complaint. I thought about it, Lieutenant. Everything works out for the best. I can accommodate a silk worker or two."

Wedemir's eyes widened, then he left. For a moment Walegrin was tempted to call him back, but the moment and the temptation passed. The night dragged toward midnight when Thrusher, still looking seedy at the edges, hauled himself up the ladder.

"You sure, Thrush?"

"Yeah, the air'll do me good. Get your sleep while you can."

Walegrin wasn't especially tired, but, as Thrusher said, a soldier learned to grab sleep when he could. He was yawning when he reached the stone-dark landing outside his room. He reached for the latchstring; it wasn't dangling where it should have been. Walegrin swore he'd pulled the string through when he shut the door, but it wouldn't be the first time he'd forgotten. He was on his knees wiggling a brass pin through the latch-hole when the door opened.

The commander gaped at Theudebourga, and she hid a yawn behind her fingers.

"I must have fallen asleep."

The commander remained on his knees. "You . . . ? What are you doing here?"

"I have nothing else to give you." She looked away. She might have been blushing, it was hard to tell in the lamplight. "You've been so kind to us."

"I have?" Walegrin got to his feet.

"When the Beysib came to get us this afternoon, they said that they were following your orders. In truth, I doubted you then, and feared for the worst as they loaded everything into a great cart. When they led us through the gates we thought we were being sent into exile. Dendorat was wild; they struck him on the head and lashed him to the cart. But they took us to a cottage and said we could pay the rent with finished silk."

Walegrin nodded, trying to recall what, exactly, Wedemir said before being assured that there was nothing to worry about.

Theudebourga did not notice his changing expression. "We haven't met Lady Kurrekai yet. Imagine, the cousin of Beysa Shupansea taking all of us under her wing. You must have been very persuasive . . . I knew from that first moment on the wharf that you were not one to leave us to our fate."

"Theudebourga—"

"Berge. Call me Berge, it's easier on the ear and tongue." He didn't call her anything. She looked at him, at the shock and sourness on his face. "Dear gods—" She lunged for the stool where she had fallen asleep. Her workbag had fallen on its side, the drop-spindle had rolled across the floor. Frantically, she grabbed for both. The thread broke and the spindle rolled behind the chest. "What use has a man like you for a withered spinster?"

Walegrin heard that she was crying. He wanted her to stop.

He wanted to tell her the truth, but his thoughts were whirling too fast to form the words he wanted to say. So Walegrin stood, blocking the doorway and feeling like an ox, while Theudebourga grew more shamed and hysterical.

"Please let me leave," she pleaded.

She had a death-grip on the sack. Wisps of unspun silk squeezed out and were tossed about on their breath. Walegrin felt them clinging to the stubble on his chin, to his eyebrows, and the tip of his nose. He became what Illyra had Seen. His thoughts froze around a single paradox: did the accommodation of good fortune lie in letting her stay, or letting her escape? What did he know about women anyway, except that the ones he got attracted to were no good for him?

Theudebourga hunched her shoulders and tried to sneak past. Her intentions were no match for Walegrin's reflexes—though the commander hadn't counted on having her so close he could feel her heartbeat.

"You don't have to leave." He lowered his arm. "You surprised me, that's all. It never occurred to me that the door would open one night and my woman would be there to greet me."

"Don't mock me."

"I'm not mocking you."

Walegrin pushed the door shut. Berge did not object.

TO BEGIN AGAIN

Robert Lynn Asprin

Without thinking, Hakiem took a long swallow of the sour, cheap wine his tankard held. Normally, he would have winced at the bitter impact of the taste, but today it passed down his throat without notice.

Leave Sanctuary!

Though the very core of his being recoiled from the idea, fighting desperately to eject it from his mind, it remained foremost in his thoughts, clinging stubbornly like some malignant parasite feeding on his brain. It had been this way since his talk with the Beysa, hounding him until he retreated to the Vulgar Unicorn, returning to his old haunt like a wounded animal seeking refuge in its lair. Even here, however, surrounded by the familiar darkness and darker half-heard conversations, there was no escape from the dread pronouncement.

Leave Sanctuary!

Lifting his tankard again, he was surprised to find it was empty.

Was that his third . . . or fourth? No matter. It wasn't enough, which was all that counted.

A brief nod at Abohorr was all that was necessary to obtain another. That notable's attentiveness was a tribute to Hakiem's rise in position and status, a rise he had never had cause to regret . . . until now.

228

Advisor to the Beysa, he thought with a grimace. At first it had seemed harmless, even desirable, to teach the ruler-in-exile the ways and thinking of her new home. Sympathy had grown into friendship, however, until he was regarded as her most trusted confidant . . . almost a surrogate father to the young girl stranded by circumstance in a foreign land. His duties had been light, and his rewards great. Then, without warning, *this*.

Lost in thought, Hakiem barely noticed the arrival of his fresh tankard, though from habit he was aware of the bartender slipping more than was his due from the pile of small coins on the table. Rather than take the offender to task for his greed, he chose instead to review the event which had led to his current state of mental confusion.

Visits from the Beysa were common enough, and more often than not, involving subjects of a trivial nature. Usually, all that was required of him was to listen while she complained or emoted about some new discomfort or minor slight, venting the hurts or frustrations her position would not let her acknowledge publicly. Thus, he was unprepared for the direction their conversation took.

"I have news for you, old friend," Shupansea announced after their normal exchange of pleasantries. "Both good and bad, I'm afraid."

Hakiem had already noticed that his royal visitor had seemed preoccupied and distracted, and was glad the cause was to be revealed without his having to draw it out of her.

"Tell me the bad news first, O Beysa," he said. "Then we can dispense with it quickly. If not, then perhaps the good news will cheer us both."

"Very well. The bad news is that I am about to lose one of my dearest and most trusted friends."

Hakiem noted that no name was mentioned, and wondered if the omission was accidental or deliberate.

"That is sad news indeed." He nodded, silently speculating on who it might be that they were discussing. "Friends are always hard to come by and impossible to replace."

"Still, the same news is good," the Beysa continued, "as it represents a promotion for that same friend . . . a chance for me to express my appreciation with a long-overdue reward.''

"So you rejoice for your friend's good fortune even though it represents a loss to you, personally. As I have said before, O Beysa, your nobility of heart surpasses the nobility of your birth. I would wager that your friend has benefited from your friendship, however brief, just as I have, and will wish you well upon parting.''

His comment was automatic, flowery politeness to fill his side of the conversation while he awaited further information. The effect of the words on Shupansea, however, was as profound as it was unexpected.

"Oh, I'm so glad you agree, Hakiem!'' she cried, seizing his hand in an uncommon display of emotion, Beysib women being usually very self-conscious about touching males. "I was afraid you'd be upset.''

"Upset? About what?'' Startled by the turn of the conversation, he practically stammered out the question, though it was now painfully clear that he himself was the subject under discussion. "I . . . I'm afraid I don't . . .''

"I'm sorry. I'm getting ahead of myself. It's so hard for me to remember court formalities when I'm talking to you.''

She released his hand and stepped back, striking a regal pose almost mocking in its severity.

"Hakiem,'' she said in her solemn, court voice. "It is with great pleasure that we hereby appoint you Royal Emissary, our Trade Ambassador to the Glorious Home of Mother Bey . . . such as it is.''

Hakiem could not have been more stunned if she had suddenly struck him.

"Ambassador? Me?''

"That's right.'' Shupansea grinned, abandoning her attempt at dignity. She was obviously delighted at her confidant's obvious surprise. "The appointment papers were just signed, and I raced the rumors through the palace so I could be the first to tell you.''

"But, O Beysa, I have no qualifications! I'm no ambassador! What would I do in a foreign court? Tell them stories?''

"You'll do what the people of this town do best,'' the Beysa informed him firmly. "Haggle. I can guarantee you the royal opponents you'll be dealing with will present little challenge to you after the training you've had here in Sanctuary."

"But I'm just a storyteller. It takes more than fine clothes to make an aristocrat!"

"That's what Kadakithis said . . . but he eventually came around to my way of thinking. It's just as well, too. The trade ship has been ready to sail for nearly a week while we argued about who the ambassador would be."

"Trade ship?"

The enormity of what was being proposed suddenly swirled up around Hakiem like a fog. Until now, he had been arguing theoretically about a preposterous idea. The mention of a ship, however, brought home the reality of what was being discussed.

"You mean I am to leave Sanctuary? Make a new home in a foreign land?"

"Well, you can't very well be a trade ambassador from here." The Beysa laughed. "Oh, I know it sounds frightening . . . but it's what I had to do when I came . . . What is it, Hakiem?"

The storyteller had suddenly collapsed into a chair, his face a mask of despair.

"O Beysa . . . I . . . I can't do it."

The smile slipped from the Beysa's face as she stiffened into a posture that had no trace of the mockery shown earlier.

"I don't recall giving you a choice," she said coldly, then softened instantly. "Oh, what's wrong, Hakiem? You've never refused me before."

"You've never asked me to leave Sanctuary before," he responded, shaking his head. "I'm not a young man . . . too old to learn new ways. I've had to change my life completely twice already. Once when . . . I first came to Sanctuary, and again when I became your advisor. I cannot make such changes again. You see me as shrewd and wily, but that's only because I know this town and the people in it. Take me out of familiar surroundings, and . . ."

"I thought I'd find you here."

Prince Kadakithis was framed in the doorway.

"Well, let me add my congratulations to those you've

already received, Hakiem." There was no effort to shake hands, but the prince's smile was warm and sincere.

"He doesn't want the position," Shupansea blurted.

"Oh?" The smile faded as Kadakithis cocked an eyebrow at the storyteller. "I should think you'd find it an honor, Hakiem . . . not to mention a noticeable improvement in your station . . . and income."

"My place is here in Sanctuary," Hakiem insisted stubbornly, his desperation making him bold in the face of royalty. "From what I understand, you yourself have questioned my effectiveness in such an assignment."

"You see?" Shupansea cried in exasperation. "I try to reward his service and do him a favor at the same time, and this is the thanks I get!"

"Highness . . ." Hakiem began, but the prince cut him short.

"I'm sure we can reach some kind of an agreement here," he said soothingly. "Let me talk with our new ambassador for a moment."

"All right."

"Alone, if you don't mind, dear."

"But . . . Oh, all right!"

The Beysa swept angrily from the room, leaving an uncomfortable silence in her wake.

"There's been a lot of water under the bridge since we first met, hasn't there, storyteller?" the prince said, making a show of inspecting the room's decor.

"That there has, Highness."

Hakiem was wary of this private audience, but he had to admit the prince had changed since that dusty afternoon he had tossed a poor storyteller a few pieces of gold. The regal brow was marked with worry lines that had not been there when he'd first arrived in Sanctuary, but he spoke and moved with a new sureness and confidence that had also been lacking in those early days.

"I'll admit I opposed the idea of your appointment when Shupansea first proposed it," the prince continued, "but after giving it considerable thought, *apart* from my fiancée's insistence, I arrived at the conclusion that you were not only acceptable for the post, but that there was no one better qualified for the position.''

"Highness?''

The storyteller was taken aback at this revelation.

"Think about it, Hakiem,'' the prince said earnestly, turning to gaze directly at his subject. "In your capacity as the Beysa's advisor, you have made yourself familiar with the Beysib culture and people, both the high and the low. In fact, you speak their language better than any non-Beysib in the town or the court.''

He paused while the ghost of a smile flitted across his face.

"While you may not have formal experience as an ambassador, your years as a storyteller will serve you well, as the bulk of diplomacy is making the untrue or unlikely sound plausible, if not desirable. These things count in your favor, but there are two points that outweigh all others.

"First, you are honest and loyal.''

The prince quickly held up a hand to restrain the storyteller's protests.

"Oh, I know you folk from Sanctuary pride yourselves in deception and shady dealings . . . which will also help you as an ambassador . . . and I have no doubts that you would have no compunctions about padding a deal or slitting a throat if you set your mind to it, but in your current position you've had many opportunities to betray the Beysa for spite or personal gain, yet to my knowledge you have not taken advantage of any of them. To my mind, that makes you trustworthy . . . notable more so than many of the advisors I've had assigned to me or appointed myself.

"Even more important, however, is the unmistakable fact that you love this town. While your feelings for Shupansea or myself might wax and wan, I cannot imagine your knowingly doing anything or agreeing to anything that would not be in Sanctuary's best interest.

"It may seem ironic or contradictory, but I firmly believe that you can best serve the interests of this town by leaving it . . . by being our eyes and ears, our watchdog, if you will, in the Beysib court during this crucial period. Will you do that for me . . . or better yet, for Sanctuary, storyteller?''

*   *   *

Hakiem grimaced into his wine at the memory.

Do it for Sanctuary.

If the prince ever decided to abandon his royal calling, there was a real future for him as a swindler or confidence man. While the request may have had the *appearance* of free will, there was really only one answer that could be given. Hakiem had had no more choice than a member of an audience having a conjuror "force" a specific card on him for the purposes of a trick or illusion.

Of course, the prince could have simply ordered him into service. In that case, Hakiem would have had the choice of leaving Sanctuary as an honored ambassador, or leaving it as a fugitive of the prince's wrath. It would seem, however, that Kadakithis had learned the value of a willing volunteer . . . however unwilling that volunteer might be in reality.

Absently, Hakiem noted the contradictory, circular nature of that observation as a gauge of the effects the wine was having on him, and was not displeased at his progress.

"May I join you, old man? . . . Or are you too busy with the 'preparations' for your voyage to spare me a few of the millions of words you spend so freely on others?"

Hakiem gaped with astonishment, uncharacteristically at a loss for words. None seemed required, however, as his visitor pulled up a chair and settled at the table like some huge black bird coming to roost.

"Jubal?" the storyteller managed at last, blurting out the question as if requiring confirmation for what his eyes already told him. "Are you . . . I mean, is this wise?"

He tore his gaze free to glance nervously about the tavern's dim interior, but no one seemed to be taking notice of the figure in their midst.

"I've found that I've been out of view long enough that no one remembers what I look like." Sanctuary's crime lord smiled without humor. "Especially with the 'changes' I've undergone since I was a 'public figure.' If anything, a disguise would draw attention to me rather than avert it . . . especially in the Vulgar Unicorn. Like this, I'm just another old man . . . like yourself."

While it appeared Jubal was correct in his analysis, Hakiem nonetheless felt distinctly uncomfortable . . . enough so to banish any effects of his earlier drinking. As long as they had known each other . . . actually, as long as Hakiem had been in Sanctuary . . . Jubal had maintained an air of secrecy about himself. Originally, he would not have left his mansion without a cloak and one of the blue hawk masks to disguise his features, and after the aging caused by the spell hired to help him heal from the wounds suffered during the Stepsons' raid on his holdings, he had not appeared in public at all. Ergo, sitting next to an ex-slaver in the Vulgar Unicorn, bereft of *any* effort to mask his identity, had Hakiem feeling that he was in close proximity to a target on one of the military's firing ranges.

"What are you doing here?"

"I've heard about your new assignment," Jubal said, his dark lips tightening into a flat smile. "Good news travels slower than bad in this town, but it still travels."

"I already gathered that from your first comments. What I want to know is why it drew you into the open. Forgive me if I find it hard to believe that you're here solely to wish me safe voyage, but in the past the only times you've sought me out is when it somehow benefited you or your operations. Of what import is my appointment to you?"

The crime lord gave a short bark of laughter and shook his head.

"Your time in court has certainly sharpened your tongue, old man, but then I guess neither of us has ever had much tolerance for small talk when it came to business. Very well, I'll come straight to the point."

He shot a quick glance around the room, then leaned forward, lowering his voice.

"I have a proposition for you. Simply put, I want to accompany you on your new assignment."

"That's absurd!"

The words slipped out before Hakiem had a chance to consider them. He did, however, have time to consider Jubal's sudden scowl at their impact.

"What's absurd about it?" the ex-slaver demanded harshly. "Is my company so repellent to you, or my advice so worthless that . . ."

"No!" the storyteller interrupted hastily. "I meant you

already have everything here in Sanctuary . . . money, power
. . . what possible reason could you have for even considering giving it all up to travel to a foreign land, one where you
are unknown and would have to start building again from
nothing? *That's* what I meant was absurd . . . the whole
idea's preposterous."

He gave a bitter snort, reaching for his tankard.

"It's preposterous for *anybody* to willingly give up their
life . . . to gamble everything on the unknown. If *I* had a
choice . . . but I don't. I *have* to go . . . for the prince, for
the Beysa, for Sanctuary. What's the comfort of one old
storyteller compared to *that*?"

"It depends on how highly you value what you're leaving," Jubal said easily, ignoring Hakiem's self-pitying comments. "It's strange that you should think I have everything
here, but then you've always taken for granted the one thing
that's always eluded me."

"And that is . . . ?" Hakiem urged, curious in spite of
himself.

"Respect." The crime lord shrugged. "I thought I had it
when I won my freedom from the gladiator arena, only to
find polite society viewed me as little better than an animal. I
couldn't find work that would earn me the kind of money
necessary for the kind of life-style I aspired to, so I took to
stealing it."

"And earned a certain type of respect in the process." The
storyteller smiled.

Jubal frowned at him. "Don't patronize me, Hakiem," he
said. "It ill becomes you. I have never been respected in this
town. Feared, to be sure, but we both know that's different
than being respected. You can't buy respect, or force it at
sword point. You have to earn it."

"So why not earn it here?" Hakiem frowned.

"Do you think I haven't tried?" The ex-slaver grimaced.
"The trouble here is that too many people know me of old,
and that knowledge makes them assume the worse. I'll tell
you, just as an example, I've been trying for months to get an
audience with your prince."

"Kadakithis? What business could you have with him?"

Jubal shot a glance around, then leaned closer, lowering his voice.

"I was going to offer him the services of my intelligence network. It's worked well enough for my criminal activities in the past, and I thought he might appreciate its value as an aid for governing this town."

"And he refused?" Hakiem frowned. "That doesn't sound like the prince."

"I never got to see him," the crime lord said. "It seems the consensus among those who control the prince's schedule is that the only way I will see him is if he presides at my trial. I tried more roundabout methods, applying leverage to a certain . . . 'friend' of the prince's who is unknown to most, but even there I was thwarted. Everyone believes it's better to buy me off than to go along with whatever I suggest or request. It's become clear to me that my organization will be more effective *and* be more acceptable if I disassociate myself from it. That's why I'm interested in accompanying you."

It occurred to the storyteller that, by employing dubious methods in his efforts to gain respectability, Jubal was proving everything his enemies believed about him. He also realized, however, that the ex-slaver had a quick temper, and that it would be wisest not to argue with him. Prematurely aged or not, the ex-gladiator was a force to be reckoned with when it came to disputes of a violent nature.

"Do you expect it will be any easier to find respect in the Beysib Empire, surrounded by a people who are physically different than us?" he asked, tactfully shifting the focus of the conversation.

"Who knows?" Jubal shrugged. "It can't be any worse than here. At least there I won't be carrying my past around my neck like a leper's bell. It will be a fresh start for me in a land where no one knows or cares anything about what I've been or done before."

"Of course, that also means they have no idea of what to guard *against* either," Hakiem observed drily.

The slaver flashed a quick grin in response.

"A land of opportunity, no matter how you look at it."

"Not if those opportunities cause problems for the ambassador," the storyteller warned. "I can't have a . . . Excuse me, what capacity were you proposing you accompany me in, anyway?''

"I had been thinking of traveling as your personal manservant," Jubal said, "but I'm open to other suggestions. I imagine that, whatever my official capacity, I will be serving as a confidential advisor to you."

Hakiem's eyebrows shot up.

"Advisor? Excuse me, but I didn't think you knew any more about the Beysib than I do."

"Think again, old man." The crime lord chuckled darkly. "Your battlefield of choice is the courts with carefully chosen words and arguments. My arena is the back alleys, gathering information from the sorts either ignored or hunted by your aristocrats. If anyone, you should know the value of a bit of street-level information when operating in a new town."

The storyteller stared thoughtfully, seriously considering Jubal's proposal for the first time. It was true that the crime lord would be a valuable ally . . . especially if none of the Beysib knew to watch or suspect what appeared to be an aged servant. Still, it was hard to believe Jubal was willing to take part in such a venture, much less accept a role subservient to Hakiem.

As if sensing the storyteller's hesitation, the ex-slaver pressed on.

"There's another thing which can make me a priceless secret weapon, old man."

"And that is . . . ?"

Jubal leaned forward, grinning smugly as he whispered.

"I've built an immunity to the bite of those snakes the Beysib women favor so."

"You have?" Hakiem's eyebrows shot up. "I didn't know that was possible . . . except for those who were conditioned from birth, that is."

"It's a secret that cost me dear." The crime lord smiled. "Far dearer than obtaining the solvent for the latest witches' brew of glue going round town. More important, I'm willing to share that secret with you if you'll include me in your plans."

"Me? I really don't think that's necessary . . . though I appreciate the offer. I've gotten used to having the snakes around, and they're harmless as long as you give them lots of room.''

Jubal stared at him for a few moments, then shook his head ruefully.

''I don't know if it's the wine or your time in court that's clouded your thinking, old man. Hasn't it ever occurred to you that those snakes are perfect tools for murder?''

''You mean assassination? But I'll be an ambassador. They wouldn't dare!''

''I wouldn't bet my life on that, if I were you,'' the ex-slaver snorted. ''You're going to be trying to establish trade with the Beysib Empire, right? That means you're going to be stepping on *someone's* livelihood. Whether you're providing better or cheaper goods, you'll be diverting money to Sanctuary that would normally go to someone else, which is going to make that someone your mortal enemy. They may not be able to attack you openly, but it's always possible to arrange a convenient 'accident.' The Beysib aren't *that* different from us.''

It had not occurred to Hakiem that there was potential danger in his mission, yet Jubal's words had the irrefutable ring of truth to them. Strangely enough, however, rather than adding to his reluctance, the possibility of an attack on Sanctuary's trade ambassador aroused in him an angry indignation which had him looking forward to the mission for the first time since it had been proposed.

If some of the Beysib thought they could block trade with Sanctuary by disposing of some court fop of an ambassador, they were in for a rude surprise.

Fast on the heels of this thought, of course, was an added awareness of the desirability of Jubal's company on this assignment.

''Well, how about it, old man?'' the crime lord said, catching the change in the storyteller's attitude. ''Do we have a deal?''

''Possibly,'' Hakiem responded warily. ''At the very least, your idea is interesting enough to discuss further . . . perhaps in more private surroundings?''

''Very well then, let's go,'' Jubal announced, rising to his feet. ''Time is short, both for decisions *and* planning. Tell me . . . I assume there will be some sort of bodyguard assigned to you . . . have you been offered your choice for that position?''

"It was offered," the storyteller admitted, also rising, "but I really don't have a preference."

"You might want to reconsider that."

A ghost of a smile flitted across Hakiem's face.

"I really don't think I can get you approved in that capacity, Jubal."

"I wasn't thinking of myself . . . you don't have to tell me how unacceptable I am to the prince. No, I was thinking about Zalbar."

"Zalbar?"

"One of the original Hell-hounds that arrived with the prince," Jubal explained. "We've had . . . dealings together in the past, and I'd trust him to guard my back . . . assuming, of course, he felt it was within his rather narrow concept of duty. Besides, like me, there's nothing left in Sanctuary for him now, and he might welcome the assignment."

Hakiem was listening with only half an ear.

As Jubal spoke, the storyteller was looking around the Vulgar Unicorn, trying to permanently brand every detail in his mind. It had suddenly occurred to him that this might be the last time he ever saw the place, the scene of the start and/or ending to so many stories over the past years. Even if he returned to Sanctuary, this tavern, as well as the town itself, would be different. As he knew all too well, each new beginning is also an ending, and on the road of life, there is no turning back.